Tyndale House Novels by Jerry B. Jenkins

Riven
Midnight Clear (with Dallas Jenkins)
Soon
Silenced
Shadowed
The Last Operative
The Brotherhood

The Left Behind® series (with Tim LaHaye)

Left Behind®
Tribulation Force
Nicolae
Soul Harvest
Apollyon
Assassins
The Indwelling
The Mark
Desecration
The Remnant
Armageddon
Glorious Appearing
The Rising
The Regime
The Rapture
Kingdom Come

Left Behind Collectors Edition

Rapture's Witness (books 1–3)
Deceiver's Game (books 4–6)
Evil's Edge (books 7–9)
World's End (books 10–12)

For the latest information on Left Behind products, visit www.leftbehind.com.

For the latest information on Tyndale fiction, visit www.tyndalefiction.com.

LEFT BEHIND
TRIBULATION FORCE
NICOLAE
SOUL HARVEST
5
APOLLYON
ASSASSINS
THE INDWELLING
THE MARK
DESECRATION
THE REMNANT
ARMAGEDDON
GLORIOUS APPEARING

TIM LaHAYE
JERRY B. JENKINS

TYNDALE HOUSE PUBLISHERS, INC., CAROL STREAM, ILLINOIS

Visit Tyndale's exciting Web site at www.tyndale.com.

Discover the latest about the Left Behind series at www.leftbehind.com.

TYNDALE, Tyndale's quill logo, and *Left Behind* are registered trademarks of Tyndale House Publishers, Inc.

Apollyon: The Destroyer Is Unleashed

Left Behind series designed by Erik M. Peterson

Published in association with the literary agency of Alive Communications, Inc., 7680 Goddard Street, Suite 200, Colorado Springs, CO 80920. www.alivecommunications.com.

Scripture quotations used by the two witnesses in this book are taken from the *Holy Bible*, King James Version.

Library of Congress Cataloging-in-Publication Data

LaHaye, Tim F.
Apollyon : the Destroyer is unleashed / Tim LaHaye, Jerry B. Jenkins.
p. cm.
ISBN 978-0-8423-2916-3 (hc)
ISBN 978-0-8423-2926-2 (sc)
I. Jenkins, Jerry B. II. Title.
PS3562.A315A56 1999
813′.54—dc21 98-32064

Repackage first published in 2011 under ISBN 978-1-4143-3494-3.

Printed in the United States of America

17 16 15 14 13 12 11
7 6 5 4 3 2 1

To Norman B. Rohrer,

friend and mentor

PROLOGUE

From Soul Harvest

RAYFORD BELIEVED the only way to exonerate Amanda was to decode her files, but he also knew the risk. He would have to face whatever they revealed. Did he want the truth, regardless? The more he prayed about that, the more convinced he became that he must not fear the truth.

What he learned would affect how he functioned for the rest of the Tribulation. If the woman who had shared his life had fooled him, whom could he trust? If he was that bad a judge of character, what good was he to the cause? Maddening doubts filled him, but he became obsessed with knowing. Either way, lover or liar, wife or witch, he had to know.

The morning before the start of the most talked-about mass meeting in the world, Rayford approached Carpathia in his office.

"Your Excellency," he began, swallowing any vestige of pride, "I'm assuming you'll need Mac and me to get you to Israel tomorrow."

"Talk to me about this, Captain Steele. They are meeting against my wishes, so I had planned not to sanction it with my presence."

"But your promise of protection—"

"Ah, that resonated with you, did it not?"

"You know well where I stand."

"And you also know that I tell you where to fly, not vice versa. Do you not think that if I wanted to be in Israel tomorrow I would have told you before this?"

"So, those who wonder if you are afraid of the scholar who—"

"Afraid!"

"—showed you up on the Internet and called your bluff before an international audience—"

"You are trying to bait me, Captain Steele," Carpathia said, smiling.

"Frankly, I believe you know you will be upstaged in Israel by the two witnesses and by Dr. Ben-Judah."

"The two witnesses? If they do not stop their black magic, the drought, and the blood, they will answer to me."

"They say you can't harm them until the due time."

"I will decide the due time."

"And yet Israel was protected from the earthquake and the meteors—"

"You believe the witnesses are responsible for that?"

"I believe God is."

"Tell me, Captain Steele. Do you still believe that a man who has been known to raise the dead could actually be the Antichrist?"

Rayford hesitated, wishing Tsion was in the room. "The enemy has been known to imitate miracles," he said. "Imagine the audience in Israel if you were to do something like that. Here are people of faith coming together for inspiration. If you are God, if you could be the Messiah, wouldn't they be thrilled to meet you?"

Carpathia stared at Rayford, seeming to study his eyes. Rayford believed God. He had faith that regardless of his power, regardless of his intentions, Nicolae would be impotent in the face of the 144,000 witnesses who carried the seal of almighty God on their foreheads.

"If you are suggesting," Carpathia said carefully, "that it only makes sense that the Global Community Potentate bestow upon those guests a regal welcome second to none, you may have a point."

Rayford had said nothing of the sort, but Carpathia heard what he wanted to hear. "Thank you," Rayford said.

"Captain Steele, schedule that flight."

Then I saw another angel ascending from the east, having the seal of the living God.

And he cried with a loud voice to the four angels to whom it was granted to harm the earth and the sea, saying, "Do not harm the earth, the sea, or the trees till we have sealed the servants of our God on their foreheads."

And I heard the number of those who were sealed. One hundred and forty-four thousand of all the tribes of the children of Israel were sealed.

REVELATION 7:2-4

CHAPTER 1

Rayford Steele worried about Mac McCullum's silence in the cockpit of *Global Community One* during the short flight from New Babylon to Tel Aviv. "Do we need to talk later?" Rayford said quietly. Mac put a finger to his lips and nodded.

Rayford finished communicating with New Babylon ground and air traffic control, then reached beneath his seat for the hidden reverse intercom button. It would allow him to listen in on conversations in the Condor 216's cabin between Global Community Potentate Nicolae Carpathia, Supreme Commander Leon Fortunato, and Pontifex Maximus Peter Mathews, head of Enigma Babylon One World Faith. But just before Rayford depressed the button, he felt Mac's hand on his arm. Mac shook his head.

Rayford shuddered. "They know?" he mouthed.

Mac whispered, "Don't risk it until we talk."

Rayford received the treatment he had come to expect on initial descent into Tel Aviv. The tower at Ben Gurion cleared other planes from the area, even those that had begun landing sequences. Rayford heard anger in the voices of other pilots as they were directed into holding patterns miles from the Condor. Per protocol, no other aircraft were to be in proximity to the Condor, despite the extraordinary air traffic expected in Israel for the Meeting of the Witnesses.

"Take the landing, Mac," Rayford said. Mac gave a puzzled glance but complied. Rayford was impressed at how the Holy Land had been spared damage from the wrath of the Lamb earthquake. Other calamities had befallen the land and the people, but to Rayford, Israel was the one place that looked normal from the air since the earthquake and the subsequent judgments.

Ben Gurion Airport was alive with traffic. The big planes had to land there, while smaller craft could put down near Jerusalem. Worried about Mac's misgivings, still Rayford couldn't suppress a smile. Carpathia had been forced not only to allow this meeting of believers, but also to pledge his personal protection of them. Of course, he was the opposite of a man of his word, but having gone public with his assurances, he was stuck. He would have to protect even Rabbi Tsion Ben-Judah, spiritual head of the Tribulation Force.

Not long before, Dr. Ben-Judah had been forced to flee his homeland under cover of night, a universal bounty on his head. Now he was back as Carpathia's avowed enemy, leader of the 144,000 witnesses and their converts. Carpathia had used the results of the most recent Trumpet Judgments to twice postpone the Israel conference, but there was no stopping it again.

Just before touchdown, when everyone aboard should have been tightly strapped in, Rayford was surprised by a knock at the cockpit door. "Leon," he said, turning. "We're about to land."

"Protocol, Captain!" Fortunato barked.

"What do you want?"

"Besides that you refer to me as Supreme Commander, His Excellency asks that you remain in the cockpit after landing for orders."

"We're not going to Jerusalem?" Rayford said. Mac stared straight ahead.

"Precisely," Fortunato said. "Much as we all know you want to be there."

Rayford had been certain Carpathia's people would try to follow him to the rest of the Tribulation Force.

Fortunato left and shut the door, and Rayford said, "I'll take it, Mac."

Mac shifted control of the craft, and Rayford immediately exaggerated the angle of descent while depressing the reverse intercom button. He heard Carpathia and Mathews asking after Fortunato, who had clearly taken a tumble. Once the plane was parked, Fortunato burst into the cockpit.

"What was that, Officer McCullum?"

"My apologies, Commander," Mac said. "It was out of my hands. All due respect, sir, but you should not have been out of your seat during landing."

"Listen up, gentlemen," Fortunato said, kneeling between them. "His Excellency asks that you remain in Tel Aviv, as we are not certain when he might need to return to New Babylon. We have rented you rooms near the airport. GC personnel will transport you."

Buck Williams sat in the bowels of Teddy Kollek Stadium in Jerusalem with his pregnant wife, Chloe. He knew she was in no way healed enough from injuries she had suffered in the great earthquake to have justified the flight from the States, but she would not be dissuaded. Now she appeared weary. Her bruises and scars were fading, but Chloe still had a severe limp, and her beauty had been turned into a strange cuteness by the unique reshaping of her cheekbone and eye socket.

"You need to help the others, Buck," she said. "Now go on. I'll be fine."

"I wish you'd go back to the compound," he said.

"I'm fine," she insisted. "I just need to sit awhile. I'm worried about Hattie. I said I wouldn't leave her unless she improved or became a believer, and she has done neither." Pregnant, Hattie Durham had been left home fighting for her life against poison in her system. Dr. Floyd Charles attended her while the rest of the Tribulation Force—including new member Ken Ritz, another pilot—had made the pilgrimage to Israel.

"Floyd will take good care of her."

"I know. Now leave me alone awhile."

Rayford and Mac were instructed to wait on the plane as Carpathia, Fortunato, and Mathews were received with enthusiasm on the tarmac. Fortunato stood dutifully in the background as Mathews declined to make a public statement but introduced Carpathia.

"I cannot tell you what a pleasure it is to be back in Israel," Carpathia said with a broad smile. "I am eager to welcome the devotees of Dr. Ben-Judah and to display the openness of the Global Community to diverse opinion and belief. I am pleased to reaffirm my guarantee of safety to the rabbi and the thousands of visitors from all over the world. I will withhold further comment, assuming I will be welcome to address the honored assemblage within the next few days."

The dignitaries were ushered to a helicopter for the hop to Jerusalem, while their respective entourages boarded an opulent motor coach.

When Rayford and Mac finished postflight checks and

finally disembarked, a Global Community Jeep delivered them to their hotel. Mac signaled Rayford not to say anything in the car or either of their rooms. In the coffee shop, Rayford finally demanded to know what was going on.

Buck wished Chloe had been able to sleep on the flight from the States. Ken Ritz had procured a Gulfstream jet, so it was the most comfortable international flight Buck had ever enjoyed. But the four of them—Ken, Buck, Chloe, and Tsion—had been too excited to rest. Tsion spent half the time on his laptop, which Ken transmitted to a satellite, keeping the rabbi in touch with his worldwide flock of millions.

A vast network of house churches had sprung up—seemingly spontaneously—with converted Jews, clearly part of the 144,000 witnesses, taking leadership positions. They taught their charges daily based on the cyberspace sermons and lessons from the prolific Ben-Judah. Tens of thousands of such clandestine local house churches, their very existence flying in the face of the all-inclusive Enigma Babylon One World Faith, saw courageous converts added to the church every day.

Tsion had been urging the local congregations to send their leaders to the great Meeting of the Witnesses, despite warnings from the Global Community. Nicolae Carpathia had again tried to cancel the gathering at the last minute, citing thousands of deaths from contaminated water in over a third of the world. Thrilling the faithful by calling Carpathia's bluff, Tsion responded publicly on the Internet.

"Mr. Carpathia," he had written, "we will be in Jerusalem as scheduled, with or without your approval, permission, or promised protection. The glory of the Lord will be our rear guard."

Buck would need the protection almost as much as Tsion. By choosing to show up and appear in public with Ben-Judah, Buck was sacrificing his position as Carpathia's publishing chief and his exorbitant salary. Showing his face in proximity to the rabbi's would confirm Carpathia's contention that Buck had become an active enemy of the Global Community.

Rabbi Ben-Judah himself had come up with the strategy of simply trusting God. "Stand right beside me when we get off the plane," he said. "No disguises, no misdirection, no hiding. If God can protect me, he can protect you. Let us stop playing Carpathia's games."

Buck had long been anonymously broadcasting his own cyberspace magazine, *The Truth*, which would now be his sole writing outlet. Ironically, it attracted ten times the largest reading audience he had ever enjoyed. He worried for his safety, of course, but more for Chloe's.

Tsion seemed supernaturally protected. But after this conference, the entire Tribulation Force, not to mention the 144,000 witnesses and their millions of converts, would become open archenemies of the Antichrist. Their lives would consist of half ministry, half survival. For all they had been through, it was as if the seven-year tribulation had just begun. They still had nearly five years until the glorious appearing of Christ to set up his thousand-year reign on earth.

What Tsion's Internet missives and Buck's underground electronic magazine had wrought in Israel was stunning. The whole of Israel crawled with tens of thousands of converted Jewish witnesses from the twelve tribes all over the world.

Rather than asking Ken Ritz to find an out-of-the-way airstrip where the Tribulation Force could slip into the country unnoticed, Tsion informed his audience—and also, of course, Carpathia & Co.—of their itinerary.

Ken had landed at the tiny Jerusalem Airport north of the city, and well-wishers immediately besieged the plane. A small cadre of Global Community armed guards, apparently Carpathia's idea of protection for Tsion, would have had to open fire to get near him. The international witnesses cheered and sang and reached out to touch Tsion as the Tribulation Force made its way to a van. The Israeli driver carefully picked his way through the crowd and south down the main drag toward the Holy City and the King David Hotel.

There they had discovered that Supreme Commander Leon Fortunato had summarily bounced their reservations and several others' by supremely commandeering the top floor for Nicolae Carpathia and his people. "I assume you have made provisions for our alternative," Tsion told the desk clerk after half an hour in line.

"I apologize," the young man said, slipping Tsion an envelope. The rabbi glanced at Buck and pulled him away from the crowd, where they opened the note. Buck looked back at Ken, who nodded to assure him he had the fragile Chloe in tow.

The note was in Hebrew. "It is from Chaim," Tsion said. "He writes, 'Forgive my trusted friend Nicolae for this shameful insensitivity. I have room for you and your colleagues and insist you stay with me. Page Jacov, and you will be taken care of.'"

Jacov was Chaim Rosenzweig's driver and valet. He loaded their stuff into a Mercedes van and soon had the Tribulation Force installed in guest rooms at Chaim's walled and gated estate within walking distance of the Old City. Buck tried to get Chloe to stay and rest while he and Ken and Tsion went to the stadium.

"I didn't come here to be on the sidelines," she said. "I know you're concerned about me, but let me decide what I'm up to."

At Kollek Stadium, Buck had been as stunned as the others at what had been arranged. Tsion was right. It had to have been God who used the rabbi's cyber pleas to pull together Israeli witnesses to handle the logistics of this most unlikely conference.

In spite of and in the midst of global chaos, ad hoc committees had arranged transportation, lodging, food, sound, interpretation, and programming. Buck could tell that Tsion was nearly overcome with the streamlined efficiency and no-frills program. "All you need worry about, Dr. Ben-Judah," he had been told, "is being prepared to inspire and inform us when you are due at the microphone."

Tsion smiled sadly. "That and praying that we all remain under the care of our heavenly Father."

"They're onto you, Rayford," Mac said over pita bread and sauce.

Rayford shook his head. "I haven't been a mystery to Carpathia for months. What are you talking about?"

"You've been assigned to me."

"I'm listening."

"I don't rate direct contact with the big man anymore. But last night I was called to a meeting with Leon. The good news is they're not onto me."

"That *is* good. But they know about the device on the plane?"

"He didn't say, but he couldn't have been clearer that you're history. If the device still works—"

"It does."

"—then I'll use it and keep you posted."

"Where will I be?"

"Anywhere but here, Ray. I'm convinced the driver was listening, the car may have been bugged, the cockpit, no question about our rooms."

"They hope I'll lead them to the others, but they'll be in plain sight in Jerusalem."

"They want to *keep* you from the others, Ray. Why do you think we've been assigned to Tel Aviv?"

"And if I leave?"

"I'm to let them know immediately. It'll be the end of you, Ray."

"But I've got to see my family, the rest of the Force."

"Not here. Carpathia's pledge is to protect Tsion and the others. Not you."

"They really think I won't go to Jerusalem?"

"They hope you will. You must not."

Rayford sat back and pursed his lips. He would not miss the job, close as it had brought him to what was going on in the camp of the enemy. He had long wondered how the end would come to this bizarre season of his life. "You're taking over?"

Mac nodded. "So they tell me. There's more good news. They like and trust David."

"Hassid? Good!"

"He's been put in charge of purchasing. Beyond all the computer stuff he's been doing, he contracts for all major purchases. Even in avionics."

Rayford squinted. Mac pulled a yellow sheet from his jacket and slid it across the table. "Don't tell me he's bought me a plane," Rayford said.

Mac snorted. "Should have thought of that. You've seen the next generation iPhones, right? David ordered a half dozen specially built. He doesn't even know yet that he won't be seeing you around anymore."

"I can't steal these, not even from Carpathia."

"You don't have to steal them, Ray. These are just the specs and where to get 'em. They're not cheap, but wait till you see what these babies can do. No more laptops or regular cells for you guys. Well, maybe the rabbi still needs a standard keyboard, but these things are solar powered, satellite connected, and contain geographic positioning chips. You can do more than just access the Internet, send and receive, and use them as phones now."

Rayford shook his head. "I suppose he thought of tracer blocks."

"Of course."

Rayford stuffed the sheet into a pocket. "What am I going to do, Mac?"

"You're going to get your tail out of this hemisphere, what else?"

"But I have to know about Amanda. Buck will tell me only face-to-face, and he's in Jerusalem."

Mac looked down. "You know how that's going to go, Ray. I'd be the last one to try to tell a man about his own wife, but you know as well as I do that everything points to what you don't want to hear."

"I haven't accepted it yet, but I have to know."

"Buck found out for sure?"

"Sounds like it."

"How can *he* be sure?"

"I told you about Hattie."

"Uh-huh."

"She knows."

"So ask her yourself, Ray. Go home."

"Like I wouldn't be noticed trying to slip out of here tomorrow morning."

"The GC can't keep track of everything. Use your people's pilot—Ritz, is it? What's he got to do the next few days?"

Rayford looked at Mac with admiration. "You're not as dumb as you look, old-timer."

Mac pulled a phone from his pocket. "Know his number?"

"Your phone scrambled? If I get detected talking to Ken Ritz on either of our phones—"

"You *are* dumber than *you* look if you think I'd risk that. I know the purchasing guy, remember?" Mac showed Rayford the phone, a generic model that had been doctored by David Hassid.

Rayford dialed Chloe's phone. "Daddy!" she exulted. "Are you here?"

Buck considered it a privilege to pray with the Israeli committee before he and Ken and Tsion headed back to find Chloe. He threw his arm around Tsion. "Are you as tired as I am?"

"Exhausted. I only hope the Lord will allow me to sleep tonight. I am ready to share his message with these dear members of the family, and all that is left before that is to talk with Eli and Moishe. You will go with me, will you not?"

"I wouldn't miss it."

"Me either," Ken said.

But the news from Chloe changed Ken's plans. "Daddy called," she whispered. "He needs a ride home tomorrow."

After she explained Rayford's situation, Ken decided to get the Gulfstream out of the Jerusalem Airport and into Ben Gurion that night. Buck was nearly despondent, wanting to talk to Rayford personally. "At least he can hear the truth about Amanda from the horse's mouth," he said.

An hour later Jacov drove as they delivered Ken to the airport. "We will see you back here Friday," Tsion said, embracing him.

Chloe fell asleep on Buck's shoulder during the after-dark ride to the Temple Mount. As they left the car, the spectacular new temple gleamed on the horizon. "I do not even want to see the new structure," Tsion said. "It is an abomination."

"I can't wait to meet the witnesses," Chloe said.

"You may not actually meet them," Tsion cautioned. "These are heavenly beings with their own agenda. They may communicate with us; they may not. We approach them with great caution."

Buck felt the usual tingle to the soles of his feet. "You know the stories, hon."

Chloe nodded. "I'm not saying I'm not scared."

The three slowed as they approached the typical crowd that gathered thirty feet from the wrought-iron fence, behind which the witnesses stood, sat, or spoke. Usually they spoke. No one had seen them sleep, and none dared get closer.

Threats on the lives of the two witnesses had ended in the ugly deaths of would-be assassins.

Buck's excitement masked his fatigue. He worried about Chloe but would not deny her this privilege. At the edge of the crowd of about forty, Buck was able to see past the fence to where Eli sat, Indian style, his back to the stone wall of a small building beyond the fence. His long hair and beard wafted softly in the breeze, but he was unmoving, unblinking, his leathery skin and burlaplike garb appearing to meld.

Moishe stood two feet from the fence, silent, unmoving, staring at the crowd. Occasionally someone shouted. "Speak! Say something!" But that made others back away, obviously fearing the violent reactions they had heard of. Moishe's feet were spread, his arms loose at his sides. Earlier in the day Buck had monitored on his computer a long monologue from Moishe. Sometimes the two traded off speaking, but this day must have been all Moishe's responsibility.

"Watch them carefully," Buck whispered to Chloe. "Sometimes they communicate without opening their mouths. I love how everyone understands them in his own language."

Commotion near the front caused several people to back away, opening a gap in the crowd. Someone said, "Carpathia! It's the potentate!"

Tsion held up a hand. "Let us stay right here," he whispered.

Buck was riveted as Leon Fortunato smoothly supervised GC guards who kept gawkers from Carpathia. The potentate appeared bemused, boldly moving to within ten feet of the fence. "Hail, Potentate!" someone shouted. Carpathia half turned, holding a finger to his lips, and Fortunato nodded to a guard, who stepped toward the crowd. They backed away farther.

"Stay here," Buck said, slipping away.

"Honey, wait!" Chloe called, but Buck moved around behind the crowd and into the shadows.

He knew he would appear to the guards as simply someone leaving. But when he was far enough away to be ignored, he doubled back through shrubbery to where he could see Carpathia's face as he stared at Moishe.

Carpathia appeared startled when Moishe suddenly spoke in a loud voice. "Woe unto the enemy of the Most High God!"

Nicolae seemed to quickly collect himself. He smiled and spoke softly. "I am hardly the enemy of God," he said. "Many say I *am* the Most High God."

Moishe moved for the first time, crossing his arms over his chest. Carpathia, his chin in his hand, cocked his head and studied Moishe. The ancient witness spoke softly, and Buck knew only he and Carpathia could hear him.

"A sword shall pierce your head," Moishe said in a haunting monotone. "And you shall surely die."

Buck shivered, but it was clear that Carpathia was unmoved. "Let me tell you and your companion something," he said through clenched teeth. "You have persecuted Israel long enough with the drought and the water turned to blood. You will lift your hocus-pocus or live to regret it."

Eli rose and traded places with Moishe, beckoning Carpathia closer. The potentate hesitated and looked back to his guards, who tentatively raised their weapons. Eli spoke with such volume that the crowd dispersed and ran, and even Tsion and Chloe recoiled.

"Until the due time, you have no authority over the lampstands of God Almighty!"

The guards lowered their weapons, and Fortunato seemed to hide behind them. Carpathia's smirk remained, but Buck was convinced he was seething. "We shall see," he said, "who will win in the end."

Eli seemed to look through Carpathia. "Who will win in the end was determined before the beginning of time. Lo, the poison you inflict on the earth shall rot you from within for eternity."

Carpathia stepped back, still grinning. "I warn you to stay away from the charade of the so-called saints. I have guaranteed their safety, not yours."

Eli and Moishe spoke in unison. "He and she who have ears, let them hear. We are bound neither by time nor space, and those who shall benefit by our presence and testimony stand within the sound of our proclamation."

Buck thrilled at the message and looked beyond the square to where Tsion stood with Chloe. The rabbi thrust his fists in the air as if he had gotten the message, and he walked Chloe back toward the car. Buck ducked out of the shrubs and headed around the other way, arriving in the parking lot seconds later.

"Did you hear that?" Tsion said.

Buck nodded. "Incredible!"

"I didn't get it," Chloe said. "What were they saying?"

"Did it sound like Hebrew to you?" Tsion said. "They spoke in Hebrew."

"I heard it in English," she said.

"Me too," Buck said. "They said that he *and she* who had ears to hear—"

"I heard," Chloe said. "I just don't understand."

"That is the first time I ever heard them add 'and she,'" Tsion said. "That was for you, Chloe. They knew we were here. We did not have to approach them, did not have to identify ourselves, did not have to face Carpathia before we were ready. We did not even have to discuss with Eli and Moishe plans for their appearance at the stadium. They said that those who would benefit by their presence and testimony stood within the sound of their proclamation."

"They're coming?" Chloe said.

"That is what I gather," Tsion said.

"When?"

"At just the right time."

CHAPTER 2

RAYFORD HAD A LOT in common with Ken Ritz and found him fascinating. Distraught over his own future—and income—and fearful of what he might learn about his late wife, Rayford nonetheless enjoyed Ken's company. More than ten years his senior, Ken was former military, gruff, to the point, and aglow in what Tsion Ben-Judah called his "first love" of Christ.

Rayford and Ken spent hours in the air on the way home bringing each other up to date on their pasts, and Rayford silently thanked God for a new friend. His relationship with Tsion was as student to mentor. To Buck he was the father-in-law. How he missed Bruce Barnes, his first friend and spiritual guide after the Rapture! Ken seemed a gift from God.

Ritz assured Rayford he could learn the Gulfstream in no time. "You guys who drive the heavies can handle these skiffs like a bike racer goin' back to a trike."

"I wish it were that easy," Rayford said, "but I'll count on you for driver's training."

"Roger. And, man, with your replacement there for Carpathia—what's his name again?"

"Mac. Mac McCullum."

"Yeah. He gives us three pilots in the Trib Force. Now we gotta talk Sawbones into gettin' out of that GC hospital before they catch onto him. That'll give us a doctor. So, three pilots, a doc, and a rabbi—sounds like the start of a joke. The only member without a specialty is your daughter, and she's what I call the voice of reason. Nobody's more reasonable than Tsion, of course, but Chloe's the voice of reason for guys like me who don't understand everything the scholar says."

Rayford told Ritz about David Hassid. "I have no idea how long he'll be safe, but he gives us another pair of eyes and ears inside. Someday both he and Mac will have to run. Then look at the lineup we'll have."

"Hot dog!" Ritz said, clapping. "I don't like bein' on the defensive, man! Let's take on that rascal!"

Rayford had never heard Nicolae referred to as a rascal, but he liked Ritz's attitude. Weary and wary after so long in Carpathia's orbit, he too longed to quit playing and get to war.

Ritz seemed to grow uncomfortable when Rayford told him about Amanda. "I'm sorry for your loss," he said, when Rayford's story came full circle to the plane crash into the Tigris that had killed her.

"So you've heard the rest, too?" Rayford asked, having left out the charges of her duplicity.

"Yes, sir. I didn't come to any conclusions, but I can imagine how it all makes you feel."

"But you didn't hear from Buck what he found out from Hattie?"

"I didn't even know she was talking. Tell you the truth, I'll be surprised if she's still kickin' when we get back."

"That wasn't what I wanted to hear."

Buck hoped staying up late would make sleep come easily in the new time zone. But his brain was on Chicago time, and he lay staring at the ceiling. Chloe slept soundly beside him, and for that he was grateful.

By dawn in Israel, when he felt Chloe stir, Buck was so exhausted he could neither move nor open his eyes. He felt the brush of her lips on his cheek but couldn't even emit a groan.

"Stay still, big guy," she whispered. "Huge day ahead."

She got up, and Buck soon smelled breakfast, but he fell asleep and didn't rouse until early afternoon.

Rayford was impressed with Ken Ritz's facility on the radio and on the ground at Palwaukee Airport at dawn in the Chicago suburbs. "You push this thing around like you own it," he said.

"It'd be a good staff plane for the Trib Force, don't you think?"

Buck's Range Rover sat gleaming behind a damaged hangar. As they approached, a young man angled toward them. "Rover cleans up pretty good, doesn't she?" he said, a shock of red hair in his face.

"Yeah," Ritz said. "You been playin' under the hood too?"

"Lucky for you. Timing was all screwed up."

"I told you that, Ernie."

"You also told me you wouldn't be back for another week. I only got into that engine 'cause I was bored."

Ritz introduced Ernie to Rayford, who remained guarded until Ritz pulled the young man close and said, "Notice anything?"

Ernie stepped toward Rayford and peered at his forehead. Ernie smiled and held his hair away from his face with both hands. Rayford embraced him. "Brother."

"There's more of us around here, including the boss man," Ritz said, "but not too many, so we're careful. Ernie here's a Ben-Judah groupie."

"You got that right," Ernie said. "I can't wait for the big meeting. It's gonna be on the Net at noon tomorrow."

"We'll be watching," Rayford said, eager to get going. Half an hour later, he and Ken pulled behind the safe house in Mount Prospect in the amazingly smooth-running Rover. "We've got to stay close to Ernie," he said. "This vehicle needs to be as travel worthy as whatever plane we wind up with."

"Did you see the front curtain move when we came by, Ray? Until he saw it was us, Floyd was probably wondering how he was gonna get Hattie underground."

"You get a lot of snoops?"

"Hardly any. The block is deserted; the roads, as you saw, nearly impassable. So far, this has been a perfect spot. You wanna see Donny's wife's grave?"

Rayford had heard how Buck and Tsion had found the place. He nodded as Dr. Floyd Charles came out, the obvious question on his face. "We tried to call you," Ritz said.

"I've been on the phone to my guy at the hospital."

"This here's Rayford Steele. I was about to show him the grave."

"Of the woman neither of us ever met, but I suppose you did, Captain."

Rayford shook his head. "Knew who she was is all. Hey, we're brothers, Doctor. Call me Ray."

"Thanks. Call me anything you want except Floyd."

"How's Hattie?"

"Not well. Sleeping."

"She going to make it?"

Dr. Charles shook his head. "I'm not optimistic. The backup at CDC in Atlanta is ridiculous. She and I both have a hunch that what's in her system was put there by the GC. If they ever get to the sample I sent, they'll disavow it or steer me wrong."

They walked back to the primitive grave and stood in silence. "Wish we could put up some kind of marker," Rayford said, "but it would be only for us anyway, and we know who she was and where she is. We don't need to draw attention to this place."

Rayford felt deep gratitude that the Tribulation Force was headquartered in what was once this woman's home. He couldn't help cataloguing in his mind the deaths in his own circle. The list grew long and ultimately led to Amanda. He had grieved so much already, and he feared he would suffer many more losses before his own number came up.

Floyd Charles gave Rayford a quick tour of the place while they brought each other up to date on their respective situations. Rayford was impressed with the house, especially the underground shelter Donny had fashioned before his own demise. The day would surely come when they would all have to live under, rather than in, the house. How soon he could not guess. Nothing was predictable anymore, save for the judgments from heaven meticulously outlined on Tsion's scriptural charts. Who would survive and for how long was all in God's control and timing.

Rayford had heard death-rattle breathing before, but the emaciated frame of his former coworker, friend, and object of flirtation strangely moved him. Rayford stood over Hattie, pitying her, hoping for her, praying for her. He wanted to know what she knew about Amanda, of course, but he was not so selfish as to wish she would stay alive only long enough to communicate that. He gently pushed her bangs off her forehead. In the dim light he couldn't tell whether a mark was there. Dr. Charles shook his head. "She's been talking a lot lately, but she hasn't come to any decision yet. At least she hasn't decided the way we'd like."

"Chloe thought she was close," Rayford said. "Lord knows she has enough information. I don't know what it'll take."

"I plead with her all the time," the doctor said. "She's stubborn. Waiting for something. I don't know. I'm at a loss."

"Pray she survives another day," Rayford said. "And wake me if she comes to."

"You want something to help you sleep?"

Rayford raised his eyebrows. "I didn't figure you for a pill pusher."

"I'm careful. Don't use 'em myself, but I'm sympathetic to globe-trotters like you."

"I've never had trouble sleeping."

"Good for you."

Rayford turned to head upstairs and stopped. "How about you, Doc? Having trouble sleeping?"

"I told you, I don't use sleeping pills."

"That's not what I asked."

Dr. Charles looked down and shook his head. "How'd you guess?"

"You look wasted, sorry to say."

Floyd nodded without expression.

"You want to talk?" Rayford said.

"You're tired."

"Hey, Doc, the way I understand it, when you leave the hospital, you're going to join us. We're like family. I make time for family."

"It's just that I didn't expect to tell anybody about this until everyone got back."

Rayford pulled out a kitchen chair. "About what?"

"I'm in your boat, Rayford."

"Free of the GC, you mean? You've been fired?"

"I've got a believer friend at the hospital. I was on the phone to him in the middle of the night, apparently when Ken was trying to reach me. He told me he didn't know where I was and didn't want to know, but he said, friend to friend, disappear."

Rayford reached to shake his hand. "Welcome to the club. You think anybody followed you here?"

"No. I made sure of that. But I've been gone from the hospital so much and was apparently suspicious enough."

"If they don't know where you are, you're safe and so are we."

Dr. Charles leaned back against the refrigerator. "Thing is, I don't want to be a burden. The GC paid well, and I never compromised my principles. I worked hard to save lives and get people well."

"In other words, you're allowed to have less of a conscience problem than I about making a living working for the enemy?"

"I wasn't implying anything."

"I know. You're worried about joining us without being able to carry your weight."

"Exactly."

"Look at me, Doc. I'm one of the charter members, and here I am without income."

"I wish that made me feel better."

"I think we can provide room and board in exchange for medical services. That puts you way ahead of me. I'm just an extra pilot now, and I've got no plane." Rayford saw the hint of a smile. But then Floyd's knees buckled. "You all right?"

"Just tired."

"When did you sleep last?"

"It's been a while, but don't worry about—"

"How long since you've slept?"

"Too long, but I'm all right."

"Ken?" Rayford called. Ritz came up from the basement. "You feel up to sitting with Hattie awhile?"

"I'm good. I got so much caffeine in me I'll be up all day anyway."

The doctor looked deeply thankful. "I'm going to take you gentlemen up on this. Thank you." He gave Ken a few instructions, then trudged upstairs.

Ken sat next to Hattie's bed with his Bible on one knee and a laptop on the other. Rayford was amused at Ken's peeking over the top of his half-glasses to be sure Hattie was all right. He was one long-legged babysitter.

A few minutes later, as Rayford stretched out on the bed

upstairs, he could hear Floyd snoring already in the next room.

Twenty-four hours before the opening evening session of the Meeting of the Witnesses, Buck, Chloe, and Tsion joined the local committee at the stadium for a final walk-through of the program. They returned to the van to find a message from Chaim via Jacov. The driver read from a scrap of paper: "Dr. Rosenzweig was summoned to the quarters of the potentate and has come back with a personal request from the Supreme Commander."

"I can't wait," Buck said.

"I beg your pardon, sir?"

"Just an expression. Can you tell us what the req—"

"Oh, no sir. I was merely asked to get you back to Dr. Rosenzweig as quickly as possible."

Buck leaned closer to Tsion. "What do you make of it? What would Fortunato want?"

"I should expect Carpathia would like to meet me. Probably for public relations or political reasons."

"Why wouldn't Carpathia have talked to Rosenzweig himself?"

"Protocol. You know that, Cameron."

"But they're old friends," Chloe said. "They go way back. Didn't Dr. Rosenzweig introduce you to Carpathia in the first place, Buck?"

Buck nodded. "No doubt Nicolae enjoys keeping him in his place."

They arrived back at Chaim's complex to find him bubbling with enthusiasm. "I am not a fool, Tsion," the old man said. "I am aware that you have pitted yourself against my friend and argued with him publicly via the Internet. But I am telling you, you have him wrong. He is a wonderful man, a godly man, if I may say. The fact that he is humbly asking for a place on the program shows his goodwill and—"

"A place on the program!" Chloe said. "Impossible! The stadium will be full of Jewish converts who are convinced Nicolae is Antichrist himself."

"Oh, sweetheart," Chaim said, smiling at her. "Nicolae Carpathia? He seeks world peace, disarmament, global unity."

"My point exactly."

Chaim turned to his protégé. "Tsion, surely you can see that the only expedient thing to do is to cordially welcome him to the stage."

"You spoke with Carpathia yourself, Chaim?"

The older man cocked his head and shrugged. "Of course not. He is a very busy man. Supreme Commander Fortunato is his most trusted—"

"Too busy for you?" Tsion said. "You are a national hero, an icon, the man who helped make Israel what she is today! Your formula was the key to Carpathia's power. How can he forget that and refuse to see an old friend like—"

"He did not refuse me, Tsion! If I had merely asked, he would have granted me an audience."

"Regardless," Tsion said, "Chloe is right. Much as I would love to humiliate him, it would be just too awkward. What kind of reception do you think he will get from the twenty-five thousand witnesses we will cram into the stadium and nearly a hundred thousand more at other sites around the city?"

"Surely, out of Christian charity, they would be cordial to the world ruler."

Tsion shook his head and leaned forward, resting his hand on his former mentor's knee. "Dr. Rosenzweig, you have been like a father to me. I love you. I would welcome you to the stadium with open arms. But Nic—"

"I am not a believer, Tsion. So why not welcome another with the same openness?"

"Because he is more than simply not a believer. He is the enemy of God, of everything we stand for. Though you are not yet a believer, we do not consider you an en—"

"Not *yet* a believer!" Chaim rocked back and laughed. "You say that with such confidence."

"I pray for you every day."

"And I appreciate that more than I can say, my friend. But I am Jewish born and bred. Though I am not religious, I do believe Messiah is yet to come. Do not hold out hope that I shall become one of your witnesses. I—"

"Chaim, Chaim! Did you not hear my evidence the night I shared it with the world?"

"Yes! It was fascinating, and no one can argue it was not

persuasive. Look at what has come of it. But surely you do not claim it is for everyone!"

Buck could feel Tsion's incredulity. "Dr. Rosenzweig," the rabbi said, "I would be so grateful if you would allow me to plead my case to you. If I could personally show you my texts, my arguments, I believe I could prove to you that Jesus Christ is the Messiah and that Nicolae Carpathia is his archenemy. I would love to just—"

"I will give you that privilege one day, my friend," Rosenzweig said. "But not the night before one of the biggest days of your life. And I must tell you, I would sooner believe Jesus was the Messiah than that Nicolae is his enemy. That is simply not the man I know."

"I have the energy and the enthusiasm tonight, Doctor. Please."

"Well," Chaim said, smiling, "I do not. I will make a deal with you, however. You grant Nicolae a place on the program during your opening night, and I will give you my full attention on these matters at a later date."

Rosenzweig sat back, appearing pleased with his suggestion. Tsion, clearly frustrated, looked at Buck, then at Chloe. He shrugged. "I do not know," he said. "I just do not know. Frankly, Doctor, I could wish that a dear, old friend like you would listen to the heart of an admirer without condition."

Rosenzweig stood and stepped to the window, where he peered through a sliver between the curtains. "Nicolae has provided the armed guards that ensure you will not suffer the way your family did and that you will not again be chased from your homeland. All I ask is that you treat the most powerful man in the world with the deference he deserves. If you choose not to, I will be disappointed. But I will not make this a condition of eventually letting you try to persuade me of your position."

Tsion stood and thrust his hands deep into his pockets. He turned his back to Buck and the others. "Well, thank you for that," he said, barely above a whisper. "I shall have to pray about what to do about Carpathia's request."

Buck couldn't imagine how Carpathia could show his face at such a meeting or what response he might get from the assembled. Why would Carpathia subject himself to it?

"Tsion," Chaim said, "I must get back to the potentate with a response tonight. I said I would."

"Chaim, I will not have an answer until I have prayed about it. If Mr. Fortunato insists—"

"It is not his insistence, Tsion. I gave my word."

"I do not have an answer."

"All I can tell him is that you are praying about it?"

"Exactly."

"Tsion, who do you think secured Kollek Stadium for you?"

"I do not know."

"Nicolae! Do you think my countrymen would have offered it? You have aligned yourself with the two at the Wailing Wall who have cursed our country, *your* country! They have boasted of causing the drought that has crippled us. They turn water into blood, bring plagues upon us. It is rumored they will appear at the stadium themselves!"

"I can only hope," Tsion said.

The men turned to face each other, both with hands spread. "My dear Tsion," Chaim said, "you see what we have come to? If Nicolae is bold enough to address a stadium full of his enemies, he must be admired."

"I will pray," Tsion said. "That is all I can say."

As they went off to bed, Buck heard Chaim on the phone with Fortunato. "Leon, I am sorry. . . ."

Late in the afternoon in Illinois, Rayford was awakened by footsteps on the stairs. The door opened. "You awake, Ray?" Rayford sat up, staring, squinting against the light. "Should I get the doc? Hattie's wakin' up."

"Does she need anything?"

"I don't think so."

"Then let him sleep. She seems OK?"

"She's trying to talk."

"Tell her I'm coming down."

Rayford staggered to the bathroom and splashed cold water on his face. His heart raced. He hurried stiff-legged down the stairs to find Ken gently giving Hattie a drink of water.

"Captain Steele!" she rasped, eyes wide. She beckoned him close. "Could you excuse us?" she asked Ken. As he stepped away she reached for Rayford. "Nicolae wants me dead. He poisoned me. He can reach anywhere."

"How do you know, Hattie? How do you know he poisoned you?"

"I knew he would." Her voice was weak and thin. She gasped for air as she spoke. "He poisoned your friend Bruce Barnes."

Rayford sat back. "You *know* this?"

"He bragged about it. Told me it was a timed-release thing. Bruce would get sicker and sicker, and if all went according to plan, he would die after he returned to the States."

"Are you strong enough to tell me more?" Hattie nodded. "I don't want to cause you to get worse."

"I can talk."

"Do you know about Amanda?"

Her lips trembled, and she turned her face away.

"Do you?" he repeated. She nodded, looking miserable. "Tell me."

"I'm so sorry, Rayford. I knew from the beginning and could have told you."

He gritted his teeth, his temples pounding painfully. "Told me what?"

"I was involved," she said. "It wasn't my idea, but I could have stopped it."

CHAPTER 3

Rayford's mind reeled. The farthest he had allowed his imagination to take him was that Amanda might have been a plant at the beginning. Hattie could have told Carpathia enough about Rayford and his first wife to give Amanda a believable story about having met Irene. But even if that was true, Amanda surely could not have faked her conversion. He would not accept that.

"Did Carpathia have her killed because she became a believer?"

Hattie stared at him. "What?"

"Hattie, please. I have to know."

"You'll hate me."

"No. I care about you. I can tell you feel bad about your part in this. Tell me."

Hattie lay panting. "It was phony, Rayford. All of it."

"Amanda?"

She nodded and tried to sit up but needed Rayford's help. "The e-mails were bogus, Rayford. I was trained to do it. I saw it all."

"The e-mails?"

"The anonymous ones to Bruce. We knew someone would find them eventually. And the ones between Nicolae and Amanda, both ways. She didn't even know they were on her hard drive. They were encrypted and encoded; she would have had to have been an expert to even find them."

Rayford hardly knew what to ask. "But they sounded like her, read the way she expressed herself. They scared me to death."

"Nicolae has experts trained in that. They intercepted all your e-mails and used her style against her."

Rayford was drained. Tears welled up from so deep inside that he felt as if his heart and lungs would burst. "She was all I believed she was?" he said.

Hattie nodded. "She was more, Rayford. She loved you deeply, was totally devoted to you. I felt so despicable the last time I saw her, it was all I could do to keep from telling her. I knew I should. I wanted to. But what I had done was so awful, so evil. She had shown me nothing but love from the first. She knew about you and me. We disagreed about everything important in life, yet she loved me. I couldn't let her know I had helped make her look like a traitor."

Rayford sat shaking his head, trying to take it all in. "Thank you, Hattie," he said. So the reason he had not seen the seal of God on Amanda's forehead, besides her grotesque and discolored death mask, was that the plane had gone down before the mark appeared on any believers.

Rayford's faith in Amanda had been restored, and he had never doubted her salvation. Even when he had been forced to wonder about how she had come to him in the first place, he never questioned the genuineness of her devotion to God.

Rayford helped Hattie lie back down. "I'll get you something to eat," he said. "And then we're going to talk about you."

"Spare me that, Rayford. You and your friends have been doing that for two years. There's nothing you can tell me that I don't know. But I just told you what I have done, and there's even more that's worse than that."

"You know God will forgive you."

She nodded. "But should he? I don't believe that in my heart."

"Of course he shouldn't. None of us deserves forgiveness."

"But you accepted it anyway," she said. "I can't do that. I know as well as God does that I'm not worthy."

"So you're going to decide for him."

"If it's up to me—"

"And it is."

"I've decided I'm unworthy and can't live with that much, um, what do you call it?"

"Grace?"

"Well, I guess, but I mean there's too much of a gap between what may be true and what should be true."

"Inequity."

"That's it. God saving me when he and I both know who I am and what I've done—that's too much of an inequity."

At quarter to five in the afternoon at Chaim Rosenzweig's estate, Tsion asked Buck and Chloe to join him in his room. Buck smiled, noticing the ever-present laptop on a small table. The three knelt by the bed. "We will pray with the committee at the stadium," Tsion said. "But in case the rush of the details gets in the way, I do not want to start the meeting without seeking the Lord."

"May I ask," Chloe said, "what message you sent back to Mr. Fortunato?"

"I merely told Chaim that I would neither acknowledge nor recognize Nicolae. Neither will I introduce him or ask anyone else to. If he comes to the platform, I will not stand in his way." Tsion smiled wearily. "As you might expect, Chaim argued earnestly, warning me not to commit such an affront to the potentate. But how can I do otherwise? I will not say what I would like to say, will not rally the believers to express their distaste for him, will not expose him for who I know him to be. That is the best I can do."

Chloe nodded. "When do you expect the witnesses?"

"I should think they are beginning to arrive even now."

"I mean Eli and Moishe."

"Oh! I have left that with the Lord. They said they would be there, and the conference extends to two more whole days and nights. You can be sure I will gladly welcome *them* to the platform whenever they choose to appear."

Buck never failed to be moved by the heartfelt prayers of Dr. Ben-Judah. He had seen the rabbi at the lowest point of grief a man could bear, reeling from the slaughter of his wife and two teenagers. He had heard him pray in the midst of terror, certain he would be apprehended on a midnight flight from Israel. Now, as Tsion looked forward to uniting with tens of thousands of new brothers and sisters in Christ from all twelve tribes of Israel and from all over the world, he was on his knees in humility.

"God, our Father," he began, "thank you for the privilege we are about to enjoy. On the front lines of battle we advance with your boldness, under your power and protection. These precious saints will be hungry to learn more of your Word. Give the other teachers and me the words. May we say what you would have us say, and may they hear what you want them to hear."

Buck was deep in his own prayer when a tap at the door interrupted them. "Forgive me, Tsion," Chaim said. "A GC escort is here."

"But I thought Jacov would drive us—"

"He will. But they tell us you have to leave immediately if you hope to reach the stadium in time."

"But it is so close!"

"Nevertheless. Traffic is already so thick that only the GC escort can ensure you will get there on time."

"Have you decided to come with us, Chaim?"

"I will be watching on television. I have asked Jacov to load a case of bottled water for you. Those two preachers at the Wall have taken credit for blood in the drinking water again. Though it supposedly has cleared since the visitors began arriving, you never know. Westerners should not risk our tap water anyway."

The GC escort proved to be two Jeeps with flashing yellow lights, each vehicle carrying four armed guards who merely stared at the Tribulation Force as they climbed into the Mercedes van. "Another bit of one-upmanship from Carpathia," Chloe said.

"If he was smart," Tsion said, "he would have left us to our own devices and let us be late."

"You would not have been late," Jacov said in his thick accent. "I would have gotten you there on time anyway."

Buck had never seen—even in New York—traffic like this. Every artery to the stadium was jammed with cars and pedestrians. Neither had he seen so many happy faces since before the Rapture. Carrying satchels and notebooks and water bottles, the pedestrians hurried along with earnest and determined looks. Many made better time than the cars and vans and buses.

Because of the conspicuous escort, the crowds recognized that the Mercedes carried Tsion Ben-Judah. They waved and shouted and gleefully pounded on doors and windows. The trailing GC vehicle shooed them away with warnings over a loudspeaker and by brandishing their automatic weapons.

"I hate to appear to be here under the aegis of the Global Community," Tsion said.

"They don't know the shortcuts anyway," Jacov said. "All three of these vehicles are equipped to go off-road."

"You know a faster way?" Tsion said. "Take it!"

"May I?"

"They won't open fire. They'll have to scramble just to keep up."

Jacov whipped the wheel to the left, flew down and up a ditch in the median, picked his way through crawling cars on the other side, and headed toward open fields. The GC Jeeps blew their sirens and bounced crazily behind him. The lead car finally caught up and pulled ahead, the driver pointing out the window and shouting at Jacov in Hebrew.

"He says to never do that again," Tsion said. "But I rather enjoyed it."

Jacov slammed on the brakes, and the trailing Jeep tore up grass stopping short of him. Jacov opened his door and stood with his head high above the roofline. The lead driver finally noticed he was leaving Jacov and slid to a stop. He waited at first, then backed up as Jacov shouted, "Unless you want trouble for making us late, you will follow me!"

Tsion looked gleefully at Chloe. "What is it your father is so fond of saying?"

"Lead, follow, or get out of the way."

As Jacov led the angry GC drivers to the stadium, it quickly became obvious that many more than twenty-five thousand hoped to get in. "Do we have monitors outside?" Tsion said.

Buck nodded. "The overflow was supposed to go to several off-site locations, but it appears they all want to stay here."

Having been shown up by Jacov, the GC soldiers leaped from their vehicles and insisted on escorting the little entourage inside the stadium. They scowled at Jacov, who told Buck he would be waiting in the van where he had dropped them off.

"Can you see a monitor?" Buck asked, looking around.

Jacov pointed to one about twenty feet away. "And I can listen on the radio."

"Does this interest you?"

"Very much. I find it confusing, but I have long been suspicious of the potentate, even though Dr. Rosenzweig admires him. And your teacher is such a wise and gentle man."

"Did you see him on television when he—"

"Everyone did, sir."

"Then this isn't totally new to you. We'll talk later."

Inside, the local committee was ecstatic. Buck loved hearing group prayer in English, Hebrew, and a few other languages he couldn't identify. All over the room he heard "Jesus the Messiah" and *"Jesu Cristo"* and *"Yeshua Hamashiach."*

On his knees next to Chloe, Buck felt her strong grip. She laid her head on his shoulder. "Oh, Buck," she said, "this is like heaven."

He whispered, "And we haven't even started."

As the stadium filled, shouts and chants resounded. "What are they saying?" Buck said.

"'Hallelujah,' and 'Praise the Lord,'" someone said. "And they're spelling out the name of Jesus."

The master of ceremonies, Daniel, addressed the group as the clock sped toward seven. "As you know, the program is simple. I will give a brief welcome and then open in prayer. I will lead in the singing of 'Amazing Grace,' and I will then introduce Dr. Ben-Judah. He will preach and teach for as long as he feels led. You twelve translators should have your copy of Dr. Ben-Judah's notes and know which of the microphones at the base of the stage is yours."

"And remember," Tsion said quietly, "I cannot guarantee I will follow the script. I will try not to get ahead of you."

People in the room nodded solemnly, and many looked at their watches. Buck heard the rumble of chants and singing above and was as excited as he had ever been. "All these people are our brothers and sisters," he told Chloe.

Three minutes before seven, as Tsion stood apart from the others, head bowed, a young man rushed in. "The other venues are empty!" he said. "Everyone is here. Everyone had the same idea!"

"How many?" someone asked.

"More than fifty thousand surrounding the stadium," he said, "at least twice as many outside as in. And they are not all witnesses. They are not even all Jewish. People are just curious."

Daniel raised his hands, and the room fell silent. "Follow me down this corridor, up the ramp, then up the stairs to the stage. You can watch from the wings, but translators go first and get into position at ground level in front of the platform. No one on the stage but Dr. Ben-Judah and me. Quiet please. Dear God in heaven, we are yours."

With one hand still raised, he and Tsion led the group toward the back of the stage. Buck peeked out to see every seat filled and people in the aisles and the infield. Many held hands. Others wrapped their arms around each other's shoulders and sang and swayed.

The interpreters slipped out and down the steps to get into position, and the crowd quieted. At seven, Daniel strode to a simple, wood lectern and said, "Welcome my brothers and sisters in the name of the Lord God Almighty, . . ."

He paused for the interpreters, but before they could translate, the stadium erupted in cheering and applause. Daniel was taken aback and smiled apologetically at the translators. "I'll wait for you," he mouthed, as the thousands continued to cheer.

When the applause finally died, he nodded to the

interpreters, and they repeated his phrase. "No! No!" came the response from the crowd. *"Nein!" "Nyet!"*

Daniel continued, ". . . maker of heaven and earth, . . ." And again the crowd erupted. He waited for the translation, but they shouted it down again.

". . . and his Son, Jesus Christ, the Messiah!"

The crowd went wild, and an aide hurried to the stage. "Please!" Daniel scolded him. "No one on the stage except—"

"No translation is necessary!" the aide shouted. "Don't use the interpreters! The crowd understands you in their own languages, and they want you to just keep going!"

As the crowd continued to exult, Daniel stepped to the front of the stage and beckoned the translators to gather before him. "You're not needed!" he said, smiling. As they dispersed, looking surprised but pleased, he went back to the microphone. "Shall we express our appreciation to these who were willing—"

Thunderous ovations rolled out of the stands.

Finally Daniel held up his hands to quiet the crowd. Every phrase from then on was greeted with resounding cheers. "You don't need to be told why you're here!" he said. "We've long been known as God's chosen people, but how about this? Would you pray with me?"

Silence descended quickly. Many knelt. "Father, we are grateful for having been spared by your grace and love. You are indeed the God of new beginnings and second chances. We are about to hear from our beloved rabbi, and our prayer is that you would supernaturally quicken our hearts and minds to absorb every jot and tittle of what you have given him to say. We pray this in the matchless name of the King of kings and Lord of lords. Amen."

A huge "Amen!" echoed from the crowd. Daniel directed the massive congregation as he began to sing quietly, "Amazing grace! how sweet the sound that saved a wretch like me! I once was lost, but now am found, was blind but now I see."

Buck could not sing. "Amazing Grace" had become his favorite hymn, a poignant picture of his faith. But twenty-five thousand believers singing it from their hearts nearly knocked him over. The mass outside added their voices. Buck and Chloe stood weeping at the beauty of it.

"When we've been there ten thousand years, bright shining as the sun, we've no less days to sing God's praise than when we'd first begun."

As the final strains trailed off, Daniel asked the crowd to sit. "The vast majority of us know our speaker tonight only as a name on our computer screens," he began. "It is my honor—"

But the assembled had come to their feet en masse, cheering, clapping, shouting, whistling. Daniel tried to quiet them, but finally shrugged and walked away as Tsion, embarrassed, hesitated. He was nudged from the wings, and the cacophony deafened Buck. He and Chloe clapped too, honoring their personal pastor and mentor. Never had Buck felt so privileged to be part of the Tribulation Force and to know this man.

Tsion stood meekly at the lectern, spreading his Bible and his notes before him. The noisy welcome continued until he finally looked up with a shy smile and mouthed his thanks, holding up both hands to request silence. At long last, the crowd settled into their seats.

"My beloved brothers and sisters, I accept your warm greeting in the name that is above all names. All glory and honor is due the triune God." As the crowd began to respond again, Tsion quickly held up a hand. "Dear ones, we are in the midst of a mountaintop experience in which anything and everything said about our God could justifiably be celebrated. But we are guests here. There is a curfew. And I trust you will forgive me if I request that we withhold expressions of praise from now until the end of the teaching."

The crowd fell deathly silent so quickly that Tsion raised his brows and looked around. "I have not offended you, have I?" A smattering of applause urged him to continue.

"Later it will be wholly appropriate if our master of ceremonies gives you an opportunity to raise your voices again in praise of our God. The Bible says, 'Let them praise the name of the Lord, for His name alone is exalted; His glory is above the earth and heaven.'

"Ladies and gentlemen," Tsion continued, spreading his feet and hunching his shoulders as he gazed at his notes, "never in my life have I been more eager to share a message from the Word of God. I stand before you with the unique privilege, I believe, of addressing many of the 144,000 witnesses prophesied in the Scriptures. I count myself one of you, and God has burdened me to help you learn to evangelize. Most of you already know how, of course, and have been winning converts to the Savior every day. Millions around the world have come to faith already.

"But let me review for you again the basics of God's plan of salvation so we may soon leave this place and get back to the work to which he has called us. You have each been assigned a location for all-day training tomorrow and the next day. On both nights we will meet back here for encouragement and fellowship and teaching."

Tsion then outlined the same evidence he had used on the controversial television broadcast that had made him a fugitive, proving from the Old Testament that Jesus was the Messiah. He recited the many names of God and finished with the powerful passage from Isaiah 9:6, "For unto us a Child is born, unto us a Son is given; and the government will be upon His shoulder. And His name will be called Wonderful, Counselor, Mighty God, Everlasting Father, Prince of Peace."

The crowd could not contain itself, leaping to its feet. Tsion smiled and nodded and waved encouragement, pointing to the heavens. "Yes, yes," he said finally. "Even I would not stifle your praise to the Most High God. Jesus himself said that if we do not glorify God, the very stones would have to cry out."

Tsion walked through God's plan of redemption from the beginning of time, showing that Jesus was sent as the spotless lamb, a sacrifice to take away the sins of the world.

He explained the truths that had so recently become clear to these initiates, that man is born in sin and that nothing he can do for himself can reconcile him to God. Only by believing and trusting in the work Christ did for him on the cross can he be born again spiritually into eternal life. "In John 14:6," Tsion said, his voice rising for the first time, "Jesus himself said he was the way, the truth, and the life, and that no man can come to the Father except through him. This is our message to the nations. This is our message to the desperate, the sick, the terrified, the bound. By now there should be no doubt in anyone's mind—even those who have chosen to live in opposition to God—that he is real and that a person is either for him or against him. We of all people should have the boldness of Christ to aggressively tell the world of its only hope in him.

"The bottom line, my brothers and sisters, is that we have been called as his divine witnesses—144,000 strong—through whom he has begun a great soul harvest. This will result in what John the Revelator calls 'a great multitude which no one could number.' Before you fall asleep tonight, read Revelation 7 and thrill with me to the description of the harvest you and I have been called to reap. John says it is made up of souls from all nations, kindreds, peoples, tribes, and tongues. One day they will stand before his throne and before the Lamb, clothed with white robes and carrying palms in their hands!"

Spontaneously, the crowd at Teddy Kollek Stadium stood as Tsion's voice rose and fell. Buck held Chloe tight and wanted to shout amen as Tsion thundered on. "They will cry with a loud voice, saying, 'Salvation belongs to our God who sits on the throne, and to the Lamb!'

"The angels around the throne will fall on their faces and worship God, saying, 'Amen! Blessing and glory and wisdom, thanksgiving and honor and power and might, be to our God forever and ever. Amen.'"

The crowd began to roar again, and Tsion did not quiet them. He merely stepped back and gazed at the floor, and Buck had the impression he was overcome and welcomed the pause to collect himself. When he moved back to the microphone, the standing thousands quieted again, as if desperate to catch every word. "John was asked by one of the elders at the throne, 'Who are these arrayed in white robes, and where did they come from?' And John said, 'Sir, you know.' And the elder said, 'These are the ones who come out of the great tribulation, and washed their robes and made them white in the blood of the Lamb.'"

Tsion waited through another reverberating response, then continued: "'They shall neither hunger anymore nor thirst anymore.' The Lamb himself shall feed them and lead them to fountains of living water. And, best of all, my dear family, God shall wipe away all tears from their eyes."

This time when the crowd began to respond, Tsion stayed in the lectern and raised a hand, and they listened. "We shall be here in Israel two more full days and nights, preparing for battle. Put aside fear! Put on boldness! Were you surprised that all of us, each and every one, were spared the last few judgments I wrote about? When the rain and hail and fire came from the sky and the meteors scorched a third of the plant life and poisoned a third of the waters of the world, how was it that we escaped? Luck? Chance?"

The crowd shouted, "No!"

"No!" Tsion echoed. "The Scriptures say that an angel ascending from the east, having the seal of the living God, cried with a loud voice to the four angels to whom it was granted to harm the earth and the sea. And what did he tell them? He said, 'Do not harm the earth, the sea, or the trees till we have sealed the servants of our God on their foreheads.' And John writes, 'I heard the number of those who were sealed. One hundred and forty-four thousand of all the tribes of the children of Israel were sealed.'

"And now let me close by reminding you that the bedrock of our faith remains the verse our Gentile brothers and sisters have so cherished from the beginning. John 3:16 says," and here Tsion spoke so softly, so tenderly that he had to be right on the microphone, and people edged forward to hear, "'For God so loved the world that He gave His only—'"

A faint rumble in the sky became a persistent *thwock-thwock-thwock* that drowned out Tsion as a gleaming white helicopter drew every eye. The crowd stared as the chopper, with GC emblazoned on the side, slowly descended, its massive blades whipping Tsion's hair and clothes until he was forced to back away from the lectern.

The engine shuddered and stopped, and the crowd murmured when Leon Fortunato bounded from the craft to the lectern. He nodded to Tsion, who did not respond, then adjusted the microphone to his own height. "Dr. Ben-Judah, local and international organizing committee, and assembled guests," he began with great enthusiasm, but immediately thousands looked puzzled, looked at each other, shrugged, and began jabbering.

"Translators!" someone shouted. "We need interpreters!"

Fortunato looked expectantly at Tsion, who continued staring straight ahead. "Dr. Ben-Judah," Fortunato implored, "is there someone who can translate? Whom are you using?"

Tsion did not look at him.

"Excuse me," Fortunato said into the microphone, "but interpreters have been assigned. If you would come forward quickly, His Excellency, your potentate, would be grateful for your service."

Buck stepped out and peered into an area near the front row in the infield where the interpreters sat. As one they looked to Tsion, but Fortunato didn't even know whom he was addressing. "Please," he said. "It isn't fair that only those who understand English may enjoy the remarks of your next two hosts."

Hosts? Buck thought. That got even Tsion's attention, and his head jerked as he glanced at Leon. "Please," Leon mouthed, as the crowd grew louder. Tsion glanced at the translators, who eyed him, waiting. He raised his head slightly, as if to give the OK. They hurried to their microphones.

"Thank you kindly, Dr. Ben-Judah," Fortunato said.

"You're most helpful, and His Excellency thanks you as well." Tsion ignored him.

With the singsong cadence necessary to keep the interpreters on pace, Fortunato addressed the crowd anew. "As supreme commander of the Global Community and as one who has personally benefited from his supernatural ability to perform miracles, it shall be my pleasure in a moment to introduce you to His Excellency, Global Community potentate Nicolae Carpathia!"

Fortunato had ended with a flourish, as if expecting cheering and applause. He stood smiling and—to Buck's mind—embarrassed and perturbed when no one responded. No one even moved. Every eye was on Fortunato except Tsion's.

Leon quickly gathered himself. "His Excellency will personally welcome you, but first I would like to introduce the revered head of the new Enigma Babylon One World Faith, the supreme pontiff, Pontifex Maximus, Peter the Second!"

Fortunato swept grandly back, beckoning to the helicopter, from which emerged the comical figure of the man Buck knew as Peter Mathews, former archbishop of Cincinnati. He had become pope briefly after the disappearance of the previous pontiff but was now the amalgamator of nearly every religion on the globe save Judaism and Christianity.

Mathews had somehow emerged from the helicopter with style, despite being decked out in the most elaborate clerical garb Buck had ever seen. "What in the world is that?" Chloe said.

Buck watched agape as Peter the Second lifted his hands

to the crowd and turned slowly in a circle as if to include everyone in his pompous and pious greeting. He wore a high, peaked cap with an infinity symbol on the front and a floor-length, iridescent yellow robe with a long train and billowy sleeves. His vestments were bedecked with huge, inlaid, brightly colored stones and appointed with tassels, woven cords, and bright blue, crushed velvet stripes, six on each sleeve, as if he had earned some sort of a double doctorate from Black Light Discotheque University. Buck covered his mouth to stifle a laugh. When Mathews turned around, he revealed astrological signs on the train of his robe.

His hands moved in circles as if to bless everyone, and Buck wondered how he felt about hearing nothing from the audience. Would Carpathia dare face this indifference, this hostility?

Peter pulled the mike up to his mouth and spoke with arms outstretched. "My blessed brothers and sisters in the pursuit of higher consciousness, it warms my heart to see all of you here, studying under the well-intentioned scholarship of my colleague and respected litterateur, Dr. Tsion Ben-Judah!" Mathews clearly expected that announcing their hero as if introducing a heavyweight boxer would elicit a roar, but the crowd remained silent and unmoving.

"I confer upon this gathering the blessings of the universal father and mother and animal deities who lovingly guide us on our path to true spirituality. In the spirit of harmony and ecumenism, I appeal to Dr. Ben-Judah and others in your leadership to add your rich heritage and history and scholarship to our coat of many colors. To the patchwork quilt that so beautifully encompasses and includes and affirms and accepts the major tenets of all the world's great religions, I urge you to include your own. Until the day comes that you agree to plant your flag under the umbrella of Enigma Babylon One World Faith, rest assured that I will defend your right to disagree and to oppose and to seek our multi-layered plural godhead in your own fashion."

Mathews turned regally and traded places with Fortunato, both clearly pretending to be unfazed by the apathy of the crowd. Fortunato announced, "And now it gives me pleasure to introduce to you the man who has united the world into one global community, His Excellency and your potentate, Nicolae Carpathia! Would you rise as he comes with a word of greeting."

No one stood.

Carpathia, a frozen smile etched on his face, had never—in Buck's experience—failed to captivate a crowd. He was the most dynamic, engaging, charming speaker Buck had ever heard. Buck himself was, of course, far past being impressed with Nicolae, but he wondered if the seal of God on the foreheads of the witnesses and their converts also protected their minds against his evil manipulation.

"Fellow citizens of the Global Community," Carpathia began, waiting for the interpreters and appearing to Buck to work hard at connecting with the crowd. "As your potentate, I welcome you to Israel and to this great arena, named after a man of the past, a man of peace and harmony and statesmanship."

Buck was impressed. Nicolae had immediately tried to align himself with a former mayor of the Holy City, one a huge percentage of this crowd would have heard of. Buck began to worry that Nicolae's power of persuasion might sway someone like Jacov. He put a hand on Chloe's shoulder and whispered, "I'll be right back."

"How can you walk out on this?" she said. "I wouldn't miss this show for the world. Don't you think Peter's getup would work on me, maybe as an evening kind of a thing?"

"I'll be with Jacov for a minute."

"Good idea."

As Buck stepped away, his cell phone vibrated in his pocket. "Buck here," he said.

"Where you goin'?"

"Who's this?"

"That was you at stage right with the blonde, right?"

Buck stopped. "I have to know who this is."

"Mac McCullum. Nice to meet ya."

"Mac! What's up? Where are you?"

"On the chopper, man! This is the best theater I've seen in ages. All this friendly folderol! You should have heard these guys on board! Swearing, cursing Ben-Judah and the whole crowd. Carpathia spit all over me, railing about the two witnesses."

"Doesn't surprise me. Hey, you sure this connection is secure?"

"Only my life depends on it, son."

"Guess that's true." Buck told Mac where he was going and why.

"Nick's a piece of work, ain't he?" Mac said.

"Chloe's particularly fond of Mathews's sartorial resplendence."

"Hey, me too! Gotta go. Don't want to have to tell 'em who I was talkin' to."

"Keep in touch, Mac."

"Don't worry. But listen, make yourselves scarce too. I wouldn't put anything past these guys."

"Wait," Buck said, a smile in his voice. "You mean we can't take Carpathia at his word? He's not a trustworthy guy?"

"All right, just watch yourselves."

CHAPTER 4

Knowing the GC brass was away from New Babylon, Rayford e-mailed David Hassid at the underground shelter. "Be where you can receive TX at six your time, brother."

At nine in the morning Chicago time, an hour before the Meeting of the Witnesses was to be broadcast live internationally via the Internet, Rayford reached David by phone. "Where are you?" he said.

"Outside," David said. "Things are pretty quiet with Abbott and Costello away."

Rayford chuckled. "I would have guessed you way too young for them."

"They're my favorites," David said. "Especially now that

they're ruling the world. What's up? I was about to watch the festivities. They've got it on the wall-sized screen in the compound."

Rayford filled him in on the latest. "Sad to say, the next time I see you may be because you need to hide out with us."

"I can't imagine escaping here, but Mac's right that it's good you slipped away. Your days were numbered."

"I'm shocked Nicolae didn't do me in months ago."

"Your son-in-law better lay low, too. His name pops up all the time. They've assigned me to locate where his webzine originates. But you know, Rayford, as hard as I work on that and as much time as I put into it, I just can't seem to break through the scramble and find it."

"No kidding."

"I'm doing my best. Honest I am. Boy it's frustrating when you can't deliver information to your boss that would cost the life of a brother. Know what I mean?"

"Well, you keep working on it, David, and I'm sure you'll at least find a misdirection that can waste more of their time."

"Great idea."

"Listen, can you walk me through hooking my laptop to a TV so we can see this meeting easier?"

David laughed. "Next you'll tell me your microdisc player is blinking twelve o'clock all day and night."

"How'd you know?"

"Just a lucky guess."

"You know we consider you a member of the Tribulation

Force," Rayford said, "though the others have not met you. You and Mac are our guys inside now, and we know well how dangerous that is."

David grew serious. "Thanks. I'd love to meet everybody and be with you all, but like you say, when that happens, it'll be because I'm running . . . and from the most technologically advanced regime in history. I may not see you until heaven. Until then, you need a plane or anything?"

"We're going to have to talk about that here. If all's fair in love and war, it might make sense for us to appropriate enemy equipment."

"You could abscond with millions' worth and not cripple the GC. You wouldn't even scratch them."

"How much longer will you be underground?"

"Not long. The new palace—yeah, it's a palace this time—is almost done. Spectacular. Wish I were proud to work here. It'd be a pretty good deal."

After David got him set up, Rayford set the TV where he, Dr. Charles, Ken Ritz, and Hattie would be able to see it. Hattie lay rocking and groaning. She refused food or medication, so Rayford merely covered her. A few minutes before ten, he asked Ken to rouse Floyd, who wanted to watch with them.

The doctor expressed alarm when he saw Hattie. "How long has she been this way?"

"About an hour," Ken said. "Should we have woken you?"

The doctor shrugged. "I'm shooting in the dark, experimenting with antidotes for a poison that hasn't been identified.

She rallies and I get encouraged, and then she reverts to this." He medicated her and fed her, and she slept quietly.

Rayford was moved to tears by the broadcast from Israel, but the men laughing at Peter Mathews's apparel awoke Hattie. She slowly and apparently painfully pushed herself up onto her elbows to watch. "Nicolae hates Mathews with a passion," she said. "You watch, he'll have him murdered someday."

Rayford shot her a double take. She was right, of course, but how did she know? Had it been in the plans as early as when Hattie worked for Carpathia? "You watch," she repeated.

When Nicolae emerged from the helicopter and joined Fortunato and Mathews onstage, Rayford's phone rang. "First chance I've had to call you, Ray," Mac said. "First off, nobody knows you're gone yet. Good job. 'Course, I can play dumb only so long. Now listen, your son-in-law and daughter—is he a good-looking kid, early thirties, and she a cute blonde?"

"That's them. Where are they? I can see the copter, but I don't see them."

"They're off camera, in the wings."

"Mac, let me tell you what Hattie told me about—"

"I've only got a second here, Ray. Let me call Buck. Will he have his phone on him, the one with the number you gave me?"

"He should, but Mac—"

"I'll check back with you, Ray."

As Buck emerged from the stadium, Carpathia's eloquence reverberated. When Buck reached the van, he saw Jacov facing front, hands on the wheel. He seemed to be peering over the crowd at the monitor while listening to the radio. Buck reached for the door handle, but Jacov had locked himself inside and recoiled at the sound, looking terrified.

"Oh, it's you," he said, unlocking the door.

"Who were you expecting?" Buck said, climbing in.

"I just didn't notice you. I apologize."

"So, what do you make of all this?"

Jacov held his hand out, palm down, to show Buck that he was trembling.

Buck offered Jacov his bottle of water. "What are you afraid of?"

"God," Jacov said, smiling self-consciously and declining the bottle.

"You don't need to be. He loves you."

"Don't need to be? Rabbi Ben-Judah teaches that all these things we have endured are the judgments of God. It seems I should have feared him long ago. But pardon me, I wish to hear the potentate."

"You know Dr. Ben-Judah is not a friend of his."

"That is clear. He has been received most coldly."

"Appropriately so, Jacov. He is an enemy of God."

"But I owe it to him to listen."

Buck was tempted to keep talking anyway, to nullify any

deleterious effect Carpathia might have on Jacov. But he didn't want to be rude, and he wanted to trust God to work in the man's heart and mind. He fell silent as Carpathia's liquid tones filled the air.

"And so, my beloved friends, it is not a requirement that your sect align itself with the One World Faith for you to remain citizens of the Global Community. Within reasonable limits, there is room for dissent and alternative approaches. But consider with me for a moment the advantages and privileges and benefits that have resulted from the uniting of every nation into one global village."

Nicolae recited his litany of achievements. It ranged from the rebuilding of cities and roads and airports to the nearly miraculous reconstruction of New Babylon into the most magnificent city ever built. "It is a masterpiece I hope you will visit as soon as you can." He mentioned his cellular/solar satellite system (Cell-Sol) that allowed everyone video access to each other by phone and Internet regardless of time or location. Buck shook his head. All this merely ushered in the superstructure necessary for Nicolae to rule the world until the time came to declare himself God.

Buck could see that Nicolae was succeeding in changing Jacov's mind. "This is hard to argue with," the driver said. "He has worked wonders."

"But Jacov," Buck said, "you have been exposed to the teaching of Dr. Ben-Judah. Surely you must be convinced that the Scriptures are true, that Jesus is the Messiah, that the disappearances were the rapture of Christ's church."

Jacov stared ahead, gripping the wheel tightly, his arms shaking. He nodded, but he looked conflicted. Buck no longer cared about rudeness. He would talk over Nicolae; he would not allow the enemy to steal this soul through slick talking.

"What did you think of the teaching tonight?"

"Most impressive," Jacov admitted. "I cried. I felt myself drawn to him, but mostly drawn to God. I love and respect Dr. Rosenzweig, and he would never understand if I became a believer in Jesus. But if it is true, what else can I do?"

Buck prayed silently, desperately.

"But, Mr. Williams, I had never before heard the verse that Dr. Ben-Judah said was the reason for this meeting. And he was interrupted, was he not? He did not finish the verse."

"You're right, he didn't. It was John 3:16, and it goes, 'For God so loved the world that He gave His only—'"

But Buck got no further than Tsion had when Jacov held up a hand to silence him. "The potentate is finishing," he said.

Carpathia seemed to be wrapping up his remarks, but something was strange about his voice. Buck had never heard him struggle to speak, but he had grown hoarse. Carpathia turned away from the mike, covered his mouth, and attempted to clear his throat. "Pardon me," he said, his voice still raspy. "But I wish you and the rabbi here all the best and welcome you, *ahem, ahem,* once again, excuse me—"

Nicolae turned pleadingly to Tsion, who was still ignoring him. "Would someone have some water?"

Someone passed a fresh bottle to the stage, where Nicolae nodded his thanks. When he opened it, the release of the pressure was magnified over the loudspeaker. But when he drank, he gagged and spit the water out. His lips and chin were covered in blood, and he held the bottle at arm's length, staring at it in horror. Jacov jumped from the car and moved closer to the monitor. Buck knew why. Even at that distance, it was obvious the bottle contained blood.

Buck followed as they heard Carpathia swearing, cursing Tsion and his "evil gaggle of enemies of the Global Community! You would humiliate me like this for your own gain? I should pull from you my pledge of protection and allow my men to shoot you dead where you stand!"

From the middle of the stunned crowd came the shouted, unison voices of Eli and Moishe. Without need of amplification, everyone within a block of the place could hear them. The crowd fell back from around them, and the two stood in the eerie light of the stadium, shoulder to shoulder, barefoot and in sackcloth.

"Woe unto you who would threaten the chosen vessel of the Most High God!"

Carpathia threw the water bottle onto the floor of the stage, and clear, clean water splashed everywhere. Buck knew the witnesses had turned only Nicolae's water to blood and that they had likely caused him to need the drink in the first place. Nicolae pointed at Eli and Moishe and screamed, "Your time is nigh! I swear I will kill you or have you killed before—"

But the witnesses were louder, and Carpathia had to fall silent. "Woe!" they said again. "Woe to the impostor who would dare threaten the chosen ones before the due time! Sealed followers of the Messiah, drink deeply and be refreshed!"

The bottle in Buck's pocket suddenly felt cold. He pulled it out and felt the sting of frigidity in his palm. He twisted off the top and drank deeply. Icy, smooth, rich, thirst-quenching nectar cascaded down his throat. He moaned, not wanting to pull the bottle from his lips but needing to catch his breath. All around he heard the sighs of satisfied believers, sharing cold, refreshing bottles.

"Taste this, Jacov!" Buck said, wiping off the top and handing it to him. "It's *very* cold."

Jacov reached for the water. "It doesn't feel cold to me," he said.

"How can you say that? Feel my hand." Buck put his hand on Jacov's arm, and Jacov flinched.

"Your hand is freezing," he said, "but the bottle feels warm to me." He held it up to the light. "Agh! Blood!" And he dropped it. The bottle bounced at Buck's feet, and he snatched it up before it emptied. It was again cold in his hands, and he couldn't resist guzzling from it.

"Don't!" Jacov said. But as he watched Buck enjoy the clean water, he fell to his hands and knees. "Oh, God, I am no better than Carpathia! I want to be a child of God! I want to be a sealed one!"

Buck squatted next to him and put an arm around his shoulder. "God wants you as part of his family," he said.

Jacov wept bitterly, then looked up at the whir of chopper blades. He and Buck stared at the TV monitor, where Tsion stood alone again on the stage. His hair and clothes flapped in the wind from the helicopter, and his notes were whipped into a funnel before scattering. Translators leapt onto the stage to retrieve them and set them back on the lectern. Tsion remained motionless, staring, having ignored the entire episode with Nicolae and the two witnesses.

The camera panned to where the witnesses had appeared, but they had left as quickly as they had come. The crowd stood, mouths open, many still drinking and passing around water bottles. When they noticed Tsion back at the lectern, they quieted and sat. As if nothing had happened since he began quoting John 3:16, Tsion continued:

"'—begotten Son, that whoever believes in Him should not perish but have everlasting life.'"

Jacov, still on his knees, hands on his thighs, seemed glued to the TV image. "What?" he cried out. "What?"

And as if he had heard Jacov, Tsion repeated the verse: "'For God so loved the world that He gave His only begotten Son, that whoever believes in Him should not perish but have everlasting life.'"

Jacov lowered his face to the pavement, sobbing. "I believe! I believe! God save me! Don't let me perish! Give me everlasting life!"

"He hears you," Buck said. "He will not turn away a true seeker."

But Jacov continued to wail. Others in the crowd had fallen to their knees. Tsion said, "There may be some here, inside or outside, who want to receive Christ. I urge you to pray after me, 'Dear God, I know I am a sinner. Forgive me and pardon me for waiting so long. I receive your love and salvation and ask you to live your life through me. I accept you as my Savior and resolve to live for you until you come again.'"

Jacov repeated the prayer through tears, then rose to embrace Buck. He squeezed him so tight Buck could hardly breathe. Buck pulled away and thrust the water bottle into Jacov's hand again.

"Cold!" Jacov exulted.

"Drink!" Buck said.

Jacov held the bottle to the light again, smiling. It was clear. "And it's full!"

Buck stared. It was! Jacov put it to his lips and tilted his head back so far that he staggered and Buck had to hold him up. He gulped, but not fast enough, and the cool clear water gushed over his face and down his neck. Jacov laughed and cried and shouted, "Praise God! Praise God! Praise God!"

"Let me look at you," Buck said, laughing.

"Do I look different?"

"You'd better." He took Jacov's head in his hands and turned him toward the light. "You have the mark," he said. "On your forehead."

Jacov pulled away and ran back toward the van. "I want to see it in the mirror."

"You won't," Buck said, following him. "For some reason we can't see our own. But you should be able to see mine."

Jacov turned and stopped Buck, leaning close and squinting. "I do! A cross! And I have one, really?"

"Really."

"Oh! Praise God!"

They climbed back into the van, and Buck dialed Chloe's phone. "This had better be you, Buck," she said.

"It is."

"I was worried about you."

"Sorry, but we have a new brother."

"Jacov?"

"Want to talk to him?"

"Of course. And don't try to get back in, hon. It's a madhouse. I'll get Tsion out as soon as I can."

Buck handed the phone to Jacov. "Thank you, Mrs. Williams!" he said. "I feel brand new! I *am* brand new! Hurry and we can see each other's marks!"

At the safe house it was midafternoon. Rayford sat staring at the screen and shaking his head. "Do you believe this?" he said over and over. "I can't believe Nicolae lost it like that."

Ken stood blocking the sun from the window. "I heard all the stories about them two witnesses, but man oh man, they are spooky. I'm glad they're on our side. They are, aren't they?"

Dr. Charles laughed. "You know as well as we do that they are, if you've been following Tsion as closely on the Net as you say you have."

"This thing's going to have the biggest TV audience in history tomorrow," Rayford said, turning to see what Hattie thought of it. She too stared at the screen, but her face was deathly pale, and she appeared to try to speak. Her mouth was open, her lips quivering. She looked terrified. "You all right, Hattie?" he said.

Floyd turned as Hattie emitted a piercing scream. She flopped onto her back, cradled her abdomen with both hands, and rolled to her side, gasping and groaning.

Dr. Charles grabbed his stethoscope and asked Rayford and Ken to hold Hattie down. She fought them but seemed to know enough to try to stay quiet so Floyd could listen for the baby's heartbeat. He looked grave. "What did you feel?" he asked.

"No movement for a long time," she said, gasping. "Then sharp pain. Did it die? Did I lose my baby?"

"Let me listen again," he said. Hattie held still. "I can't tell with just a stethoscope," he said. "And I don't have a fetal monitor."

"You could tell if it was there!" Hattie said.

"But I can't be sure if I hear nothing."

"Oh, no! Please, no!"

Floyd shushed her and listened carefully again. He felt all around her abdomen and then lay his ear flat on her belly. He straightened up quickly. "Did you tighten your abdominal muscles on purpose?" She shook her head. "Did you just feel a labor pain?"

"How would I know?"

"Cramping? Tightening?"

She nodded.

"Phone!" Floyd barked, and Ken tossed him his. The doctor dialed quickly. "Jimmy, it's me. I need a sterile environment and a fetal monitor. . . . Don't ask! . . . No, I can't tell you that. Assume I'm within fifty to sixty miles of you. . . . No, I can't come there."

"How 'bout Young Memorial in Palatine?" Ken whispered. "There's a believer there." Rayford looked up, surprised.

Floyd covered the phone. "How close?"

"Not that far."

"Thanks, Jimmy. Sorry to bother you. We found a place. I owe you one."

The doctor began barking orders. "Decide who's gonna drive, and the other get me two blankets."

Rayford looked at Ken, who shrugged. "I'm easy," he said. "I can drive or—"

"Sometime today, gentlemen!"

"You know where it is, you drive," Rayford said, and he dashed upstairs. When he returned with the blankets, the Rover idled near the door, and Dr. Charles backed out of the house with Hattie in his arms. She squirmed and cried and screamed.

"Should you move her?"

"No choice," Floyd said. "I'm afraid she's about to spontaneously abort."

"No!" Hattie screeched. "I'm only staying alive for my baby!"

"Don't say that," Rayford said as he squeezed past and opened the car door.

"Yes, say that," the doctor said. "Whatever it takes, keep fighting. Ray, get one blanket on the backseat and put the other over her as soon as I get her in there."

He wrestled Hattie into the car, her head near the far rear door. When Rayford draped the other blanket over her, Floyd got in and lay her feet across his lap. Rayford jumped into the front seat, and Floyd said, "Don't hold back, Ken. Get us there as fast as you can."

Apparently that was all Ken needed to hear. He gunned the engine and backed out the way he had pulled in. He slid to a dusty stop, then spun over the ruts in the torn-up road in front of the house. They bumped and banged and nearly rolled a couple of times as he set a course for Palatine.

"Am I bouncin' too much?" he asked.

"You're not going to do either of them any more harm. Speed is more important than comfort now!" Floyd said. "Ray, help me."

Rayford twisted in his seat and grabbed Hattie's wrist as the doctor wrapped both arms around her ankles. They steadied her as Ken pushed the car to its limits. Only one short stretch of paved road existed between the house and the hospital. Ken opened the Rover all the way over that quarter mile, and when he hit dirt at the end of it, the vehicle nearly went airborne.

When the hospital came into view, Floyd said, "Find Emergency."

"Can't do that," Ken said. "I don't know the woman's name. I just saw her mark, and she works up front near Reception, not in Emergency. I say we pull up there and let me run in and find her. If she can get us an operating room, the fastest way would be to take Hattie right through the front door."

Floyd nodded, and Ken steered up onto the sidewalk near the entrance. "Go, Ken. Ray, help me with her."

Rayford jumped out and opened the door near Hattie's head. She was unconscious. "I don't like this," the doctor said.

"Let me take her," Rayford said. "Just push her toward me, and then you lead the way in and talk to the woman if Ken's found her."

"I've got her, Ray."

"Just do it!"

"You're right," Floyd said, and he pushed as Rayford pulled and gathered Hattie to him. She felt as light as a little girl, despite her pregnancy. He wrestled with the blanket and charged up the steps behind Floyd. The woman with the mark of the cross on her forehead followed Ken toward the door, terror on her face.

"You brothers are going to get me in trouble," she said. "What have we got here?"

"She's about to miscarry," Floyd said. "Are you certified in the OR?"

"Years ago. I've been behind a desk since—"

"I can't trust anyone else. Lead us to an OR now."

"But—"

"Now, dear!"

The receptionist, a teenager, stared at them. The woman said, "Point those eyes elsewhere and keep your mouth shut. Got it?"

"Didn't see a thing," the girl said.

"What's your name, ma'am?" Floyd said as they followed her down a corridor.

"Leah."

"I recognize your risk, Leah. We appreciate it."

Leah peered at Hattie as she opened the operating room door and pointed at the table. "I'm not *her* sister, apparently."

Floyd stared at her. "So we let her die, is that it?"

"I didn't mean that, Doctor. You *are* a doctor?" He nodded. "I just meant, you're going to a lot of trouble and danger for someone who isn't, you know—"

"One of us?" he said, rushing to the scrubbing area. He grabbed a gown from a stack and headed to the sink. "Scrub with me. You're going to assist."

"Doctor, I—"

"Let's go, Leah. Now."

She stepped beside him at the sink. Ken stood near the still unconscious Hattie. Rayford felt useless, waiting between the table and the scrub room. "Are we messing up the sterile environment in here?" he asked.

"Try not to touch anything," Floyd said. "We're breaking a lot of rules."

"I wasn't implying—," Leah began.

"Faster," Floyd said, scrubbing more quickly than Rayford imagined it could be done. "We want to give this girl every chance to become one of us before she dies."

"Of course. I'm sorry."

"Let's concentrate on the patient. As soon as you're ready, I want you to paint her with Betadine from sternum to thighs, and I mean paint. Use a liter if you have to. You don't have time to be precise, so just don't miss a thing. And have a fetal monitor on her by the time I get in there. If that baby is alive, I may try to take it C-section. You'll have to handle anesthesia."

"I have no experience—"

"I'll walk you through it, Leah. How about we rise to the occasion?"

"I'm going to lose my job."

"Humph," the doctor said. "I hope that's the worst thing that happens to you. You see the people in this room? I lost mine the other day. So did Captain Steele. Ken lost his home."

"I know him. He was a patient here."

"Really?" He followed her into the operating theater.

"And how about the patient?" she asked, quickly applying the fetal monitor.

"Hattie too. We're all in the same boat. Prep her."

Ken and Rayford moved closer to the door. Floyd checked the fetal monitor and shook his head. He hooked her to other various monitors. "Actually, her respiration is not bad," he said. "BP's low. Pulse high. Go figure."

"That's weird, Doctor."

"She's been poisoned."

"With what?"

"I wish I knew."

"Doctor, did you call her Hattie?"

He nodded.

"She's not who I think she is, is she?"

"I'm afraid so," he said, moving into position. "You ever hear of another Hattie?"

"Not in this century. Does her, um, boyfriend know what's going on, or should we plan a trip to a gulag somewhere when he finds out?"

"He did this to her, Leah. When you got the mark you became his archenemy, so now you're on the front lines, that's all."

"That's all?"

Rayford watched, praying for Hattie as Floyd positioned the glaring overhead light. "Dilated. Seven or eight centimeters."

"No section then," Leah said.

"The baby's gone," he said. "I need an IV line, Ringer's lactate solution, forty units of oxytocin per liter."

"Incomplete abortion?"

"See how fast it all comes back to you, Leah? Normally

she would deliver in an hour or two, but as far along as she is, this will be quick."

Rayford was impressed with Leah's speed and efficiency.

Hattie came to. "I'm dying!" she wailed.

"You're miscarrying, Hattie," Doctor Charles said. "I'm sorry. Work with me. We're worried about you now."

"It hurts!"

"Soon you won't feel a thing, but you're going to have to push when I tell you."

Within minutes, Hattie was wracked with powerful contractions. *What,* Rayford wondered, *might the offspring of the Antichrist look like?*

The dead baby was so underdeveloped and small that it slipped quickly from Hattie's body. Floyd wrapped it and pieces of the placenta, then handed the bundle to Leah. "Pathology?" she asked.

Floyd stared at her. "No," he whispered firmly. "Do you have an incinerator?"

"Now I cannot do that. No. I have to put my foot down."

"What?" Hattie called out. "What? Did I have it?"

Leah stood with the tiny bundle in her hands. Floyd moved to the head of the operating table. "Hattie, you expelled a very premature, very deformed fetus."

"Don't call it that! Boy or girl?"

"Indeterminate."

"Can I see it?"

"Hattie, I'm sorry. It does not look like a baby. I don't advise it."

"But I want—"

Floyd pulled off his gloves and laid a hand gently on her cheek. "I have grown very fond of you, Hattie. You know that, don't you?" She nodded, tears rolling. "I'm begging you to trust me, as one who cares for you." She looked at him wonderingly. "Please," he said. "I believe as you do that this was conceived as a living soul, but it was not viable and did not survive. It has not grown normally. Will you trust me to dispose of it?"

Hattie bit her lip and nodded. Floyd looked to Leah, who still appeared resolute. He placed the baby in a carrier and carefully examined Hattie. He beckoned Leah with a nod. "I need you to assist me with a uterine curettage to eliminate the rest of the placental tissue and any necrotic decidua."

"Worried about endometritis?"

"Very good."

Rayford could see by the look on her face and the set of her jaw that Leah was not going to dispose of the fetus. Apparently Floyd gathered that too. After performing the procedure on Hattie, he gently picked up the wrapped body. "Where?" he said.

"End of the hall," she whispered. "Two floors down."

He walked out, and Hattie sobbed aloud. Rayford approached and asked if he could pray for her.

"Please," she managed. "Rayford, I want to die."

"No you don't."

"I have no reason to live."

"You do, Hattie. We love you."

CHAPTER 5

BUCK GREW NERVOUS in the van, waiting for Chloe and Tsion. He assumed she would hustle Tsion from the stage; thousands would have given anything for a moment with him, not to mention committee members who might want a word. And no one knew how Carpathia might respond to what had happened on stage. He initially blamed it on Tsion, but then the witnesses had appeared.

Buck thought Nicolae should realize that Tsion had no miraculous powers. Nicolae's quarrel was with the two witnesses. It was his own fault, of course. He had not been invited, or even welcomed, on stage. And the gall to have Fortunato and the pompous Peter the Second precede him! Buck shook his head. What else could one expect from Antichrist?

Buck dialed Chloe's number but got no answer. A busy signal he could understand. But no answer? A recorded voice spoke in Hebrew. "Jacov, listen to this. What is she saying?"

Jacov was still beaming, having craned his neck and leaned out the window to see others' marks. He often pointed to his own and learned that fellow believers always smiled and seemed to enjoy pointing heavenward. The day would come, Buck knew, when the sign of the cross on the forehead would have to say everything between tribulation saints. Even pointing up would draw the attention of enemy forces.

The problem was, the day would also come when the other side would have its own mark, and it would be visible to all. In fact, according to the Bible, those who did not bear this "mark of the beast" would not be able to buy or sell. The great network of saints would then have to develop its own underground market to stay alive.

Jacov put the phone to his ear, then handed it back to Buck. "If you want to leave a message, press one."

Buck did. "Chloe," he said, "call me as soon as you get this. The crowd out here hasn't thinned a bit, so I don't want to have to come and find you and Tsion. But I will if I don't hear from you in ten minutes."

As soon as he ended the call, his phone chirped. "Thank God," he said and flipped it open. "Yeah, babe."

Heavy static and mechanical noise. Then he heard, "Jerusalem Tower, this is GC Chopper One!"

"Hello?"

"Roger, tower, do you read?"

"Hello, this isn't the tower," Buck said. "Am I getting a cross frequency?"

"Roger, tower, this is a confidential transmission, so I'm using the phone rather than the radio, roger?"

"Mac, is that you?"

"Roger, tower."

"You in the chopper with the other three?"

"Ten-four. Checking coordinates to return to pad at King David, over."

"You trying to tell me something?"

"Affirmative. Thank you. No head winds?"

"Is it about Tsion?"

"Partly cloudy?"

"And Chloe?"

"Ten-four."

"Are they in danger, Mac?"

"Affirmative."

"Have they been taken?"

"Not at this time, tower. ETA five minutes."

"They're on the run?"

"Affirmative."

"What can I do?"

"We'll come in from the northwest, tower."

"Are they outside the stadium?"

"Negative."

"I'll find them in the northwest corner?"

"Affirmative, that's a go. Assistance, tower. Appreciate your assistance."

"Am I in danger too?"

"Ten-four."

"I should send someone else?"

"Affirmative and thank you, tower. Heading that way immediately."

"Mac! I'm going to send someone they may not recognize, and I'm going to be waiting for him to bring them out the northwest exit. Am I all right with that?"

"As soon as we can, tower. Over and out."

"Jacov, run in and find Tsion and Chloe and get them out of the stadium through the northwest exit."

Jacov reached for the door handle. "Up or down?" he said. "There is an exit at ground level and one below."

"Bring them out from below, and stop for no one. Do you have a weapon?"

Jacov reached under the seat and pulled out an Uzi. He stuffed it in his waistband and covered it with his shirt. Buck considered it obvious, but in the darkness and with the press of the crowd, maybe it would go undetected. "Someone must have assigned GC guards to grab Tsion. They don't have him yet, but it won't be long. Get them out of there."

Jacov ran into the stadium, and Buck slid behind the wheel. The crowd was finally, slowly, starting to move. It was as if people didn't want to leave. Clearly they hoped for a glimpse of Tsion. Buck didn't understand their conversations, but the occasional English phrase told him most were discussing the humiliation of Carpathia.

As Buck maneuvered the van carefully through the crowd

he heard a chopper. He feared it brought more GC guards. He was surprised that the helicopter looked just like the one that had borne Carpathia. He grabbed his phone and hit the last-caller callback button.

"McCullum."

"Mac! It's Buck. What are you doing back here?"

"Ten-four, Security. We'll check out the southeast quadrant."

"I sent a man to the northwest corner!"

"Affirmative, affirmative! *I'll* check southeast, but then I'm taking my cargo to base, over."

"Might they be southeast now?"

"Negative! *I'll* cover southeast!"

"But what can you do if they're there?"

"Roger, I can create the diversion, Security, but then we're gone, copy?"

"I'm confused but trusting you, Mac."

"Just keep your people out of southeast, Security. I'll handle."

Buck tossed the phone onto the seat and tilted his outside mirror to watch the chopper. Leon Fortunato announced over the helicopter's loudspeakers, "We have been asked by Global Community ground security forces at the stadium to help clear this area! Please translate this message to others if at all possible! We appreciate your cooperation!"

The mass of people did not obey. As word spread that Carpathia's own helicopter hovered over one corner of the stadium trying to clear the area, hundreds started that way, staring into the sky. That cleared a path for Buck, who drove quickly to the northwest corner. As people streamed out, they were drawn to the helicopter and immediately began moving that way to check out the commotion.

Buck pulled near the stadium. He ignored waving armed guards, opened his door, and stepped up on the floorboard to locate the underground exit. He found the dimly lit ramp where trucks had delivered equipment the day before. On tiptoes he saw a shaft of light appear as a door burst open and someone sprinted up the ramp.

Guards moved in for a closer look as Buck realized it was Jacov. What was he running from? Why was he ignored? Was the GC watching for Tsion? As Jacov passed the guards, he appeared to spot the van. Less than fifty feet away, he looked straight at Buck. He pulled the Uzi from under his shirt and sprayed bullets into the sky as he turned left.

The guards gave chase, guns drawn, and hundreds in the area screamed and dived for cover. Buck instinctively lowered his body, now watching over the top of the van. A couple hundred feet away, Jacov turned and fired more bullets into the air. The guards returned fire, and Jacov ran off again.

Buck had not heard the van doors open, but he heard them shut and Chloe and Tsion scream, "Go, Buck! Drive! Go, now!"

He dropped into the seat and slammed the door. "What about Jacov!"

"Go, Buck!" Chloe hollered. "He's creating a diversion!"

Buck laughed as he floored the accelerator and bounced

over a curb. "So is Mac!" he said. "What a team! Where do we pick up Jacov?"

Tsion lay on the floor of the backseat, panting. Chloe lay across the seat itself. "He said he would meet us at Chaim's," Tsion managed.

"They were shooting at him!"

"He said he would not draw their fire until he was out of range. He was sure he'd be all right."

"Nothing is out of their range," Buck said, putting distance between them and the stadium. Most traffic, emergency and otherwise, headed toward instead of away from Kollek Stadium now. Roadblocks kept many civilian cars at bay as GC vehicles tried to get through. Buck was virtually ignored going the other direction.

"If they're after you, Tsion, we don't dare go back to Chaim's."

"I cannot think of a safer place," Tsion said. "Carpathia will not threaten me there. Your wife was brilliant. She figured it out before it happened. She saw the guards coming for me, but she didn't like their looks."

"They were pressing their earpieces hard against their ears," Chloe said, "while releasing the safety locks on their weapons. I figured Carpathia or Fortunato told them to get revenge on Tsion and do it in the middle of a crowd so it would look like an accident. They got so close that I heard one tell the supreme commander where we were."

"I'm still worried about Jacov," Buck said.

"He was resourceful," Chloe said. "He jogged through

the tunnel near us, saying, 'I'm looking for familiar faces to follow me quickly to safety.' We stepped out from a utility room and—"

"I immediately saw the mark on his forehead," Tsion said. "Praise the Lord! You must tell us later what happened."

Chloe continued, "He said you were bringing the van to the underground exit. He peeked out and saw the guards at the top of the ramp, then said he would create a diversion and we should follow twenty seconds later. He backed up and ran, bursting through that door!"

"It worked," Buck said, "because he even distracted me. I didn't see you get in the van."

"Nobody saw us," Chloe said. "Oh!"

"What?"

"Nothing," she said, hissing.

"What, Chlo'? Are you all right?"

"Just not used to running," she said.

"Nor am I," Tsion said. "And I would like to get off this floor as soon as it is safe, too."

"You cannot keep her here," Leah told Dr. Charles. "It's impossible. I'm sorry. We could try to sneak her into a room, and I know it would be better for her, but if you think you'll ever need this facility or my help again, you'd better get her out of here now."

"Give me another sedative then," Floyd said. "I want her out before we go."

Hattie slept all the way to the safe house, and Dr. Charles put her to bed near the TV, where they were quickly brought up to date on the activity in Jerusalem. "His Excellency the potentate, Nicolae Carpathia, will address the world in twenty minutes," the announcer said. "As most of you saw on live television in the Eastern Hemisphere and many saw on a Cell/Sol Internet hookup that covered the rest of the globe, an attempt to poison His Excellency was foiled. The potentate is healthy, though shaken, and wishes to assure global citizens he is all right. We expect his remarks may also cover what sort of retribution he might exact from the perpetrators of the attempt on his life."

The journalist in Buck wished he was still at the stadium. He would have loved to have seen how long Mac kept Carpathia, Fortunato, and the clownish Mathews in the air while giving Tsion a chance to escape. He wished he could see for himself the water and blood on the stage and ask eyewitnesses if anyone saw the two from the Wailing Wall come or go.

He had learned not to baby Chloe; she was as brave and strong as he was. But she was also carrying their child, and she had been through a horrible physical ordeal that had left her wounded. This trauma couldn't have been good for her.

Buck was relieved to see Israeli rather than GC guards at Chaim's gates. Admittedly, it was this same force that had been behind the massacre of Tsion's family and the chasing of him from his homeland. But now he was here as Chaim's guest, and Chaim was just short of deity in Israel.

As soon as they were inside, a pale, trembling Chaim greeted them with embraces and demanded to know where Jacov was. Buck left the explaining to Tsion, knowing Chaim would need assurances that his protégé had not planned the disgracing of Carpathia. "You assured me you would remain neutral," Chaim said. "Otherwise I would not have urged him to attend."

"You knew he was coming and did not tell me?" Tsion said.

"He wanted an element of surprise. Surely you must have expected him."

"I had hoped he would wait until tomorrow or the next night. You should have prepared me."

"You appeared more than prepared."

Tsion sat wearily. "Chaim, the man interrupted the quoting of Scripture. It was as if he had planned his entrance for the worst possible instant. I am going to hold you to your promise to hear me out, and very soon. I am not up to it this evening, but as a brilliant and reasonable man, you will not be able to refute the evidence I have for Jesus as Messiah and Carpathia himself as Antichrist."

Rosenzweig settled into a large, soft chair and sighed heavily. "Tsion, you are as a son to me. But what you just said could get you killed."

"How well I know!"

"Of course, and I am still grieved and heartbroken over

your losses. But to come to Israel to proclaim the deity of Jesus is as foolhardy as those troublemakers at the Wall playing tricks with our water and our weather. And, Tsion, calling Nicolae the Antichrist when he is visiting the Holy City is the height of arrogance and insensitivity. I have told you before, I would sooner believe Carpathia was the Messiah and one of those two so-called witnesses the Antichrist."

Tsion sat shaking his head wearily, and Buck took the occasion to beg off for the evening. "If you'll excuse us . . ."

"Of course," Chaim said.

"I would like to know when Jacov arrives, no matter when," Buck said.

"Thank you for your concern," the older man said. "We will get word to you."

Rayford kept one eye on the television while trying to reach someone in Israel. Neither Buck's nor Chloe's phone was answered, and he couldn't raise Mac either. Forgetting himself for a moment, he swore under his breath. Hattie roused. "That's the Rayford Steele I once knew," she said, her voice airy and weak.

"Ah, I'm sorry, Hattie. That's not like me. I'm worried about what's happened over there, and I want to be sure everybody's all right."

"It's nice to know you're still human," she whispered. "But you never were and you never will be as human as I am."

"What does that mean?"

"I'm going to kill Nicolae."

"I'm sorry about your baby, Hattie, but you don't know what you're saying."

"Rayford, would you lean closer?"

"I'm sorry?"

"Don't be afraid of me. I'm not going to be around much longer anyway."

"Don't say that."

"I just don't have the energy to talk louder, so would you lean closer?"

Rayford felt conspicuous, though it was only the two of them in the room. He pursed his lips, looked around, and turned his ear to her. "Go ahead," he said.

"Rayford, I was not with that man long enough for him to have affected me this much. I know I was no better or worse than the next girl. You knew that as well as anybody."

"Well, I—"

"Just let me finish, because Floyd obviously drugged me and I'm about to fall asleep. I'm telling you, Nicolae Carpathia is evil personified."

"Tell me something I don't know."

"Oh, I know you people think he's the Antichrist. Well, I *know* he is. I don't think he has an ounce of truth in him. Everything that comes out of his mouth is a lie. You saw him acting like he was a friend of Mathews? He wants him dead. He told me that himself. I told you he poisoned Bruce. He sent people to murder me *after* I was poisoned, just to make sure. The poison had to have killed my baby. Anyway,

I hold him responsible. He made me do things I should never have done. And you know what—while I was doing them, I enjoyed it. I loved his power, his appeal, his ability to persuade. When I was making Amanda look like a plant, I actually believed I was doing the right thing. And that was the least of it.

"I want to die, Rayford. And I don't want to be forgiven or go to heaven to be with God or any of that stuff. But I will fight this poison, I will work with Floyd, I will do whatever I have to do to stay alive long enough to kill that man. I have to get healthy, and I have to somehow get to where he is. I'll probably die in the process with all the security he's got. I don't care. As long as I get to be the one who does it."

Rayford put a hand on her shoulder. "Hattie, you need to relax. Doc Charles did give you more anesthetic before we brought you home, so you may not even remember what you're saying here. Now, please, just—"

Hattie wrenched away from Rayford's hand, and her frail fingers grabbed his shirt. She fiercely pulled him closer and rasped in his face, spittle landing on his cheek. "I'll remember every word, Rayford, and don't think I won't. I will do this thing if it's the last thing I do, and I hope it will be."

"All right, Hattie. All right. I won't argue with you about it now."

"Don't argue with me about it ever, Rayford. You'll be wasting your time."

Carpathia would soon be on the screen, and Hattie was quickly dozing again. Rayford was glad she would be spared his image and whatever he would say about his debacle in Israel. Something cold ran through Rayford's soul. She had forced him to face himself.

Rayford was relieved beyond description to find out that Amanda was all he believed her to be: a loving, trustworthy, loyal wife. But since discovering what Carpathia had done to Bruce, to Amanda, to Hattie, he was again battling with his own desires. He had once prayed for the permission, the honor, of being the one assigned to assassinate Carpathia at the halfway point of the Tribulation. Now, truth be told, he found himself angling to be in position at that time.

He knew he had to talk sense to Hattie, to keep her from doing something so reckless and stupid. But that was also why he would not confide in Mac or Tsion or his daughter and son-in-law, why he would not say a word to his new friend, Ken, or to Floyd, about his own murderous leanings. They would, of course, want to show him the folly of his ways. But he wanted to entertain the thoughts longer.

Only when Buck was alone with Chloe in the privacy of one of Chaim Rosenzweig's guest rooms did he realize how worried he had been about her. Trembling, he gathered her in his arms and held her close, careful not to hug her too tight because of her injuries. "When I didn't know where you were," he began, "all I could think of was how I felt after the earthquake."

"But I wasn't lost this time, darling," she said. "You knew where I was."

"You didn't answer your phone. I didn't know if someone had grabbed you, or—"

"I turned it off when we were being chased. I didn't want it to give us away. That reminds me, I never turned it back on."

She started to pull away. "Don't worry about it now," he said. "It doesn't have to be on now, does it?"

"What if Daddy tries to call? You know he had to be watching."

"He can reach me on my phone."

"Where is it?"

"Agh! I left it in the van. I'll go get it."

Now it was her turn to not let him go. "I'll just turn mine on," she said. "I don't want to be apart from you again right now either."

Their mouths met, and he held her. They sat on the edge of the bed and lay back, her head resting in the crook of his arm. Buck imagined how silly they looked, staring at the ceiling, feet flat on the floor. If she was as tired as he, it wouldn't be long before she nodded off. This probably wasn't the time to bring up a delicate subject, but Buck had never been known for his timing.

As had become the custom, Global Community Supreme Commander Leon Fortunato introduced His Excellency,

Potentate Nicolae Carpathia, to the international television audience. Rayford was stunned at how straightforward and overt Leon was in telling his own story. Tsion had warned Rayford that Nicolae's supernatural abilities would soon be trumpeted and even exaggerated, laying a foundation for when he would declare himself God during the second half of the Tribulation. So far the widespread pronouncements had been circumspect, and Nicolae himself had personally made no such claims. But on this day, Rayford had to wonder how Nicolae would respond to Fortunato's obsequious opening. And he also had to concede that the pair had done a masterful, if not supernatural, job of choreographing the ultimate spin on Nicolae's most public embarrassment.

CHAPTER 6

"I'M WORRIED ABOUT YOU," Buck said.

"I'll be all right," Chloe said. "I'm glad I came, and I'm doing better than I thought I would. I knew it was a little early for me to take such a trip, but it's worked out."

"That's not what I'm worried about."

She pulled away from him and rolled onto her side to look at him. "What then?"

There was a knock at the door. "Excuse me," Tsion said. "But did you want to watch the Carpathia response on television?"

Chloe started to get up, but Buck stopped her. "Thanks, Tsion. Maybe in a little while. If we miss it, you can recap it for us in the morning."

"Very well. Good night, loved ones."

"Buck Williams," Chloe said. "I don't know when I've felt so special. You've never missed a breaking news story in your life."

"Don't make me out to be too altruistic, hon. I have no magazine to write for anymore, remember?"

"You do too. You have your own."

"Yeah, but I'm the boss and I sign the checks. There's no money for any checks, so what am I going to do—fire myself?"

"Anyway, you chose me over the latest news."

Buck rolled toward her and kissed her again. "I know what he's going to say anyway. He'll have Fortunato on first to sing his praises, then he'll act all humble and self-conscious and attack Tsion for embarrassing him after all he's done for the rabbi."

Chloe nodded. "So what's on your mind?"

"The baby."

She raised her brows at him. "You too?"

He nodded. "What're you thinking?"

"That we weren't too smart," she said. "Our baby will never reach five, and we'll be raising him, or her, while we're trying to just stay alive."

"Worse than that," he said. "If we were trying just to survive, we might hole up somewhere safe. The baby might be relatively secure for a while. But we've already declared ourselves. We're enemies of the world order, and we're not going to just sit by and protest in our minds."

"I'll have to be careful, of course," she said.

"Yeah," he said, snorting. "Like you have been so far."

She lay there silently. Finally she said, "Maybe I'll have to be more careful, hmm?"

"Maybe. I just wonder if we're doing right by the little one."

"It's not like we can change our minds now anyway, Buck. So what's the point?"

"I'm just worried. And there's nobody else I can tell."

"I wouldn't want you telling anyone else."

"So tell me not to worry, or tell me you're worrying with me, or something. Otherwise I'm going to get all parental on you and start treating you like you don't have a brain."

"You've been pretty good about not doing that, Buck. I've noticed."

"Yeah, but sometimes I ought to do more of it. Somebody's got to look out for you. I like when you keep track of *me* a little. I don't feel demeaned by it. I need it and appreciate it."

"To a point," she said.

"Granted."

"And I'm also quite good at it."

"And subtle," he said, draping his arm over her.

"Buck," she said, "we really should watch Carpathia, don't you think?"

He shrugged, then nodded. "If we're going to have any chance of thwarting anything he does."

They padded out to where Tsion and Chaim sat watching TV. "No word on Jacov yet?" Buck asked.

Chaim shook his head. "And I am none too pleased."

"I merely asked him to go in and get them," Buck said. "Playing decoy and drawing the gunfire was his idea. I wasn't happy about it either."

"The *what?!*" Chaim demanded.

Rayford was strangely buoyed, despite Hattie's threats against Carpathia. In his mind that showed a level of sanity that, according to Dr. Charles, she had not had in weeks. He didn't consider himself a lunatic, despite his own admittedly unrealistic wishes to be God's hit man. What he longed for, down deep, was that Hattie get healthy enough to change her mind about God. She knew the truth; that wasn't the issue. She was the epitome of a person who could know the truth without acting on it. That was what Bruce Barnes had told Rayford was his own reason for having been left behind. As for Rayford, he had missed the point—despite his first wife's efforts to explain it—that nothing he did for himself could earn God's favor. As for Bruce, he knew all that. He knew salvation was by grace through faith. He simply never made the transaction, thinking he could slide by until later. Later came sooner, and he was left without his family.

Ken appeared at the top of the basement stairs. "Doc and me was wonderin' if you wanted to watch down here," he said. "He thinks maybe Hattie'll rest better that way."

"Sure," Rayford said, rising quickly. He tried dialing

Chloe and Buck one more time without success and left the phone on his chair.

As he left the room, Hattie called out to him. "Would you leave that on, Rayford?"

"Don't you want to sleep?"

"Just leave it on low. It won't bother me."

"My people are calling around looking for Jacov," Chaim whispered as Leon Fortunato's benign smile graced the screen. "If anything happened to him, I don't know—"

"I believe no harm can come to him, Chaim. He has become a believer in the Messiah and even has the mark of a sealed tribulation saint on his forehead, visible to other believers."

"You're saying you can see it and I cannot?"

"That's what I'm saying."

"Poppycock. How arrogant."

"Can you see our marks?" Chloe asked.

"Pish-posh, you have no marks," Chaim said.

"We see each other's," Tsion said. "I see Buck's and Chloe's plain as day."

Chaim waved them off bemusedly, as if they were putting him on. And Fortunato was introduced.

"I'd better try to call Daddy before Carpathia comes on," Chloe said. She hurried to the bedroom and came back with her phone. She showed it to Buck. The readout showed

Rayford had called since they were in the bedroom. She dialed his number.

Rayford thought he heard his phone ring upstairs but decided he was mistaken when it did not ring again. Looking around the basement, he wondered how a big, lanky man like Ken Ritz could live in a tiny, dark, dank spot like this. Ritz was slowly expanding it in his spare time, pointing toward the day when the entire Tribulation Force might have to live down there. Rayford didn't want to even think about that.

Was it Rayford's imagination, or was Fortunato looking more dapper? He had not noticed while watching him at the stadium. But that was on a jerry-built setup from his laptop that wasn't as clear as this live, satellite transmission directly to Ken's TV. Television usually didn't flatter a stocky, middle-aged man, but Fortunato appeared trimmer, more bright eyed, healthier, and better dressed than usual.

"Ladies and gentlemen of the Global Community," he began, looking directly into the camera as if the lens was his audience's eyes (as Carpathia had long modeled), "even the best of families has its squabbles. Since His Excellency, Potentate Carpathia, was reluctantly swept to power more than two years ago, he has made tremendous strides in making the entire earth one village.

"Through global disarmament, vast policy changes in the former United Nations and now the Global Community, he has made our world a better place to live. After the devastating vanishings, he brought about peace and harmony. The only blips on the screen of progress were the result of things outside his control. War resulted in plagues and death, but His Excellency quickly broke the back of the resistance. Atmospheric disasters have befallen us, from earthquakes to floods and tidal waves and even meteor showers. This was all due, we believe, to energy surpluses from whatever caused the vanishings.

"There remain pockets of resistance to progress and change, and one of the more significant movements in that direction revealed its true nature earlier this evening before the eyes of the world. His Excellency has the power and the obvious right to retaliate with extreme measures to this affront to his authority and the dignity of his office. In the spirit of the new society he has built, however, His Excellency has an alternative response he wishes to share with you this evening.

"Before he does that, however, I would like to share a personal story. This is not secondhand or hearsay, not a legend or an allegory. This happened to me personally, and I assert the veracity of every detail. I share it because it bears on the very issue the potentate will address, spirituality and the supernatural."

Fortunato told the world the story of his resurrection at the command of Carpathia, a story Rayford had heard too many times. Fortunato concluded, "And now, without further ado, your potentate and, to me may I say, my deity, His Excellency, Nicolae Carpathia."

Chloe had been talking quietly on the phone during Fortunato's bouquet to Carpathia. While Leon uncharacteristically stumbled while both making way for Carpathia and bowing deeply to him, Chloe hung up.

"Hattie lost her baby," she said sadly.

"You reached your dad?"

"Hattie answered. She sounded fairly lucid, all things considered."

Chloe suddenly laughed, making Buck jerk to see the TV. Fortunato tried to back out of Carpathia's presence while bowing and tripped over a light cord. Out of camera range he had apparently tumbled and rolled heavily, distracting even the usually unflappable Carpathia and causing him to temporarily lose contact with the lens.

Carpathia quickly recovered and grinned magnanimously and condescendingly. "Fellow citizens," he began, "I am certain that if you did not see what happened earlier this evening at Teddy Kollek Stadium in Jerusalem, you have by now heard about it. Let me briefly tell you my view of what occurred and outline my decision of what to do about it.

"Let me go back to when I first reluctantly accepted my role as secretary-general of the United Nations. This was not a position I sought. My goal has always been to merely serve in whatever role I find myself. As a member of the lower parliament in my home country of Romania, I served many years for my constituents, championing their view—and mine—for peace and disarmament. My rise to the presidency of my motherland was as shocking to me as it was to the watching world, only slightly less so than my elevation to secretary-general—which has resulted in the world government we enjoy today.

"One of the hallmarks of my administration is tolerance. We can only truly be a global community by accepting diversity and making it the law of the land. It has been the clear wish of most of us that we break down walls and bring people together. Thus there is now one economy highlighted by one currency, no need for passports, one government, eventually one language, one system of measurement, and one religion.

"That religion carries the beautiful mystery of being able to forge itself from what in centuries past seemed intrinsically contradictory belief systems. Religions that saw themselves as the only true way to spirituality now accept and tolerate other religions that see themselves the same way. It is an enigma that has proven to somehow work, as each belief system can be true for its adherents. Your way may be the only way for you, and my way the only way for me. Under the unity of the aptly named Enigma Babylon One World Faith, all the religions of the world have proved themselves able to live harmoniously.

"All, that is, save one. You know the one. It is the sect that claims roots in historic Christianity. It holds that the vanishings of two and a half years ago were God's doing. Indeed, they say, Jesus blew a trumpet and took all his favorite people to heaven, leaving the rest of us lost sinners to suffer here on earth.

"I do not believe that accurately reflects the truth of Christianity as it was taught for centuries. My exposure to that wonderful, peace-loving religion told of a God of love and of a man who was a teacher of morals. His example was to be followed in order for a person to one day reach eternal heaven by continually improving oneself.

"Following the disappearances that caused such great chaos in our world, some looked to obscure and clearly allegorical, symbolic, figurative passages from the Christian Bible and concocted a scenario that included this spiriting away of the true church. Many Christian leaders, now members of Enigma Babylon, say this was never taught before the disappearances, and if it was, few serious scholars accepted it. Many others, who held other views of how God might end life on earth for his followers, disappeared themselves.

"From a small band of fundamentalists, who believe they were somehow stranded here because they were not good enough to go the first time, has sprung up a cult of some substance. Made up mostly of former Jews who now have decided that Jesus is the Messiah they have been looking for all their lives, they follow a converted rabbi named Tsion Ben-Judah. Dr. Ben-Judah, you may recall, was once a respected scholar who so blasphemed his own religion on an international television broadcast that he had to flee his home country.

"I come to you tonight from the very studio where

Dr. Ben-Judah desecrated his own heritage. While in exile, he has managed to brainwash thousands of like-minded megalomaniacs so desperate for something to belong to that they have become his marionette church. Using a feel-good psychological approach to morality, Dr. Ben-Judah has used the Internet for his own gain, no doubt fleecing his flock for millions. In the process he has invented an us-against-them war in which you, my brothers and sisters, are 'them.' The 'us' in this charade call themselves true believers, saints, sealed ones—you name it.

"For months I have ignored these harmless holdouts to world harmony, these rebels to the cause of a unified faith. While advisers urged me to force their hand, I believed tolerance was in order. Though Dr. Ben-Judah continually challenged all we stand for and hold dear, I maintained a policy of live and let live. When he invited tens of thousands of his converts to meet in the very city that had exiled him, I decided to rise above personal affronts and allow it.

"In a spirit of acceptance and diplomacy, I even publicly assured Dr. Ben-Judah's safety. Though I was well aware that the Global Community and I as its head were the avowed enemies of this cult, I believed the only right and proper thing to do was to encourage its mass meeting. I confess it was my hope that in so doing these zealots would see that there was value in compromise and tolerance and that they would one day choose to align themselves with Enigma Babylon. But it would have had to have been their choice. I would not have forced their hand.

"And how was my magnanimity rewarded? Was I invited to the festivities? Asked to welcome the delegates? Allowed to bring a greeting or take part in any of the pageantry?

"No. Through private diplomatic channels I was able to secure the promise that Dr. Ben-Judah would not restrict my presence or prohibit my attendance. I traveled to Israel at my own expense, not even burdening Global Community finances, and dropped in to say a few words at what has been called the Meeting of the Witnesses.

"My supreme commander was met with the rudeness of utter silence, though he comported himself with élan regardless. The most revered Supreme Pontiff Peter the Second, the pope of popes as it were, was received in no less a quietly hostile manner, despite being a fellow clergyman. No doubt you agree this had to have been a well-planned and executed mass response.

"When I myself addressed the crowd, though they were still obeying their mind-controlling leader and not responding, I sensed they wanted to. I had the clear feeling, and a public speaker develops antennae for these things, that the crowd was with me, was sympathetic, was embarrassed by their leader and wanted to welcome me as warmly as I was welcoming them.

"Though Dr. Ben-Judah was ostensibly ignoring me from just a few feet away, he somehow signaled someone to release some sort of agent in the air, an invisible dust or powder that instantly parched my throat and resulted in a powerful thirst.

"I should have been suspicious when I was immediately presented with a bottle from someone in the crowd. But as a trusting person, used to being treated as I treat others, I naturally assumed an unknown friend had come to my aid.

"What a disappointment to have been callously ambushed by a bottle of poisonous blood! It was such an obvious public assassination attempt that I called Dr. Ben-Judah on it right there. As a pacifist not skilled in warfare, I had played right into his hands. He had hidden in the crowd the two elderly lunatics from the Wailing Wall who have so offended the Jews in the Holy Land and have actually murdered several people who have attempted to engage them in debate. With hidden microphones turned louder than the one I was using, they shouted me down with threats and turned my humble act of diplomacy into a fiasco.

"I was whisked away for medical attention, only to find that had I swallowed what they gave me, I would have died instantly. Needless to say, this is an act of high treason, punishable by death. Now, let me say this. My wish is that we still come together in a spirit of peace and harmony. Let it be said that these words from the Scriptures came first in this context from me: 'Come now, and let us reason together.'

"There is no doubt in my mind that the whole of this ugly incident was engineered and carried out by Dr. Ben-Judah. But as a man of my word and lacking any physical evidence that would tie him to the assassination attempt, I plan to allow the meetings to continue for the next two nights. I will maintain my pledge of security and protection.

"Dr. Ben-Judah, however, shall be exiled again from Israel within twenty-four hours of the end of the meeting the night after tomorrow. Israeli authorities are insisting on this, and I would urge Dr. Ben-Judah to comply, if for no other reason than his own safety.

"As for the two who call themselves Eli and Moishe, let this serve as public notification to them as well. For the next forty-eight hours, they shall be restricted to the area near the Wailing Wall, where they have posted themselves for so long. They are not to leave that area for any purpose at any time. When the meetings in the stadium have concluded, Eli and Moishe must leave the Temple Mount area. If they are seen anywhere outside their area of quarantine in the next forty-eight hours or in the Temple Mount area after that time, I have ordered that they be shot on sight.

"Some eyewitnesses have testified that the murders they have committed might somehow be convoluted into some sort of self-defense. I reject this and am exercising my authority as potentate to deny them trial. Let me be clear: Their appearance anywhere but near the Wailing Wall for forty-eight hours or their showing their faces in public anywhere in the world after that shall be considered reason to kill. Any Global Community officer or private citizen is authorized to shoot to kill.

"I know you will agree that this is a most generous response to an ugly attack and that allowing the meetings to continue proves a spirit of accommodation. Thank you, my friends, and good night from Israel."

Rayford looked up as Ken Ritz rocked back and slapped his thighs. "I don't know about you boys," Ritz said, "but I got me some tinkerin' to do. For one thing, I gotta find out how we can get us some of those millions the rabbi's been fleecin' off the flock. With none of us having any income anymore, we're going to need some cash."

"You got a minute, Ray?" Floyd said, rising.

"Sure, Doc."

They climbed the stairs, and Floyd bent over the sleeping Hattie for a moment. "Seems fine for now," he said. "But can you imagine postpartum blues on top of what she's already going through?"

"You get that even with a miscarriage?"

"It makes more sense with a miscarriage if you think about it."

Rayford turned off the TV and followed Floyd to the porch. They both carefully surveyed the horizon and listened before talking. Rayford had grown used to that since he'd arrived. At Global Community headquarters it was a matter of knowing whom you could talk to. Out here knowing you were not being spied on was paramount.

"I've got a problem, Rayford, but I hardly know you."

"Friendships, acquaintances, everything has to necessarily be telescoped these days," Rayford said. "You and I could live together the rest of our natural lives, and it would be less than five years. If you've got something on your chest, you might as well shoot. You want to criticize me, fire away. I can take it. My priorities are different than they used to be, needless to say."

"Aw, no, it's nothing like that. In fact, I figure you've got cause to scold me a bit after today."

"For snapping at me in the heat of battle? Hey, I've done my share of that. In medical emergency situations, you're in charge. You bark at whomever you have to bark at."

"Yeah, but even though I know Tsion is sort of our pastor, you're the chief. I need you to know that I know that and respect it."

"There's no time for hierarchy anymore, Doc. Now what's on your mind?"

"I've got a Hattie problem."

"We all do, Floyd. She was an attractive, bright girl once. Well, maybe more attractive than bright, but you're seeing the worst of her just now, and I think she's coming around. You might appreciate her more in a few weeks."

"Just so you know, I got the drift that she and you used to work together and that, while you never actually had an affair—"

"Yeah, OK. Not proud of it, but I acknowledge it."

"Anyway, this isn't about her being in a bad way and being so difficult. I'm moved by how you all seem to care so much for her and want her to become a believer."

Rayford sighed. "This business of her believing but not wanting to accept has me buffaloed. She's even halfway logical about it. She's not one who has to be convinced she's unworthy, is she?"

"She's so convinced she refuses to accept what she knows is free."

"So, what's your problem, Doc? You think she's a lost cause spiritually?"

Floyd shook his head. "I wish it was that easy. My problem makes zero sense. You said yourself there's nothing attractive about this girl. It's obvious that when she was healthy she was a knockout. But the poison has done its work, and the illness has taken its toll. She makes no sense when she talks, and spiritually she's bankrupt."

"So you want to throw her out, and that makes you feel guilty?"

Floyd stood and turned his back to Rayford. "No, sir. What I want is to love her. I *do* love her. I want to hold her and kiss her and tell her." His voice grew quavery. "I care so much for her that I've convinced myself I can love her back to health in every way. Physically and spiritually." He turned and faced Rayford. "Didn't expect that one, did you?"

As Buck and Chloe lay in bed, Buck said, "Will you be able to sleep if I go out for a while?"

She sat up. "Out? It's hardly safe."

"Carpathia is too focused on Eli and Moishe to worry about us right now. I want to see if I can find Jacov. And

I want to see what the witnesses will do in response to Nicolae's threats."

"You know what they'll do," she said, lying back down. "They'll do what they want until the due time, and woe to the one who tries to make points with the potentate by trying to kill them before that."

"Just the same, I'd like—"

"Do me this favor, Buck. Promise you won't leave this place until I'm sound asleep. Then I'll worry only when I have to, if you're not here when I wake up in the morning."

Buck dressed and went looking to see if Tsion was still up. He wasn't, but Rosenzweig was on the phone. "Leon, I insist on talking with Nicolae. . . . Yes, I know all about your cursed titles, and I remind you that I knew Nicolae as a friend before he was His Excellency and the potentate of this and that. Now please, put him on the phone. . . . Well, then *you* tell me what has happened to my driver!"

Rosenzweig noticed Buck, motioned for him to sit, and hit the speaker button on the phone. Leon was in mid-threat. "Our intelligence sources tell us your man turned."

"Turned what? He's not Jewish anymore? Not Israeli? Doesn't work for me? What are you talking about? He's been with me for years. If you know where he is, tell me and I will come get him."

"Dr. Rosenzweig, all due respect, sir, I'm telling you your man is one of them. We wanted GC guards to personally escort Rabbi Ben-Judah back to Jacov's vehicle, but he came running from the stadium firing off a high-powered weapon.

Who can say how many guards and innocent civilians were killed."

"I can. None. It would have been all over the news. I heard the same story. Your people were coming after Ben-Judah to exact revenge for the embarrassment to Nicolae and might have done who-knows-what to him if he had not slipped away on his own."

"He wasn't on his own. He was with Buck Williams's wife, who has proven to be an American subversive who escaped from one of our facilities in Minnesota, where she had been detained for questioning." Rosenzweig glanced at Buck, who sat shaking his head slowly as if wondering where they dreamed up this stuff. Fortunato continued, "She was suspected of looting after the earthquake."

"Leon, is Jacov alive?" There was a pause. Rosenzweig grew irate. "I swear, Leon, if something has happened to that young man—"

"Nothing has happened to him, Doctor. I'm trying to train you to address me properly."

"Oh, for the sake of heaven, Leon, are there not more important things to worry about right now? Like people's lives!"

"Supreme Commander, Dr. Rosenzweig."

"Supreme Nincompoop!" Rosenzweig shouted. "I am going out to search for my Jacov, and if you have any information that would help me, you'd better give it to me now!"

"I don't need to be spoken to that way by you, sir."

And Leon hung up.

Rayford put an arm on Floyd's shoulder as they went back into the house. "I'm no love counselor," he said, "but you're right when you say this one makes no sense. She's not a believer. You're old enough to know the difference between pity and love and between medical compassion and love. You hardly know her, and what you know is not that pretty. It doesn't take a scientist to see that this is something other than what you think it is. You lonely? Lose a wife in the Rapture?"

"Uh-huh."

"Better tell me about her."

CHAPTER 7

BUCK PEEKED IN on Chloe before heading out with Chaim. She appeared sound asleep.

"Do you mind driving?" Chaim asked. "It has been so long since I was allowed."

"Allowed?"

Chaim smiled wearily. "Once you become, how shall I say it, a personality in this country, especially in this city, you are treated like royalty. I cannot go anywhere unescorted. I was not even famous when first you did the cover story on me."

"You were revered, however."

Chaim checked with his gateman, Jonas, for the latest word on Jacov. "Stefan?" Buck heard him say. Then something urgent and frustrated in Hebrew.

Chaim directed Buck to the last stall in the garage, and Buck slid behind the wheel of an ancient sedan. "I don't want everyone to know I am coming. The Mercedes is well known. You drive a stick shift, do you not?"

Buck feathered the throttle and quickly caught on to the vagaries of the manual transmission. He worried more about the bald state of the tires. "Any idea where we're going?"

"Yes, I am afraid I do," Chaim said. "Jacov is an alcoholic."

Buck shot him a double take. "You have an alcoholic as your driver?"

"He's dry. Recovering they call it. But in times of crisis, he reverts."

"Falls off the wagon?"

"I do not know that expression."

"It's an old Americanism. Early in the twentieth century the Women's Christian Temperance Union would roll the Temperance Wagon into town, decrying the evils of alcohol and calling on offenders to give it up and get on the wagon. When a sober man went back to drinking, it was called falling off the wagon."

"Well, I'm afraid that is what has happened here," Chaim said, pointing where Buck was to turn. As they moved into smaller neighborhoods with houses and buildings closer together, Buck began noticing things he hadn't seen on the drive from Chaim's to the stadium. Jerusalem had grown seedy. How he had loved to visit this city just a few years before! It had had its rundown areas, but overall it had been kept with pride. Since the disappearances, certain types of crime and lewd activity had sprung up that he never expected to see in public here. Drunks staggered along, some with their arms slung around ladies of the evening. As Buck drove farther into the city he saw strip clubs, tattoo parlors, fortune-telling shops, and triple-X-rated establishments.

"What has happened to your city?"

Chaim grunted and waved dismissively. "This is something about which I would love to speak to Nicolae. All that money spent on the new temple and moving the Dome of the Rock to New Babylon! *Ach!* This Peter the Second fellow wearing the funny costumes and welcoming the Orthodox Jew into the Enigma Babylon faith. I am not even a religious man, and I wonder at the folly of it. What is the point? The Jews have maintained for centuries that they worship the one true God, and this somehow now fits with a religion that accepts God as man and woman and animal and who knows what else? And you see what effect it has had on Jerusalem. Haifa and Tel Aviv are worse! The Orthodox are locked away in their gleaming new temple, slaughtering animals and going back to the literal sacrifices of centuries gone by. But what impact do they have on this society? None! Nicolae is supposed to be my friend. If he will see me, I will inform him of this, and things will change.

"When my Jacov—a wonderful, spirited man, by the way—falls off the wagon, as you put it, he winds up on the same street in the same bar and in the same condition."

"How often does this happen?"

"Not more than twice a year. I scold him, threaten him, have even fired him. But he knows I care for him. He and his wife, Hannelore, still grieve over two little ones they lost in the disappearances."

Buck was chagrined to realize he had pushed Jacov spiritually without getting to know him. He just hoped Chaim was wrong about Jacov and that they would not find him where the old man expected to.

Chaim pointed Buck to a parking place in the middle of a row of cars and vans that lined a crowded street. It was after midnight now, and Buck was suddenly overcome with fatigue. "The Harem?" he said, reading the neon sign. "You sure this is only a bar?"

"I'm sure it is not, Cameron," Rosenzweig said. "I don't want to think about what else goes on in there. I've never been inside. Usually I wait out here while my security chief goes in and drags Jacov out."

"That's why I'm here?"

"I would not ask you to do that. But you may need to help me with him because if he resists, I am no match for him. He will not hurt me, even when drunk, but a little old man cannot make a thick mule of a young man go anywhere he does not want to go."

Buck parked and sat thinking. "I'm hoping you're wrong, Dr. Rosenzweig. I'm hoping Jacov will not be here."

Chaim smiled. "You think because he became a believer he will not get drunk after being shot at? You are too naive for an international journalist, my friend. Your new faith has clouded your judgment."

"I hope not."

"Well, you see that green truck there, the old English Ford?" Buck nodded. "That belongs to Stefan of my valet staff. He lives between here and Teddy Kollek Stadium, and he is Jacov's drinking partner. Stefan does not suffer as Jacov does. He can hold his liquor, as we like to say. He was off work today, but if I was a man of wagers, I would bet Jacov ran to him while escaping the Global Community guards. Naturally shaken and scared out of his wits, he no doubt allowed Stefan to take him to their favorite place. I cannot hold this against Jacov. But I want him safe. I don't want him making a spectacle of himself in public, especially if he is a fugitive from the GC."

"I don't want him to be here, Dr. Rosenzweig."

"I don't either, but I am not a young man with stars in his eyes. Wisdom is supposed to come with age, Cameron. I wish less came with it, frankly. I have gained wisdom I cannot now recall. I have what I call 'mature moments,' where I recall in detail something that happened sixty years ago but cannot remember that I told the same story half an hour before."

"I'm not even thirty-three yet, and I have my share of those."

Chaim smiled. "And your name again was?"

"Let's go look for Jacov," Buck said. "I say he's not in there, even if Stefan is."

"I hope Jacov is," Chaim said, "because if he is not, that means he is lost or caught or worse."

Dr. Floyd Charles's story was so similar to Rayford's it was eerie. He too had had a wife serious about her faith, while he, a respected professional, played at the edges of it. "Fairly regular church attendee?" Rayford asked from experience. "Just didn't want to get as deep into it as your wife?"

"Exactly," Floyd said. "She was always telling me my good works wouldn't get me into heaven, and that if Jesus came back before I died, I'd be left behind." He shook his head. "I listened without hearing, you know what I mean?"

"You're telling my story, brother. You lose kids too?"

"Not in the Rapture. My wife miscarried one, and we lost a five-year-old girl in a bus accident her first day of school." Floyd fell silent.

"I'm sorry," Rayford said.

"It was awful," Floyd said with a thick voice. "Gigi and I both saw her off at the corner that morning, and LaDonna was happy as she could be. We thought she would be shy or scared—in fact, we kinda hoped she would be. But she couldn't wait to start school with her new outfit, lunch box, and all. Gigi and I were basket cases, nervous for her, scared. I said putting her on that big old impersonal bus made me feel like I was sending her off to face the lions. Gigi said we just had to trust God to take care of her. Half an hour later we got the call."

Rayford shook his head.

"Made me bitter," Floyd said. "Drove me farther from God. Gigi suffered, sobbed her heart out till it almost killed me. But she didn't lose her faith. Prayed for LaDonna, asked God to take care of her, to tell her things, all that. Real strain on our marriage. We separated for a while—my choice, not hers. I just couldn't stand to see her in such pain and yet still playing the church game. She said it wasn't a game and that if I ever wanted to see LaDonna again, I'd 'get right with Jesus.' Well, I got right with Jesus all right. I told him what I thought of what he let happen to my baby girl. I was miserable for a long time."

They sat at the kitchen table, where Rayford could hear Hattie's steady, rhythmic breathing. "You know what convinced me?" Floyd said suddenly.

Rayford snorted. "Besides the Rapture, you mean? That got my attention."

"I was actually convinced before then. I just never pulled the trigger, know what I mean?"

Rayford nodded. "You knew your wife was right, but you didn't tell God?"

"Exactly. But what convinced me was Gigi. She never stopped loving me, through it all. I was a rascal, man. Mean, nasty, selfish, rude, demeaning. She knew I was grieving, suffering. The light had gone out of my life. I loved LaDonna so much it was as if my heart had been ripped out. But when I was trying to cover the pain by working all hours and being impossible to my coworkers and everyone else, Gigi knew just when to call or send a note. Every time, Rayford, every stinkin' time, she would remind me that she loved me, cared about me, wanted me back, and was ready to do whatever I needed to make my life easier."

"Wow."

"Wow is right. She was hurting just as bad as I was, but she would invite me for dinner, bring me meals, do my laundry—and she was working too—clean my apartment." He chuckled. "Humiliated me is what she did."

"She won you back?"

"She sure did. Even lifted me out of my grief. It took a few years, but I became a happier, more productive person. I knew it was God in her life that allowed her to do that. But I still thought that if there was anything to this heaven and hell business, God would have to look kindly on me because I was helping people every day. I even had the right motive. Oh, I loved the attention, but I helped everybody. I did my best work whether the patient was a derelict or a millionaire. Made no difference to me. Somebody needed medical attention, they got my best."

"Good for you."

"Yeah, good for me. But you and I both know what it got me when Jesus came back. Left behind."

Floyd checked on Hattie. Rayford got them Cokes from the refrigerator. "I don't want to bad-mouth an old friend," Rayford said, "but I suggest you think about the kind of woman your wife was before you consider Hattie as a replacement."

Floyd pursed his lips and nodded.

"I'm not saying Hattie couldn't become that kind of person," Rayford added.

"I know. But there's no evidence she wants to be."

"Know what I'm gonna do?" Rayford said, rising. "I'm gonna call my daughter and tell her I love her."

Floyd looked at his watch. "You know what time it is where she is?"

"I don't care. And she won't either."

Buck and Chaim got stares from both men and women as they approached The Harem. The place was much bigger inside than it looked from outside. Several rooms, each packed with people shoulder to shoulder—some dancing, some kissing passionately—led to the main bar where women danced and people ate and drank.

"Ach!" Rosenzweig said. "Just as I thought."

As they made their way in, Buck looked carefully for Jacov and averted his eyes every time he was met with a "what are you looking at" glare. Not all the couples were made up of both sexes. This was not the Israel he remembered. The smoke was so thick that Buck knew he'd have done less damage to his lungs if he himself was smoking.

Buck did not realize Chaim had stopped in front of him, and he bumped into the old man. "Oh, Stefan!" Rosenzweig chided, and Buck turned in time to see a young man with a sloshing drink in his hand. His dark hair was wet and matted, and he laughed hysterically. Buck prayed he was alone. "Is Jacov with you?" Rosenzweig demanded.

Stefan, in midcackle, could barely catch his breath. He bent over in a coughing jag and spilled some of his drink on Rosenzweig's trousers.

"Stefan! Where's Jacov?"

"Well, he's not with me!" Stefan shouted, straightening up and laughing more. "But he's here all right!"

Buck's heart sank. He knew Jacov had been sincere in his conversion, and God had proved it with the seal on his forehead. How could Jacov desecrate his own salvation this way? Had his brush with the GC been more gruesome than Buck could imagine?

"Where?" Rosenzweig pressed, clearly disgusted.

"In there!" Stefan pointed with his drink, laughing and coughing all the while. "He's up on a table having the time of his life! Now let me through so I don't have an accident right here!" He lurched off, laughing so hard tears ran down his face.

Chaim, appearing overcome, strained to see into the main room, from which music blared and strobe lights flashed. "Oh, no!" he moaned, backing into Buck. "He's totally drunk. This shy, young man who hardly looks you in the eye when he greets you is carrying on in front of everyone! I can't take this. I'll bring the car up. Could you just get him down off that table and drag him out? You're bigger and stronger than he is. Please."

Buck didn't know what to say. He'd never been a bouncer, and while he had once enjoyed the nightlife himself, he had never liked loud bars, especially ones like this. He jostled past Chaim as the old man hurried out. Buck shouldered his way through several clusters of revelers until he came to dozens whose attention was on the crazy young Israeli holding forth atop a table. It was Jacov all right.

Rayford hurried to the basement and found Ken with Donny Moore's telescope in his lap and his microscope on the desk. Ken was reading Donny's technical journals. "Kid was a genius, Ray. I'm learning a ton that's gonna help us. If you can get this stuff to your other pilot and your inside techie over there, they can have us up to speed when their cover is blown and we're all just tryin' to stay alive. What can I do you for?"

"I want to go with you Friday to Israel."

"You barely escaped. Didn't your friend Mac say you were as good as dead if you had stayed?"

"It's not like me to run. I can't hide from Carpathia for the rest of my life anyway, short as it may be."

"What the heck's got into you, Ray?"

"Just talked with Chloe. I smell trouble. No way Nicolae is going to let them out of Israel alive. We have to go get them."

"I'm game. How do we do it?"

Buck quit excusing himself; he was being cursed anyway. Finally, he was close enough to hear Jacov, but he was railing in Hebrew and Buck understood none of it. Well, almost none. Jacov was shouting and gesturing and trying to keep people's attention. They laughed at him and seemed to curse him, whistling and throwing cigarette butts at him. Two women splashed him with their drinks.

His face was flushed and he looked high, but he was not drinking, at least then. Buck recognized the word *Yeshua*, Hebrew for Jesus. And *Hamashiach*, the word for Messiah.

"What's he saying?" he asked a man nearby. The drunk looked at him as if he were from another planet. "English?" Buck pressed.

"Kill the English!" the man said. "And the Americans too!"

Buck turned to others. "English?" he asked. "Anyone know English?"

"I do," a barmaid said. She carried several empties on a tray. "Make it quick."

"What's he saying?"

She looked up at Jacov. "Him? Same thing he's been saying all night. 'Jesus is the Messiah. I know. He saved me.' All that nonsense. What can I tell you? The boss would have thrown him out long ago, but he's entertaining."

Jacov was little more than entertaining. His motive might have been pure, but he was having zero impact. Buck moved close and grabbed his ankle. Jacov looked down. "Buck! My friend and brother! This man will tell you! He was there! He saw the water turned to blood and back again! Buck, come up here!"

"Let's go, Jacov!" Buck said, shaking his head. "I'm not coming up there! No one is listening! Come on! Rosenzweig is waiting!"

Jacov looked amazed. "He is here? Here? Have him come in!"

"He was in. Now let's go."

Jacov climbed down and eagerly followed Buck out, accepting cheers and slaps on the back from the merry-makers. They were near the front door when Jacov spotted Stefan heading the other way. "Wait! There's my friend! I must tell him I'm leaving!"

"He'll figure it out," Buck said, steering him out the door.

In the car Rosenzweig glared at Jacov. "I was not drinking, Doctor," he said. "Not one drop!"

"Oh, Jacov," Rosenzweig said as Buck pulled away from the curb. "The smell is all over you. And I saw you atop the table."

"You can smell my breath!" he said, leaning forward.

"I don't want to smell your breath!"

"No! Come on! I'll prove it!" Jacov breathed heavily into Rosenzweig's face, and Chaim grimaced and turned away.

Rosenzweig looked at Buck. "He had garlic today, but I do not smell alcohol."

"Of course not!" Jacov said. "I was preaching! God gave

me the boldness! I am one of the 144,000 witnesses, as Rabbi Ben-Judah says! I will be an evangelist for God!"

Chaim slumped in his seat and raised both hands. "Oy," he said. "I wish you *were* drunk."

After hearing what had gone on behind the scenes in Israel, Ken agreed it was likely Carpathia would manufacture "some tragedy outside his control, somethin' he can blame on somebody else, but no matter how you slice it, people we care about are gonna die."

"I don't want to be foolhardy, Ken," Rayford said. "But I'm not going to hide here and just hope they get out."

"I been sky-jockeyin' that son-in-law of yours since the disappearances, and you'd have to go some to be more foolhardy than that boy. We're gonna hafta get in touch with your copilot over there though. I can teach you a lot about the Gulfstream, but nobody can put it down without a runway."

"Meaning?"

"You're gonna be looking at a quick pickup, right? Probably from this Rosen-whatever estate?"

"Yeah, I'm going to suggest to Tsion that he announce plans for Saturday, something Carpathia will believe he wouldn't want to miss. Then we get in there after midnight Friday and get them out of there."

"Unless they meet us somewhere near the airport, we're going to have to drop in and get 'em. And that means a chopper."

"Can't we rent one? I could ask David Hassid, our guy inside the GC, to have one waiting for us at Jerusalem or Ben Gurion."

"Fine, but we're gonna need two fliers. No way McCullum can get away to help us."

"What am I, chopped liver?"

Ken smacked himself in the head. "Listen to me," he said. "What an idiot! You're trained in a copter, then?"

"Mac brought me up to speed. I land near the complex and shuttle them to you at the airport, right?"

"You'd better get a layout of the place before we go. You're going to have precious little time as it is, puttin' one of them noisy jobs down in a residential area. Somebody sees you in their yard, the gendarmes'll be there before you can get airborne again."

"Does your wife know where you've been?" Rosenzweig asked Jacov as Buck pulled in front of his apartment building.

"I called her. She wants to know what in the world I'm talking about."

"Why did you go to that awful place first?"

"I escaped to Stefan's house. He wanted to go. I thought, what better place to start preaching?"

"You're a fool," Rosenzweig said.

"Yes I am!"

Buck tossed Jacov his cell phone. "Call your wife so you don't scare her to death when you walk in."

But before Jacov could dial, the phone rang. "What's this?" he said. "I didn't do that."

"Push Send and say, 'Buck's phone.'"

It was Chloe. "She needs to talk with you right away, Mr. Williams."

Buck took the phone and told Jacov, "Wait here until we can warn your wife you're coming."

Chloe told Buck about the call from her father and his request for a schematic of Rosenzweig's estate. "I'll bring it up when it's appropriate," Buck whispered.

Later, when he finally drove through the gates at Chaim's place, the time didn't seem right to raise the issue of the schematic. Rosenzweig was still a Carpathia sympathizer and would not understand. He might even spill the beans. Buck remained in the car as Rosenzweig got out.

"You're not coming in?"

"May I borrow your car for a while?"

"Take the Mercedes."

"This will be fine," Buck said. "If Chloe is still up, tell her she can call me."

"Where are you going?"

"I'd rather not say. If you don't know, you don't have to lie if anyone asks."

"This is entirely too much skullduggery for me, Cameron. Be safe and hurry back, would you? You and your friends have another big day tomorrow. Or I should say today."

Buck drove straight to the Wailing Wall. As he expected, after the squabbling between the two witnesses and Carpathia and the threats Nicolae made on international television, huge crowds pressed near the fence where Eli and Moishe held court. The GC was well represented, armed guards ringing the crowd.

Buck parked far from the Temple Mount and moseyed up like a curious tourist. Moishe and Eli stood back-to-back with Eli facing the crowd. Buck had never seen them in that position and wondered if Moishe was somehow on the lookout. Eli was speaking in his forceful, piercing voice, but at that moment he was competing with the head of the GC guard unit and his bullhorn. The guard was making his announcement in several languages—first in Hebrew, then in Spanish, then in an Asian tongue Buck couldn't place. Finally, he spoke a broken English with a Hebrew accent, and Buck realized the GC guard was an Israeli.

"Attention, ladies and gentlemen! I have been asked by the Global Community supreme commander to remind citizens of the proclamation from His Excellency, Potentate Nicolae Carpathia—" here the crowd erupted into cheering and applause—"that the two men you see before you are under house arrest. They are confined to this area until the end of the Meeting of the Witnesses Friday night. If they leave this area before that, any GC personnel or private citizen is within his rights to detain them by force, to wound them, or to exterminate them. Further, if they are seen anywhere, repeat anywhere, after that time, they shall be put to death."

The crowd near the fence cheered wildly again, laughed,

taunted, pointed fingers, and spat toward the witnesses. But still the crowd hung back at least thirty feet, having heard of, if not seen, those whom the witnesses had killed. While many claimed the two capriciously murdered people who got too close, Buck himself had seen a mercenary soldier charge at them with a high-powered rifle. He was incinerated by fire from the witnesses' mouths. Another man who had leaped toward them with a knife had seemed to hit an invisible wall and fell dead.

The witnesses, of course, seemed unaffected by the proclamation or the guard with the bullhorn. They remained motionless and back-to-back, but there was a vast difference between how they now appeared and how they had looked when Buck first saw them. Because of the incredible interest drawn to them by the meetings televised from Kollek Stadium and their being mentioned by both Leon Fortunato and Carpathia himself, the news media had converged upon this place.

Gigantic klieg lights illuminated the area, a glaring spotlight bathing the witnesses. But neither squinted nor turned from the glare. The extra light only served to emphasize their unique features: strong, angular faces, deep-set dark eyes in craggy sockets under bushy brows.

No one ever saw them come or go; none knew where they were from. They had appeared strange and weird from the beginning, wearing their burlap-like sackcloth robes and appearing barefoot. They were muscular and yet bony, with leathery skin; dark, lined faces; and long, scraggly hair and beards. Some said they were Moses and Elijah reincarnate, but if Buck had to guess, he would have said they were the two Old Testament characters themselves. They looked and smelled centuries old, a smoky, dusty aroma following them.

Their eyes were afire, their voices supernaturally strong and audible for a mile without amplification.

An Israeli shouted a question in Hebrew, and the GC guard translated it into all the languages. "He wants to know if he would be punished for killing these men now, where they stand." The crowd cheered anew as each people group understood what he said. Finally, the GC guard answered.

"If someone was to kill them this very night, he would be punished only if an eyewitness testified against him. I don't know that there are any eyewitnesses here at all."

The crowd laughed and agreed, including the other guards. Buck recoiled. The GC had just given permission for anyone to murder the witnesses without fear of reprisal! Buck was tempted to warn anyone so foolish that he had personally seen what happened to previous would-be assassins, but Eli beat him to it.

Barely moving his lips but speaking so loudly he seemed to be shouting at the top of his lungs, Eli addressed the crowd. "Come nigh and question not this warning from the Lord of Hosts. He who would dare come against the appointed servants of the Most High God, yea the lampstands of the one who sits high above the heavens, the same shall surely die!"

The crowd and the guards stumbled back at the force of his voice. But they soon inched forward again, taunting.

Eli erupted again. "Tempt not the chosen ones, for to come against the voices crying in the wilderness is to appoint one's own carcass to burn before the eyes of other jackals. God himself will consume your flesh, and it will drip from your own bones before your breath has expired!"

A wild, cackling man brandished a bulky, high-powered rifle. Buck held his breath as the man waved it above the crowd, and the rest screamed warnings at him. The weapon had a sight on the stock that identified it as a sniper's rifle with kill power from a thousand yards. *Why,* Buck wondered, *would a man with such a weapon risk showing it within reach of the witnesses and their proven power to destroy?*

The GC guard stepped between the man and the wrought-iron fence, behind which the witnesses stood. He spoke to the man in Hebrew, but it was clear he did not understand. "English!" the man screamed, but he did not sound American. Buck couldn't make out his accent. "If you do this thing," the guard started over in English, "as a service to the Global Community, you must take full responsibility for the consequences."

"You said there were no eyewitnesses!"

"Sir, the whole world is watching on television and the Internet."

"Then I'll be a hero! Out of my way!"

The guard did not move until the man leveled the weapon at him. Then the guard skipped into the darkness, and the man stood alone, facing the fence. And nothing else. The witnesses were gone.

"Threaten to burn my flesh, will you?" the man raged. "Face this firepower first, you cowards!"

The GC guard came back on the bullhorn, speaking urgently. "We shall search the area behind the fence! If the two are not there, they are in violation of the direct order of the potentate himself and may be shot at will by anyone without fear of indictment!"

CHAPTER 8

THOUGH IT WAS NOW the wee hours of Thursday morning on the Temple Mount, the atmosphere was festive. Hundreds milled about, chattering about the gall of two old men to defy Carpathia and make themselves vulnerable to attack by anyone in the world. They were fair game, and within minutes they would surely be dead.

Buck knew better, of course. He had sat under the teaching of Bruce Barnes and then Tsion Ben-Judah, and he knew what the witnesses meant by "the due time." Bible prophecy called for the witnesses to be given the power by God to prophesy one thousand, two hundred and threescore days, clothed in sackcloth. Both Bruce and Tsion held that those days were counted from the time of the signing of an agreement between Antichrist and Israel for seven years of peace—

which also coincided with the seven-year tribulation. Such an agreement had been signed only a little more than two years before, and 1,260 days divided by 365 equaled three and a half years. Buck calculated that the due time was more than a year away.

Suddenly, from high on the hillside called the Mount of Olives came the loud preaching of the two in unison. The crowds began to run that way, murder in their throats. Despite the confusion and noise and armed guards engaging their weapons while on the run, the witnesses spoke with such volume that every word was clear.

"Harken unto us, servants of the Lord God Almighty, maker of heaven and earth! Lo, we are the two olive trees, the two candlesticks standing before the God of the earth. If any man will hurt us, fire proceedeth out of our mouths and devoureth our enemies. If any man dare attempt to hurt us, he must in that manner be killed! Hear and be warned!

"We have been granted the power to shut heaven, that it rain not in the days of our prophecy. Yea, we have power over waters to turn them to blood and to smite the earth with all plagues, as often as we will.

"And what is our prophecy, O ye generation of snakes and vipers who have made the holy city of Messiah's death and resurrection likened unto Egypt and Sodom? That Jesus of Bethlehem, the son of the Virgin Mary, was in the beginning with God, and he was God, and he is God. Yea, he fulfilled all the prophecies of the coming Messiah, and he shall reign and rule now and forevermore, world without end, amen!"

The rabid cries of angry Israelis and tourists filled the air. Buck followed, his own panting filling his ears. No media lights had reached the witnesses, and nothing illuminated them from the sky, yet they shone bright as day in the dark grove of olive trees. It was an awesome, fearful sight, and Buck wanted to fall to his knees and worship the God who was true to his word.

As the crowd reached the base of the sloping hill and slipped in the dewy grass, Buck caught up. "It is ours to bring rain," the witnesses shouted, and a freezing gush of water poured from the skies and drenched the crowd, including Buck. The place had not seen a drop in twenty-four months, and the people craned their necks, pointed their faces to the sky, and opened their mouths. But the rain had stopped the instant it began, as if Eli and Moishe had opened and shut a tap in one motion.

"And it is ours to shut heaven for the days of our prophecy!"

The crowd was stunned, complaining and murmuring, grumbling threats anew. As they started again toward the illumined pair on the hillside, now less than a hundred yards away, the prophets stopped them with their voices alone.

"Stand and hear us, O ye wicked ones of Israel! You who would blaspheme the name of the Lord God your maker by sacrificing animals in the temple you claim to have erected in his honor! Know ye not that Jesus the Messiah was the lamb that was slain to take away the sins of the world? Your sacrifices of animal blood are a stench in the nostrils of your God!

Turn from your wicked ways, O sinners! Face yourselves for the corpses you already are! Advance not against the chosen ones whose time has not yet been accomplished!"

But sure enough, as Buck watched in horror, two GC guards rushed past him and past the crowd, weapons raised. Slipping and sliding on the moist hillside, their uniforms became muddy and grass stained. They crawled combat style up the hill, illuminated by the light radiating from the witnesses.

"Woe unto you who would close your ears to the warnings of the chosen ones!" the witnesses shouted. "Flee to the caves to save yourselves! Your mission is doomed! Your bodies shall be consumed! Your souls shall be beyond redemption!"

But the guards pressed on. Buck squinted, anticipating the awfulness of it. The crowd chanted and raised fists at the witnesses, urging the guards to open fire. Gunshots resounded, echoing, deafening, the exploding cartridges producing yellow and orange bursts from the barrels of the weapons.

The witnesses stood side by side, gazing impassively at their attackers, who lay on their bellies a hundred feet down the slope. The crowd fell silent, as did the rifles, everyone staring, wondering how the guards could have missed from such close range. The guards rolled onto their sides, ejecting shell magazines and replacing them with loud clicks. They opened fire again, filling the valley with violent explosions.

The witnesses had not moved. Buck's eyes were locked on them as blinding white light burst from their mouths, and they appeared to expectorate a stream of phosphorous vapor directly at the guards. The attackers had no time to even recoil as they ignited. Their weapons remained supported by the bones of their arms and hands as their flesh was vaporized, and their rib cages and pelvises made ghastly silhouettes against the grass.

Within seconds the white heat turned their rifles to dripping, sizzling liquid and their bones to ash. The would-be assassins smoldered in piles next to each other as the crowd fled in panic, screaming, cursing, crying, nearly knocking Buck over as they pushed past. His emotions conflicted, as always, when he saw humans die. The witnesses had declared that when the attackers died, their souls would be lost. It wasn't as if they hadn't been warned.

Horrified at the loss of life and the eternal damnation the guards had gambled against and lost, Buck felt his knees weaken. He couldn't take his eyes off the witnesses. The brightness of their killing fire still burned in his eyes, and it was as if the light that had shone from them was now gone. In the darkness, blinking against the spots and streaks that remained, he made out that they were slowly descending the mount. Why, he wondered, did they not just appear wherever they wanted to go, as they had seemed to transfigure themselves into the stadium the night before and from the Temple Mount to the Mount of Olives just now? They were beyond figuring, and as they neared him, he held his breath.

He knew them. He had talked to them. They seemed to know the people of God. Should he say anything? And what does one say? Good to see you again? What's up? Nice job on those guards?

When he was close to them before, he had the wrought-iron fence between them. Of course, nothing could protect anyone from beings like this who carried the firepower of God himself. Buck fell to his knees as they passed within ten feet of him, and he looked up as he heard them murmuring.

Moishe said, "The Lord of hosts hath sworn, saying, Surely as I have thought, so shall it come to pass; and as I have purposed, so shall it stand."

At the words of God, Buck dropped face first into the grass and wept. God's very thoughts would come to pass, and his purposes would stand. No one could come against the anointed ones of God until God decided it was time. The witnesses would carry on their ministry during the great and terrible day of the Lord, and no pronouncement or sentence or house arrest by anyone would get in the way of that.

If only Chaim Rosenzweig could have seen this, Buck thought as he made his way back to the parking lot at the Temple Mount.

Finally back at Chaim's complex, Buck was waved in by Jonas, the gateman, who also unlocked the door for him, since no one else was awake. Buck peeked in on Chloe, grateful to find her still asleep. Then he walked out onto the veranda off their room and let his eyes grow accustomed to the dark again.

He was on the side of the main house opposite the driveway where Jonas now served as night watchman. He had seen him stroll the property every half hour or so before. Buck waited until Jonas came by again, then checked out the possibilities just past the railing of the patio.

Up one side was a metal drainpipe, old but still intact and solid. On the other side was a wire, embedded into the stucco with wire brads. The wire, he assumed, was either for telephone or television. Regardless, it would not support him. The drainpipe, however, had protruding seams every few feet that made it a natural for climbing. If, that is, a man was fearless.

Buck had never put himself in that category, but he was reluctant to arouse Rosenzweig's suspicions by asking for house plans, and he was certain he had never seen a passageway to the roof. He had to know whether a chopper could set down there, and this was the only way he knew to find out.

Buck rubbed his hands until they felt sufficiently dry. He tied his canvas shoes tighter and hitched up his pants. Standing on the edge of the railing, he hoisted himself up and began shinnying up the drainpipe. When he was ten feet above the veranda and passing a small, mottled glass window on the third floor, he made the mistake of looking down. He still had ten feet to go to reach the roof, but even if he fell from where he was, the railing was likely to cut him in two.

He was not in trouble, but a wave of panic showed up on the doorstep of his mind. There was no wiggle room here, no leeway, no margin for error. A slip, a weak section, a fright that knocked him off balance would leave him no options. He would drop and could only hope to land close enough to the middle of the patio to keep from flopping over the rail. If he hit the ground, he was dead. If he hit the patio, he was probably dead.

So, now what to do? Proceed and finish the mission, or quickly move back to safety? He decided he would be just as safe up ten feet, so he kept going. Three feet from the roof he felt precarious, but also knew the only danger he could be in now would be of his own making. If he got wobbly, scared, panicky, or looked down, he would freeze because he had made himself look. As he lifted his left leg over the lip at the flat roofline, he gained a mental picture of himself, a human fly, by his own design hanging from the edge of the roof of a three-story building.

I'm an idiot, he decided, but he felt much better with the roof solidly beneath him. It was a bright, starry night now, crisp and calm. He detected utility boxes, fans, exhausts, ductwork, and vents here and there. What Rayford, or whoever, would need, he decided, was a fairly large, unencumbered area in which to set down a chopper.

Buck tiptoed across the roof, knowing that footsteps from above are often magnified below, and found pay dirt on the other side. In fact, to his surprise, he discovered an ancient helipad. The markings were faded, but whatever this building had been before it was bequeathed to the national hero, it had required a landing area for a helicopter. He assumed Rosenzweig knew that and could have easily saved him this adventure.

He also deduced that if someone once used the helipad,

there had to be easy access to and from it within the house. Buck looked and felt around the area until he found a heavy, metal door. It was rusted and bent, but it was not locked. He could only imagine how the creaking and groaning of metal would sound inside if he was not careful in forcing it open.

Buck played with it for several minutes, getting it to budge just a fraction each time. When he felt he had sufficiently prepared it for a wider push, he set his shoulder against it and wrapped his fingers around the edge to keep it from moving too far too fast. With a grunt and one driving step, he made the door move about eight inches. It made a noise, but not much of one. He assumed no one had heard it. If guards came running or if he roused someone inside, well, he'd just quickly identify himself and explain what he was up to.

Buck tried to slither through the opening, but he needed another couple of inches. These he accomplished by nudging the door a quarter inch or so at a time. When he finally got through, he found himself at the top of a wood staircase, musty and dusty and cobwebbed. It was also creaky, as he learned with his first step on the top landing. He felt for a light switch in the pitch-dark, not hoping for much. Finding nothing, he gingerly felt for the edge of the top step with a tentative foot. He was startled when something brushed his forehead. He nearly fell back on the stairs but held himself by pressing against the hoary wood walls. He had to fight to keep his balance, the backs of his legs pressing against the steps.

Feeling around in the dark, he grabbed a single, swaying bulb with a twist switch in its housing. Was it possible it still worked? How fortunate could a man be in one night? He turned the switch, and the light sprang to life. Buck quickly shut his eyes against the intrusion and heard the telltale pop of the filament breaking. He should have expected nothing less from a bulb that probably hadn't been used in years.

He opened his eyes to a halo of yellow residue from the brief flash. Blinking, he tried to reproduce behind his eyelids the image that had to have been temporarily projected and burned there. He kept his eyes shut until his brain drew a rudimentary block picture of three more steps down to a large door.

Buck didn't know what else to do but trust his split-second vision. He felt his way down the stairs and found he had been correct. Another landing presented itself, and he felt the door. This one was wood—big, heavy, solid. He found the knob, and it turned freely. But the door did not budge. And he could tell it was not stuck. It felt locked, dead-bolted. His fingers found the lock above the handle. There would be no opening this door without a key. He would have to get back into his room the way he had come.

Buck was encouraged, however, as he retraced his steps. Somehow he would find that door from inside the house and broach with Chaim the subject of a key.

When he reached the drainpipe, he was forced to look down before swinging out over the ledge and heading back. That was a mistake. Now he would have to talk himself into and through this. And how long had he been gone? He decided to wait through one more guard walk-around to be sure. He soon realized he must have just missed one because nearly half an hour later Jonas shuffled by and out of sight again.

Buck gripped the top of the pipe with both hands, swung his lead leg over the side until he felt the lip of the first seam, and climbed straight down. He was about to reach the top of the patio railing outside his and Chloe's room when he was certain he saw something below in his peripheral vision. If he had to guess, he thought he saw the curtain move.

Was Chloe awake? Had she heard him? Could she see him? He didn't want to scare her. But what if this was GC? What if they had already infiltrated the place? It could also be Chaim's own security. Might they take action before he was able to identify himself?

Buck hung from the drainpipe, feeling like an idiot, his feet pigeon-toed on a seam. He should have just dropped lightly onto the patio and reentered the room. But he had to be sure no one was at the window. He let go with one hand and leaned down as far as he could. Nothing.

He spread his knees and tried to lower his head to get a sight line. Were the curtains open? He thought he had left through a shut drape. As he tried to peer farther, first one foot, then the other, slipped off the seam, and his fingers supported his full body weight. He could only hope no one was watching through the window because no one he knew—certainly not himself—could hang for long that way.

As Buck's fingers gave way, he dropped straight down, his

nose inches from the glass door. When his feet hit the patio, he found himself staring into another pair of eyes, wide and terrified and set in a ghostly pale face.

Besides being startled at the image, Buck's weight made his knees bend as he landed, but he was so close to the door that they banged into it, driving him off his feet and straight back into the railing. The top caught him just above his backside and his weight carried him backward over the rail. He grabbed the wrought iron as he flopped, desperate to keep from hurtling all the way to the ground on his head.

With a loud grunt, Buck saw the sky as he flipped back, and his feet soon followed. He hung from the top of the rail by his hands, upside down, the back of his head pressed against the bars and his feet dangling near his face. It was all he could do to hang on, knowing his life was in his own hands.

Meanwhile, of course, Chloe was screaming.

Buck forced his feet back up until he was balanced, teetering painfully on his seat, the rail digging into his back. With a desperate pull, he forced his torso up until the weight of his legs brought him back onto the patio. "It's just me, babe," he said, as Chloe stared wide-eyed out the window.

He rubbed his back as she slid open the door. "What in the world?" she said over and over. "I nearly gave birth."

Buck tried to explain as he undressed, more ready for bed than he had been in a long time. A quick knock at the door was followed by, "Everything all right in there, ma'am? We heard a scream."

"Yes, thank you," she managed, then giggled. The guard

went away muttering, "Newlyweds!" and Buck and Chloe laughed till they cried.

"Anyway," Buck said, stretching out on his tender back, "I found an old helipad, and—"

"I know all about that," Chloe said. "I asked Chaim about it when he finally got home."

"You did?"

"I did."

"But I don't want him to know we're planning anyth—"

"I know, super sleuth. I just asked him about the history of the place to see what I could learn. It used to be an embassy. Ergo, the—"

"Helipad."

"Right. He even showed me the door that leads to it. There's a key on a nail embedded in the doorjamb right next to it. I'll bet even you could unlock the door with it."

"I'm such a dork," he said.

"You're *my* dork. Scare me to death, why don't you. If I'd had a weapon, I'd have killed you. I thought about running out there and pushing you over."

"What kept you?"

"Something told me it had to be you. You didn't look too dangerous there you know, rear end aloft."

"You're bad. So you want to know where I went?"

"I figured you went to the Wall; that's why I didn't call."

"You know me too well."

"I knew you'd want to see what they made of Carpathia's threat. Big crowd?"

Rayford had trouble sleeping, a rarity for him. He kept looking at his watch, figuring what time it was in Israel, and trying to decide when to call Buck or Chloe. He knew they would likely try to tell him things had settled down and that they didn't sense the same danger he did. But he had worked more closely with Carpathia than Buck had. He knew the man too well. Besides, he wanted to talk to Tsion. Though the rabbi felt the confidence of God as his protection, one couldn't be too careful. Scripture was clear that for a time the sealed ones of God were invulnerable to harm from the actual judgments of God. But no one was clear on whether that protection extended past the 144,000 converted Jewish evangelists to Gentiles like Rayford and his family, who had become tribulation saints.

And though the 144,000, of whom Tsion was clearly one, were protected against the judgments, it seemed unlikely that none of them would die by other causes in the meantime. Rayford grew desperate to get them out of Israel, but come dawn in the Chicago area, he finally fell asleep. When he awoke late that morning, he knew his counterparts in the Holy Land would be well on their way to the evening's meeting, which he would have to watch via the Internet again.

Once again, Buck had slept several hours, and Chloe had let him. "You're on a different schedule than I am," she explained.

"If you're going to be up all hours playing Spiderman, you need your rest. Seriously, Buck, I need you healthy. You've been going full speed for months, and someone has to look out for you."

"I'm trying to look out for *you*," he said.

"Yeah, well, start by not prowling around my balcony in the middle of the night."

Chaim had negotiated with Fortunato that Jacov not be charged in connection with the incident the night before if Chaim agreed to not have him serve as Tsion's driver anymore. But Jacov put up such a fuss at the prospect of not getting to go that Dr. Rosenzweig finally agreed to follow only the letter of the agreement. Buck drove. Jacov rode along and brought a guest: Stefan.

When they arrived at the stadium early that afternoon, with the requisite GC escort this time leading them through the shortcuts Jacov had discovered, Jacov emerged from the van with such glee and anticipation etched on his face that Buck couldn't help but smile.

Chloe had agreed to stay at the compound, and Buck was worried. He had expected more debate from her, and now he wondered if she was suffering more than she let on. She had been shaken, of course, by the escape from the GC the night before, and he only hoped she realized that similar incidents couldn't be good for her or the unborn baby.

News reports all day carried the story that the two preachers at the Wailing Wall had callously disregarded the directive handed down by the potentate himself. Reports said that when Global Community forces tried to apprehend them and bring them to justice, the pair murdered two guards. Eyewitnesses on the Mount of Olives said the two concealed flamethrowers in their robes that they produced when the guards were within feet of them. The weapons had not been recovered, though the preachers had spent since just before dawn through the present time in their usual spots near the Wailing Wall.

Live shots from there showed huge crowds deriding them, taunting them, and yet keeping a healthier-than-usual distance. Buck asked Tsion, "Why doesn't Nicolae drop a bomb on them or attack them with missiles or something? What would happen, being that it's a year before the appointed time?"

"Even Nicolae knows the sacred nature of the Temple Mount," Tsion said as he disembarked from the van. He hurried inside to escape a rushing, cheering crowd. "I would love to greet them all," he said, "but I fear the mayhem." He found a place to sit. "Anyway," he concluded, "Carpathia would not sanction violence there, at least if it could be traced to him. His threat to kill them if they remain there after the end of tomorrow night's meeting is some sort of ruse. Frankly, I'm glad he's gone public with it. I expect the two to flout his authority by being right there right then."

Jacov and Stefan looked much different than they had in the wee hours. It appeared Rosenzweig was right that Stefan was better able to hold his liquor. He seemed none the worse for wear and proved pleasant. They went off to find good seats, Jacov asking Buck to "pray for my wife, who will be watching on TV at home. She worries about me, thinking I have lost my mind. I told her, it's not what I've lost but what I've found!"

GC guards looked menacingly at anyone connected with the program, as if silently expressing that they were only doing what they were commanded. If they had it their way, was the implication, they would destroy the lot of those who opposed their potentate.

No fireworks were expected this second night. Surely Nicolae and his people knew better than to make another appearance. But because of the noise the previous night's controversies had engendered, the crowd was bigger than ever. The converts were back, but more curious skeptics were on hand too.

Again the evening began with a simple greeting, the hearty singing of a hymn, and the introduction of Tsion Ben-Judah. He was greeted with wave upon wave of cheers and applause, all of which he largely ignored, except to smile and raise his hands for silence. Buck again stood in the wings and watched and listened in awe to the man who had become a spiritual father to him—the rabbi who had come to Jesus through studying the prophecies of the Old Testament now led a flock of millions over the Internet. Here he stood, a smallish, plainspoken man with a Bible and a pile of meticulous notes. And he held the massive crowd in his palm.

"You have learned much today, I understand," Tsion began. "And tonight is a time for more instruction. I have warned you in advance of many judgments, from the seven seals to the seven trumpets and eventually to the seven vials that will finally usher in the Glorious Appearing of our Lord and Savior, Jesus Christ.

"I have traced the beginning of the seven-year tribulation period from the signing of the unholy alliance between the one-world system and the nation of Israel. By following the judgments that have befallen the world since then, I have calculated that we are waiting on a precipice. We have endured all seven Seal Judgments and the first three of the seven Trumpet Judgments. The middle, or fourth, Trumpet Judgment is next in God's timing.

"To prove to the wondering world and to the unconvinced that we can know whereof we speak, I will tell you now what to expect. When this occurs, let no man deny that he was warned and that this warning has been recorded in the Scriptures for centuries. God is not willing that any should perish but that all should come to repentance. That is the reason for this entire season of trial and travail. Though he waited as long as his mercy could endure and finally raptured his church, still he rains judgment after judgment down upon an unbelieving world. Why? Is he angry with us? Should he not be?

"But no! No! A thousand times no! In his love and mercy he has tried everything to get our attention. All of us remaining on the earth to this day were delinquent in responding to his loving call. Now, using every arrow in his quiver, as it were, he makes himself clearer than ever with each judgment. Is there doubt in anyone's mind that all of this is God's doing?

"Repent! Turn to him. Accept his gift before it is too late. The downside of the judgments that finally catch some people's attention is that thousands also die from them. Don't risk falling into that category. The likelihood is that three-fourths of us who were left behind at the Rapture will die—lost or redeemed—by the end of the Tribulation.

"I want to tell you tonight of the fourth Trumpet Judgment in the hope that it will not take that catastrophe to finally convince you. For it could just as easily kill you."

CHAPTER 9

JUST AFTER NOON on Thursday in Chicago, Rayford and Ken joined Doc Charles and Hattie to watch the Meeting. The pilots had their flight plans out and doodled with charting their course to the Middle East. Assuming word got to Tsion, he would announce something official or ceremonious for Saturday, and that would trigger Rayford and Ken's attempt to get to Israel. They would plan to arrive around midnight Friday and pick up their passengers shortly thereafter.

Rayford's head jerked up as all four watchers heard Tsion say, "I plan to summarize all this in a small thank-you session to the local committee on Saturday at noon, when we meet near the Temple Mount."

"Bingo!" Rayford said. "Teach me the Gulfstream this afternoon, so I can share the load both ways."

"Long as you're confident of chopper duty. Got one lined up?"

"That part'll be easy. Hoo, boy, back in the battle!"

Hattie gave Rayford a long look. "You like this stuff?"

"Funny *you* would ask that," he said, "knowing how you feel about Carpathia."

"I expect to die going after him. You act like you can't lose."

"We've already won," Ritz said. "It's just a matter of going through the motions. The Bible's already told the story, and as Tsion says, 'We win.'"

Hattie shook her head and rolled onto her side, her back to them. "You're pretty glib for dealing with a man like Nicolae."

Ken caught Rayford's eye. "You realize when we have to leave, with the time change and all? Well, 'course you do. You been flyin' these routes a lot longer'n I have."

Buck found it hard to believe all that had happened in the twenty-four hours since Tsion had last addressed the crowd. He missed Chloe but felt more settled and at peace than he had in a long time.

"The earth groans under the effects of our fallen condition," Tsion began. "We've all lost loved ones in the Rapture and in the ten judgments from heaven since then. The great wrath of the Lamb earthquake devastated the globe, save for this very country and nation. The first three Trumpet Judgments alone scorched a third of the earth's trees and grass, destroyed a third of the oceans' fish, sank a third of the world's ships, and poisoned a third of the earth's water—all as predicted in the Scriptures.

"We know the sequence of these events, but we don't know God's timing. He could pile many of these judgments into one day. All I can say with certainty is what comes next. As you see, these get progressively worse. The fourth Trumpet Judgment will affect the look of the skies and the temperature of the entire globe.

"Revelation 8:12 reads, 'Then the fourth angel sounded: And a third of the sun was struck, a third of the moon, and a third of the stars, so that a third of them were darkened. A third of the day did not shine, and likewise the night.'

"Regardless of whether it means one-third of each star or a third of all stars, the effect will be the same. Day or night, the skies will be one-third darker than they have ever been. Not only that, but I take from this passage that one-third more of the day will be dark. So the sun will shine only two-thirds the time it used to. And when it *is* shining, it will be only two-thirds its usual brightness.

"Prophecy indicates that more scorching and parching of the earth comes later, so it's likely the darkening and resultant cooling is temporary. But when it occurs, it will usher in—for however long—winterlike conditions in most of the world. Prepare, prepare, prepare! And when depressed friends and neighbors and loved ones despair due to the darkness and gloom, show them this was predicted. Tell them it is God's way of getting their attention."

Tsion summarized the teaching that had gone on during the day at various sites around the city and urged the audience to preach boldly "until the Glorious Appearing fewer than five years away. I believe the greatest time of harvest is now, before the second half of the Tribulation, which the Bible calls the Great Tribulation.

"One day the evil world system will require citizens to bear a mark in order for them to buy or sell. You may rest assured it will not be the mark we see on each other's foreheads!"

Tsion went on to outline practical suggestions for storing goods. "We must trust God," he concluded. "He expects us to be wise as serpents and gentle as doves. That wisdom includes being practical enough to prepare for a future that has been laid out for us in his Word.

"Tomorrow night I'm afraid I have a difficult message to bring. You may get a preview of it by reading Revelation 9."

As Tsion began wrapping up his teaching for the night, Buck's phone vibrated.

"It's Mac. Are you where you can talk?"

Buck turned away from the backstage wing and moved to a quiet area. "Shoot."

"Do you have an evacuation plan, you and your wife and Ben-Judah?"

"We're working on it."

"You'll need it. I'm telling you, boy, these guys are crazy. Carpathia spends half his day fuming about the two witnesses and the other half plotting to kill Mathews."

"Mathews bothers him more than Tsion does?"

"I wouldn't give a nickel for Peter Mathews's future. And Carpathia thinks he's got Tsion's number. Whatever that Saturday deal is, be careful. Nicolae's got his troops so fired up that they know they could take out Tsion and never suffer for it. Nicolae would paint it as a setup, dissension among the ranks of the believers or something, and he would still look like a hero."

"This connection is secure, right, Mac?"

"Of course."

"We'll be long gone before that rally."

"Good! Need anything? I'm in contact every day with David Hassid."

"Rayford's trying to get a chopper to get us from Jerusalem to one of the airports."

"You can't just sneak out and get a ride?"

"We trust hardly anyone, Mac."

"Good for you. I'm going to recommend David get you a chopper that looks like ours."

"White, with GC on it?"

"Nobody'll mess with you if they see that."

"Until we leave it on the runway and fly off in a Gulfstream."

"Ritz has a Gulf? I'm jealous."

"Come with us, Mac."

"You know I'd love to. But somebody has to be the ears here."

"We're not going to be able to watch tomorrow night's meeting, are we?" Rayford said as Ken ran him through the paces of the Gulfstream over Palwaukee Airport.

"Sure we are. Hook your iPhone to my satellite tracking system, and I can force it to lock onto the Internet feed. It'll be a little tricky, bouncin' around up there, but you'll at least be able to hear it."

Rayford completed a fourth consecutive smooth landing, and Ritz pronounced him ready. As they sat in a rebuilt hangar finalizing their route, the young mechanic approached. "Captain Steele," Ernie said. "I took a call while you were in the air. Was your phone off or something?"

"Yeah," Rayford said, turning it back on. "I didn't want to be distracted."

"I heard you had one of them wake-up features where it'll ring even when it's off."

"Yeah, but you can override that too."

"Cool. Anyways, a Miss Hattie Durham wants you to call her."

Rayford called her on the drive back to the safe house. "I wouldn't care if Floyd said you were fit to run a marathon, Hattie. You're not going with us, at least not on my plane."

"Your plane?" Ritz said, laughing from behind the wheel of the Rover.

"Or Ken's plane, I mean."

"It ain't mine either, Bro!" Ken said.

"Whoever's plane. Anyway, Hattie, there's no way Floyd would release you to travel. Let me talk to him."

"He doesn't even know I'm calling. I know what he'd say. That's why I haven't said anything to him. And don't you either, Rayford."

"Hattie, you're acting like a child. You think I'd let you go with us on a dangerous mission, sick as you've been? You know me better than that."

"I thought maybe you owed me."

"Hattie, this discussion is closed. You want a ride to the Middle East so you can kill Carpathia, find it elsewhere."

"Let me talk to Ken."

"He's not going to—"

"Just let me talk to him!"

Rayford handed the phone to a puzzled-looking, scowling Ritz. "Yeah, doll," he said. "No, sorry, that's just an expression we old flyboys use. . . . Well, sure, I'd like to be a doll too. . . . Oh, no ma'am. I can't see any way. Well, now, I hate to have you think less of me, but the truth is if I could be manipulated by the poutin' of a spoiled pretty little girl, I wouldn't be lookin' back on two divorces now, would I? . . . You can beg and cry for someone else, honey, 'cause I sure ain't gonna be responsible for you overseas not forty-eight hours after you miscarried. . . . Now I'm awful sorry for you, and, like everybody else in your life, I got sort of a soft spot for you. But that's the reason I'm not going to be party to any foolishness like this. . . . Well, I understand that. I'd like to kill him myself. But I got a job to do, and it's dangerous enough as it is. I'm gettin' people outta there, not worryin' about killing anybody. At least this trip. How 'bout you get yourself healthy, and I'll see about running you over there for Nicolae target practice another time. . . . No, I'm not poking fun at you. You are being a little silly here though, don't you think?"

Ritz shook his head and flapped the phone shut as he handed it back to Rayford. "Little spitfire hung up on me. You gotta like her spunk, though. And she *is* a gorgeous thing, ain't she?"

Rayford shook his head. "Ritz, you've got to be on the feminists' top ten most wanted list. Man, what a throwback!"

Rayford nearly panicked when he didn't see Hattie in her bed as they walked in. "She in the bathroom?" he asked Floyd.

"I wish," the doctor said. "She's walking somewhere."

"Walking!"

"Calm down. She insisted on walking around and wouldn't let me help her. She's on the other side."

Rayford checked the empty, more damaged half of the duplex. Hattie walked slowly on the uneven floor of an unfurnished room, her arms folded. He just stared at her, not asking the obvious question. She answered it anyway.

"Just trying to build my strength."

"Not for this trip."

"I've resigned myself to that. But Ken promised to—"

"Ken was talking through his hat, and you know it. Now would you please do yourself and all of us a favor and follow Doc's orders."

"I know my body better. It's time I started building back up. He said himself I may be out of the woods with the poison, whatever it was. But that's only because my baby took the brunt of it. Nicolae has to pay for that."

Hattie was suddenly short of breath. "See?" Rayford said. "You're overdoing it." He helped her back to the other side of the house, but she refused to lie down.

"I'll just sit awhile," she said.

Floyd was visibly angry. "She's going to be a whole lot of fun to deal with while you guys are gone."

"Come with us," Ken said. "She looks like she's getting pretty self-sufficient to me."

"Not a chance. She may not know how sick she is, but I do."

"Let's hope we're not bringing you back any more wounded," Ken said.

Rayford nodded. "I've already seen enough casualties in this war to last me a lifetime."

Mac confirmed to Buck that the plot against both the witnesses and Tsion was set for Saturday noon near the Temple Mount. "They can't believe Tsion has played right into their hands. They're planning what will appear to be a terrorist bombing that should kill anyone within two hundred feet of the Wall."

"Tsion thought Carpathia wouldn't try anything at a site so sacred to the Jews."

"It would never be traced to him. They're already trying to pin it on Mathews. Funny thing is, Mathews wants the credit for it. He says the witnesses and Tsion are the greatest enemies to religion he has ever seen. He's livid. You're going to be gone, right?"

"By 1:00 a.m."

"Perfect. A replica chopper's been delivered, and as far as I know, everything's in place. And your host is none the wiser?"

"Rosenzweig's still holding out for Carpathia's being a misunderstood good guy. He'll be as surprised as anyone when we disappear in the middle of the night. He's usually one of the first to bed, so we're all going to make sure of that. We can't pack or do anything that might tip him off until we're sure he's asleep. If worse comes to worse, though, he'd keep quiet until we were long gone."

A strange wrinkle in the Friday night plan was that everyone, it seemed, wanted to go to the stadium. The threats against the witnesses, the public feud between Carpathia and Ben-Judah, everything had come to a head. The place would be jammed. While Chloe had assured Buck she was glad to have taken a night off, she wanted to be there and promised to be careful and take it easy. Yes, she said, she would even sit through the meeting.

Jacov was back on driving detail, Dr. Rosenzweig deciding

the sanction against him was ludicrous. "But what if the GC escort sees him behind the wheel?" Buck asked, not wanting to create unnecessary turmoil.

"Then they can report it to Fortunato, and I will insist on talking personally with Nicolae. But, Cameron, they don't care. They will see him brazenly behind the wheel and will assume a new deal has been made. You know his wife will be along."

"What?"

"And Stefan."

"Oh, Chaim! This is getting to be a circus."

"And their boss."

"Their boss? Now who's that?"

Chaim smiled at him. "You don't know who my driver and valet's boss is?"

"You? You want to go?"

"I not only want to, I shall. And I want us all jammed into that Mercedes, just like a school trip. It will be festive and grand!"

"Chaim, this is not advisable."

"Don't be silly. You and Tsion have been begging me to go. I have been watching. I am intrigued. I might even give Tsion his audience tonight."

"Tonight?"

"Tonight. He is speaking on some more terrible things supposedly coming from the heavens. He will be in a mood to keep going and to try to convince his old friend that Jesus is the Messiah."

"But he'll be very tired later, Chaim. And won't you be also?"

"Too tired for a good debate? You don't know the Jews, Cameron. And you certainly don't know your own rabbi. I'm surprised at you! A good, ah, missionary, ah, what do you call it, evangelist like you and you want now to postpone the appointment with a prospective convert?"

"Are you really?"

"Probably not, but who is to say? You must not treat lightly the curious, am I right?"

Buck shook his head. "Under normal circumstances. But you are just having fun with us."

"A promise is a promise, my young friend. I am a man of my word."

"You know Tsion must prepare for the noon meeting at the Temple Mount tomorrow."

"That is not until noon! He is a dozen or so years older than you, my friend, but he is almost thirty years younger than I. He is robust. And who knows? If he is right, he has the power of God on him. He will survive. He can talk to an old man until the wee hours and still be prepared for his little get-together tomorrow. And I will be there too."

Buck was frantic by the time he got alone with Tsion. The rabbi was less concerned about Rosenzweig's presence in the stadium than with his plan to be at the Temple Mount the next day.

"But we'll be gone by then," Buck said. "He'll know that meeting is off. We need to make sure everyone knows we're

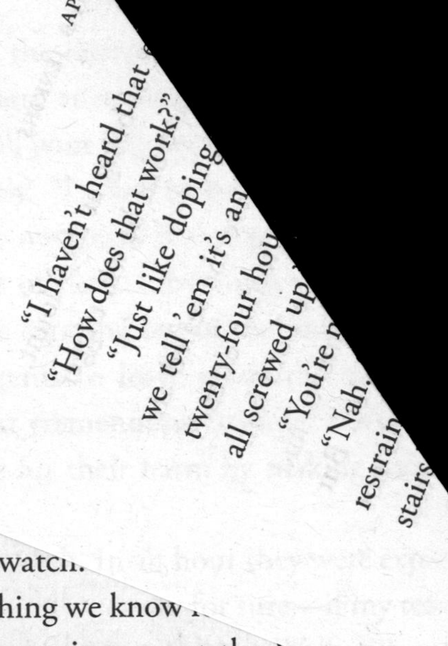
APOL
"I haven't heard that
"How does that work?"
"Just like doping
we tell 'em it's an
twenty-four hou
all screwed up
"You're n
"Nah.
restrain
stairs

gone so no one ma
Nicolae could be
the attack anywa

Tsion nodd
protected, but
beyond the
self has cha
he can in
he has g
want to be
assumptions."

Buck looked at his watch.
at the stadium. "One thing we know
is right—is that the two witnesses at the wa
harmed, regardless of what Nicolae engineers tomorro

"If they're there," Tsion said, smiling.

"Oh, they'll be there," Buck said.

"What makes you say that?"

"Because Nicolae warned them not to appear in public under penalty of death. What would be more public than where they have stood for more than two years?"

"You have a point," Tsion said, patting Buck on the shoulder. "You must have a good teacher."

Rayford was on the phone to Dr. Floyd Charles at the safe house as Ken piloted the Gulfstream over the Atlantic. "I'm tempted to slip her a Mickey, medical-school style," Floyd said.

expression in ages," Rayford said.

somebody's drink," Floyd said, "only innocuous IV. I could put her out for rs, but then her immune system would be ."

ot really considering it?"

She's driving me batty though. I had to physically her to keep her from doing laps up and down the ."

"The stairs!"

"That's what I said. I'm glad she's feeling stronger, and ironically this murderous rage she feels toward Carpathia seems to be speeding her recovery. But I can't have her expending the exertion necessary to climb stairs while she's this weak. Honestly, Ray, it's like trying to corral a toddler. I look up, and there she goes again."

"How about downstairs?"

"Downstairs what?"

"Could she just walk downstairs?"

"Ray, I've been through medical school, and I don't know how a person goes downstairs without going up too."

"You could carry her up and let her walk down. Maybe it would tire her out without overexerting her."

There was a pause long enough for Rayford to have to ask if Floyd was still there.

"I'm here," he said. "I'm just thinking what a good idea that is."

"Left you speechless, did it? Every once in a while even pilots come up with something useful."

"Problem is, Ray, I look for reasons to touch her, to hold her, to comfort her. Now you're telling me to pick her up and carry her, and you want me to rethink my feelings for her?"

"Get a grip, Doc. You're no teenager anymore. I hoped your obsession with her wasn't purely physical, but I should have known. You hardly know her, and what you know drives you batty by your own admission. Just behave yourself until we can get back and help you keep your senses."

"Yeah, yeah."

"I mean it now."

"I know. I hear you."

"And, Doc, remember that our absolute, number one, top priority with her is her soul."

"Yeah."

"I didn't hear any enthusiasm there, Floyd."

"No, I got it."

"If you care a whit about her beyond your adolescent need to have her in your arms, you'll want above all else to make her part of the family."

"Buck, we've got a problem," Chloe said, pulling him into an empty room. "I just casually walked through our route to the helipad so there'd be no surprises, and that key is gone."

"What?"

"The key Rosenzweig had on a nail on the frame next to the access door. It's gone."

"Does he suspect we're up to something?"

"How could he? I was as casual and subtle as I could be. He brought it up. I only asked him about the history of the house."

"Did that door look as solid to you from inside as it felt to me from the outside?"

"It's like a brick wall, Buck. If we had to break through it or knock it down, we'd wake the dead, not to mention the guard staff and Chaim himself."

"We've got to find the key or get him to tell us what he did with it."

"You think Jacov would know anything about it?"

Buck shrugged. "If I asked him, he'd sure know something was going on. I can't get between them."

"But he's a brother, Buck."

"Brand new. I'm not saying he'd betray us on purpose."

"You heard about his wife?"

"That she's going along tonight, yes. How does she feel about his faith?"

"So you haven't heard."

"No."

"Chaim said Jacov claims his wife is now a believer too. Chaim thought it was humorous and asked me to use my Jesus vision tonight to see if she had the secret mark too."

Buck shook his head. "Talk about a soul harvest. I'm praying for Rosenzweig himself."

Jacov's wife, Hannelore, proved to be a German-born Jew, sandy haired and small with shy, azure eyes. She joined Jacov, Stefan, Buck, Chloe, Tsion, and Chaim in the driveway, and the guard staff opened the doors of the Mercedes for them. Chloe embraced her tightly, and though she was a stranger, reached up to brush Hannelore's hair from off her forehead.

Buck hugged her too, whispering, "Welcome to the family."

"My wife, she does not understand English too good," Jacov said.

"Well, how about it?" Chaim said, his eyes bright. "Does she have the—" and here he lowered his voice an octave and growled—"secret mark?"

"As a matter of fact, she does, Dr. Rosenzweig," Chloe said, clearly not amused at his teasing.

"Oh, good then!" he exulted, moving to the front passenger seat. "You are all one big happy family then, are you not? And how about you, Stefan? Have you joined the ranks of the tribulation saints?"

"Maybe tonight!" Stefan said. "Almost last night!"

"My, my," Chaim said. "I shall be left in the minority, shall I not?"

Only Jacov and Chaim fit in the front seat, so Hannelore sat directly behind Jacov with Chloe in the middle and Tsion behind Chaim. Buck and Stefan crammed into the rear compartment. Jacov had begun to pull slowly down the driveway when Jonas stepped in front of the car and signaled that Chaim should lower his window. He spoke urgently to Chaim in Hebrew.

Buck, with his face inches from Tsion's head, whispered, "What's going on?"

Tsion turned toward the window and spoke softly. "They've gotten a call from Leon. He's sending a helicopter. The roads are more jammed than ever; the stadium is already full. They had to open the gates two hours ahead." He listened some more. "The gateman told Fortunato there were seven of us, too many for a helicopter anyway. Apparently Fortunato told him to tell Chaim we were on our own if we refused GC assistance. Chaim is saying the gateman did the right thing. Just a minute. He's whispering. Oh, no."

"What?"

"Fortunato has warned that Jacov not be in our party. Chaim is angry, demanding that the gateman get Leon back on the phone."

Jonas signaled that Jacov should pull the vehicle to the guardhouse at the gate. A phone was extended to Chaim, who immediately began arguing passionately in Hebrew.

"Then I will speak in English, Leon. I thought you knew every language in the world, as your boss seems to. I may call him potentate because I have always admired him, but I will not even call you *sir*, let alone supreme whatever-you-are. Now you listen to me. I am a personal friend of the potentate. He has pledged the security of my guests. I will be sitting with Jacov in the stadium tonight, and—yes, out in the crowd! I will not hide backstage. . . . To you he may be only a driver or a valet. To me he is part of my family, and he will not be threatened. Running from your guards and shooting harmlessly into the air may have been foolhardy, but he would not have done it if he didn't feel our guests were in danger from the very people who had promised their safety!"

Tsion reached up and laid a hand on Rosenzweig's shoulder as if to calm him. Buck could see the blood rise on the back of the old man's neck and the veins bulge in his temple. "I need not remind you that it was not so long ago that Rabbi Tsion Ben-Judah lost his family for merely expressing his beliefs on television! He was chased from his homeland like a common criminal! . . . Yes, I know how offensive it must have been for the Jews! I am a Jew, Leon! That's more than I can say for you. . . . Tsion assures me his belief is founded on more than faith but also scholarship, but that is not the point! . . . No! I am not one of them, as you say. But if I find that Nicolae looks upon these devout and passionate seekers of God with the contempt that you do, I might just become one of them!

"Now we are proceeding to the stadium in my well-known vehicle. We will take our chances with the traffic because we know shortcuts, and I also assume Tsion's followers will make way for us. . . . As a compromise to you, yes, I will use an alternate driver—" Chaim signaled quickly for Jacov and Stefan to switch places—"but we are on our way, and we expect the protection pledged by the potentate himself.

". . . Am I sorry? Sorry that you make so much of titles,

Leon. But no, not sorry that I have offended you. You have offended me, how about that? I have tried to keep my wits about me and have maintained as normal a lifestyle as possible despite the accolades and the wealth that have come with my formula. . . . I am not insisting on some new title or a higher pedestal, and frankly it does not wear well on you either. We are pulling away, Leon, and my new driver seems unaware that I am on a cord phone! Good-bye!"

He laughed. "Stefan, you snake! You nearly pulled the phone away from the cord!"

"I'm a snake?" Stefan said, smiling. "You put me in the target seat!"

Chaim wrenched around in the seat. "Tsion, my son, you know what Leon was saying when we pulled away?"

"I can only imagine."

"That he would be happy to work on a more appropriate title for a man of my station! Have you ever encountered anyone so out of touch with the point of a conversation?"

"Never," Tsion said.

Buck was awestruck that such a dangerous ride could turn so festive.

CHAPTER 10

RAYFORD HANDLED the bulk of the flying across the Atlantic, scheduling his arrival to allow the least amount of time on the ground. Mac had informed him that Carpathia and his entourage were still at the King David, but that the Condor 216 was hangared at Ben Gurion in Tel Aviv. Rayford figured security was tighter at Ben Gurion, but Carpathia was being ferried about on a GC chopper primarily out of Jerusalem Airport.

"You still takin' chopper duty with me waiting at the airstrip with these turbines hot?" Ken said.

"As long as nobody knows I'm AWOL yet. If the word is

out about me and I get spotted absconding with a GC chopper, mission's over."

"Well, make up your mind, Ray. I mean, I'm a good soldier, and I'll do what I'm told. But I gotta be told."

"Help me out here, Ken. I've still got my high-level security ID, but . . ."

"But if they do know and you get caught, how am I going to get our people back to the Gulfstream?"

Rayford shook his head. "I've got to try Mac one more time."

"You fly; I'll punch in the numbers. I'm going to have way too many flight hours otherwise."

Ken handed the phone to Rayford. "Man, I'm glad you called," Mac said. "I got the third degree about you for an hour. They don't suspect anything on my part, but they think you're in Jerusalem."

"As long as they're not setting up a dragnet in the U.S."

"I'd rather they were, Ray. They look hard enough in Jerusalem, they're gonna find you."

"They won't think I'd be stupid enough to be at an airport."

"Maybe not, but stay aboard that Gulfstream."

"You just answered a very important question for us, Mac. Thanks."

"What? *You* were going to do the chopper work? Not smart. Anyway, as good as your teacher was, I never thought you got that good at it."

"This is better anyway. Ken's been to Rosenzweig's. If we

don't draw too much attention to ourselves, we should be able to pull this off. Where's Carpathia going to be?"

"No air plans, and he's sure not going to crash the stadium party again. He's staying close to the King David tonight, and I've charted a midmorning flight to New Babylon out of Tel Aviv. He's going to be a long way from here before anything violent goes down."

"How're you getting him to Tel Aviv?"

"Helicopter out of Jerusalem Airport."

"If these choppers are identical, how will I know which one we're supposed to borrow?"

"They're supposed to be side by side, facing south. Take the one to the west. Nobody's standing guard over them like they are the Condor at Gurion."

"Have you seen the one David had delivered?"

"No, but it's there. The airport called asking what they were supposed to do with it. You'd have been proud of me, Ray. I adopt this major attitude. I tell the guy, 'Just what do you think you're supposed to do with a backup chopper? Stay the blazes away from it! If I find out anybody but my crew lays a finger on it, heads are gonna roll.' Got his attention."

"You're the best, Mac. Here's what we'll do then. I'll land the Gulfstream and play it like I'm there on business, stopping for fuel and a system check. Ken will walk down to the chopper and take off while I'm refueling. Will he be seen?"

"Not if he heads due south, lights off till he's away from the field. It would be only blind luck if somebody saw him. The tricky part is going to be taking off again, what, twenty minutes later. You don't want to get cleared too long before he sets down with your passengers or you'll look suspicious. Obviously you'll coordinate that by secure phone so the tower can't eavesdrop. Taxi down to the far end of the runway where it's darker, and Ken can land, again without lights. Somebody may see all that, but you're a quarter mile from anyone who can hurt you, so get going. If you're lucky, nobody will see the chopper go or come. The guy who ferried it down here for me is staying in Haifa. I told him I'd call him if I needed him. Otherwise, he's taking it back to New Babylon after we leave."

"Pray for us, Mac. We think we're ready, but you never know."

"I will, Ray. Every waking moment. Let me talk to Ken a second." Ray handed him the phone.

"Well, thank you, sir," Ken said. "I look forward to meeting you, too, though the way I understand it, that would happen if your tail was in as much trouble as Rayford's here. You be careful now, and we'll be in touch."

Buck was continually amazed at the resourcefulness of his wife. Despite her youth, Chloe knew people. She knew when to act, when to speak, when not to. She waited until they were nearly at the stadium, stuck in traffic, to bring up the missing key.

"You know, Dr. Rosenzweig," she began, "I was getting

our suitcase down from the hall closet and noticed that key you showed me the other day is missing."

"Oh, it is not missing if I know where it is, is it?"

She laughed. "No. I just wanted to tell you, in case you didn't know."

"Were you afraid I would accuse you of having taken it?" he said, his eyes alive with humor.

Chloe shook her head. "I just noticed," she said. "That's all."

"It is in safekeeping," he said. She shrugged, doing a good job, Buck thought, of pretending it was no concern of hers. "It just seemed foolish of me to leave it hanging right there all these years. A security risk, you know?"

"Oh?" she said. "I should think it would be more of a security risk if you hung it outside." That tickled the old man so that the car bounced and swayed as he laughed. "In the States," she continued, "we don't have many doors that can be key-locked both inside and out."

"Really? They are common here, especially for doors hardly ever used. I imagine in the embassy days of the compound that door was used frequently and was likely locked or unlocked with a key only on the outside." Chloe appeared more interested in the teeming crowds outside the van. "Jacov," Chaim said, "you do still have that key, do you not?"

"I do!" he shouted from the rear next to Buck. "And right now it's digging into my leg through my pocket!"

Chaim leaned back toward Chloe as if with a secret. "I am certain that is the only key I have for that lock. I can't imagine needing that exit, but it seems reckless to not have copies made. Jacov will take care of that Monday."

She nodded and turned to catch Buck's eye. What was he supposed to do, he wondered, pickpocket it? He did not want Jacov to know of their escape until they were long gone. Rosenzweig either, despite his escalating war of words with Leon Fortunato.

As Stefan was directed into a private parking spot next to the west entrance, Buck found himself grateful that this was the last night of the conference. It had been beyond anything he could have imagined, but where would they put all these people? Every night the crowds grew. Now people were shoulder to shoulder, the stadium full, crowds milling about outside and spilling into traffic. The news media, admittedly controlled by the Global Community, was everywhere. Clearly this was Nicolae's way of monitoring every detail.

The entourage filed into the staging area, where the local committee waited. Buck was impressed with the authoritative tone Tsion suddenly effected. He must have felt like the shepherd he was and that the tens of thousands inside and outside the stadium were his flock. The previous two days he had deferred to the master of ceremonies and the local committee and merely appeared on stage and preached when it was his turn. Now he seemed to take charge, at least of certain details.

"Buck," he said, beckoning him with a raise of his chin. As Buck approached, Tsion gripped his elbow and pulled him toward the emcee. "You know Daniel, of course."

Buck nodded and shook hands with him. "Daniel, listen," Tsion continued, "I want five seats in the reserved section held for my guests. They will include Dr. Rosenzweig, two of his staff members, one of their wives, and Buck's wife. Understood?"

"Of course."

"And I would like Buck cleared to be backstage as usual." He turned to Buck. "Chloe will be all right without you?"

"More than all right, sir. The question is how will I get along without her."

Tsion was apparently too focused to see the humor. "Daniel, I would like Dr. Rosenzweig recognized in an understated, dignified manner. He has not asked for this. It is merely a courtesy appropriate to his standing within the country."

"I'll handle it."

"After your greeting and welcome, announce the Saturday rally for the local committee at the Temple Mount, recognize Dr. Rosenzweig, pray, lead in a hymn, and get me on. No fanfare this time. They know who I am."

"But, sir—"

"Please, Daniel. We are on the front lines here, and it is becoming increasingly dangerous. We are enemies of the world system and will have many opportunities to expose them down the road. Making a fuss over me serves no purpose and merely—"

"Begging your pardon, Doctor. Mr. Williams, I'm sure you agree that these people will be eager to express themselves on what may be the last time they have opportunity to see Dr. Ben-Judah in person. Please let me—"

"If they respond spontaneously, I will accept it in the spirit offered. But I want no grand introduction. You should be able to do it without even using my name. Take that as a personal challenge."

Daniel looked crestfallen. "Oh, sir, are you sure?"

"I know you can handle it."

Rayford, with nothing but water in view, took a call from Floyd Charles. "What's up, Doc?" he said.

"Never heard that one before," Floyd said. "I hate to bother you, but this seemed important. Hattie's spent a lot of time on the phone with a kid named Ernie, a friend of Ken's."

"I met him."

"She apparently happened onto him when she was trying to reach you out there."

"Yeah, so?"

"Well, she'd like to see him."

"Does she know he's got to be ten years younger than she is?"

"So about the same age difference as Buck and your daughter?"

Rayford paused. "What, you're worried about a relationship? Have you talked to this kid?"

"Yeah. He's a believer. Seems nice enough."

"He's a mechanical whiz, but him and Hattie? Don't even worry about it. She's your patient, Floyd, but she's also a grown woman. We don't have any authority over her."

"That's not what I'm worried about, Rayford. She'd like him to come here."

"Whoops!"

"That's what I thought. We don't want him knowing where we are, do we?"

"No. He's a brother and all, but we don't know who he knows, whether he's mature enough to keep his mouth shut, that kind of thing."

"That's what I thought. Just checking."

"Don't let her even hint at where we're located."

"Gotcha. I might reward her for good behavior and run her out to Palwaukee in a day or two. She can put a face to a name that way, anyway."

"We'll be home before that, Doc. We'll make a picnic of it. The whole Tribulation Force, except David and Mac, of course, together at last."

After the group prayed backstage, Tsion stood by himself, head down, eyes closed. Buck couldn't decide whether Tsion was more or less nervous than usual. He kept an eye on Tsion until Daniel walked past him to the podium. Tsion looked up at Buck and waved him over.

"Stand with me, Cameron, would you?" Buck felt honored. He stepped up next to Tsion in the wings as they watched Daniel welcome the crowd and make his announcement about Saturday's rally. "Most of you will have gone home, but if you live locally or can make it, please feel free. Remember, however, that this is just a thank-you to the local committee." He then had Dr. Rosenzweig stand to warm applause.

"How will you get the key?" Tsion asked.

"I'm not sure yet, but I may simply ask Jacov for it and tell him to ask no questions. I believe he will trust me until I can explain."

Tsion nodded. "I feel a particular burden tonight, Cameron," he whispered suddenly. Buck didn't know what to say. When Tsion bowed his head again, Buck put an arm around his shoulder and was shocked to find the man trembling.

Daniel prayed, then led the singing of "Holy, Holy, Holy."

"Excellent choice," Tsion murmured, but he did not sing. Buck tried to and nodded when Tsion said, "Pray for me."

The song ended. Tsion looked to Buck, who lifted a fist of encouragement in his face. Daniel said, "And now I invite you to listen to a message from the Word of God." Buck was thrilled to see the crowd rise and clap. No shouting, no cheering, no whistling. Just a long and respectful and enthusiastic season of applause that seemed to overwhelm Tsion. He waved shyly and, when he had finished arranging his notes, stepped back until the applause died out.

"God has put something on my heart tonight," he said.

"Even before I open his Word, I feel led to invite seekers to come forward and receive Christ." Immediately, from all over the stadium and even outside, lines of people, many weeping, began streaming forward, causing the saints to burst into applause again. "You know the truth," Tsion said. "God has gotten your attention. You need no other argument, you need no other plea. It is enough that Jesus died, and that he died for thee."

The seekers kept coming. Tsion asked believers to pray with anyone who wanted them to, and for an hour it seemed that anyone within the sound of Tsion's voice—other than Global Community personnel—came looking for salvation.

"The Global Community Broadcasting Network is beaming this all over the world and onto the Internet," Tsion said. "I'm sure they believe that any thinking person will see through our message and that the GC has nothing to fear by letting us proclaim it. They will say ours is not the message of ecumenism and tolerance that they promote, and I say they are right. There is right and wrong, there are absolute truths, and some things cannot and should not and shall not ever be tolerated.

"The GC Network will not turn us off, lest they appear afraid of our message, of the truth of God, of a converted rabbi who believes Jesus Christ is the long-sought Messiah. I applaud the courage of the Global Community administration and unapologetically take advantage of their largesse. At no cost to us, our message is broadcast to every nation of the world. We have not needed translators here, and reports tell us the same miracle of understanding has happened on television as well. If you understand neither Hebrew nor English but still understand every word I'm saying, I'm happy to tell you that God is working in your mind. Most of this message is in English, though I read Scripture in Hebrew, Greek, and Aramaic. I have been amused to discover that even my coworkers are unaware of this. They hear all of it in their own tongues.

"God is also working in your heart. You do not have to be with us physically to receive Christ tonight. You need not be with anyone else, pray with anyone else, or go anywhere else. All you need is to tell God that you acknowledge that you are a sinner and are separated from him. Tell him you know that nothing you can do for yourself will earn your way to him. Tell him you believe that he sent his Son, Jesus Christ, to die on the cross for your sins, that he was raised from the dead, has raptured his church, and is coming yet again to the earth. Receive him as your Savior right where you are. I believe millions all over the world are joining the great soul harvest that shall produce tribulation saints and martyrs, a multitude that cannot be numbered."

Tsion looked spent and stepped back to pray. When the people who had come forward finally began to disperse and head back to their seats, Tsion moved back to the lectern. He arranged his notes yet again, but his shoulders sagged and he seemed to breathe heavily. Buck was worried about him.

Tsion cleared his throat and drew in a huge breath, yet his voice was suddenly weak. "My text tonight," he managed, "is Revelation 8:13." All over the stadium, tens of thousands of Bibles opened, and the unique sound of onionskin pages turning filled the air. Tsion hurried back to Buck while people looked for the passage.

"Are you all right, Tsion?"

"I think so. Are you willing to read the passage for me if I need you to?"

"Certainly. Right now?"

"I prefer to try, but I'll call on you if I need you."

Tsion made his way back to the podium, looked at the passage, then lifted his eyes to the crowd. He cleared his throat. "Bear with me," he said. "This passage warns that once the earth has been darkened by a third, three terrible woes will follow. These are particularly ominous, so much so that they will be announced from heaven in advance."

Tsion cleared his throat yet again and Buck stood ready if needed. He wished Tsion would simply ask his assistance. But suddenly he smelled the dusty, smoky robes of the two witnesses and was startled when Eli and Moishe stepped up beside him. He turned as if in a dream and found himself staring into Eli's endless eyes. Buck had never been so close to the prophets and had to resist the urge to touch them. Eli's eyes bore into his. "Show thyself not to thine enemy," he said. "Be sober, be vigilant; because your adversary the devil, as a roaring lion, walketh about, seeking whom he may devour."

Buck could not speak. He tried to nod, to indicate he had heard and understood, but he could not move. Moishe leaned between him and Eli and added, "Whom resist stedfast in the faith."

They moved past him and stood directly behind Tsion. The crowd seemed so stunned that they didn't cheer or applaud but pointed and stood and leaned forward to listen. Moishe said, "My beloved brethren, the God of all grace, who hath called us unto his eternal glory by Christ Jesus, after that ye have suffered a while, make you perfect, stablish, strengthen, settle you."

To Buck it appeared as if Tsion might fall over, but he merely made way for the two. Neither stepped close to the microphone, however. Moishe loudly quoted Tsion's passage so that every ear could hear, in the stadium and on global television.

"'And I beheld, and heard an angel flying through the midst of heaven, saying with a loud voice, Woe, woe, woe, to the inhabiters of the earth by reason of the other voices of the trumpet of the three angels, which are yet to sound!'"

All around Buck came the sound of the engaging of high-powered GC rifles. Guards dropped to one knee to raise their weapons and take a bead on the two witnesses. He wanted to shout, "It's not the due time, you fools!" but he worried for Tsion's safety, for Chloe's and their friends', for his own.

But no one fired. And just when it appeared one or two might squeeze their trigger, Eli and Moishe strode off the stage, past Buck, and past the very guards who had them in their sights. The guards scrambled away from them, some falling, their weapons clattering on the concrete floor.

Buck heard Tsion say from the podium, "If we never meet again this side of heaven or in the millennial kingdom our Savior sets up on earth, I shall greet you on the Internet and teach from Revelation 9! Godspeed as you share the gospel of Christ with the whole world!"

The meeting ended early, and Tsion, as frightened as Buck had ever seen him, hurried directly to him. "Get our passengers into the van as quickly as possible!"

CHAPTER 11

RAYFORD AND KEN sat silently during the bizarre telecast from Israel, where it was not yet nine o'clock, as they streaked toward the Middle East Friday night.

"Still on schedule to touch down at midnight," Rayford said. "Oh, sorry, Ken. I didn't mean to wake you."

Ken massaged his eye sockets with his thumbs. "Wasn't really sleeping," he said. "Just thinking. You know, if everything Ben-Judah says is true, we're soon gonna spend half our time just trying to stay alive. What're we gonna do when we can't buy or sell 'cause we don't have the mark?"

"Like Tsion said, we have to start stockpiling now."

"You realize what that means? We're going to be a whole

separate, like invisible, society of believers. There may be a billion of us, but we're still going to be in the minority, and we're still going to be seen as criminals and fugitives."

"Don't I know it!"

"We won't be able to trust anybody with the other mark."

"Don't forget, there'll be a lot of people with neither mark."

Ken shook his head. "Food, power, sanitation, transportation—all controlled by the GC. We'll be scrambling around, scratching out an existence in a huge, underground black market. How much money have we got?"

"The Trib Force? Not much. Buck and I made good salaries, but that's gone. Tsion and Chloe have no sources of income either. We can hardly expect Mac and David to have to worry about us, though I'm sure they'll do what they can. I haven't talked to Floyd about any reserves he might have had."

"I have a good bit stashed away."

"So do Buck and I, but nothing like we're going to need for aircraft and fuel, let alone survival."

"This ain't gonna be pretty, is it, Ray?"

"You can say that again, but please don't."

Ken pulled a yellow legal pad from his flight bag. Rayford noticed the pages were dog-eared with handwriting on more than half of them. "I know we never signed anything or made any pledges when we joined," Ken said, "but I been doin' a lot of thinkin'. I was never one for socialism or communism or even communal living. But it seems to me we're going to be pretty much a commune from now on."

"In the New Testament sense, like Tsion says."

"Right, and I don't know about you, but I don't have a problem with that."

Rayford smiled. "I've learned to believe the Bible completely," he said. "If that's what you're asking."

"I don't know what you're going to do about future members and all that, but we may have to get formal about giving everything we have to the cause."

Rayford pursed his lips. So far that had not been an issue. "Sort of like asking everybody to make all their resources available to everybody else?"

"If they're serious about joining."

"I'm willing, and I know Buck and Chloe and Tsion would be. It's just that we bring relatively little materially. Between Buck and me we wouldn't have more than a million dollars. That used to sound like a lot, but it won't last long, and it won't finance any offensive against Carpathia."

"You'd better get that converted to gold—and fast."

"Think so?"

"I'm 90 percent precious metal," Ritz said. "As soon as we went to three currencies, I could see what was coming. Now we're down to one, and no matter what happens, I've got a tradable commodity. I got absolutely obsessed with saving when I turned forty. Don't even know why. Well, I mean, I do now. Tsion believes God works in our lives even before we acknowledge him. For almost twenty years I've been living alone and running charters. I've been a miser. Never owned a new car, made clothes last for years. Wore a cheap watch. Still do. I don't mind telling you, I've made millions and saved almost 80 percent of it."

Rayford whistled through his teeth. "Did I mention the annual dues for being a member of the Tribulation Force?"

"You joke, but what else am I gonna do with millions' worth of gold? We've got, what, less than five years left. Vacations seem frivolous just now, wouldn't you say? Bottom line, Ray, I want to buy a couple of these Gulfstreams, then I want to put in an offer on Palwaukee."

"The airport?"

"It's virtually a ghost strip now anyway. Owner tells me I run more flights out of there than anybody. I know he'd like to sell, and I'd better do it before Carpathia makes it impossible. The place would come with several small planes, a couple of choppers, fuel tanks, tower, sundry equipment."

"You *have* been thinking, haven't you?"

Ken nodded. "About more than that, too." He held up his notepad. "This here's filled with ideas. Farming co-ops, a sea-harvesting operation, even private banking."

"Ken! Back up! Sea harvesting?"

"I read about Carpathia doling out royalties to his ten guys—the ten kings, Tsion calls 'em—for the rights to harvest their waterways for food and oil, and I got thinking they were onto something. He could easily shut down somebody's farm, bomb it, raid it, burn it, confiscate equipment, all that. But how can he patrol all the oceans? We get believers who have fishing experience and equipment—I'm talking about commercial guys here—and we provide 'em a market of millions of saints. We somehow coordinate this, help process the shipping and billing, take a reasonable percentage, and finance the work of the Tribulation Force."

Rayford checked his settings and then turned to stare at Ken. "Where do you come up with this stuff?"

"Thought I was a clod-kicker, didn't you?"

"I knew better because Mac likes to play that role and he's smart as a whip. But do you have background in this, or—?"

"You wouldn't believe me if I told ya."

"I'd believe anything right now."

"London School of Economics."

"Now you're putting me on."

"Told ya. You don't believe me."

"What're you, serious?"

"It was thirty-five years ago, but, yeah. Mustered out of the air force, planned to go commercial but wanted to bum around Europe first. Wound up liking England; I *really* don't remember the whys of that now, but I knocked over LSE with my high school records."

"You did well in high school?"

"Salutatorian, baby. Made the speech and everything. Thought I was gonna be an English teacher. I only talk like this 'cause it's easier, but yours truly is eminently cognizant of the grammatical parameters."

"Amazing."

"I amaze myself sometimes."

"I'll bet you do."

The departing crowd seemed festive, but Buck could not see his party and didn't want to lose sight of Tsion. The rabbi stood chatting with Daniel and the local committee, but he looked agitated and distracted, as if he wanted to be on his way. Buck scanned the stadium, especially the reserved section, but he didn't see any of the five he was looking for. He thought autograph seekers or well-wishers might surround Rosenzweig, perhaps even zealous believers who would try to convert him. But there were no clusters, just lines of people happily filing out under the stern watch of GC guards.

Buck looked back to Tsion and the others backstage. That group seemed to be thinning too, and he didn't want Tsion left alone. He was among the most recognizable people in the world, so he wouldn't be able to blend into any crowds.

Buck hurried to Daniel, but Tsion, now deadly serious, intercepted him. "Cameron, please! Get the others and let's go! I want to speak with Chaim tonight, but nothing must get in the way of our schedule. Everything is set, and we can't leave Rayford and Ken exposed."

"I know, Tsion. I'm looking for the others, but—"

Tsion gripped Buck's arm. "Just go and find them and let's get to the van. I have a terrible feeling I can only assume is from the Lord. We need to get to Chaim's place. The GC surely has it under surveillance, so we can give them a false sense of security once they know we're there and seem to be settling down for the night."

Daniel and only four or five committee members remained backstage. "I don't want to leave you alone, Tsion. With no eyewitnesses, the GC could do anything they wanted with you and blame someone else."

"Go, Cameron. Please. I'll be fine."

"Daniel," Buck said, "would you keep an eye on Tsion until I get back?"

Daniel laughed. "Babysit the rabbi? I can handle that!"

Buck, stern faced, pulled Daniel close and whispered in his ear. "He may be in grave danger. Promise me."

"I will not let him out of my sight, Mr. Williams."

Buck jogged up the ramp and across the stage, jumping to ground level. He could see less from there than on the stage, so he began to climb back up. A GC guard stopped him. "You can't go up there."

Buck reached for his ID. "I'm with the program committee," he said.

"I know who you are, sir. I would advise your not going up there."

"But I need to get through there to get to our van, and I'm trying to find my party."

"You can get to your van the way everyone else is getting out."

"But I can't leave without my people, and we have to rendezvous with someone backstage first."

Buck began to climb the stage again when the guard called him down. "Sir, don't make me use force. You are not allowed to go back up that way."

Buck avoided eye contact to keep from further agitating the guard. "You don't understand. I'm Cam—"

"I know who you are, sir," the guard said severely. "We all know who you are, who makes up your party, and with whom you are rendezvousing."

Buck looked him full in the face. "Then why won't you let me pass?" The guard tipped his uniform cap back, and Buck saw the sign of the cross on his forehead. "You're, you're a—?"

"Just tonight," he whispered. "Standing here. People in the crowd began to notice, and of course I saw their marks too. I had to pull my hat low to keep from being exposed. I'm as good as dead if I'm discovered. Let me come with you."

"But you're in a strategic spot! You can affect so many things! Fellow believers will not give you away. They'll know what you're doing. Is Tsion in danger?"

The guard raised his weapon at Buck. "Move along!" he barked, then lowered his voice again. "Your party is already in the van. Snipers are waiting for a clear shot of Ben-Judah backstage. I doubt you could get him out."

"I have to!" Buck hissed. "I'm going back there!"

"You'll be shot!"

"Then fire at me out here! Draw attention! Yell for help! Do something!"

"Can't you call him?"

"He doesn't carry a phone, and I don't know the emcee's number. Do what you have to do, but I'm going."

"My job is to keep *everyone* away from backstage."

Buck pushed past him and took the steps two at a time. From behind he heard the guard yell, "Wait! Stop! Assistance!" As Buck reached the stage, he stole a glance back to see the guard on his walkie-talkie, then cocking his weapon. Buck dashed backstage and headed straight for Tsion, who stood precariously with only Daniel now. Daniel saw Buck and moved away, as if his job was over. Buck was about to scream at him to stay close, when gunfire erupted.

Tsion and Daniel immediately went down, as did a few stragglers several feet away. GC guards ran for the stage at the sound of the gunfire. Buck rushed to help Tsion up. "Daniel, help me get him into the van!"

They shouldered through panicky people and out to the Mercedes. Outside people screamed and pushed to get as far from the stadium as they could. The back door and the backseat side door stood open. Buck jumped in the back as Daniel pushed Tsion in and shut the door.

They all kept their heads below window level until Stefan pulled out onto the street. From inside the stadium came the *pop pop pop* of more shooting, and Buck could only pray that the GC was not taking out its frustration by creating more martyrs.

Tsion wept as he watched the crowds sprint from the area. "This is what I feared," he said. "Bringing these people into the enemy camp, leading them to the slaughter."

Chaim was strangely quiet. He neither spoke nor seemed to move. He sat facing straight ahead. At a traffic light he seemed distracted when Stefan took his hands off the wheel, made fists with both hands, and shook them before his own face as if celebrating. Chaim glanced at him and looked away.

The light changed, but a GC guard still held the traffic, letting a line go from the other way. Stefan took the moment to turn the rearview mirror toward himself. He pushed his hair back and stared at his forehead. Chaim looked at him with a bored expression. "You can't see your own, Stefan. Only others can see yours."

Stefan turned around in his seat. "Well?" he said.

"Yes," Chloe said, and Tsion nodded.

Stefan tried to shake hands with everybody behind him, and Chaim raised both hands in resignation, shrugging and shaking his head. "I won't know for sure unless it happens to me."

Buck saw GC guards running toward the intersection. "Go, Stefan!" he said.

Stefan turned back to see the traffic director still holding him. "But—"

"Trust me, Stefan! Go now!"

Stefan stomped on the accelerator, and the Mercedes shot forward. The guard stepped in front of it with both arms raised but leaped aside as Stefan bore down on him.

"Get us to Chaim's as fast as you can," Buck said. Stefan rose to the challenge.

"So, Ken," Rayford said, "as an economics expert, do you still trust the banks?"

"I didn't trust the banks *before* Carpathia came to power."

"Where'd you stash your bullion then?"

"Some bullion. Mostly coins. Who's got change for a brick of gold?"

Rayford snorted. "Who's got change even for a gold piece? You'd have to buy out a store to keep from getting hundreds in change."

"I hope it doesn't come to actually having to spend the gold as currency. As for where I put it, let's just say if I do buy Palwaukee, I'll be buyin' one valuable piece of real estate."

"You're not saying . . ."

"I know what you're thinkin'. Guy who's s'posed to know money loses out on more millions by putting it where it can't grow."

"Exactly. Even I have a little portfolio."

"Only recently have I put all of it underground. Right under my Quonset hut. For years I stored only the gain. After the Rapture, which I knew only as the disappearances then, I could see what was going to happen to the economy." Ken laughed.

"What?"

"I thought I'd lost it all in the earthquake. Dang near killed myself goin' after it, my stash that is. Ground was all broke up, and my bullion and boxes of coins slipped through one fissure and wound up twenty feet lower'n I'd buried 'em. It could have just as easily been a hundred feet or all the way to the center of the earth. I didn't know it meant that much to me, I honestly didn't. Digging through that cave-in was about the dumbest thing a man could do after a quake, all those aftershocks rumblin' and such. But I was in such a state that I figured if I couldn't find my gold, I might's well die anyway. I'd be buried underground either way. I found it, and I was like a schoolkid who found his long-lost marbles. That's when I knew I had it bad. Started gathering that from your son-in-law."

"How?"

"I thought he'd got religion, and while I didn't buy any of it, I couldn't argue that he sure had different priorities than me or anybody else I knew. I mean, I knew he'd bought the whole package, that was for sure. My future was tied up in the security of my assets. His whole life was trustin' in Jesus. Man, that sounded stupid, but he wore it well. I envied him, I really did. After that earthquake I wound up in the hospital with my brains 'bout hangin' out, and all I could think of was that I could not picture the Williams kid scratching through the rubble for his possessions. Then he showed up, and was off on another of his wacky capers."

"I wish this were just a caper," Rayford said. "No matter how you slice it, this is going to be a long night."

"Should we put down in Greece or Turkey instead of trying to go all the way back tonight? There's a coupla guys I trust over there, one in each country. Not believers yet, I don't guess, but they'd never give us up, if you know what I mean."

Rayford shook his head. "We get enough fuel, I'd just as soon scoot all the way back."

"Your call."

As Stefan pulled into Chaim's complex, the old man asked Stefan in Hebrew to say something to Jonas, the gateman. When Jonas also responded in Hebrew, Buck asked Tsion what they were saying. The rabbi put a finger to his lips. "Later," he said.

Inside they watched the coverage and commentary on TV while one by one, so as not to be obvious, Tsion, Buck, and Chloe slipped away to pack. They surreptitiously synchronized watches.

Buck sensed Chaim was now as eager to pursue the spiritual discussion as Tsion was. Perhaps more so, as Tsion had escape on his mind. Buck knew, however, that winning souls was more important to Tsion than his own life. He would not pass up this opportunity to plead his case for Rosenzweig's heart.

Buck needed to beg the key from Jacov and was glad for the chance to leave the two old friends to talk in private. But when he went looking for his new brother, he learned Jacov was off for the rest of the night. "Where can I find him?" he asked.

"At home, I presume," another staff member told him in broken English. He provided the number, and Buck dialed him. No answer.

"Where else might he be?" Buck asked.

The man spoke conspiratorially. "You did not hear it from me, but there is a bar called The Harem. It is in the—"

"I know where it is," Buck said. "Thanks."

He hurried back into the house and interrupted Chaim and Tsion. "I'm sorry," he said, "but I need a word with Jacov, and he is not at his apartment."

"Oh," Chaim said. "He said something about going to Hannelore's mother's. He will be at the Temple Mount tomorrow though."

"I really want to speak to him tonight."

Chaim gave him the woman's name, and Buck looked it up. A German woman answered his call and put Jacov on the line. "It will be hard for me to get away tonight, Mr. Williams," he said. "Hannelore's mother is not taking this well, and we have agreed to stay and talk about it. Please pray for us."

"I will, but Jacov, I need that key."

"Key?"

"The one you're having duplicated for Dr. Rosenzweig."

"He needs it sooner?"

"I need it, and I need you to trust me enough not to ask why."

"You're afraid of intrusion? The door was left locked. It is the strongest in the house."

"I know. I need it, Jacov. Please."

"I don't even have it. I left it with Stefan. I am working tomorrow, but I am off again Monday. He said he would get it copied then."

"And where does he live?"

"Near the stadium, but I saw on the news they are allowing no traffic into there tonight."

"We've been watching, and I didn't see that."

"It was just on. A Global Community guard was murdered right after the meeting. That must have been the shooting we heard. The GC is looking for the killers. They believe it was done by one or more of the witnesses at the meeting."

"Jacov, listen to me. I told you what that shooting was about."

"But you didn't say a guard was shot. Were some of the witnesses armed? Maybe they were protecting you when they thought the guard was really shooting at you."

"Oh, please, God, I hope not."

"You never know, my friend. Anyway, you will not get into Stefan's neighborhood tonight without being stopped. And you know they will recognize you."

"Jacov, I need a favor."

"Oh, Mr. Williams, I want to help you, but I cannot go to Stefan's tonight. We are trying to convince my mother-in-law that this whole thing was not Stefan's idea. She has always hated him, blaming him for everything bad I have ever done. Now she is saying she wishes he and I were still drunks and not crazy religious people, enemies of the potentate. She is threatening to take Hannelore from me."

"I just need you to not mention to Dr. Rosenzweig that I asked for the key." There was a long silence. "I realize I am asking you to keep something from your—"

"From the man I owe my life to. He has been like a father to me. You must tell me all about this for me to agree to that. If I kept something from him that caused him harm, I would never forgive myself. Why would you need that key and for him to not know about it?"

"Jacov, you know he is not a believer yet."

"I know! But that does not make him our enemy! I pray I will be the one who gets to preach to him, and yet the rabbi himself is Dr. Rosenzweig's friend."

"He is not our enemy, Jacov, but he is naive."

"Naive. I do not know that word."

"He is still a friend of the potentate."

"He doesn't know better yet."

"That's what I mean by naive. If we use that key to slip away early, before the GC knows we're gone, we cannot risk that he might say something to Nicolae or his people."

Jacov was silent another moment. "I did not know what I was getting into," he said finally. "I would never go back, and I do believe. But I never thought I would have anything to do with fighting Nicolae Carpathia."

"Jacov, can you get word to Stefan that I desperately need that key? Maybe he could sneak out and bring it. He is known in that neighborhood, and it would not be unusual for him to come to work, even at this hour, would it?"

"I'll try. But now you have two who must keep your secret."

"Will he?"

"I believe he will. But what will Dr. Rosenzweig think when he knows we helped you escape and never told him?"

Buck thought about suggesting that they tell Rosenzweig the Tribulation Force threatened them. But it was one thing, he decided, to use any and all means to deceive Carpathia and his minions. It was another to start lying to the man they were trying to reach for God. Buck looked at his watch. It was nearly eleven. The odds were against Stefan getting to him in time anyway.

"Jacov, can we break through that door?"

"Not easily. Mr. Williams, I need to go."

Rayford was an hour outside Jerusalem Airport, casually checking in with towers along the way who would pick him up on their radar screens anyway. He identified his craft by type and call numbers only, and no one asked more details. "ETA Jerusalem Airport for refueling at 2400 hours," he said.

"Ten-four, Gulf. Over and out."

He dialed Chloe. "Everything a go, hon?"

"We're a little squirrelly here, Dad. I won't bore you with the details, but stay on track. Somehow we'll be waiting on the roof at 12:30."

"I can't wait to see you, sweetheart."

"I miss you too, Dad. I'll call if we have a problem."

"Ditto. Ken will be in the bird, so I'll see you aboard the Gulfstream."

Buck lightly tapped on the door where Tsion and Chaim sat talking quietly but animatedly. Tsion gave Buck a look as if he really picked the wrong time to intrude. "I'm very sorry, gentlemen, but Tsion, I need a word."

"Not at all!" Rosenzweig said. "I need a moment myself. Let me leave you. I want to ask your wife if she would like to ride with me tomorrow to the Temple Mount. Jacov and I are going a little later."

He stepped past Buck, smiling but clearly distracted. Buck apologized to Tsion.

"Buck, I know our time is short, but he is so close!"

"Close enough that we can trust him?" Buck brought Tsion up-to-date.

Tsion reached to turn the TV back on. On the screen appeared the face of the very GC guard who had fired over Buck's head, intentionally missing. Beneath his photograph were the years of his birth and death. "I got him killed," Buck said, his throat constricted.

"You likely saved my life," Tsion said. "Praise God he is in heaven now. Buck, I know this is hard, and I never want to grow callous to the high price we are called to pay. No one would put much stock in our futures now. I don't know how long the Lord will spare any of us to do his work. But I fear if we let Carpathia hurt or kill or even detain any of us tonight, it will be a terrible blow to the cause. You know I don't care about my own life anymore. My family is in heaven, and I long to be there too. But I don't believe God would have us die needlessly. There is so much to do.

"Yes, we must confide in Chaim, I'm afraid. He asked the gateman if his video surveillance equipment was running.

The man told him not until midnight, as usual. And Chaim told him to turn it on now."

A wave of panic hit Buck in his gut. Might the camera have picked him up the night before? "We have to tell him then," Buck said. "If his security people hear a chopper and see it's GC, they won't know what to do."

"That's what we want, Cameron, just enough confusion to get going. Surely they wouldn't fire on a helicopter that looks like Carpathia's own. But it wouldn't be long before they called to ask about it, and the GC would know we had used one of their machines."

"How can we convince Chaim without making him think we're overreacting?"

"He was there tonight, Buck. And you should hear his reaction. I'm telling you, he's close."

"What's holding him back?"

"His admiration and love for Carpathia."

Buck grunted. "Then let's tell him what Rayford heard on the Condor 216."

"About me, you mean?"

"And about him."

"Will he believe it?"

"That's up to him, Tsion. It will go against everything he believes and feels about Carpathia."

"So be it."

It was pushing midnight when Rayford entered Israeli airspace, on schedule. He checked in with the Ben Gurion tower in Tel Aviv, then was cleared for landing at Jerusalem Airport for refueling. "It's been a while since I've been this scared," he said.

"Really?" Ken said. "This kind of terror is becoming a weekly occurrence for me."

Rosenzweig rejoined Buck and Tsion with Chloe in tow. She was in her pajamas and robe, drawing a confused stare from Buck. "Dr. Rosenzweig is insisting I get my rest for the baby's sake," she said. "Can't argue with that. I just came to say good-night."

Buck knew she would race back to change, but he said, "Stay with us a minute, hon. We need to tell Chaim something, and you may need to corroborate it with what you have heard from your dad."

CHAPTER 12

"JERUSALEM TOWER, this is Gulfstream Alpha Tango, over."

"Tower, go ahead, Alpha Tango. Initiate landing sequence."

Rayford plugged in the coordinates and put down in the busier-than-usual airstrip. To appear as casual as possible, he asked about it. The tower informed him that the wealthier commuters from the big meeting at Kollek Stadium were flying small craft to Tel Aviv for their international flights home.

"Any delay on a refuel?"

"Negative, Alpha. You're clear."

"See the choppers?" Ray said as he lined up his approach.

"I see one," Ken said. "White with black block letters on the side."

"Don't kid me."

"I'm not. It's GC all right, but there's only one."

"I don't like it, Ken."

"Why hasn't Mac called if there's a glitch?"

Rayford shook his head. "I don't want to call him. He may not be where he can talk."

"But he might not know one of his birds is gone. Ever think of that?"

Rayford punched in Mac's number. "McCullum."

"Mac! It's me. What's going on?"

"Yes, hello, Sergeant Fitzgerald. Of course you may proceed."

"We're good to go?"

"No need to wait, Sergeant. That's affirmative."

"All my eggs are in your basket, Mac."

"You're welcome, Sergeant. Good-bye."

"Take your phone, Ken!" Rayford shouted over the scream of the engines as Ritz opened the door.

Ken smacked himself in the head and grabbed the phone out of his bag. "Another mature moment," he said. "Don't leave me out there hitchhikin' now."

"Don't worry." Rayford wished he had rearview mirrors on the side of the plane so he would know when Ken got to the chopper.

Chaim Rosenzweig had never looked older to Buck. He was tired, of course. It was late. But his wispy white hair, independent of control, haloed a grayish, drawn face. Buck, Tsion, and Chloe had quickly revealed to him conversations Rayford had overheard on the Condor. Chaim appeared unable to speak after hearing that his requests for Tsion's safety following his first TV broadcast had been laughed at.

"You realize," Chloe said, "that you are the first outside person who knows about the bugging device on that plane. We're putting lives in your—"

Rosenzweig waved her off sadly. "To think that Nicolae himself would say one thing and do another, looking me in the eyes, he did, and lying. He could have prevented the slaughter of your family, Tsion. Oh God, oh God, oh God! How could I have been so blind? I know you tried to tell me."

"Doctor," Tsion said quickly, "you and I will continue our discussion by phone or e-mail or in person, God willing, but we must leave now. Our sources tell us that the GC is planning a terrorist attack at the Temple Mount tomorrow, and we want to be long gone by then."

"Of course," Chaim said. "I understand. I will have you driven to—"

"It's all arranged," Buck said. "We need to be on the roof in ten minutes."

"Of course, go. I will cover for you. Don't worry about me."

Chloe went to change, and Buck told Chaim the disposition of the key. "Break it down," he said wearily. "Tools are in the utility room."

"Buck!" Chloe cried as she moved toward the door. "You're on TV! Turn it up!"

". . . Community forces believe videotape reveals this man as the likely killer of a GC guard earlier this evening at the Meeting of the Witnesses at Kollek Stadium. He has been identified as an American, Cameron Williams, a former employee of the GC publishing division. Williams is reportedly staying with Rabbi Tsion Ben-Judah at the home of Israeli Nobel Prize–winner Dr. Chaim Rosenzweig. Supreme Commander Leon Fortunato went on to say . . ."

Tsion and Buck followed Rosenzweig toward the utility room. As soon as Buck saw where they were headed, he brushed past the old man, flipped on the light, and grabbed a hammer, a shovel, and a concrete block. "Do you have a sledgehammer?"

"If you don't see it, I don't have it," Chaim said. "We need to hurry." The phone rang. "That will be the GC," he said. Jonas the gateman spoke over the intercom in Hebrew, but Buck understood "Rosenzweig" and "Fortunato."

"Have someone bring me the phone," Rosenzweig said. "I'm in the back hallway." He turned to Buck and Tsion and gestured that they should lead the way to the access door. When he got the cordless phone, he dismissed the valet and talked as he followed Buck.

"Of course he's here, Leon," he said. "And sound asleep. Don't even think of invading my household in the middle of the night. You have my word he will be here in the morning. You can question him then. I will even be happy to bring him to you. . . . Oh, Leon, that is patent nonsense, and you know it. He is no more a murder suspect than I am. Your man was shot by one of your own. . . . Have you found a murder weapon? Fingerprints? Check the bullets, and they will trace to your weapons. I have known Mr. Williams for years and have never seen him with a weapon. I'm warning you, Leon. These are my guests, and I will not wake them! . . . Yes, I warned you! You are not *my* supreme commander. . . . Now you are threatening me? You know my standing in this country and, may I say, with Nicolae! If I tell people you used gestapo tactics in the middle of the night. . . . Crime? You would charge me with a crime for speaking disrespectfully to you? You call me at midnight, *after* midnight, and tell me to hold my guest as a murder suspect, and you expect me to respect you? I'll tell you what, Leon, you come personally at a reasonable hour, and I will make my guest available to you. . . . Well, I promise you, Leon, you send anyone tonight, and I will not answer the door."

Buck waved furiously at Chaim to move away so the sound of the banging wouldn't be heard over the phone. Chaim nodded and hurried away, and Buck drove the claw of the hammer behind the top hinge of the heavy door. Chloe showed up with two bags and left to get Tsion's.

Tsion drove the shovel in and around the doorknob, but neither man was getting far. "Step back a second, Tsion," Buck said, and he hefted the concrete block above his head. The weight almost carried him over backward. He slammed it against the upper half of the door and heard a resounding crack. A couple more shots, he believed, and he'd break through the wood.

Rayford was refueling when the call came from Ken. "I'm away," he said.

"Godspeed."

He kept an eye on his watch, tempted to call Chloe and keep her on the phone until they were aboard the chopper. But he didn't want to be a distraction. The missing helicopter already had him puzzled, but if that wasn't a clear go message from Mac, he didn't know what was. He couldn't wait to hear what that was all about.

"Get all the lights off!" Buck hollered, as he finally smashed through the thick wood. He heard Chaim hurry around flipping switches.

Over the intercom Chaim urgently told his gateman something in Hebrew. "What'd he say?" Chloe said, joining Buck and Tsion at the broken doorjamb in the dark. Each had a heavy bag.

"He told him no one gets in. Everyone's asleep. That won't keep them out long."

"Let's go," Buck said. "I hear a chopper."

"It's your imagination," Chloe said. "I think it's GC in the driveway."

"You're both paranoid," Tsion said, climbing through the broken door.

"I've got your bag, hon," Buck said.

"Buck! Don't baby me."

"It's the baby I'm thinking of. Now go."

"We never said good-bye to Chaim!"

"He'll understand. Go. Go."

As she stepped through the door, Chaim returned. "I'm waiting for word from the gate," he whispered. "A GC vehicle just pulled up."

Buck reached for him in the darkness and embraced him fiercely. "On behalf of all of us—"

"I know," Chaim said. "I'm so sorry about all this. Let me know when you are safe."

A nervous tingle swept over Rayford's body. After fueling and paying with Ken Ritz's international debit card, Rayford deliberately taxied the Gulfstream away from ground traffic about two hundred yards from where Ken would land the chopper. From where he sat he would be able to see the helicopter and get next to it as it landed.

His phone chirped. "Rayford, it's Mac. I'm finally alone. Listen and don't say anything. Leon took it on himself to get my chopper guy out of Haifa and put him in the air. They had some kind of incident near the stadium and didn't want to risk using me because of tomorrow's flight back on the

Condor. I thought they'd have it back in time, and when they didn't and you called, I gave you the go-ahead to use Chopper One. Yes, that means your guy is in Carpathia's ride, but no one's the wiser if he gets it back quick. I was in a car with Leon, and that's why I sounded so strange.

"Here's the problem. Leon's got a couple of cars on their way to Rosenzweig's with a trumped-up charge against Buck. I heard 'em say a video proves it's bogus, but truth never stopped 'em before. Apparently the old man is not going to let them in, and they're afraid your people are on the run. Leon's asking for the chopper to light up the neighborhood. If he sees your guy, he's gonna think it's me until he asks and finds out it's not.

"I'm going to do what I can to misdirect, Ray, short of giving myself away. Just wanted you to know what you're dealing with. I've got another few seconds here if you've got any questions."

"Thanks, Mac. Bet you're glad this isn't a wrong number. Has this guy got weapons?"

"Two armed guys are with him, yes."

"What's Ken supposed to do if he encounters him?"

"Play cool like he's supposed to be there, but evade as soon as possible. That kid knows I'm not in the air."

"I'd better get off in case Ken's trying to reach me."

"We were both right," Chloe whispered as they stepped out into the cool night air. Two GC vehicles were being stalled outside the gate, and a chopper illuminated the ground with a huge light. "Doesn't Ken know where we are?"

"I can't imagine," Buck said. "But we can't flag him down without giving ourselves away to those guys. C'mon, Ken! Right here, man!"

Suddenly, from right above them, GC Chopper One descended, whipping their hair and clothes. Ken opened the door and shouted, "Let's go, let's go, let's go!" Buck threw their bags in and helped Chloe climb aboard. He didn't dare peek down to see what kind of attention they were drawing from the guards on the ground.

Tsion and Buck leaped aboard. Ken was on the phone. "We're not alone, Ray! Two on the ground, one in the air! . . . All right, I'm going!" Ken swept up and away, heading north.

Tsion, Buck, and Chloe huddled together, holding hands and praying. Buck wondered how long it would be before the ground troops alerted the other helicopter. Three minutes later, with Ken speeding toward Jerusalem Airport, he found out. From over the radio came an urgent call. "GC Chopper One, this is Chopper Two, over."

Ken hollered into the phone, "Don't worry, Ray, I won't answer it. Anyway, I thought *we* were Chopper Two. . . . Tell me later. I'm on my way. . . . Mac's voice? How can I do that? I only talked to him on the phone once! . . . All right, I'll try! I'm comin' fast, so be ready!"

"Chopper Two to Chopper One, do you copy?"

"Go ahead, Two," Ken said, lowering his voice and effecting a Southern accent.

"I didn't know you were airborne, Cap."

"Roger, Two." Ken clicked the microphone as he spoke. "I . . . bad . . . connection . . . you . . . over?"

"Repeat, Cap?"

A frantic voice broke in. "McCullum is not in the air, Chopper Two! He's with us! Find out who that is!"

"Chopper Two to Chopper One, identify yourself, over."

Ken hesitated.

"Identify, Chopper One, or risk a charge of air piracy."

"This is Chopper One, go ahead."

"Identify yourself, pilot."

"Bad connection, come back."

The Chopper Two pilot swore. "Demand immediate descent and surrender, One."

"En route to Tel Aviv, Two. See you there."

"Negative! Put down at Jerusalem Airport and stay aboard!"

"Negative yourself, Two. See you at Ben Gurion."

Chopper Two put out a call for assistance to all aircraft in that sector.

"Now what?" Buck said.

"Lights off and stay low," Ken said.

"Not too low."

"High enough to clear power lines," Ken said. "Low enough to stay under radar."

"We gonna be all right?"

"Depends on where he was when he first called. If he was still in Chaim's neighborhood, we've got a pretty good lead on him. I doubt he'll stay this low or go this fast. No way he's dumb enough to believe we're going to Ben Gurion. Somebody's bound to spot us, and then he'll chase us to the airstrip. No time for restroom stops or seat changes at the airport, if that's what you're asking."

Rayford sat near the runway listening to the radio traffic and resisting the urge to coach Ken. If he didn't know enough to stay low and push the chopper's limits, nothing Rayford could say would help.

The radio came to life again with a report from a small, fixed-wing plane that had sighted the low-flying GC chopper with its lights off.

"Chopper Two is in pursuit. Chopper One, you are breaking international aviation law by running without lights, high speeds at low altitude, and hijacking of government aircraft. Proceed directly to Jerusalem Airport and remain on board or suffer the consequences."

Airport personnel swept into action, emergency vehicles cruising the runways. "Attention please. Jerusalem Airport is temporarily closed due to an emergency. Be advised, all landing sequences and takeoffs are suspended until further notice. Cessna X-ray Bravo, you copy?"

"Roger."

"Piper Two-Niner Charley Alpha?"

"Roger."

"Gulfstream Alpha Tango?"

"Roger," Rayford said, but he did not shut down. He hoped Ken would understand why he was waiting at the wrong end of the runway. This would be a takeoff without clearance and in the wrong direction.

And here came the chopper. Ken wouldn't have time to talk on the phone, and the radio was not an option. Rayford checked his gauges. He was ready.

Ken started to put down at the original spot.

"Gulfstream's up there!" Buck shouted. "And you've got security coming on the ground!"

Ken hopped the craft back up and set down near Rayford. The door of the Gulfstream hung open. Buck, Chloe, and Tsion set themselves to jump out of the chopper. "Hold tight a second," Ken shouted. "They see us board the Gulf now, they can block him easy! I'm going to have to play cat and mouse with 'em, make 'em think Ray's not involved!"

As security vehicles approached, Ken leapfrogged them, hovering just above where he had first set down, two hundred yards from the Gulfstream. "Put down right there, Chopper One!" came the voice from Chopper Two on the radio. "And do not disembark. Repeat, do not disembark."

Ken put down but kept the blades whirring as the ground vehicles headed his way. "Shut it down, One!" the radio blared. Buck and the others saw Chopper Two descending from Rayford's end of the field, right toward them.

"Stay out of sight, and forget your bags, people," Ken said. "If I get you close, you're going to make a run for the Gulf."

"We're still going to try to do this?" Chloe said. "It's hopeless!"

"It's never hopeless as long as I'm breathin'," Ken said.

Rayford stared out the cockpit windshield of the Gulfstream, imagining that any second Ken and all that was left of his own family would be surrounded by armed GC guards. They would never expose him, but dare he just sit and wait to leave when the airport reopened? His body boiled with frustration, wanting to do something, anything.

Ken was a creative, resourceful, smart guy. And it did appear he still had those blades spinning. What was he going to do? Let Chopper Two chase him some more? There was no hope in that.

"Shut it down, One!" the command came again. "You are surrounded with no possible escape!"

Chopper Two was within thirty feet of Ken, also on the ground now with blades engaged. Rayford watched, amazed, as Ken went straight up about a hundred feet, then pointed the nose of the chopper at the Gulfstream and seemed to fall right in front of it. It hit the tarmac at such an angle that it slid fifty feet and spun to a stop next to the open door.

"Let's go kids!" Ken shouted. "Right now!"

He smacked the door open with a running back–like stiff-arm and grabbed Buck, tugging him past the front seat and out. Buck waited on the ground and caught Tsion as Ken handed him off. Tsion charged up the steps of the Gulfstream and stood ready to shut the door.

Buck was grateful Ken took a little more time with Chloe. "Go all the way in!" he said. "Tsion's got the door!"

Rayford watched in horror as GC vehicles raced his way yet again. He had to get airborne. Betting ground control could not see people boarding his plane, he got on the radio. "Gulf Alpha Tango to ground control, requesting permission to get out of the way of this activity."

"Roger, Gulf. Just stay out of the way of security vehicles."

Rayford started rolling, though he knew only two had boarded. The Gulfstream screamed and whined as he slowly moved forward, edging past Chopper One, his door dragging on the pavement and throwing sparks. He couldn't leave the ground until everyone was aboard, then he had to pressurize the cabin before getting too high.

Buck's brain went into slow motion, and a kaleidoscope of images raced through his mind. In what seemed the next millisecond he remembered taking a bullet to his heel in Egypt while diving with Tsion aboard a Learjet piloted by Ken. Now while whirling to grab the door as the Gulfstream edged by, he saw clearly through the struts of the chopper that GC men sprinted toward them, taking aim.

Buck screamed, "Ken! Ken! Go! Go! Go!" as Ritz caught up to him. Buck pumped his legs as fast as he could, and Ken loped right behind with those long limbs. The Gulfstream picked up steam, and Buck felt the pull of the power on his body. He glanced back at Ken, whose face was inches from his, desperate determination in his eyes.

Buck was about to leap up the steps when Ken's forehead opened. Buck felt the heat and smelled the metal as the killing bullet sliced his own ear on the way by, and his face was splashed by Ken's gore. The big man's eyes were wide and vacant as he dropped out of sight.

Buck was yanked along, sobbing and screaming, his arm caught in the wire that supported the open door. He wanted to jump off, to run back to Ken, to kill someone. But he was unarmed, and Ken had to have been dead before he hit the ground. In spite of himself, despite his grief and horror and anger, Buck's instincts turned to his own survival.

The Gulfstream was now speeding along too fast for Buck's legs to keep up. Tsion leaned out as far as he could, straining with all his might to pull the door up and Buck with it. But the more he pulled, the more entangled Buck became. Chloe was helping now, crying and screaming herself, and Buck worried about the baby.

He lifted his feet to keep from scraping the leather off his shoes and burning his feet. The Gulfstream was at takeoff speed, the door stuck open, Buck pinned in the support—and he knew Rayford had no choice but to throttle up.

Buck tried to swing forward and catch a foot on the step, but the momentum and the wind made him unable to move. He was nearly horizontal now, and the vibration in the aluminum skin of the plane changed when the wheels left the ground. He squinted against the wind and grit that stung his eyes, and he could see Rayford would be lucky to clear the ten-foot fence in the grass at the wrong end of the runway.

The plane lumbered over the fence, and Buck felt as if he could have lowered a toe and brushed it. One thing was sure: He was not going to get into that plane now that it was in the air. The door would have to be shut mechanically. He could wait for that to sever his arm and fall to his death, or he could take his chances in the underbrush on the far side of the fence.

Buck pulled and twisted and jerked until his elbow cleared the wire. The horrified faces of his wife and his pastor were the last images he saw before he felt himself fall, cartwheeling, hitting the tops of tall bushes, and lodging himself, scraped and torn and bleeding, in the middle of a huge thicket.

His body shuddered uncontrollably, and he worried about going into shock. Then he heard the Gulfstream turn, and he knew Chloe would never let her father leave without him. But if they came back, if they landed to look for him, they were all as good as dead. Ken was already gone. That was enough for one night.

Painfully, he wrenched himself free and knew his injuries would require attention. No bones seemed broken, and as he stood, shivering in the cool of the night, he felt the bulge in his pocket. Was it possible? Had his phone survived?

He didn't dare hope as he flipped it open. The dial lit up. He hit Rayford's number.

"Buck?" he heard. "Is it really you?"

Buck barked, his voice raw, "It's me and I'm all right. Go on, and I'll hook up with you later."

Rayford wondered if he was dreaming. He was certain he had killed his own son-in-law. "Are you sure, Buck?" he shouted.

Chloe, who had collapsed in despair, now grabbed the phone out of Rayford's hand.

"Buck! Buck! Where are you?"

"Past the fence in some nasty underbrush! I don't think they saw me, Chlo'! Nobody's coming this way. If they saw me running for the plane, they have to think I made it aboard."

"How did you survive?"

"I have no idea! Are you all right?"

"Am *I* all right? Of course! Ten seconds ago I was a widow! Is Ken with you?"

"No."

"Oh, no! They've got him?"

"He's gone, Chloe."

CHAPTER 13

RAYFORD DECIDED to fly north as fast as he could, guessing that GC forces would assume he was heading west. "Tsion, dig through Ken's stuff and see if he has any record of friends of his in Greece. He mentioned our putting down there or Turkey if necessary."

Tsion and Chloe opened Ken's flight bag. "This is painful, Rayford," Tsion said. "This brother flew me to safety when there was a bounty on my head."

Rayford could not speak. He and Ken had clicked so quickly that he had made an instant friend. Because of their hours together in the air, he'd spent more time with him than anyone but Buck. And being closer to Ken's age, he felt a true kinship. He knew violence and death were the price of this period of history, but how he hated the shock and grief of the losses. If he began thinking of all the tragedy he had suffered—from missing out on the Rapture with his wife and son, to the loss of Bruce, Loretta, Donny and his wife, Amanda . . . and there were more—he would go mad.

Ken was in a better place, he told himself, and it sounded as hollow as any platitude. Yet he had to believe it was true. The loss was all his. Ken was finally free.

Rayford was bone weary. He was not supposed to be handling the flight back. Ken had reserved his hours behind the controls so he could pilot the Tribulation Force back to the States.

"What *is* all this?" Chloe asked suddenly. "He's got lists and ideas and plans for businesses, and—"

"I'll tell you later," Rayford said. "He was quite the entrepreneur."

"And brilliant," Tsion said. "I never figured him for this kind of thinker. Some of this reads like a manifesto of survival for the saints."

"No names though? Nothing that looks like a contact in Greece? I'm going to start that way, just in case. I can't fly much farther anyway."

"But we can't land without a local contact, can we, Dad?"

"We shouldn't."

"Can Mac help?"

"He'd call me if he was free to talk. I'm sure they've involved him in this fiasco. Pray he'll somehow misdirect them."

Buck's facial lacerations were deep but below the cheekbones, so there was little bleeding. His right thumb felt as if it had been pulled back to his wrist. He could not stop the bleeding from his left ear where the bullet that had killed Ken had sliced it nearly in half. He quickly took off his shirt and undershirt, using the latter to wipe his face and sop his ear. He put his shirt back on, hoping he wouldn't appear so monster-like that he would scare off anyone who might help him.

Buck crept to the airport edge of the underbrush but didn't dare get near the fence. Though no searchlights pointed that way, the fence provided a perfect background for any watchful eye to detect movement. He sat with his back to a large bush to catch his breath. His ankles and knees were tender, as was his right elbow. He must have taken the brunt of the crash into the spiky plant on his right side. He tilted his cell phone toward the light to see his foggy reflection in the lighted dial.

Feeling a sting below the cuff, Buck pulled his pant legs up a few inches to find both shins bleeding into his socks. His muscles ached, but under the circumstances he felt fortunate. He had his phone, and he could walk.

"We might have found something," Tsion said. In Rayford's peripheral vision he could see the rabbi showing a phone directory page to Chloe.

"That looks Greek to me. What do you think, Dad? He's got a number for a Lukas Miklos, nickname Laslos."

"What city?"

"Doesn't say."

"Any other notations? Can you tell if it's a friend or a business contact?"

"Try the number. It's all we've got."

"Wait," Tsion said. "There's a star by the name and an arrow pointing down to the word *lignite.* I don't know that word."

"I don't either," Rayford said. "Sounds like a mineral or something. Dial him up, Chloe. If I'm landing in Greece, I've got to start initial descent in a few minutes."

Buck couldn't remember the name of Jacov's mother-in-law. And he never caught Stefan's last name. He didn't want to call Chaim; his place had to be crawling with GC. He walked in the darkness, staying in the shadows, and made a huge loop around the airport and onto the main road. There he could either hitchhike or flag a taxi. Not knowing where else to turn, he would go to the Wailing Wall. Nicolae had publicly warned Moishe and Eli to disappear from there by the end of the stadium meeting, which told Buck they would be there for sure.

"Yes, hello, ma'am," Chloe said. "Does anyone there speak English? . . . English! . . . I'm sorry, I don't understand you.

Does anyone there—" She covered the phone. "I woke her. She sounds scared. She's getting someone. Sounds like she's waking him up.

"Yes! Hello? Sir? . . . Are you Mr. Miklos? . . . Do you speak English? . . . Not so good? Do you understand English? . . . Good! I am sorry to wake you, but I am a friend of Ken Ritz's from America!" Chloe covered the phone again. "He knows him!"

Chloe asked where he lived, whether there was an airstrip in town, and if they could visit him and talk about Ken if they landed there. Within minutes, Rayford was in touch with the tower at Ptolemaïs in northern Greece.

"Macedonia," Tsion said. "Praise God."

"We're not safe yet, Tsion," Rayford said. "We're depending on the kindness of a stranger."

For the first time, Buck was grateful the Global Community had chosen the American dollar as its currency. He was cash rich, and that might keep eyes averted and mouths closed. Somewhere deep in his wallet, too, was his ever-useful phony identity . . . as long as he could keep from being searched and having both IDs exposed.

"Mr. Miklos was suspicious," Chloe reported. "But once I convinced him we were friends of Ken's, he even told me what to tell the tower. Tell them you're Learjet Foxtrot Foxtrot Zulu. That's the plane of one of his suppliers. He runs a mining company. He will be there to meet us."

"This looks nothing like a Lear," Rayford said.

"He said the tower won't even pay attention."

When Buck reached the road, he was surprised to see traffic still heavy. Witnesses must have still been streaming out of Jerusalem. And all the air traffic told him the airport had reopened already. He saw no roadblocks. The GC had to assume he had boarded the Gulfstream.

He moved to the side of the road leading into Jerusalem, which was much less congested than the other side. He waved his bloody undershirt at empty cabs coming from the airport, trying to show more white than red. He straightened up and tried to look sober and healthy. Buck lucked out on the fourth cab, which rumbled off the road and skidded in the gravel.

"You got money, mate?" the cabby said before unlocking the back door.

"Plenty."

"Not many pedestrians coming this way. First I've seen in weeks."

"Lost my ride," Buck said, getting in.

"A mite cut up now, ain't ya?"

"I'm all right. Got caught in some thorns."

"I should say."

"You an Aussie?"

"How'd you guess? Where to, mate?"

"The Wailing Wall."

"Ah, you won't get within a half mile of it tonight, sir."

"That so?"

"Big doings. You know the story of those two—"

"Yeah, what about 'em?"

"They're there."

"Yeah."

"And they're not supposed to be, ya know."

"I know."

"Word is the potentate is still in Jerusalem but not near the Wall. Huge crowd there with weapons. Civilians and military. Big mess. I'm a fan of the potentate, mind ya, but offerin' a bounty on the heads of these two wasn't wise."

"Think not?"

"Well, look what you've got now. Somebody's gonna kill 'em tonight and want to be made the hero. That's both citizens and guards. Who's to say they won't turn the guns on each other?"

"You think those two will buy it tonight?"

"Have to. They've planted themselves in their usual spot, got the whole city up in arms about the bloody water and the drought, takin' credit for it and all. Proud of it they are. They've killed a lot of mates who've tried to take 'em out, but what chance have they got now? They've put themselves behind that iron fence there, in a cage for target practice."

"I say they're still there and alive come daybreak."

"You don't say."

"If they are, would you do something for me?"

"Depends."

"If I'm right, and you've got to admit it's against all odds—"

"Oh, I'll grant ya that."

"—you find a Bible and read the book of Revelation."

"Oh, you're one of them, are you?"

"Them?"

"The witnesses. I've taken at least three loads of 'em to the airport tonight, and every last one of 'em's wanted to get me to join ranks. You gonna try to save me, mate?"

"I can't save you, friend. But I'm surprised God hasn't gotten your attention by now."

"Oh, I can't deny somethin' strange is happening. But I've got a pretty good gig going, if you know what I mean, and I don't guess God would look kindly on it. Lots of money on the other side of the street, ya know."

"Worth more than your soul?"

"Just might be. But I'll tell ya what. If those two are still there come mornin', I'll do what you say."

"Got a Bible?"

"I told ya. Had three carloads of your type tonight. Got three Bibles. Wanna make it four?"

"No, but I could use one of those if you can spare it."

"I'm a businessman, mate. I'll sell it to ya."

Rayford parked the jet at the end of a runway with similar-sized craft, and he and Chloe and Tsion walked cautiously into the mostly deserted terminal. A middle-aged couple eyed them warily from a dark corner. He was short and stocky with full, dark, curly hair. She was heavyset, her hair in curlers under a scarf.

After shy handshakes, Lukas Miklos said, "Ken Ritz gave you my name?"

"We found you in his address book, sir," Rayford said.

Miklos flinched and sat back. "How do I know you knew him?"

"I'm afraid we have bad news for you."

"Before you start with the bad news, I must know I can trust you. Tell me something about Ken that only a friend would know."

Rayford looked at the others and spoke carefully. "Former military, flew commercially, owned his own charter company for many years. Tall, late fifties."

"Did you know he used to fly one of my suppliers, when first I began serving energy plants?"

"No, sir. He did not mention that."

"He never spoke to you of me?"

"Not by name. He mentioned he knew someone in Greece who might provide hospitality on our way from the States."

"To where?"

"To Israel."

"And you were there for what?"

"For the Meeting of the Witnesses."

Miklos and his wife looked at each other. "Are you believers?"

Rayford nodded.

"Turn your face to the light."

Rayford turned.

Miklos looked at him, then at his wife, then turned his face to the light and pulled the curls back from his forehead. "Now you're not going to tell me this is Dr. Ben-Judah?"

"It is, sir."

"Oh, oh!" Miklos said, slipping off the chair and onto his knees on the tile floor. He took Ben-Judah's hands in his and kissed them while his wife clasped her hands before her face and rocked, her eyes closed. "I knew you looked familiar from the TV, but it's really you!"

"Now, now," Tsion said. "It's nice to meet you too, but I'm afraid the news is not good about our brother Ken."

The cabby stopped in an alley behind a nightclub, where he apparently had an arrangement. A bouncer met him. "No, he's not a john, Stallion. And he ain't comin' in either. Get him a turban and a neck scarf, and I'll pay you later." Stallion reached in and grabbed the Aussie by the throat. "You'll get your cut, you overgrown child," the cabby said. "Now get the clothes and let me get outta here."

A minute later Stallion tossed the gear through the back window of the cab and pointed threateningly at the driver. "I'll be back," the Aussie said. "Trust me."

Buck pulled the rolled cap over his head and tucked the scarf under it, covering his ears and the back of his neck. If he held his head a certain way, it also covered most of his face. "Where does he get this stuff?"

"Sure you want to know?"

"Some drunk's going to be surprised when he wakes up."

Buck's ear had stopped bleeding, but he still needed medical attention. "Know where I can get antibacterial and a stitch or two without a lot of questions?"

"Cash leaves a lot of questions unasked, mate."

At three o'clock in the morning, as close as they could get to the Temple Mount, Buck paid the Aussie handsomely. "For the ride," he said. "For the Bible. And for the clothes."

"How about a little something for the medical services?"

Buck had paid cash at a backstreet clinic, but he guessed the lead alone was worth a few dollars.

"Thanks, mate. And I'll keep my promise. I'll be listening to the news. Wouldn't surprise me if they're dead already."

Lukas Miklos owned a late-model luxury car and lived in an opulent home that was being repaired after the earthquake. He begged the Trib Force to stay a week, but Rayford told him they simply needed a good day's rest and would be on their way the next evening.

"Ken didn't know you were a believer, did he?"

Miklos shook his head as his wife apologetically returned to bed. Rayford and Tsion stood when she did, and she smiled shyly and bowed. "She runs the office," Miklos explained. "Gets there before I do."

He settled back in an easy chair. "Ken told me in an E-mail what had happened to him. We thought he was crazy. I knew the Carpathia regime opposed this rapture theory, and the Global Community sent me so much business, I did not want to appear to even know someone who opposed them."

"You did a lot of business with the GC?"

"Oh, yes. And we still do. I have no guilt about using the enemy's money. Their energy consultants buy tremendous quantities of lignite for their thermoelectric plants. Ken always said lignite grows on trees in Ptolemaïs. I wish it did! But he's right. It is plentiful, and I am one of the major suppliers."

"Why didn't you tell Ken you had become his brother?"

"Why, Mr. Steele, it happened only the other day, watching Dr. Ben-Judah on TV. We have been unable to reach Ken. He probably has an e-mail message from me on his computer."

Buck walked as close to the Temple Mount as he could get before having to sidle through the jostling crowd. No one dared get within two hundred feet of Eli and Moishe, including GC guards—especially GC guards. Many civilians were armed too, and the atmosphere crackled with tension.

Buck felt safe and nearly invisible in the darkness, though he drew anger and was shoved as he kept working his way through the crowd. Occasionally, on tiptoes, he could see Eli and Moishe bathed in glaring TV lights. Again without amplification, they could be heard throughout the area.

"Where is the king of the world?" Eli demanded. "Where is he who sits on the throne of the earth? Ye men of Israel are a generation of snakes and vipers, blaspheming the Lord your God with your animal sacrifices. You bow to the enemy of the Lord, the one who seeks to defy the living God! The Lord who delivered his servant David out of the paw of the lion, and out of the paw of the bear, will deliver us out of the hand of this man of deceit."

The crowd laughed, but none advanced save Buck. He stayed on the move, feeling every sting and ache and pain, but eager to be close to these men of God. As he neared the front he found the crowd less belligerent and more wary. "Be careful, man," some said. "Watch yourself. Not too close now. They have flamethrowers behind that building."

Buck would have found that funny and the bravado of the witnesses invigorating, but Ken's awful death was too much with him. He instinctively wiped his face as if Ken's blood were still there, but his hand raked across his stitches and he nearly wept.

Moishe took over the speaking. "The servant of Satan comes to us with a sword, and with a spear, and with a shield.

But we come in the name of the Lord of hosts, the God of the armies of his chosen, whom thou hast deceived. You shall be impotent against us until the due time!"

The crowd hissed and booed and cried out, "Kill them! Shoot them! Fire a missile at them! Bomb them!"

"O men of Israel," Eli responded. "Do you not care for water to drink or rain for your crops? We allow the sun to bake your land and turn the water into blood for as long as we prophesy, that all the earth may know that there is a God in Israel. And all this assembly shall know that the Lord saveth not with sword and spear: for the battle is the Lord's, and he has given you into our hands."

"Show them! Kill them! Destroy them!"

The crowd gasped and drew back as Buck reached the front and stepped ten feet closer to the fence than anyone else. He was still far from the witnesses, but after what had happened the night before, he appeared brave or foolish. The crowd fell silent.

Moishe and Eli stood side by side now, not moving, hands at their sides. They stared past Buck, appearing resolute in their challenge to Carpathia. He had given permission for anyone to kill them if they showed their faces anywhere after the meetings. And now they stood where they had appeared every day since the signing of the agreement between the Global Community and Israel.

Buck felt drawn to them in spite of his desperation to remain unrecognized. He stepped yet closer, causing the crowd to deride him and laugh at his foolhardiness.

Neither witness opened his mouth, but Buck heard them both in unison. It was as if the message was for him alone. He wondered whether anyone else heard it.

"For whosoever will save his life shall lose it; but whosoever shall lose his life for Christ's sake and the gospel's, the same shall save it."

They knew about Ken? Were they consoling Buck?

Suddenly Moishe looked to the crowd and shouted, "For what shall it profit a man, if he shall gain the whole world, and lose his own soul? Or what shall a man give in exchange for his soul? Whosoever therefore shall be ashamed of Jesus Christ and of his words in this adulterous and sinful generation; of him also shall the Son of Man be ashamed, when he cometh in the glory of his Father with the holy angels."

And just as suddenly the two spoke in unison again, softer, without moving their lips, as if just to Buck. "There be some of them that stand here, which shall not taste of death, till they have seen the kingdom of God come with power."

Buck had to speak. He whispered, his back to the crowd so none could hear. "We want to be among those who do not taste death," he said. "But we lost another of our own tonight." He couldn't go on.

"What'd he say?" someone blurted.

"He's gonna get himself torched."

The two spoke directly to Buck's heart again. "There is no man that hath left house, or brethren, or sisters, or father, or mother, or wife, or children, or lands, for Jesus' sake, and the gospel's, but he shall receive an hundredfold now in this time, houses, and brethren, and sisters, and mothers, and children, and lands, with persecutions; and in the world to come eternal life."

God *had* provided for Buck a place to live and new brothers and sisters in Christ! How Buck wished he could come right out and ask the witnesses what he should do, where he should go. How was he going to reunite with his wife when he was a fugitive from the GC? Would he have to be spirited out the way he had rescued Tsion?

A GC bullhorn warned him to retreat. "And to the two who are under arrest. You have sixty seconds to surrender peacefully. We have strategically placed concussion bombs, mines, and mortars with kill power in a two-hundred-yard radius. Evacuate now or stay at your own peril! The clock begins when the last translation of this announcement has ended. In the meantime, the ranking officer of the Global Community, under direct authority of the supreme commander and the potentate himself, will offer to escort the fugitives to a waiting vehicle."

As the announcement was translated into several languages, the crowd gleefully dispersed, sprinting out of range of the explosives and crouching behind cars and concrete barriers. Buck slowly backed away, never taking his eyes from Moishe and Eli, whose jaws were set.

From the right a lone GC guard, decked out in military ribbons but unarmed and with his hands in the air, hurried toward the witnesses. When he was within ten yards, Eli shouted so loudly that the man seemed paralyzed from the sound wave alone. "Dare not approach the servants of the Most High God, even with an empty hand! Save yourself! Find shelter in caves or behind rocks!"

The GC man slipped and fell, then fell again as he scrambled to get away. Buck picked up his pace too but was still walking backward, his eyes on the witnesses. From a branch high above him came two loud, echoing reports from a rifle. The sniper was less than fifty feet from Eli and Moishe, and what happened to the bullets Buck could not say. A burst of flame shot from Moishe's mouth straight to the soldier, who somehow kept a grip on his weapon until his flaming body slammed to the stony ground. Then the rifle bounced twenty feet away. He burned quickly into a pile of ashes as if in a kiln, and his rifle melted and burned too.

Silence fell over the area as guards, crowd, and Buck waited for the igniting of the threatened weapons. Buck was now back with the rest of the onlookers, huddled beneath the low-slung roof of a portico across the way. When he was sure the minute had long passed, the air grew cold as winter. Buck shivered uncontrollably as those around him groaned and wept in fear. A wind kicked up and howled, and people tried to cover exposed skin and huddle together against the frigid blast. Hail fell as if a cosmic truck had unloaded tons of golf ball–size spheres of ice all in one dump. In ten seconds the downpour stopped, and the area was ten inches deep in melting ice.

The power that supplied electricity for the TV lights popped and sizzled and blew out, plunging the area into darkness. In three locations simultaneously, what appeared to be boxes of explosives burned, emitted a series of muffled pops, then disintegrated into ash.

Such was the extent of the murderous attack on the witnesses.

Two helicopters aimed gigantic searchlights on the Temple Mount as the temperature rose, Buck guessed, into the nineties. The shin-deep hail turned to water in an instant, and the sound of it running away was like a babbling brook. Within minutes the mud turned to dust as if it were the middle of the day and the sun had baked it.

And all the while, the crowd whimpered and whined every time the circling choppers lit up the area near the Wall. Eli and Moishe had not moved an iota.

As he and Chloe and Tsion headed off to the guest rooms, Rayford thanked Lukas Miklos for his hospitality. "You are an answer to prayer, my friend."

Tsion promised to send Miklos a list of believers in Greece. "And Mr. Miklos, would you pray with us for Chloe's husband, Captain Steele's son-in-law?"

"Certainly," Miklos said, following their lead to hold hands and bow his head. When his turn came, he said, "Dear Jesus Christ, protect that boy. Amen."

CHAPTER 14

BUCK, THRILLED but also grieving and exhausted, caught another cab to within two blocks of Chaim Rosenzweig's. Still wearing his headgear, he walked close enough to see that the GC were long gone. The gateman, Jonas, dozed at his post.

Knowing neither Jonas nor Chaim professed faith yet, Buck hesitated. He knew Chaim was at least learning the truth about Carpathia and would not turn Buck in. Jonas was a gamble. Buck didn't know if the man spoke or understood English, having heard him speak only Hebrew. The man had to know some English, didn't he? Serving as the first contact with visitors?

Emboldened by the exhilarating challenges of Eli and

Moishe, Buck took a deep breath, gently touched an itching stitched wound below his eye, and walked directly to the gatehouse. He didn't want to startle the man, but he had to wake him. He tossed a pebble at the window. Jonas did not stir. Buck knocked lightly, then more loudly. Still he did not rouse. Finally Buck opened the door and gently touched Jonas's arm.

A burly man in his late fifties, Jonas leaped to his feet, eyes wild. Buck whipped off his disguise, then realized his face had to look horrible. Red, blotched, swollen, stitched, he looked like a monster.

Jonas must have taken the removal of the headdress as a challenge. Unarmed, he grabbed a huge flashlight from his belt and reared back with it. Buck spun away, wincing at the very thought of a blow to his tender face. "It's me, Jonas! Cameron Williams!"

Jonas put his free hand to his heart, forgetting to lower the flashlight. "Oh, Mr. Williams!" he said, his English so broken and labored that Buck hardly recognized his own name. Finally Jonas put the light away and used both hands to help communicate, gesturing with every phrase. "They," he said ominously, pointing outside and waving as if to indicate a sea of people, "been looked for you." He pointed to his own eyes.

"Me personally? Or all of us?"

Jonas looked lost. "Personal?" he said.

"Just for me?" Buck tried, realizing he was copying Jonas and pointing to himself. "Or for Tsion and my wife?"

Jonas closed his eyes, shook his head, and held up one

hand, palm out. "Not here," he said. "Tsion, wife, gone. Flying." He fluttered his fingers in the air.

"Chaim?" Buck said.

"Sleeps." Jonas demonstrated with a hand to his cheek and his eyes shut.

"May I go in and sleep, Jonas?"

The man squinted at this puzzle. "I call." He reached for the phone.

"No! Let Chaim sleep! Tell him later."

"Later?"

"Morning," Buck said. "When he wakes up." Jonas nodded, but still had his hand on the phone as if he might dial. "I'll go in and sleep," Buck added, acting it out like charades. "I'll leave a note on Chaim's door so he won't be surprised. OK?"

"OK!"

"I'll go in now?"

"OK!"

"All right?"

"All right!"

Buck watched Jonas while backing away and heading for the door. Jonas watched him too, let go of the phone, waved, and smiled. Buck waved, then turned and found the door locked. He had to go back and explain to Jonas that he would have to let Buck in. Finally, for the first time since the chopper had left the roof hours before, Buck could relax. He left a note on Chaim's door with no details—just that he was in the guest room with much to tell him and that he would likely see him late morning.

Buck looked at himself in the bathroom mirror. It was worse than he thought, and he prayed the so-called clinic he had visited at least had a modicum of sterility. The stitching looked professional enough, but he was a mess. The whites of his eyes were full of blood. His face was a patchwork of colors, none close to his complexion. He was glad Chloe didn't have to see him like this.

He locked the bedroom door, let his clothes fall by the bed, and stretched out painfully. And heard the soft chirp of his phone. It had to be Chloe, but he didn't want to stand up again. He rolled over, reached for his pants, and as he struggled to free the phone from the back pocket, his weight shifted, and he tumbled out of bed.

He wasn't hurt, but the racket woke Chaim. As Buck answered his phone, he heard Chaim crying over the intercom: "Jonas! Jonas! Intruders!"

By the time it was sorted out, he and Chloe were up-to-date, Chaim had heard the whole story, and the sun was beginning to peek over the horizon. It was agreed that Chloe and Tsion and Rayford would go on home to Mount Prospect and that Chaim would work on finding a way for Buck to get back when he had recuperated.

Chaim was even angrier than Buck had seen him on the phone to Leon. He said the TV news had been running and rerunning the videotape of Buck talking with the GC guard who was killed a few seconds later. "The tape makes it obvious you were unarmed, that he was fine when you left him, and that you neither turned around nor returned. He fired over your head, and moments later he was spun around by bullets from high-powered rifles at close range. We all know they had to have come from the weapons of his own compatriots. But it will never get that far. It will be covered up, he will be accused of working with you or for you, and who knows what else will come of it?"

The "what else" turned out to be a news story concocted by the GC. Television reports said that an American terrorist named Kenneth Ritz had hijacked Nicolae Carpathia's own helicopter to stage an escape by the Tsion Ben-Judah party from house arrest at Chaim Rosenzweig's. The reports claimed Rosenzweig had hosted Ben-Judah, murder suspect Cameron Williams, and Williams's wife and had agreed to lock them under house arrest for the GC. Scenes of Dr. Rosenzweig's roof access door, "clearly broken from the inside show conclusively how the Americans escaped."

A Global Community spokesman said Ritz was shot and killed by a sniper when he opened fire on GC forces at Jerusalem Airport. The other three fugitives were at large internationally, and it was assumed that Williams, a former employee of the Global Community, was an accomplished jet pilot.

The stateside members of the Tribulation Force followed the news carefully, keeping in touch with Chaim and Buck as often as possible. Rayford was amazed at the improvement in Hattie after such a short time. Her illness and despair and stubbornness had synthesized into a fierce hatred and determination. She grieved the loss of her child so deeply that Rayford was haunted by her stifled wails in the night.

Chloe, too, battled anger. "I know we should expect nothing less from the world system, Daddy," she said, "but I feel so helpless I could explode. If we don't find a way to get Buck back here soon, I'm going over there myself. Have you ever wished you could be the one God uses to kill Carpathia when the time comes?"

"Chloe!" Rayford said, hoping his response sounded like scolding rather than a cover for the fact that he had prayed for that very privilege. What was happening to them? What were they becoming?

Word came from Buck that Jacov had helped him get set up undercover with Stefan. Rayford felt better about that than his staying with Chaim. It was clear Global Community security forces believed Buck had escaped with the others, but living under an alias in a lower middle-class neighborhood made him less vulnerable and gave him a chance to heal. He told Rayford by phone that within a few weeks he would attempt to return to the States commercially, probably from a major European airport. "Since they're not looking for me over here, I should be able to slip out under a phony name."

Meanwhile, Rayford had stayed in touch with Mac McCullum and David Hassid and used David's leads to replace everyone's computers and add to their bag of tricks cell phones that could both access the Internet and were solar-powered and satellite-connected globally.

Tsion often expressed to Rayford his satisfaction with his new computer—a light, thin, portable laptop with every handy accessory he could even dream of needing. It was the latest, fastest, most powerful model on the market. Tsion spent most of every day communicating with his international flock, which had exploded even before the meetings in Israel and now multiplied exponentially every day.

With Hattie improving physically if not mentally, Dr. Floyd Charles had time to take Ken's place as the Tribulation Force's technical adviser. He installed scrambling software that kept their phones and computers untraceable.

The toughest chore for Rayford was dealing with his emotions over Ken. He knew they all missed him, and Tsion's message at a brief memorial service left them all in tears. Chloe spent two days on the Internet searching for surviving relatives and turned up nothing. Rayford informed Ernie at Palwaukee, who promised to pass the word to the staff there and secure Ken's belongings until Rayford could get there to assess them. He said nothing to Ernie about Ken's gold stash, knowing that the two, while fellow believers, had not known each other long.

Buck bought a computer so he could log onto the Net and study under Tsion without having to strain to see the tiny screen of his phone. But he was unable to find untraceable software that would allow him to communicate with Chloe except by phone. He missed her terribly but was pleased to hear she and the unborn baby were healthy, though she admitted Doc had expressed some concern over her fragility.

She kept busy building a business model based on Ken Ritz's notes. Within a month, she told Buck, she hoped to run the business by computer, networking believers around the globe. "Some will plant and reap," she said. "Others will market and sell. It's our only hope once the mark of the beast is required for legal trade." She told him her first order of business was enlisting growers, producers, and suppliers. Once that was in place, she would expand the market.

"But what about when you have a baby to take care of?" he said.

"I hope my husband will be home by then," she said. "He has nothing to manage but a little alternative Internet magazine, so I'll teach him."

"Teach him what? Your business or child care?"

"Both," she said.

Late one Friday she mentioned to Buck on the phone that Rayford was planning to visit Palwaukee Airport the next day. "He's going to look at Ken's planes and try to get to know this Ernie kid better. He might be a good mechanic, but Ken hardly knew him."

That night Buck logged on to find Tsion's teaching for the day. The rabbi seemed down, but Buck realized that people who didn't know him personally probably wouldn't notice.

He wrote about the heartbreak of losing friends and family and loved ones. He didn't mention Ken by name, but Buck read between the lines.

Tsion concluded his teaching for the day by reminding his readers that they had recently passed the twenty-four-month mark since the signing of the peace pact between the Global Community (known two years before as the United Nations) and the State of Israel. "I remind you, my dear brothers and sisters, that we are but a year and a half from what the Scriptures call the Great Tribulation. It has been hard, worse than hard, so far. We have survived the worst two years in the history of our planet, and this next year and a half will be worse. But the last three and a half years of this period will make the rest seem like a garden party."

Buck smiled at Tsion's insistence at always ending with a word of encouragement, regardless of the hard truth he had to convey. He closed by quoting Luke 21: "'There will be signs in the sun, in the moon, and in the stars; and on the earth distress of nations, with perplexity, the sea and the waves roaring; men's hearts failing them from fear and the expectation of those things which are coming on the earth, for the powers of heaven will be shaken. Then they will see the Son of Man coming in a cloud with power and great glory. Now when these things begin to happen, look up and lift up your heads, because your redemption draws near.'"

The next morning at seven in Israel, Buck was watching a television news report of Nicolae Carpathia's response to Eli and Moishe, who were still wreaking havoc in Jerusalem.

The reporter quoted Supreme Commander Leon Fortunato, speaking for the potentate, "His Excellency has decreed the preachers enemies of the world system and has authorized Peter the Second, supreme pontiff of Enigma Babylon One World Faith, to dispose of the criminals as he sees fit. The potentate does not believe, and I agree, that he should involve himself personally in matters that should be under the purview of the Global Community's religious division. His Excellency told me just last night, and I quote, 'Unless, that is, we discover that our Pontifex Maximus is impotent when it comes to dealing with those who use trickery and mass hypnosis to paralyze an entire country.'"

Of course, it being a "balanced" broadcast, Buck was not surprised to see a furious Peter Mathews spitting a reply. "Oh, the problem is mine now, is it? Has His Excellency finally ceded authority to where it belongs? Of course, not until it was proven his military had no power over these impostors. When the two lie dead, the rains will fall again in Israel, clear, pure, refreshing water will cascade once more, and the world will know where the true seat of power resides."

A week before, Buck had gotten Chaim to visit the preachers at the Wall, and the old man admitted coming away shaken by the experience and more disillusioned with Carpathia. "But still, Cameron, as long as Nicolae upholds his end of the bargain and honors the pact with Israel, I will trust him. I have no choice. I want to and I need to."

Buck had pressed him. "If he should betray Israel, what would you think of all you have heard and learned from

Tsion and what you know from what my father-in-law heard behind the scenes? Might you defect and join us?"

Rosenzweig would not commit. "I am an old man," he said, "set in my ways. I regret I am a hard sell. You and your fellow believers are most impressive, and I hope against hope you are not proven right in the end, for I will be most miserable. But I have cast my lot with the world I can touch and feel and see. I am not ready to throw over intellectualism for blind faith."

"That is what you think Tsion has done?"

"Please don't tell him I said that. Tsion Ben-Judah is a brilliant scholar who does not fit the image I have of believers. But then neither do any of you in his immediate circle. That should tell me something, I suppose."

"God is trying to get your attention, Dr. Rosenzweig. I hope it doesn't take something drastic."

Rosenzweig had waved him off. "Thank you for caring."

Now Buck sat shaking his head at the TV report, knowing it was eleven at night in Illinois and that his family and friends would not have seen this yet. He wished he could leave them a message on e-mail that would tell them to be sure to watch. But he couldn't transmit from this location without leaving Stefan and himself exposed to the GC.

He thought about calling or texting a message, but Chloe had begun sleeping so lightly that she always answered, even text beeps in the middle of the night. She needed her sleep.

With his housemate off at work, Buck stepped out into the morning sunshine. He felt such a longing to be back at the safe house that he nearly wept. He squinted at the brilliance of a cloudless sky and enjoyed the pleasant warmth of a windless day. And suddenly it seemed someone pulled a shade down on the heavens.

With the sun still riding high in the clear sky, the morning turned to twilight and the temperature plummeted. Buck knew exactly what it was, of course: the prophecy of Revelation 8:12. The fourth angel had sounded, "and a third of the sun was struck." The same would befall a third of the moon and the stars. Whereas the sun shone for around twelve hours every day in most parts of the world, it would now shine no more than eight, and at only two-thirds its usual brilliance.

Even knowing it was coming did not prepare Buck for the awe he felt at God's power. A lump formed in his throat, and his chest grew tight. He hurried into the empty house and fell to his knees. "God," he prayed, "you have proven yourself over and over to me, and yet I find my faith strengthened all the more every time you act anew. Everything you promise, you deliver. Everything you predict comes to pass. I pray this phenomenon, publicized all over the world by Tsion and the 144,000 witnesses, will reach millions more for you. How can anyone doubt your power and your greatness? You are fearsome but also loving and gracious and kind. Thank you for saving me. Thank you for Chloe and our baby, and for her dad and Tsion and Doc. Thank you for the privilege of having known Ken. Protect our people wherever they are, and give me the chance to meet Mac and David. Show us what to do. Guide us in how to serve you best. I give myself to you again, willing to go anywhere and do anything you ask. I praise you for Jacov and Hannelore and Stefan and these new brothers and sisters who have taken me in. I want Chaim for you, Lord. Thank you for being such a good and great God."

Buck was overcome, realizing that the darkening would affect everything in the world. Not just brightness and temperatures, but transportation, agriculture, communications, travel—everything that had anything to do with him and his loved ones reuniting.

He wanted to warn the Tribulation Force, but he waited until seven o'clock in the morning Chicago time. They liked to rise with the sun, but it wasn't going to rise for them. Buck wondered what darkened stars looked like. It wouldn't be long.

He dialed Chloe and woke her up.

Rayford had awakened early and looked at his watch. It was quarter to seven and still dark. He lay staring at the ceiling, wondering if they were in for some bad weather or just a cloudy day. At seven he heard Chloe's phone ring. It would be Buck, and Rayford wanted to talk to him. He would give her a few minutes, then go down and give her the high sign.

Rayford lay back and breathed deeply. He wondered what Palwaukee would produce that day. Did he dare raise with young Ernie the subject of hidden treasure? That would depend on how their conversations went. He assumed it would take a while to develop trust. Ernie was very young.

Chloe sounded agitated. And she was calling for him. He sat up. It was way too early for anything with her baby. Was something wrong with Buck? "Dad! Come down here!" He dragged on a robe.

She met him at the bottom of the stairs, the cell phone to her ear. "Look a little dark for seven?" she said. "Buck says the sun was struck at seven in the morning over there. While we were sleeping. Talk to Daddy, hon. I'm going to start getting people up around here."

To Buck, Rayford sounded stunned. "Incredible," he said, over and over. "We're going to have to determine what this means to all our solar-powered stuff."

"I thought Doc was already working on that."

"He was. We just didn't like his conclusions. For some reason, the sum is not equal to its parts in a deal like this. You can't just figure you're going to have a third less power. He put his big calculator to it and said it's a third less power on top of being a third less time every twenty-four hours. He sketched out a model of what it will mean just to us, and we didn't like it. Couldn't argue with it and couldn't store much power in advance, but we sure hope he's wrong."

"He won't be," Buck said. "Smart guys never are. Hang on

a second, Rayford. I've got another call. Oh, it's Rosenzweig. I'd better call Chloe back."

"I'll tell her. Watch your phone power now."

"Right." He hit the switch. "Dr. Rosenzweig!"

"Cameron, I need to see you. I need some counsel."

"You want to meet now?"

"Can you manage it?"

"I suppose you know what's really happening," Buck said.

"Of course I do! I was at the last meeting when Tsion spoke of this prophecy."

"You admit it's too obvious to be anything else."

"What thinking man would not know that?"

Thank you, God! Buck thought.

"The problem, and what I need to talk to you about, is what do I say? The media is all over this and wants a comment for tomorrow's broadcasts. I told a half dozen that I am a botanist, and the best I can tell them is what it will mean to photosynthesis."

"What will it mean, by the way?"

"Well, it will bollix it all up, if you want my technical response. But the newspeople are reminding me that I have always spoken out on scientific subjects, even outside my area of expertise. You will recall Nicolae had me speculating on the causes of the disappearances. I almost convinced myself with that spontaneous atomic reaction blather."

"You almost convinced me too, Doctor, and I was an international news correspondent."

"Well, I just heard from Fortunato, and he wants

me to corroborate the Global Community view of this phenomenon."

"How can I help?"

"We need to strategize. I am considering bursting their bubble. I might imply that I will endorse their view—wait till you see it—and when I get on the air, I will say what I want. I owe at least that to Leon."

"You're worried what Carpathia will think."

"Of course."

"It will be a test of your relationship."

"Exactly. I'll find out how free a citizen I am. I have given Leon nothing short of grief for making it appear I had worked with him on detaining the three of you. I could have exposed the whole strong-arm regime, but Nicolae apologized personally and asked that I not embarrass him."

"He did? You never told me that."

"It didn't seem appropriate. You have no idea how close I came to telling him that I would trade a friend's free passage out of the country for my agreeing to let that news report slide. I just couldn't muster the courage to ask."

"Probably wise," Buck said. "I can't see him making that kind of trade. Finding out I've been here right under their noses would have infuriated him."

"I did have the audacity to ask if he had considered that his tactics against Ben-Judah and his people might be the reason for all the plagues and judgments. He chided me for buying into all that fiction. Now I must meet with you, Cameron."

"Can we meet somewhere private?"

Rosenzweig suggested a dank, underground eatery appropriately called The Cellar. Buck asked for a table in the corner under a dim light where they could look at Chaim's document without being disturbed. Rosenzweig produced a printout of the official Global Community assessment of what had struck that morning. It was all Buck could do to keep from howling.

The document contained all kinds of legalese, insisting on its confidentiality, its for-your-eyes-only nature, its personal direction to Dr. Chaim Rosenzweig only, and all this under penalty of prosecution by the supreme commander of the Global Community under the authority of His Excellency, blah, blah, blah.

It read: "Dr. Rosenzweig, His Excellency wishes me to convey his deep personal appreciation for your willingness to endorse the official policy statement of the Global Community Aeronautics and Space Administration regarding the natural astronomical phenomenon that occurred 0700 hours New Babylon time today."

"Of course, I agreed only to review it, but Leon proceeds with his typically presumptuous tone. Anyway, here's the party line."

Buck read, "The GCASA is pleased to assure the public that the darkening of the skies that began this morning is the result of an explainable natural phenomenon and should not be cause for alarm. Top scientific researchers have concluded that this is a condition that should rectify itself in forty-eight to ninety-six hours.

"It should not significantly affect temperatures, except in the short run, and the lack of brightness should not be misconstrued as lack of solar power and energy. While there may be some short-term impact on smaller solar-powered equipment such as cell phones, computers, and calculators, there should be no measurable impact on the power reserves held by Global Community Power and Light.

"As for what happened in space to cause this condition, experts point to the explosion of a massive star (a supernova), which resulted in the formation of a magnetar (or super-magnetized star). Such a heavenly body can be up to fifteen miles across but weigh twice as much as the sun. It is formed when the massive star explodes and its core shrinks under gravity. The magnetar spins at a tremendous rate of speed, causing the elements in its core to rise and become intensely magnetic.

"Flashes from such events can emit as much energy as the sun would produce in hundreds of years. Normally these bursts are contained in the upper atmosphere, which absorbs all the radiation. While we have not detected harmful levels of radiation, this flash clearly occurred at an altitude low enough to affect the brightness of the sun. Current readings show a decrease in light between 30 and 35 percent.

"The GCASA will maintain constant watch on the situation and report significant changes. We expect the situation to normalize before the end of next week."

Rosenzweig shook his head and looked into Buck's eyes. "A convincing piece of fantasy, no?"

"I'd buy it if I didn't know better," Buck said.

"Well, this is not my field, as you know. But even I can see through this. The creation of a magnetar would have no effect on the brightness of the sun, moon, or stars except maybe to make them brighter. It would affect radio waves, maybe knock out satellites. If it happened low enough in our atmosphere, as they imply, to affect earth, it would probably knock the earth off its axis. Whatever this was, it was not the creation of a magnetar from a supernova."

"What do you mean, 'Whatever this was'? You know as well as I do what it was."

"As a matter of fact, I think I do."

Dr. Rosenzweig tried out on Buck what he planned to say live on the air when asked about the event. "I'll even carry the document solemnly in my hand, rolled up and dog-eared, as if I have been agonizing over it for hours."

"I love it," Buck said. He phoned the States, something that grew increasingly difficult as the hours of darkness continued and would become nearly impossible within days.

Chloe answered. "Yes, dear," she said. "Your phone call from Chaim lasted this long?"

"No, sorry. Got tied up. I just wanted to tell you to watch for him on the news with his assessment of what happened."

"What *is* his assessment?"

"I don't want to spoil it for you. Just make sure nobody misses it. It'll make your day."

"We're having power problems here already, Buck, and this connection isn't the best."

"Save enough to watch Chaim. You'll be glad you did."

CHAPTER 15

EATING A LATE DINNER that evening, Tsion shared with the Stateside Tribulation Force his joy over a wildly successful effort by many believers on the Internet. "I merely put out a simple request—you all saw it—for translators in various countries to interpret the daily messages in their own languages. You can imagine how much of the web is made up of Asian language groups, Spanish, German, and others.

"Well," he added with a twinkle, "not only did I get far more volunteers than I needed, but some very advanced computer types are offering free software downloads that automatically translate into other languages. It's Pentecost on the Net. I'm able to type in unknown tongues!"

Rayford was always warmed by the joy Tsion took in his work and ministry. He had sacrificed as much as anyone in their little group—a wife and two children. Chloe had lost her mother and brother and now two friends. Rayford had lost two wives, his son, his pastor, and more new acquaintances than he wanted to think about. Everybody around the table, Doc Charles and Hattie included, had reason to go mad if they allowed themselves to dwell on it.

Momentary smiles were all they could muster when Tsion shared a story like that or someone made the occasional wry comment. Raucous laughter or silliness just didn't have a place in their lives anymore. Grief was wearying, Rayford thought. He looked forward to that day when God would wipe away all tears from their eyes, and there would be no more war.

That was one reason he looked forward with relish to the ten o'clock news event that had been trumpeted on the GC Broadcasting Networks all day. The GC was bringing together experts who would speak to the official statement of the government related to the darkness that had already begun to take its toll. Buck had insinuated that Chaim would be entertaining. Although Rayford couldn't imagine a belly laugh, he looked forward to the diversion.

"I just hope," Tsion said, "that we detect some movement in Chaim's spirit. When I was laying out all the prophecies again for him, I challenged him. I said, 'Chaim, how can a man with such a mind as yours ignore the mathematical impossibility of so many dozens of prophecies referring to just one man unless he is the Messiah?' He started with the typical argument about not knowing whether the Bible is authentic. I said, 'My mentor! You would doubt your own Torah? Where do you think I am coming up with this stuff?' I tell you, young people, it won't be long for Chaim. I just don't want him to wait too long."

Rayford, just three or so years younger than Tsion, loved being referred to as a young person.

Hattie spoke up, her voice stronger than ever. "Do you still feel that way about me, Dr. Ben-Judah? Or have I convinced you I am a lost cause?"

Tsion put his fork down and pushed his plate away. "Miss Durham," he said quietly, "are you sure you want to hear my thoughts on your situation in front of the others?"

"Go for it," she said, just short of gleeful. "I have no secrets, and I know you people sure don't."

Tsion entwined his fingers. "All right, since you brought it up and gave me permission. You and I rarely interact. I hear what you say and know where you stand, and you know that my whole life is now dedicated to proclaiming what I believe. So my views are not a mystery to you either. You are nearly twenty years my junior and we are of opposite sexes, and so there is a generational and gender barrier that has perhaps caused me to be less frank with you than I might have been with someone else.

"But it might surprise you to know how frequently during each day God brings you to my mind."

Rayford thought Hattie looked more than surprised. She

had a glass of water suspended between the table and her lips, and her bemused smile had frozen.

"Again, I do not intend to embarrass you—"

"Oh, you can't embarrass me, Doc. Let me have it." She smiled as if she had finally reeled in a big one.

"If you would permit me to speak from my heart. . . ."

"Please," she said, setting her glass down and settling herself as if ready to enjoy this. Rayford thought she enjoyed being in Tsion's spotlight.

"I feel such compassion for you," Tsion said, "such a longing for you to come to Jesus." And suddenly he could not continue. His lips trembled, and he could not form words.

Hattie raised her eyebrows, staring at him.

"Forgive me," he managed in a whisper, taking a sip of water and collecting himself. He continued through tears. "Somehow God has allowed me to see you through his eyes—a scared, angry, shaken young woman who has been used and abandoned by many in her life. He loves you with a perfect love. Jesus once looked upon his audience and said, 'O Jerusalem, Jerusalem, the one who kills the prophets and stones those who are sent to her! How often I wanted to gather your children together, as a hen gathers her chicks under her wings, but you were not willing!'

"Miss Durham, you know the truth. I have heard you say so. And yet you are not willing. No, I do not consider you a lost cause. I pray for you every bit as much as I pray for Chaim. Because Jesus went on to say about the hard-hearted people of Jerusalem, 'I say to you, you shall see Me no more till you say, "Blessed is He who comes in the name of the Lord!"'

"I look at you in your fragile beauty and see what life has done to you, and I long for your peace. I think of what you could do for the kingdom during these perilous times, and I am jealous to have you as part of our family. I fear you're risking your life by holding out on God, and I do not look forward to how you might suffer before he reaches you.

"I'm sorry if I embarrassed you, but you asked."

Hattie sat shaking her head, and Rayford had the impression she was more surprised than embarrassed. She did not respond except to go from shaking to nodding. "What time is that news thing?" she asked.

"Right now," Chloe said, and everyone cleared his own dishes.

Buck settled in front of the television in Jerusalem with his notebook, fascinated by the foreboding dusk at dawn. He was grateful that both Jacov and Stefan were off and had showed up to watch the press conference with him.

"Press conference" was a misnomer, of course, now that the Global Community owned the media. Only in underground publications like Buck's did readers get objective substance. That was what made Chaim's appearance so intriguing. If he had the guts to follow through on what he told Buck he would say, it would be the most controversial thing on television since Tsion's startling testimony. No, Rosenzweig had not become a believer, at least not yet. But he had clearly grown tired of being used by the GC regime.

The program began with what had become the obligatory fawning over the panelists. It seemed every time the GC wanted to persuade the populace of some cockamamie theory, it paraded pedigreed know-it-alls before the camera and buttered them up.

The host introduced the head of GCASA, the head of GCP&L, various and sundry scientists, authors, dignitaries, and even entertainment personalities. Each luminary had smiled shyly during the recitation of his or her litany of achievements and qualifications.

Buck snorted aloud when the host actually used the phrase "And last, but certainly not least." The camera panned to the tiny Albert Schweitzer–looking man on the end, and the scrolling legend along the bottom of the screen bore his name. Chaim looked neither shy nor humble, but rather bemused, as if this whole thing was a bit much.

Chaim tilted his head back and forth as if mocking himself as the plaudits rambled on and on: former professor, writer, botanist, winner of the Nobel Prize, honorary this, honorary that, speaker, diplomat, ambassador, personal friend and confidant of His Excellency the potentate. Chaim drew circles with an open hand as if they should wrap it up. The host finished, "Once *Global Weekly*'s Man of the Year and inventor of the formula credited with making Israel a world power, Dr. Chaim Rosenzweig!"

There was no studio audience, and even the GC press corps was against applauding. So the energetic intro died a conspicuous, awkward death, and the show moved on.

The host first read the entire GC statement while the text scrolled on the screen. Buck's tension mounted when—as he feared—the host began by asking for the opinion and comment of the first expert on the left. He would continue in the same order they had been introduced. Buck worried that viewers would lose patience and nod off from boredom by the time they got around to Chaim. One advantage to the GC-controlled media: Despite five hundred channel choices, this was on every station.

Buck had to remind himself that even for millions who ignored what they considered the ravings of a madman like Tsion Ben-Judah, the sudden darkness was frightening. They tuned in for answers from their government and likely considered this the most important program they had ever watched. Buck only hoped they would stay around for the last guy. The payoff would be worth it.

Everyone on the panel, of course, praised the fast and efficient and thorough work of the GCASA and assured the public that this was a minor event, a temporary condition. "As alarming as the darkness is," a woman on the management staff of Global Community Power and Light said, "we agree it will have negligible impact on the quality of life as we know it, and it should correct itself in a matter of days."

When at long last they got to Chaim, Buck felt a sense of community with his people in the States. The idea that they were all watching the same thing made the miles shrink momentarily, and he longed to have his wife cuddling next to him.

"Well," Chaim began dramatically, "who am I to add to or detract from anything said by any of these brilliant aficionados of interplanetary galactic astronomical phenomena? As for the dear woman who promises this will have no impact on our quality of life, let me say how disappointed I am. Our quality of life the last few years has been nothing to write home about.

"I am but a simple botanist who happened upon a combination that turned out to be magic water, and suddenly my opinion is sought on everything from the price of sausage to whether the defiant preachers at the Wailing Wall are real or make-believe.

"You want my opinion? OK, I will give it to you. To tell you the truth, I don't know. I don't know who turned the lights out, and I'm not sure I want to know who the two gentlemen are at the Wall. I just wish they would bring back the pure water and let it rain once in a while. Is that too much to ask?

"But let me tell you this, now that I have your attention. I do have your attention, don't I?"

The camera, panning back to the speechless host, exposed the shocked expressions of the other guests. It was clear they thought Rosenzweig had finally stepped off the edge.

"As should come as no surprise to anyone, I am not a religious man. A Jew by birth, of course, and proud of it.

Wouldn't have it any other way. But to me it's a nationality, not a faith. All that to say this: Many, myself included, were horrified to hear what happened to the family of my beloved protégé and former student who grew up to be the respected linguistic and biblical scholar, Rabbi Tsion Ben-Judah.

"I confess, in my heart of hearts I had to wonder if he hadn't brought this on himself. Condone the killings? Never as long as I live. But would I advise a man to go on international television, from the very land where the name Jesus Christ is anathema to your neighbors, and tell the world you had become a turncoat? A Christ follower? A believer that Jesus is the Messiah?

"Madness.

"I was doubly horrified when he became a fugitive, exiled from his own homeland, his life worth nothing. But did I lose respect for him? Admire him less? How could I? Knowing such risks, taking such stands!"

"Thank you, Dr. Rosenz—," the host began, obviously getting instructions through his earpiece.

"Oh, no you don't," Rosenzweig said. "I have earned the right to another minute or so, and I demand that I not be unplugged from the air. I just want to say that I am still not a religious man, but my religious friend, the aforementioned rabbi, has spoken to the very issue we address today. Now you may rest easy. I have come back to the point.

"Ben-Judah was ridiculed for his beliefs, for his contentions that scriptural prophecy could be taken literally. He said an earthquake would come. It came. He said hail and blood and fire would scorch the plants. They did. He said things would fall from the sky, poisoning water, killing people, sinking ships. They fell.

"He said the sun and the moon and the stars would be stricken and that the world would be one-third darker. Well, I am finished. I don't know what to make of it except that I feel a bigger fool every day. And let me just add, I want to know what Dr. Tsion Ben-Judah says is coming next! Don't you?" And he quickly added the address of Tsion's Web site.

The host was still speechless. He looked at Chaim, brows raised.

"Go ahead now," Chaim said. "Pull the plug on me."

Rayford was frustrated that he had not made it to Palwaukee that day. And he wouldn't make it the next day either, or the next. The reduction of solar power affected every facet of an already difficult existence including the transmission of Tsion's lessons. Dr. Rosenzweig's endorsement of Tsion's teaching resulted in the most massive number of hits on what was already a site ten times more popular than any other in history. And yet broadcasting Tsion's daily messages became an arduous chore that forced Rayford to delay any other activity.

Repeated failures on the Internet were blamed on the solar problems. Believers all over the globe rallied to try to copy and pass the teaching along as necessary, but it became impossible to track the success of that effort.

Chloe's efforts at building a private marketplace in anticipation of the mark of the beast nearly ground to a halt. Over the next several weeks, seasons were skewed. Major Midwest cities looked like Alaska in the dead of winter. Power reserves were exhausted. Hundreds of thousands all over the world died of exposure. Even the vaunted GC, having conveniently ignored adjusting their initial assessment, now looked for someone to blame for this curse. Confused in the tragic panic surrounding the crisis was the role of Ben-Judah. Had he predicted it, as Rosenzweig had asserted, or had he called it down from heaven?

Peter the Second decried Ben-Judah and the two preachers as reckless practitioners of black magic, proving it by showing live shots of the Wailing Wall. While snow swirled and drifted and Israelis paid top dollar for protective clothing, stayed inside, and used building material for fuel, there stood Eli and Moishe in their same spot. They were still barefoot! Still clad only in their loose-hanging sackcloth robes, arms bare. With only their deeply tanned skin, their beards, and long hair between them and the frigid temperatures, they preached and preached and preached.

"Surely," the self-ascribed supreme pontiff railed, "if there is a devil, he is master of these two! Who other than deranged, demonic beings could withstand these elements and continue to spout irrational diatribes?"

Nicolae Carpathia himself was strangely silent and his visage scarce. Finally, when the Global Community seemed powerless, he addressed the world. During a brief season of solar activity at midday in the Middle East, Mac was able to place a call to Rayford, who answered a cell phone with ancient batteries that had been recharged by a generator. The connection was bad, and they couldn't talk long.

"Watch the potentate tonight if you can, Ray!" Mac shouted. "We're warm as toast even in the snow here because he has marshaled all the energy we need for the palace. But when he goes on TV he's going to be wearing a huge parka he had shipped in from the Arctic."

Mac was right. Rayford and Floyd worked to store as much energy as they could from various sources so they could watch on the smallest TV in the safe house. The whole lot of them huddled to watch and stay warm, Hattie continuing to maintain, "I don't know about the rest of you, but I'm only getting what I deserve."

Tsion said, "My dear, you will find that none of the sealed of the Lord will die due to this judgment. This is an attention-getter aimed at the unbelievers. We suffer because the whole world suffers, but it will not mortally harm us. Don't you want the same protection?"

She did not answer.

Buck, shivering underground with Stefan and Jacov, could not find the power to watch Carpathia on TV. The group listened on a radio with a signal so weak they had to hold their collective breath to hear him.

In Mount Prospect, Rayford, Tsion, Chloe, Floyd, and Hattie watched as Carpathia came on TV in a bare studio, clapping his mittens and bouncing on his toes as if freezing to death. "Citizens of the Global Community," he intoned, "I applaud your courage, your cooperation, your sense of loyalty and togetherness as we rise to the challenge of enduring yet another catastrophe.

"I come to you at this hour to announce my plan to personally visit the two preachers at the Wailing Wall, who have admitted their roles in the plagues that have befallen Israel. They must now be forced to admit that they are behind this dastardly assault on our new way of life.

"Apparently they are invulnerable to physical attack. I will call upon their sense of decency, of fairness, of compassion, and I will go with an open mind, willing to negotiate. Clearly they want something. If there is something I can bargain with that will not threaten the dignity of my office or harm the citizens I live for, I am willing to listen and consider anything.

"I shall make this pilgrimage tomorrow, and it will be carried on live television. As the Global Community headquarters in New Babylon naturally has more power reserves than most areas, we will record this historic encounter with the hope that all of you will be able to enjoy it when this ordeal is finally over.

"Take heart, my beloved ones. I believe the end of this nightmare is in sight."

"He's going personally to the Wall?" Buck said. "Is that what I just heard?"

Stefan nodded. "We should go."

"They won't let anybody near the place," Jacov said.

"They might," Buck said. He suggested the three of them bundle up as thickly as possible and find a location with a clear view of the wrought-iron fence. "We can build a shelter there that looks like just a wood box."

"We're down to our last few sheets of plywood for fuel now," Stefan said. "That green stuff in the cellar."

"We'll bring it back with us," Buck said, "and use it for fuel later."

The plan proved his most foolhardy yet. His face was still tender in spots and numb in others since getting the stitches out several weeks before. He had not expected to have to deal with frostbite in Israel. He and his two compatriots found a stairway that led to an abandoned building with a sealed door, fewer than a hundred yards from the Wall. With Carpathia expected at noon, they built their shelter in the pitch-blackness of the morning. If others ventured out in the howling blizzard, Buck and his friends didn't see them.

They were raw and cold by the time they climbed into their rough-hewn box with slits for viewing. Buck, ever the journalist, just had to see what the thing might look like to a passerby. "I'll be right back," he said.

"You're going out in this again?" Jacov said.

"Just for a minute."

Buck jogged a hundred feet from the staircase and tried to make out the box in the blowing snow and low output from a nearby light pole. *Perfect,* he thought. It would draw no one's attention. As he trudged back, he squinted in the darkness toward the Wall, knowing the witnesses were there but unable to see them. He detoured to get closer.

From what he could tell, they were not by the fence. He drew closer, confident he could not surprise or frighten them and that they would know in their spirits he was a believer. He stepped as close to the fence as he had ever been, recalling one of the first times he had ever conversed with them from just a few feet away.

A break in the wind allowed him to see the two, sitting, their backs against the stone building. They sat casually, elbows on knees, conversing. They were not huddled, still impervious to the elements. Buck wanted to say something, but nothing came to mind. They didn't seem to need encouragement. They didn't seem to need anything.

When in unison they glanced up at him standing there, he just nodded with his stiff neck, like a kid in a binding snowsuit, and raised both fists in support. His heart leapt when he saw them smile for the first time, and Eli raised a hand of greeting.

Buck ran back to the shelter. "Where you been, man?" Jacov said. "We thought you got lost or frozen or something."

Buck just sat, wrapping his arms around his knees, hunching his shoulders, and shook his head. "I'm fine," he said.

GC troops kept crowds several blocks away, once the motor coach arrived bearing Nicolae and his entourage. The wind and snow had stopped, but the noonday sun hardly warmed the area.

Carpathia remained on the bus as TV personnel set up lights and sound and cameras. Finally they signaled the potentate, and several of his top people, led by Fortunato, disembarked. Carpathia was the last to appear. He approached the fence, behind which the two witnesses still sat.

As the world watched on television, Carpathia said, "I bring you cordial greetings from the Global Community. I assume, because of your obvious supernatural powers, that you knew I was coming."

Eli and Moishe remained seated. Moishe said, "God alone is omnipotent, omniscient, and omnipresent."

"Nonetheless, I am here on behalf of the citizens of the earth to determine what course we might take to gain respite from this curse on the planet."

The witnesses stood and stepped forward. "We will speak to you alone."

Carpathia nodded at his minions, and Fortunato, clearly reluctant, led them back to the motor coach.

"All right then," Carpathia said, "shall we proceed?"

"We will talk with you alone."

Carpathia looked puzzled, then said, "These people are merely television technicians, cameramen, and so forth."

"We will talk with you alone."

Nicolae cocked his head in resignation and sent the TV

crew away as well. "May we leave the cameras running? Would that be all right?"

"Your quarrel is not with us," Eli said.

"Beg pardon? You are not behind the darkness, the resultant global chaos?"

"Only God is omnipotent."

"I am seeking your help as men who claim to speak for God. If this is of God, then I plead with you to help me come to some arrangement, an agreement, a compromise, if you will."

"Your quarrel is not with us."

"Well, all right, I understand that, but if you have access to him—"

"Your quarrel is not w—"

"I appreciate that point! I am asking—"

Suddenly Moishe spoke so loudly that the sound meters had to have maxed out. "You would dare wag your tongue at the chosen ones of almighty God?"

"I apologize. I—"

"You who boasted that we would die before the due time?"

"Granted, I concede that I—"

"You who deny the one true God, the God of Abraham, Isaac, and Jacob?"

"In the spirit of ecumenism and tolerance, yes, I do hold that one should not limit his view of deity to one image. But—"

"There is one God and one mediator between God and man, the man Christ Jesus."

"That is a valid view, of course, just like many of the other views—"

"It is written, 'Beware lest any man spoil you through philosophy and vain deceit, after the tradition of men, after the rudiments of the world, and not after Christ.'"

"Do you not see that yours is such an exclusivisti—"

"Your quarrel is not with us."

"We are back to that again, are we? In the spirit of diplomacy, let me suggest—"

But the two witnesses turned away and sat down again.

"So, that is it, then? Before the eyes of the world, you refuse to talk? To negotiate? All I get is that my quarrel is not with you? With whom, then, is it? All right, fine!"

Carpathia marched in front of the main camera and stared into it from inches away. He spoke wearily, but with his usual precise enunciation. "Upon further review, the death of the Global Community guard at the Meeting of the Witnesses was not the responsibility of any of the witnesses or any member of Dr. Ben-Judah's inner circle. The man killed by GC troops at the airport was not a terrorist. My good friend Dr. Chaim Rosenzweig was at no time and in no way holding Ben-Judah or his people at our behest. As of this moment, no one sympathetic to Dr. Ben-Judah and his teachings is considered a fugitive or an enemy of the Global Community. All citizens are equally free to travel and live their lives in a spirit of liberty.

"I do not know with whom I am or should be negotiating, but I assure whoever it is that I stand willing to make whatever other concessions would move us closer to the end of this plague of darkness."

He turned on his heel, sarcastically saluted the two witnesses, and reboarded the motor coach. As the TV crew rushed to gather their equipment, the witnesses spoke in unison from where they sat, clearly loud enough for anyone, even Carpathia, to hear.

"Woe, woe, woe unto all who fail to look up and lift up your heads!"

Two days later, the sun rose bright and full and the earth began to thaw. Buck made plans to fly home freely under his own name. "I can't fly directly to Chicago commercially," he told Rayford, "even with the reconstruction of Midway. I have to go through Europe."

"Any connections through Athens?"

"I'll check. Why?"

Rayford asked that he check on Lukas Miklos. "I'll see if he can greet you at the airport. It won't delay your trip home, and it'll really encourage him."

In Mount Prospect, Tsion told Rayford he was working on what would be his most dramatic and ominous warning yet. Meanwhile he broadcast worldwide over the Internet: "Because of the proven truth of Luke 21, I urge all, believers and unbelievers alike, to train your eyes on the skies. I believe this is the message from the two witnesses."

Doc Charles dug out and cleaned up Donny Moore's telescope, and with millions around the world, began monitoring the heavens. But when Tsion announced in one of his daily messages that he was planning to build a Web site that would allow others to watch the skies through the same telescope, Rayford received a frantic call from David Hassid in New Babylon.

"Glad I caught you," he said breathlessly. "How far along are you on that telescope Web site idea?"

"Couple of days yet. Won't take our people long."

"You don't want to do that. A little software and a bright astronomer could just about pinpoint where you guys are."

Rayford put a hand atop his head. "Thanks for that, David. I never would have thought of it."

"Anyway, the potentate himself has authorized the purchase of a colossal telescope, and I get to work with the guys who will man it. Several can monitor it at once through various computers."

"Well, David, you know what we're looking for."

"I sure do."

CHAPTER 16

THE FOLLOWING WEEK, news programs reported that stargazers from around the globe were tracking what appeared at first to be a shooting star. But this one, first seen during nighttime hours in Asia, did not streak across the sky for a second or two and disappear. Neither was this hurtling object in an orbital trajectory.

Astronomers were fond of explaining that, due to the distance from the earth of even the nearest stars, much of the activity seen from earth actually occurred years before and were just being seen now.

But after several hours of every amateur and professional telescope jockey in the world tracking it, it was becoming clear that this was no ordinary star. Neither was this an event that had happened years before. Experts unable to identify it agreed it was tiny, it was falling straight, and it had been descending a long time. It radiated little heat but seemed to emit its own light as well as reflecting light from stars and the sun, depending on the time of day.

The more closely it was studied, the less a threat it appeared to Earth. The head of GCASA said it had every chance of burning up as it hit Earth's atmosphere. "But even if it remains intact, it has a high probability of landing harmlessly in water. From what we are able to speculate about its mass and density, if it was to hit land, it would suffer far more damage than it could inflict. In all likelihood, it would be vaporized."

Still, none seemed able to turn their telescopes from it. Eventually the unidentified falling object was projected to land somewhere in an uninhabited region of the Fertile Crescent, near what many believed was the cradle of civilization.

GC scientists reached the projected touchdown point in time to see the impact, but they reported that it appeared to slip past the earth's surface into a deep crevice. Aerial studies of the area showed the impossibility of vehicular or foot traffic to more closely evaluate the object and its effect or lack thereof on the earth's crust.

As planes circled and shot still pictures and videotape, however, a geological eruption registered high on the Richter scale of seismology sensors all over the world. This thing that fell to earth, whatever it was, had somehow triggered volcanolike activity deep beneath the earth's surface.

The shock wave alone blew the surveillance planes off course and forced their pilots to fight to stay airborne and escape the area. Astounding scientists, the first evidence of what happened beneath the earth was a mushroom cloud a thousand times bigger and launched with that much more power and speed than any in history produced by bombs or natural phenomena. Also unique about this eruption was that it came from the crevice below sea level rather than from the typical volcanic mountain.

Cameras a thousand miles from the source of the cloud picked up images of it within twelve hours. Rather than being carried on indiscriminate winds, this cloud—massive and growing, fed from the belching earth—spread equally in all directions and threatened to block the sun all over the globe.

And this was no smoky cloud that thinned and dissipated as it traveled. The thick fumes that gushed from the ground were dense and black like the base of a gasoline fire. Scientists feared the source of the smoke was a colossal fire that would eventually rise and shoot flames miles into the air.

Early the following Monday afternoon in Jerusalem, Buck was devastated to learn that his flight to Athens and then on to the States had been cancelled. The billowing cloud of smoke that blanketed the earth had affected daylight again. Buck had looked forward to a two-hour layover during which he would meet Lukas Miklos. He was then to switch planes and fly nonstop the rest of the way to Chicago's Midway Airport. He was to proceed from there to Mount Prospect only after determining that he would not lead any enemies to the safe house. He and the Stateside members of the Tribulation Force had developed options to misdirect tails and shake them free.

Instead Buck hurried to Chaim Rosenzweig's home under the cover of darkness. "Be wary of Carpathia's claim that you are not still a suspect," Chaim said. "Nicolae is not speaking to me. Leon is fuming. While they cannot casually renege on their agreement, they will soon find some justification."

"Don't worry. I'm so eager to see Chloe, I may fly under my own power."

"Be careful of Enigma Babylon."

"What's Peter up to now?"

"You haven't heard?"

Buck shook his head. "Too busy getting ready to go."

Chaim turned on the TV. "I could quote this by heart, I've heard it so many times today. It's the only thing in the news outside the smoking volcano."

Mathews, in full clerical regalia again, spoke to the camera. "The Global Community may have a tacit agreement with black-magic religious terrorists, but the time has come to enforce the law. Enigma Babylon One World Faith is *the* accepted religion for the whole world. As much as it is in my power—and a careful reading of the Global Community charter reveals that this clearly falls within my purview—I will prosecute offenders. So that all may be clear, I consider exclusivist, intolerant, one-way-only beliefs antithetical to true religion. If, because of misplaced diplomacy, the Global Community administration feels it must allow diversions from cosmic truth, Enigma Babylon itself must go on the offensive.

"To be an atheist or an agnostic is one thing. Even they are welcome beneath our all-inclusive banner. But it is illegal to practice a form of religion that flies in the face of our mission. Such practitioners and their followers will suffer.

"As a first initiative in a sweeping effort to rid the world of intolerance, it shall be deemed criminal, as of midnight Tuesday, Greenwich Mean Time, for anyone to visit the Web site of the so-called Tribulation Force. The teachings of this cult's guru, Dr. Tsion Ben-Judah, are poison to people of true faith and love, and we will not tolerate this deadly toxin pushed like a drug.

"Technology is in place that can monitor the Internet activity of any citizen, and those whose records show they have accessed this site after the deadline shall be subject to fine and imprisonment."

A Global Community reporter interrupted. "Two-part question, Supreme Pontiff: One, how does imprisoning people for what they access on the Web jibe with tolerance, faith, and love? And two, if you can monitor everyone's Internet activity, why can't you trace where Ben-Judah transmits from and shut him down?"

"I'm sorry," one of his aides said as Peter the Second was ushered away, "but we established in advance that we would not have time for questions."

I'd like to get a peek at that reporter's forehead, Buck thought. It made him wish his cover had not been blown and that he was still working from the inside.

It was early morning in the Chicago area as Rayford pulled away from the safe house in Buck's Range Rover. Despite the smoky skies, he felt he had to get to Palwaukee and check on the condition of Ken Ritz's Suburban. It seemed in better shape than the Rover. The Trib Force could use it, but Rayford didn't know how a dead man's belongings should be disposed of, especially those of a man with no living kin.

Rayford suddenly heard a voice, as if someone were in the car with him. The radio was off and he was alone, but he heard, clear as if from the best sound system available: "Woe, woe, woe to the inhabitants of the earth, because of the remaining blasts of the trumpet of the three angels who are about to sound!"

His phone chirped. It was David from New Babylon. "Captain Steele, I'm outside right now, and I don't know what kind of spin we're going to put on this one, but I'll bet my life it'll never make the news."

"I heard it. It doesn't have to make the news."

"Everybody in here saw it before we heard it. Well, at least our equipment detected it. We can't see a thing through this cloud of smoke. But because we have huge radio receivers pointed at the sky anyway, it was plain as day here. I asked a Turkish guy what language it was in, and he said his own. Well, I heard it in English, so you know what I think."

"You *saw* the angel?"

"OK, we worked all night because somebody's probe detected something. The digital facsimile made it look like some sort of heavenly body, a comet or something. He gets it all tracked in and measured and whatnot, and we all start studying it. Well, I'm no astronomer so I haven't got a clue what I'm looking at. I tell 'em it looks real small to me, and not very thick. They're all congratulating me because it gave the lead guy an idea. He says, 'All right, let's assume it's closer and smaller. A lot smaller.' So he turns the dials and resets the probe, and all of a sudden the computer is spitting out images we can see and understand. It looked transparent and sorta humanlike, but not really. Anyway, we're following this thing, and then the boss says to point *all* the radio satellite dishes at it and try to track it that way, the way we do the stars in the daylight. Next thing you know, we hear the announcement.

"Well, it's all staticky and crackly, and we miss the first word, but of course I've been reading Dr. Ben-Judah's stuff, so I know what it is. Because the next two words are the same, and clear. I'm telling you, Captain, it freaked out *everybody*, and I mean everybody. Guys were on the floor, crying.

"They've been playing the tape over and over in there, and I even copied it on my dictation machine. But you know what? It records only in Greek. Everybody heard it in his own language, but it was Greek."

Buck heard the angel and mistook it for the TV until he saw the look on Chaim's face. The old man was terrified. How could he, or anyone, doubt the existence of God now? This was no longer about ignorance. It was about choice.

Rayford parked near the hangar where Ken Ritz had lived before moving to the safe house. There, his head under the hood of Ritz's Suburban, was Ernie, the new believer. He looked up and squinted through the haze as Rayford approached. Ernie smiled, shook his hand with enthusiasm, and pushed his greasy hat back on his head. The mark on his forehead stood out clearly as if he was proud of it, but he was also shivering.

"That was scary, wasn't it?" he said.

"Shouldn't be to those of us who knew it was coming," Rayford said. "You have nothing to fear. Not even death. None of us wants to die, but we know what comes next."

"Yeah," Ernie said, adjusting his hat again. "But still!"

"How's Ken's car doing?"

Ernie turned back to the engine. "Pretty good shape for all it's been through, I'd say."

"You find this therapeutic?"

"I'm sorry," Ernie said. "I was never much of a student. What's that mean?"

"Does it help you remember Ken without it being too painful for you?"

"Oh, well, I didn't really know him that long. I mean, I was shocked, and I'll miss him. But I just did stuff for him. He paid me, you know."

"But you both being believers—"

"Yeah, that was good. He put me onto that Ben-Judah guy's Web site."

A car pulled up to the rebuilt tower across the way and two men—in shirts and ties—got out. One was tall and black, the other stocky and white. The first went into the tower. The other approached Ernie and Rayford. Ernie emerged from under the hood again and pulled his cap low across his brow. "Hey, Bo!" he said. "D'ya hear that voice out of the sky?"

"I heard it," Bo said, obviously disgusted. "If you believe it was a voice from the sky, you're loopier than I thought."

"Well, what was it then?" Ernie said, as Bo studied Rayford.

"Those crazy fundamentalists again, playing with our minds. Some kind of loudspeaker trick. Don't fall for it."

Ernie emitted an embarrassed laugh and looked self-consciously at Rayford.

"Howdy," Bo said, nodding to Rayford. "Can I help you with something?"

"No thanks. Just a friend of Ken Ritz."

"Yeah, that was awful."

"Actually I just came by to see about his belongings. I don't believe there were any living relatives."

Ernie straightened up and turned around so quickly that even Bo seemed taken aback. It was clear both wanted to say something, but each looked at the other and hesitated. Then they both spoke at once.

Bo said, "And so you just thought you'd come by and see what you could—"

While Ernie was saying, "No, that's right. No relatives. In fact, he told me just a week or so ago that—"

Ernie conceded the floor first, and the man backed up and finished his thought: "—you'd come by and see what you could make off with, is that it?"

Rayford recoiled at such insensitivity, especially on the part of a stranger. "That's not it at all, sir. I—"

"Where do you get off calling me *sir*? You don't know me!"

Caught off guard, Rayford's old nature took over. "What, am I talking to an alien? How does polite society refer to strangers on your planet, *Bo*?" He hit the name with as much sarcasm as he could muster. Rayford was much taller, but Bo was built like a linebacker. With his blond crewcut, he looked the part too.

"Why don't you just take your opportunistic tail out of here while it's still part of your body?" Bo said.

Rayford was boiling and repenting of his attitude even as he spewed venom. "Why don't you mind your own business while I talk privately with Ernie?"

Bo stepped closer to Rayford and made him wonder if

he would have to defend himself. "Because Ernie's on my payroll," Bo said, "and everything on this property is my business. Including Ritz's effects."

Rayford took a deep breath and regained control of his emotions. "Then I'll be happy to talk to Ernie on his own time, and—"

"And on his own property," Bo added.

"Fine, but what gives you the right to Ken Ritz's stuff?"

"What gives *you* any right to it?"

"I haven't claimed any right to it," Rayford said. "But I think its disposition is a valid question."

Ernie looked ill. "Um, Bo, sir, Ken told me that if anything ever happened to him, I could have his stuff."

"Yeah, right!"

"He did! The planes, this car, his personal junk. Whatever I wanted."

Rayford looked suspiciously at Ernie. He didn't want to question a fellow believer, especially in front of an outsider, but he had to. "I thought you told me you two hardly knew each other."

"I'll handle this," Bo said. "That's bull, Ernie, and you know it! Ritz was part owner of this airport and—"

Rayford cocked his head quickly. That didn't mesh with what Ken had told Rayford about wanting to buy the place.

Bo must have noticed Rayford's reaction and assumed he knew more than Bo thought. "Well," he adjusted, midstream, "he made an offer anyway. Or was going to. Actually, yeah, an offer was made. So if there are assets in his estate, they would be the property of Palwaukee ownership."

Rayford felt his blood boil again. "Oh, that makes a lot of sense. He dies before your deal is consummated, so you take his estate in exchange for what? You're going to change the name of the place to Ritz Memorial? You take his assets and he gets what, posthumous ownership while you run it for him and take the profits?"

"So, what's your stake in this, smarty-pants?"

Rayford nearly laughed. Was he back on the playground in fourth grade? How had he come to a shouting match with a total stranger?

"As I said, I made no claim, but my stake now is to be sure nothing happens to my friend's legacy that he didn't intend to happen."

"He intended for me to have it," Ernie said. "I told you that!"

"Ernie," Bo said, "stick to your grease-monkeying and keep your nose outta this, will ya? And wipe that smudge off your forehead. You look like a snot-nosed rugrat."

Ernie tugged down on his cap and whirled around to busy himself under the hood again. He was muttering, "I'm takin' the stuff he said I could have, I'll tell you that right now. You're not bullyin' me into giving up what I know is rightfully mine. No way."

Rayford was disgusted with Ernie's obvious lies but even more so that he was ashamed of the mark of God.

And then it hit him. Only other believers could see the

mark. Was Rayford arguing with a fellow tribulation saint? He looked quickly at Bo's forehead, which, because of his haircut and his complexion and the breadth of his face, had been right in front of Rayford's eyes the whole time.

Even in the dense smog, Bo's skin was as clear as a baby's.

Buck felt restless. He sat across from Chaim Rosenzweig in the parlor of his estate and was nearly overcome with compassion for the man. "Doctor," he said, "how can you see and know and experience all we have endured—all of us, even you—these last few years and yet still resist the call of God on your life? Don't be offended. You know I care for you, as does Tsion and my wife and her father. You told an international audience on TV that Ben-Judah was proven correct in his interpretations of what is to come. Forgive me for being so forward, but the time is growing short."

"I confess I have been troubled," Rosenzweig said, "especially since Ben-Judah stayed with me. You have heard my arguments against God in the past, but no, not even I can deny he is at work today. It is too plain. But I have to say I don't understand your God. He seems mean-spirited to me. Why can he not get people's attention through wonderful miracles, as he did in the Bible? Why make things worse and worse until a person has no choice? I find myself resisting being forced into this by the very one who wants my devotion. I want to come willingly, on my own accord, if at all."

Buck stood and pulled back the drape. The skies were growing darker, and he heard a low rumble in the distance. Should he stay away from the window? The weather had not portended rain. What was the noise? He could see no more than ten feet through the heavy smoke.

"Doctor, God has blessed you beyond what any human deserves. If your wealth of friends, education, knowledge, creativity, challenge, admiration, income, and comfort do not draw you to him, what else can he do? He is not willing that any should perish, and so he resorts to judgments that will drive them to him or away from him forever. We're praying you will choose the former."

Rosenzweig appeared older than his age. Weary, drawn, lonely, he looked like he needed rest. But life was hard everywhere. Buck knew everything would head downhill from here. The old man crossed his legs, appeared uncomfortable, and set his feet flat on the floor again. He seemed distracted, and he and Buck had to raise their voices to even hear each other.

"I must tell you that your praying for me means more than I can s—" He furrowed his brow. "What *is* that noise?"

The rumble had become higher pitched and had developed a metallic sound. "It's like chains clanging together," Buck said.

"A low-flying craft?"

"The airports are closed, Doctor."

"It's getting louder! And it's darker! It's dark as night out there. Open that drape all the way, Cameron, please. Oh, my heavens!"

The sky was black as pitch and the racket deafening. Buck spun to look at Chaim, whose face matched Buck's own terror. Metal against metal clanged until both men covered their ears. Rattling, thumping against the windows now, the rumble had become a cacophony of piercing, irritating, rattling, jangling that seemed it would invade the very walls.

Buck stared out the window, and his heart thundered against his ribs. From out of the smoke came flying creatures—hideous, ugly, brown and black and yellow flying monsters. Swarming like locusts, they looked like miniature horses five or six inches long with tails like those of scorpions. Most horrifying, the creatures were attacking, trying to get in. And they looked past Buck as if Chaim was their target.

The old man stood in the middle of the room. "Cameron, they are after me!" he screamed. "Tell me I'm dreaming! Tell me it's only a nightmare!"

The creatures hovered, beating their wings and driving their heads into the window.

"I'm sorry, Doctor," Buck said, shuddering, his arms covered with gooseflesh. "This is real. It's the first of the three woes the angels warned about."

"What do they want? What will they do?"

"Tsion teaches that they will not harm any foliage like locusts usually do, but only those who do not have the seal of God on their foreheads." Chaim paled, and Buck worried he might collapse. "Sit down, sir. Let me open the window—"

"No! Keep them out! I can tell they mean to devour me!"

"Maybe we can trap one or two between the screen and the window and see them more clearly."

"I don't want to see them! I want to kill them before they kill me!"

"Chaim, they have not been given the authority to kill you."

"How do you know?" He sounded like a schoolboy now, doubting the doctor who's told him a shot won't hurt bad.

"I won't tell you they won't torment you, but the Bible says the victims they attack will want to die and be unable to."

"Oh, no!"

Buck turned a crank that swung open the window. Several creatures flew near the screen, and he quickly shut the window. Now trapped between, they flew crazily, straining, fighting, banging off each other. The harsh metallic sound increased.

"Aren't you the least bit curious?" Buck said, fighting to not turn from the sight of them. "They are fascinating hybrids. As a scientist, don't you want to at least see—"

"I'll be right back," Chaim cried, and he hurried away. He returned looking ridiculous, dressed head to toe in beekeeping garb: boots, bulky canvas body smock, gloves, hat with face mesh and material covering his neck. He carried a cricket bat.

Bloodcurdling screams rose above the clamor. Chaim rushed to the other window, threw back the drape, and fell to his knees. "Oh, God," he prayed, "save me from these creatures! And don't let Jonas die!"

Buck looked over Chaim's shoulder out to the gate. Jonas lay writhing, screaming, thrashing, slapping at his legs and torso, trying to cover his face. He was covered with the locusts. "We've got to get him inside!" Buck said.

"I can't go out! They'll attack me!"

Buck hesitated. He believed he was invulnerable to the creatures' stings, but his mind had trouble communicating that to his legs. "I'll go," he said.

"How will you keep the creatures out?"

"I can only do the best I can. Do you have another bat?"

"No, but I have a tennis racket."

"That'll have to do."

Buck headed downstairs with the racket. Chaim called after him, "I'm going to lock myself in this room. Be sure you've killed or kept out all of them before coming back in. And put Jonas in the front guest room. Will he die?"

"He'll wish he could," Buck said.

He waited at the front door. The smoke that had hung over the city for days was gone, having left just as dense a spread of the ghastly beings. Praying for courage, Buck opened the door and ran to Jonas, who now lay quivering and twitching.

"Jonas! Let's get you inside."

But he was unconscious.

Buck set the racket down and used both hands to grab the big man by the shoulder and roll him over. His face showed one welt, and he was beginning to swell. A barrel-chested, beefy man, Jonas was going to be difficult to move. Buck tried to remember the fireman's carry, but he couldn't get enough leverage to get Jonas off the ground.

The locusts, too tame a description for these revolting beasts, flew menacingly around Buck's head, and some even landed. He was astonished at their weight and thickness. And while he was relieved they didn't sting or bite, he heard their hisses and believed they were trying to drive him away from Jonas. When one hovered over Jonas's face, Buck snatched up the racket and stepped into a full, hard backhand, sending the locust rocketing through a window at the front of the house. The sensation of beast on strings felt as if he had smacked a toy metal car. His first order of business, if he ever got back into the house, was to board up that window and get rid of that animal.

Buck tucked the racket under his arm and resorted to pulling Jonas by his wrists, on his back, up to the house. About ten feet from the stairs, their progress stopped, and Buck discovered Jonas's waistband and belt had torn up grass as he slid. Buck spun him around and tucked the man's ankles under his own arms and kept going. When he reached the steps, he sucked it up, bent at the knees, and lifted Jonas up onto his shoulders. He believed the man outweighed him by a hundred pounds.

In the house he plopped Jonas into a chair, from which he nearly toppled before rousing enough to at least keep his balance. Another locust flew in before Buck could shut the door, and he smacked it with the racket as well. It skittered across the floor and rebounded off the wall, rattling as it rolled.

It lay stunned, its segmented abdomen heaving. Buck's first target chose that moment to attack, and Buck knocked it out of the air again.

He tried stepping on one and found its shell unbreakable. He nudged both onto the face of the racket with his foot and shoveled them out the door, slamming it shut before more could invade. He covered the broken window and helped the staggering Jonas to the front guest room. There Jonas stretched out on the bed, incoherent and groaning and tearing at the buttons on his shirt.

Knowing there was no remedy for the torture and agony the man would endure, Buck reluctantly left him and returned to the parlor upstairs. Like a person perversely drawn to a train wreck, Buck wanted a close look at these things, with a glass barrier between him and them.

Before unlocking the door, Chaim demanded that Buck double- and triple-check that he was not accidentally bringing a locust in with him. Buck found Chaim still shrouded in the beekeeper getup and wielding the cricket bat. After demanding to know Jonas was still alive, Chaim grabbed Buck's arm and dragged him to the window. Angry locusts, trapped between glass and screen, were front and center, ready for study. Buck knew that any unbeliever on the street had already suffered Jonas's fate and that it couldn't be long before the locusts would begin finding their way into homes and apartments. This was going to be the worst horror yet.

CHAPTER 17

RAYFORD GRABBED ERNIE by the collar and pulled him close, feeling the rage of a parent against a threat to his family.

"So you're an impostor, hey, Ernie?"

Rather than fighting, Ernie tried to hold his hat on with both hands. Rayford let go of his collar and drove his hand directly under the bill of the cap. Ernie flinched, obviously thinking he was about to take an uppercut to the nose, and released his grip just enough so Rayford sent his cap flying.

No wonder Ernie's mark had appeared so prominent. He had refreshed it with whatever he had used to create it in the first place. "You'd fake the mark, Ernie? The mark of the sealed of the Lord? That takes guts."

Ernie paled and tried to pull away, but Rayford grabbed the back of his neck and with his free hand pressed his thumb against Ernie's bogus mark. The smudge rubbed off. "You must have studied Tsion's teaching really well to replicate a mark you've never seen."

"What the heck is that?" Bo asked, seeming frozen to his spot.

"He faked the mark of—"

"I know all about that," Bo said, his eyes wide with fear. He pointed past Rayford. "I mean that!"

Rayford looked into the distance where the cloud of smoke was turning into a swarming wave of locusts. Even from a few hundred yards, they looked huge. And what a racket!

"I hate to tell you this, gentlemen, but you're in big trouble."

"Why?" Bo cried. "What is it?"

"One of your last warnings. Or another trick by the fundamentalists. You decide."

"Do what you want, Bo!" Ernie said. "I'm gettin' outta here!"

He lit out for the tower, which apparently appealed to Bo too. When Ernie had trouble opening the door, Bo skidded into him, plastering him against it. They both went down, Ernie holding his knee and whimpering.

"Get up and get in there, you sissy," Bo said.

"Yeah, well, so are you, you big sissy boy! Sissy boy Bo!"

Bo yanked the door open, and it banged Ernie's head. He swore and spun on his seat and kicked it shut as Bo was trying to get in. Bo dropped to one knee, sucking his slammed fingernail, and Ernie jumped up and stepped over him into the safety of the tower.

Rayford arrived at the door and tried to help Bo up, but Bo wrenched away. The locusts swarmed Bo. He kicked and screamed and ran in circles, and when Ernie opened the door to taunt him and laugh at him, he too was attacked. The black man who had been in the car with Bo appeared in the doorway, staring in horror at the suffering man and boy.

He shook his head slowly and looked up at Rayford. They noticed each other's marks immediately, and Rayford knew his was genuine because the locusts left him alone.

Rayford helped him fight off the locusts and haul the two onto a landing at the bottom of the stairs. As Bo and Ernie shook and swelled and fought for breath, Rayford accepted the man's handshake.

"T. M. Delanty," he said. "I go by T."

"Rayf—"

"I know who you are, Captain. Ken told me all about you."

"Sorry to sound rude," Rayford said, "but it's odd he never mentioned you." Odder still, Rayford thought, was their getting acquainted with two suffering victims at their feet.

"I asked him not to. It's great to know he was what I thought he was—a man of his word."

Rayford wanted to talk with T, but he felt obligated to do something for Bo and Ernie. "Anyplace we can put these guys?"

T nodded to a reception area with couches and chairs but otherwise empty. "I understand they're not going to die, but they're going to wish they could?"

Rayford nodded. "You study, do you?"

"I'm in Tsion's cyberclass, like pretty much every other believer in the world."

"I'd better check on Tsion and the others," Rayford said, pulling out his phone.

Chloe answered. "Oh, Dad! It's horrible! Hattie's already been attacked." Rayford heard her screaming in the background.

"Can Doc help?"

"He's trying, but she's cursing God and already wants to die. Tsion says this is just the beginning. He believes she'll be in torment for five months. By then *we're* going to want to put her out of her misery ourselves."

"We can pray she'll become a believer before that."

"Yeah, but Tsion doesn't think that guarantees instant relief."

That sounded strange to Rayford. He would have to ask Tsion about that later. "Everybody else all right?"

"Think so. I'm waiting to hear from Buck."

Buck was surprised to learn he had more capacity for revulsion. As he and Chaim knelt by the window, their faces inches from the locusts, he saw Scripture come to life. He couldn't imagine an uglier, more nauseating sight than the creatures before him. Tsion taught that these were not part of the animal kingdom at all, but demons taking the form of organisms.

As he took in their unique characteristics, he felt for Chaim. They both knew his protective covering would not save him in the end. These things were here to attack him, and time was on their side. They would find a way in, and when that happened, they would show no mercy.

"Good heavens, look at them!" Chaim said.

Buck could only shake his head. Contrasted with the beauty of God's creation, these mongrels were clearly from the pit. Their bodies were shaped like miniature horses armed for war. They had wings like flying grasshoppers. When one alighted on the window, Buck edged closer.

"Chaim," Buck said, his own voice sounding distant and fearful, "do you have a magnifying glass?"

"You want a closer look? I can hardly stand to peek at them!"

"They look like horses, but they don't have snouts and mouths like horses'."

"I have a very powerful magnifier in my office, but I'm not leaving this room."

Buck ran off and got it from the study near Chaim's bedroom. But as he dashed back he heard a dreadful, inhuman howl and the bumps and bangs of someone thrashing on the floor. The someone, of course, was Chaim Rosenzweig, and the howl was human after all.

One of the locusts had found a way in and had locked itself onto Chaim's wrist, between his glove and sleeve. The old man lay jerking as if in the throes of a seizure, wailing and crying as he slammed his hand on the ground, trying to dislodge the brute.

"Get it off me!" he bellowed. "Please, Cameron, please! I'm dying!"

Buck grabbed the thing, but it seemed stuck as if by suction. It felt like an amalgam of metal, spiny protrusions, and insect slime. He dug his fingers between its abdomen and Chaim's wrist and yanked. The locust popped free, twisted in his hand, and tried stinging him from one end and biting him from the other.

Though it had no effect on him, Buck instinctively threw it against the wall so hard it dented the plaster and rattled noisily to the floor.

"Is it dead?" Chaim cried. "Tell me it's dead!"

"I don't know that we can kill them," Buck said. "But I stunned a couple of other ones, and this one is immobile right now."

"Smash it," Chaim insisted. "Stomp on it! Smack it with the bat!" He rolled to his side in convulsions. Buck wanted to help him, but Tsion had been clear that he found in the Scriptures no mention of relief to the victims of a sting.

The magnifying glass lay on the floor a few feet from the unmoving locust. Keeping an eye on the creature, Buck held the glass over it, illuminated by the chandelier directly above. He nearly vomited at the magnified ugliness.

It lay on its side, appearing to regroup. The four horselike legs supported a horse-shaped body consisting of a two-part abdomen. First was a preabdomen in the torso area made up of seven segments and draped by a metallic breastplate that accounted for the noise when it flew. The posterior consisted of five segments and led to the scorpionlike stinger tail, nearly transparent. Buck could see the sloshing venom.

Its eyes were open and seemed to glare at Buck. In a strange way, that made sense. If Tsion was right and these were demons, they were madly conflicted beings. They would want to kill believers, but they were under instructions from God to torment only unbelievers. What Satan meant for evil, God was using for good.

Buck held his breath as he moved the glass and his own face closer to the locust. He had never seen a head like that on any living thing. The face looked like that of a man, but as it writhed and grimaced and scowled at Buck, it displayed a set of teeth way out of proportion. They were the teeth of a lion with long canines, the upper pair extending over the lower lip. Most incongruous, the locust had long, flowing hair like a woman's, spilling out from under what appeared to be a combination helmet and crown, gold in color.

Though no larger than a man's hand, the grossly overgrown combination insect, arthropod, and mammal appeared invincible. Buck was encouraged to know he could temporarily shock them with a hard blow, but he had neither killed nor apparently even injured any.

He had no idea how to toss the thing out of the house

without letting in dozens more. Buck scanned the room and noticed a heavy vase holding a large plant. Chaim was already incoherent, crawling to the door. "Bed," he said. "Water."

Buck pulled the plant from the vase and laid it on the floor, muddy roots and all. He turned the vase over and set it atop the locust, which had just begun to move about again. Within a minute he heard the metallic whirring as it banged again and again against the inverted vase.

It tried to escape through a small hole in what had become the top of its makeshift prison, but it could only poke its head through. Buck staggered and nearly fell when it seemed to shout, as if crying for help. Over and over it repeated a phrase Buck could not understand.

"Do you hear that, Dr. Rosenzweig?" Buck asked.

Chaim lay by the door, panting. "I hear it," he rasped, groaning, "but I don't want to! Burn it, drown it, do something to it! But help me to bed and get me some water!"

The creature called out in a mournful keen what sounded to Buck like "A bad one! A bad one!"

"These things speak!" Buck told Chaim. "And I think it's English!"

Rosenzweig shook as if the temperature had dropped below freezing. "Hebrew," he said. "It's calling out for Abaddon."

"Of course!" Buck said. "Tsion told us about that! The king over these creatures is the chief demon of the bottomless pit, ruler over the fallen hordes of the abyss. In the Greek he has the name Apollyon."

"Why do I care to know the name of the monster that

killed me?" Rosenzweig said. He reached up for the doorknob but could not unlock the door with his gloves on. He shook them off but could no longer raise an arm.

Buck got him up, and as they lumbered out of the parlor, he looked back at the locust trying to squeeze out of the vase. It looked at him with such hatred and contempt that Buck nearly froze.

"Abaddon!" it called out, and the tiny but gravelly voice echoed in the hallway.

Buck kicked the parlor door shut and helped Chaim into his bedroom. There Buck peeled the rest of the beekeeper garb off Chaim and helped him lie back atop the covers on his bed. Convulsions racked him again, and Buck noticed swelling in his hands and neck and face. "C-c-could y-y-you g-g-g-et me some w-water, p-please!"

"It won't help," Buck said, but he got it anyway. Parched himself, he poured into a glass some from the bottle he found in the refrigerator and quenched his own thirst. He grabbed a clean glass and returned. He set the bottle and the glass on a stand next to the bed. Chaim appeared unconscious. He had rolled on his side, covering his ears with a pillow, as the haunting cries continued from the parlor.

"Abaddon! Abaddon! Abaddon!"

Buck laid a hand on the old man's shoulder. "Can you hear me, Chaim? Chaim?"

Rosenzweig pulled the pillow away from his ear. "Huh? What?"

"Don't drink the water. It's turned to blood."

Rayford and T. M. Delanty stood outside the empty reception area at the base of the Palwaukee Airport tower, peering in at Bo and Ernie, who cursed each other as they writhed on the floor.

"Is there nothing we can do for them?" T asked.

Rayford shook his head. "I feel sorry for them and for anybody who has to endure this. If they had only listened! The message has been out there since before the Rapture. What's their story, anyway? Ernie had me convinced he was a believer—had the mark and everything."

"I was shocked to see him attacked," T said, "but part of that had to have been my fault. For days he sounded interested, said Ken was urging him to log on and check out what Tsion Ben-Judah was teaching. He asked so many questions, especially about the mark, that between what he learned from Tsion and what Ken and I said about it, he was able to fake it."

Rayford looked out. The sky was still filled with the locusts, but all but a few had moved away from the door. "I never thought about anyone being able to counterfeit the mark. I figured the mark, distinguishable only by another believer, was a foolproof test of who was with us and who wasn't. What do we do now—try the smudge test on anybody who's bearing the mark?"

"Nope," T said. "Don't have to."

"Why's that?"

"You're not testing *my* mark, are you? Why do you assume I'm legit?"

"Because you weren't attacked."

"Bingo. For the next ten months, that is our litmus test."

"Where are you getting ten months?"

"You haven't read Dr. Ben-Judah today?"

Rayford shook his head.

"He says the locusts have five months to find their prey and sting them and that the victims suffer for five months. He also believes, though he admitted it was just conjecture, that the locusts bite a person once, and then they move on."

"Have you taken a look at these things?" Rayford said, studying one on the other side of the window.

"Do I want to?" T said, approaching. "I didn't even like reading about them in Dr. Ben-Judah's lessons. Oh, boy, look at that! That is one ugly monstrosity."

"Be glad they're on our side."

"Talk about irony," T said. "Ben-Judah says they're demons."

"Yeah, but they're moonlighting for God for a while."

Both men cocked their heads. "What's that sound?" Rayford said. "Tsion said their flight would sound like horses and chariots riding into battle, but I hear something else."

"Are they chanting?" T said.

They cracked the door an inch or so, and a locust tried to squeeze through. Rayford shut the door on it, and it squirmed and flailed. He released the pressure, and it flew back out. "That's it!" Rayford said. "They're chanting something."

The men stood still. The cloud of locusts, on its way to fresh targets, called out in unison, "Apollyon, Apollyon, Apollyon!"

"Why would God do this to me?" Chaim whined. "What did I ever do to him? You know me, Cameron! I am not a bad man!"

"He did not do this, Dr. Rosenzweig. You did it to yourself."

"What did I do that was so wrong? What was my sin?"

"Pride, for one," Buck said, pulling up a chair. He knew there was nothing he could do for his friend but keep him company, but he was past gentility.

"Proud? I am proud?"

"Maybe not intentionally, Doctor, but you have ignored everything Tsion has told you about how to connect with God. You have counted on your charm, your own value, your being a good person to carry you through. You get around all the evidence for Jesus being the Messiah by reverting to your educational training, your confidence only in what you can see and hear and feel. How many times have you heard Tsion quote Titus 3:5 and Ephesians 2:8-9? And yet you—"

Chaim cried out in pain. "Quote them to me again, Cameron, would you?"

"'Not by works of righteousness which we have done, but according to His mercy He saved us. . . . For by grace you have been saved through faith, and that not of yourselves; it is the gift of God, not of works, lest anyone should boast.'"

Chaim nodded miserably. "Cameron, this is so painful!"

"Sad to say, it will get worse. The Bible says you will want to die and won't be able to commit suicide."

Chaim rocked and cried in anguish. "Would God accept me if I relent only to ease my torture?"

"God knows everything, Doctor. Even your heart. If you knew you would still suffer, worse and worse for five months, regardless of your decision, would you still want him?"

"I don't know!" he said. "God forgive me, I don't know!"

Buck turned on the radio and found a pirate station broadcasting the preaching of Eli and Moishe from the Wailing Wall. Eli was in the middle of a typically tough message. "You rant and rave against God for the terrible plague that has befallen you! Though you will be the last, you were not the first generation who forced God's loving hand to act in discipline.

"Harken unto these words from the ancient of days, the Lord God of Israel: I have withholden the rain from you, when there were yet three months to the harvest: and I caused it to rain upon one city, and caused it not to rain upon another city: one piece was rained upon, and the piece whereupon it rained not withered.

"So two or three cities wandered unto one city, to drink water; but they were not satisfied: yet have ye not returned unto me. . . .

"I have smitten you with blasting and mildew: when your

gardens . . . increased, the palmerworm devoured them: yet have ye not returned unto me. . . . I have sent among you the pestilence after the manner of Egypt: your young men have I slain with the sword, . . . yet have ye not returned unto me. . . . I have overthrown some of you, as God overthrew Sodom and Gomorrah, and ye were as a firebrand plucked out of the burning: yet have ye not returned unto me. . . .

"Therefore thus will I do unto thee, O Israel: and because I will do this unto thee, prepare to meet thy God, O Israel. For, lo, he that formeth the mountains, and createth the wind, and declareth unto man what is his thought, that maketh the morning darkness, and treadeth upon the high places of the earth, The Lord, The God of hosts, is his name. . . .

"Thus saith the Lord unto the house of Israel, Seek ye me, and ye shall live: . . . Ye who turn judgment to wormwood, and leave off righteousness in the earth, Seek him that maketh the seven stars and Orion, and turneth the shadow of death into the morning, and maketh the day dark with night: that calleth for the waters of the sea, and poureth them out upon the face of the earth: The Lord is his name. . . .

"Therefore the prudent shall keep silence in that time; for it is an evil time. Seek good, and not evil, that ye may live: and so the Lord, the God of hosts, shall be with you, as ye have spoken. Hate the evil, and love the good, and establish judgment in the gate: it may be that the Lord God of hosts will be gracious unto the remnant of Joseph. . . .

"Though ye offer me burnt offerings and your meat offerings, I will not accept them: neither will I regard the peace offerings of your fat beasts. Take thou away from me the noise of thy songs; for I will not hear the melody of thy viols.

"But let judgment run down as waters, and righteousness as a mighty stream."

"Wow," Buck said.

"Please, Cameron!" Chaim said. "Turn it off! I can take no more."

Buck sat another two hours with Chaim, helpless to ease his suffering. The man thrashed and sweated and gasped. When finally he relaxed a moment, he said, "Are you sure about this getting worse and worse until I despair of my life?"

Buck nodded.

"How do you know?"

"I believe the Bible."

"It says that? In those words?"

Buck knew it from memory. "'In those days men will seek death and will not find it,'" he said. "'They will desire to die, and death will flee from them.'"

CHAPTER 18

DURING THE ENSUING five months, the demon locusts attacked anyone who did not have the seal of God on his or her forehead. And for five months after that, those among the last bitten still suffered.

The starkest picture of the interminable suffering came from Hattie's ordeal at the Tribulation Force's safe house in Mount Prospect, Illinois. Her torment was so great that everyone—Rayford, Tsion, Chloe, and Floyd—begged her to give in to Christ. Despite her anguished screams at all hours of the day and night, she stubbornly maintained that she was getting what she deserved and no less.

Listening to her around the clock became so stressful to

the Force that Rayford made an executive decision and moved her to the basement where Ken had lived. As weeks passed she became a shell of even the unhealthy frame she had been. Rayford felt as if he were visiting a living corpse every time he went down there, and he soon quit going alone. It was too frightening.

Doc Charles tried to treat her symptoms, quickly discovering it was futile. And the rest took turns delivering her meals, which were rarely touched. She ate much less than should have been required to keep her alive, but as the Bible predicted, she did not die.

It got to where Rayford had to visit Hattie with one of the others, and even then he didn't sleep well afterward. Hattie was skeletal, her dark eyes sunk deep into her head. Her lips stretched thin and taut across teeth that now looked too big for her mouth.

Eventually she could not speak, but communicated by a series of grunts and gestures. Finally she refused to even turn and look when someone came down.

Hattie finally forced herself to talk when Chloe somehow located her sister Nancy, working at an abortion clinic out west. All the other members of Hattie's family had died in various ways before the plague of locusts. Now Hattie spoke to her sister for the first time in months. Nancy had somehow avoided for a few months the sting of a scorpion locust, but now she too was a victim.

"Nancy, you must believe in Jesus," Hattie managed,

though she spoke as if her mouth was full of sores. "It's the only answer. He loves you. Do it."

Floyd had overheard Hattie's end of the conversation and asked Rayford and Tsion to join him in talking to her. But she was more belligerent than ever. "But it's so obvious you know the truth," Tsion said. "And the truth shall set you free."

"Don't you see I don't want to be free? I only want to stay alive long enough to kill Nicolae, and I will. Then I don't care what happens to me."

"But we care," Rayford said.

"You'll be all right," she said, rolling over and turning her back to them.

Chloe, getting toward the end of her pregnancy, finally couldn't navigate the stairs. She told Rayford that the prayer of her life now was that Buck would somehow make it home before the baby was born.

Tsion was busier than ever. He passed on miraculous reports from the 144,000 witnesses who had fanned out to serve as missionaries to every country, not just their own. Stories poured in of obscure tribal groups understanding in their own languages and becoming tribulation saints.

Tsion wrote to nearly a billion Web site visitors every day that this was the last period during the end of time when believers would have any semblance of freedom. "Now is the time, my dear brothers and sisters," he wrote. "With everyone else vulnerable to the attacks of the locust hordes, they must stay inside or venture out only with bulky protective gear. This is our chance to put into place mechanisms that will allow us to survive when the world system requires its own mark one day. We will be allowed to neither buy nor sell without the mark, and it is a mark that once taken seals the fate of the bearer for all time—just as the mark we now bear has sealed us for eternity.

"I beg of you not to look upon God as mean or capricious when we see the intense suffering of the bite victims. This is all part of his master design to turn people to him so he can demonstrate his love. The Scriptures tell us God is ready to pardon, gracious and merciful, slow to anger, and abundant in kindness. How it must pain him to have to resort to such measures to reach those he loves!

"It hurts us to see that even those who *do* receive Christ as a result of this ultimate attention-getter still suffer for the entire five months prescribed in biblical prophecy. And yet I believe we are called to see this as a picture of the sad fact that sin and rebellion have their consequences. There are scars. If a victim receives Christ, God has redeemed him, and he stands perfect in heaven's sight. But the effects of sin linger.

"Oh, dear ones, it thrills my heart to get reports from all over the globe that there are likely more Christ followers now than were raptured. Even nations known for only a minuscule Christian impact in the past are seeing great numbers come to salvation.

"Of course we see that evil is also on the rise. The Scriptures tell us that those who remain rebellious even in light of this awful plague simply love themselves and their sin too much. Much as the world system tries to downplay it, our society has seen catastrophic rises in drug abuse, sexual immorality, murder, theft, demon worship, and idolatry.

"Be of good cheer even in the midst of chaos and plague, loved ones. We know from the Bible that the evil demon king of the abyss is living up to his name—Abaddon in Hebrew and Apollyon in Greek, which means Destroyer—in leading the demon locusts on the rampage. But we as the sealed followers of the Lord God need not fear. For as it is written: 'He who is in you is greater than he who is in the world. . . . We are of God. He who knows God hears us; he who is not of God does not hear us. By this we know the spirit of truth and the spirit of error.'

"Always test my teaching against the Bible. Read it every day. New believers—and none of us are old, are we?—learn the value of the discipline of daily reading and study. When we see the ugly creatures that have invaded the earth, it becomes obvious that we too must go to war.

"Finally, my brethren, with the apostle Paul I urge you to 'be strong in the Lord and in the power of His might. Put on the whole armor of God, that you may be able to stand against the wiles of the devil. For we do not wrestle against flesh and blood, but against principalities, against powers, against the rulers of the darkness of this age, against spiritual hosts of wickedness in the heavenly places.

"'Therefore take up the whole armor of God, that you may be able to withstand in the evil day, and having done all, to stand. Stand therefore, having girded your waist with truth, having put on the breastplate of righteousness, and having shod your feet with the preparation of the gospel of peace; above all, taking the shield of faith with which you will be able to quench all the fiery darts of the wicked one.

"'And take the helmet of salvation, and the sword of the Spirit, which is the word of God; praying always with all prayer and supplication in the Spirit, being watchful to this end with all perseverance and supplication for all the saints—and for me, that utterance may be given to me, that I may open my mouth boldly to make known the mystery of the gospel.'

"Until next we interact through this miracle of technology the Lord has used to build a mighty church against all odds, I remain your servant and his, Tsion Ben-Judah."

Buck knew that Jacov and Hannelore and Stefan had grown in their faith when they insisted on moving into the Rosenzweig estate and caring for Chaim and Jonas for several months. They brought with them Hannelore's mother, who had received Christ the day the locusts attacked. Even in her suffering she read and studied and prayed, often pleading with Chaim and Jonas to also come to Christ. Even after Jonas did, Chaim remained resolute.

Unable to find a commercial flight that had a full crew, Buck desperately searched among the saints to find someone who might charter him back to the States for the birth of his child. At wit's end, he tried calling Mac in New Babylon but was unable to get through. He tried e-mailing him a heavily coded message, and an hour later received a lengthy reply.

> I'm still looking forward to meeting you, Mr. Williams. Of course, your father-in-law has told me all about you, but don't worry, I didn't believe a word of it.
>
> How do you like the e-mail system David has set me up with here? He's built into it all the safeguards you could imagine. If someone walked in on me right now, they wouldn't be able to read what I've just written.
>
> I gather you need a charter flight out of there. Try Abdullah Smith in Jordan. The name looks weird, but he has his reasons. And he is a believer. Mention my name and he'll charge you double (just kidding). If he can handle the job, he'll take care of you.
>
> I'll copy this to your people so they'll know what's going on here. David Hassid and I had to fake locust stings to keep from revealing ourselves. In the process we discovered several other clandestine believers in the ranks here. Carpathia and Leon are quarantined in a fallout shelter that has served to keep out the locusts too, though almost everyone else, including the ten rulers and even Peter the Second, have been stung and are suffering. When you see Carpathia on the news telling everyone that the stories of poisonous bites are exaggerated while he sits there with a locust on his shoulder as

a pet, don't believe it. It's a trick of photographic technology. Of course, the real things probably wouldn't bite Nicolae or Leon out of professional courtesy.

A few of us believers have been able to pretend we are simply recuperating more quickly, so we don't lie around the infirmary twenty-four hours a day listening to the agony. Carpathia has sent me on some missions of mercy, delivering aid to some of the worst-off rulers. What he doesn't know is that David has picked up clandestine shipments of literature, copies of Tsion's studies in different languages, and has jammed the cargo hold of the Condor 216 with them. Believers wherever I go unload and distribute them.

Word has gotten back to Leon that all this Christian literature is flooding the globe, and he's furious about it. So is Peter the Second. I hope someday they both find out how it was transported. But not yet. Pray for us. We're your eyes and ears in New Babylon, and light as I try to make it all sound, we're in very precarious positions. Subversives are punished by death here. Two close members of Peter Mathews's staff were executed for mentioning to Global Community personnel something Peter thought was private. Carpathia heard about the executions and sent him a note of congratulations. Of course, Peter is on Nicolae's hit list, or at least for sure on Leon's. Leon believes there's no need for *any* religion because we have His Excellency the potentate to worship.

I say that with irony, but Leon is dead serious. David was in the room when Leon suggested passing a law that people have to bow in Nicolae's presence. That may be the end of me.

The believers here cannot meet for fear of suspicion and detection, but we encourage each other in subtle ways. Fortunately, David has been elevated to a position that puts him on a level close to the senior pilot (yours truly), so we are expected to interact a lot. We love the late Ken Ritz's idea for the believers' commodity co-op, for lack of a better handle, and we think your wife will make an absolutely smashing CEO. You know who her direct competition will be, of course. Carpathia himself is personally (really) taking charge of global commerce, effective immediately. You heard it here first. He wants those ten kings in his hip pocket, doesn't he?

You know, Mr. Williams, I heard something on the Condor a few days before the locusts attacked that proved one of Dr. Ben-Judah's points. Remember when he wrote that this period is not just a grand war between good and evil, but also a war between evil and evil? I think his point was that we were to love each other and make sure the crises don't turn us on each other and spur fights between good and good. But anyway, Mathews and Saint Nick and the ever-present Leon-my-whole-Fortunato-is-tied-to-you-Excellency are aboard the Condor 216. (I finally figured out the significance of Carpathia's obsession with that number, by the way. Well, actually David told me. He thought everybody knew. Your quiz for the week.)

So on the plane ol' Mathews is really putting the screws to Carpathia. He's demanding this and urging that and begging for more share of the taxes for all the wonderful stuff Enigma Babylon is going to do for the Global Community. Nicolae is yessing him and uh-huhing him to beat the band. Mathews takes a bathroom break and Nicolae tells Fortunato, "If you don't have him hit, I'll do the job myself."

Of course Leon tells him, "He's outlived his usefulness, and I'm working on it."

Well, didn't mean to ramble, but with all the afflicted here, I've got more alone time than I'll probably ever have again. All the best with the little one. We'll pray you get home in time and that Mama is up and around in time to get back to work and make a parent out of you. Greet everyone for me.

In the name of Christ, Mac M.

Still grieving the loss of Ken Ritz, missing his interaction with Mac McCullum, and reeling from the attempted infiltration of the bumbling Ernie, Rayford took his time getting to know T. M. Delanty. While Ernie and the irrepressible Bo were ensconced at Arthur Young Memorial Hospital in Palatine, Rayford made several trips to the Palwaukee Airport to sift through Ken's things. As often as not, he'd see T.

They shared life stories over a couple of lunches, and Rayford knew they had taken a step toward potential friendship when he mustered the courage to ask, "What does T. M. stand for?"

T gave him a you-had-to-ask-didn't-you? look. "If I wanted people to know that, I wouldn't have resorted to initials."

"Sorry. Just wondered why you go by T, that's all."

"I've got a crummy first name, what can I tell you? My mother was African-American and my father Scotch-Irish. Heavy on the Scotch, sad to say. She named me after an old schoolteacher of hers. Tyrola made a good last name, but if you were hung with that moniker, what would you go by?"

"I'd go buy a ticket out of town, T. Sorry I asked. Middle name wasn't an option?"

"Mark."

Rayford shrugged. "What's wrong with that?"

"Nothing, except do I look like a Mark? Admit it, I look like a T."

Tyrola Mark Delanty was the only member of his small

church to be left behind at the Rapture. "I was suicidal," he said. "And I can't say I've had much fun, even since I finally got right with God. Lost a wife of fourteen years and six kids, my whole extended family, friends, church people, everybody."

Rayford asked whom he met with now.

"There are about thirty believers in my neighborhood. More all the time. Neighborhood is overstating it, of course. We're all living in our original homes, but they're worthless. Just happened to not fall over, so there are living spaces."

After a few meetings, Rayford and T finally got around to the subject of Ken and Palwaukee and Bo and Ernie. It turned out that T was the major owner of the airport, having bought it from the county a couple of years before the Rapture. "Never made much money at it. Low margin, but it was turning. Ken and several other regulars flew out of here. Ken lived here, as you know, until the earthquake when he moved in with you guys."

Bo was the only son of a wealthy investor who owned 5 percent of the business but who had died in a car wreck when the Rapture took drivers from cars in front and in back of his. "In the ensuing chaos, Bo shows up as the sole heir, trying to act like a board member and a boss. I humored him until he brought Ernie on. I fought it at first. He was a nineteen-year-old who had dropped out of school when he was fourteen but reputed to be a natural mechanic. Well, it turned out he was, and he helped a lot around here. I only put it together the day of the locust attack that Ernie and Bo had a scheme going."

"Why would they have wanted Ernie to infiltrate our group?"

"Rumor was that Ken had a lot of money. Ernie was trying, I think, to get in good with him. He and Bo would have run some scam on him and tried to cash in. When Ken was killed, they went into high gear. You saw the sad result of that comical effort."

Rayford studied T, trying to decide whether to ask what he thought of the rumors about Ken's wealth. He decided not to pursue it yet, but T made the question moot. "The rumors were true, you know."

"As a matter of fact, I do know," Rayford said. "How did *you* know?"

"Ken really wanted to buy the airport, and I really wanted to sell it. That was my hope all along, but now I had a different motive. Rebuilding it after the earthquake really strapped me, and I needed to cash out. I wanted to pour a little money into our tiny congregation and see if we couldn't accomplish something for God in the few years we have left. I asked Ken if he could afford market value for the airport, and he assured me he could."

"Did he happen to say where he banked?"

T smiled. "We're still feeling each other out, aren't we? Still playing cat and mouse."

"I was just wondering," Rayford said.

"Yes, I think we're both up to speed."

"What do you think should be done with Ken's assets, T?"

"Used for God. Every last dime. That's what he would have wanted."

"I agree. Does that money belong to anyone else? Legally, I mean?"

"Nope."

"And you have access to it?"

"You want to dig with me, Rayford?"

"I don't know. What're you paying?"

"Unless Ken told you you could have it, I believe rightfully it's mine. It was left on my property. I'm not sure where, and I'm not sure how much. But I'd sure like to get at it before Bo and Ernie recuperate."

Rayford nodded. "Your little church can make use of all that?"

"Like I said, we want to see if we can do something significant. We wouldn't build a church or fix up our homes."

"Any inkling how much you're talking about?" Rayford said.

"Maybe over a million."

"Would it surprise you to know it's probably five times that?"

"Are we negotiating, Rayford? You want some of this, think you're entitled to it, what?"

Rayford shook his head. "I'd like to be able to buy his planes. I have no claim on his money or anything else."

"I'll tell you what," T said. "If there's half as much money as you think there is, I'll give you his planes."

"How much for the Gulfstream?"

"If there's as much as you say there is, you can have that one too."

"And can I fly out of here?"

"You can house 'em, keep 'em up, and live here with 'em if you want."

"And may a Jordanian fly my son-in-law in here within twenty-four hours, no questions asked?"

"You got it, brother."

Rayford broached the subject of a world commodity co-op among believers, coordinated out of the Tribulation Force safe house. "Any interest in getting behind that, delivering, running charters, that type of thing?"

"Now *that* I could get excited about," T said. "My little band of believers too, I'll bet."

Buck met Abdullah Smith in an outdoor café run by a young woman on the tail end of her recuperative season. Abdullah was as secretive and quiet as just about anyone Buck had ever met. But he had a clear mark on his forehead and was healthy. He embraced Buck with vigor despite being a laconic conversationalist.

"The name McCullum is all I need to hear, sir. We are brothers, the three of us. I fly. You pay. Nothing more need be said."

And it wasn't. At least by Abdullah. Buck told him he was

making one last social call and would meet him at the airport in Amman at six that evening. "I would appreciate a stop in northern Greece, and then straight to the Chicago area."

Abdullah nodded.

The streets of Jerusalem were largely deserted. Buck had never grown used to the sobbing and howling he heard on every corner. It seemed many suffered in every household. He heard that thousands in Jerusalem had slit their wrists, tried to hang themselves, drunk poison, stuck their heads in gas ovens, put plastic bags over their heads, sat in garages with cars running, even jumped in front of trains and leaped off buildings. They were severely injured, of course, and some were left looking like slabs of butchered meat. But no one died. They just lived in torment.

Buck found Rosenzweig's home a little quieter, but even Chaim begged to be put out of his misery. Jacov reported that Chaim had taken no nourishment—none—for more than a week. He was trying to starve himself to death or develop a fatal case of dehydration. He looked terrible, emaciated and wan.

Jonas and Jacov's mother-in-law were more stoic. Though clearly suffering, they did what they could to help themselves. They slept, they ate, they got up and around. They tried medication, though it seemed to make no difference. The point was in trying. They looked forward to the day they would be free from the effects of the sting. Jonas, in particular, was childlike in his excitement over reading the Bible with Jacov and having Tsion Ben-Judah's daily cyberspace message read to him.

Chaim merely wanted to die. Buck sat on his bed until the old man cried out in agony. "Everything hurts, Cameron. If you cared a whit about me, you would free me from this misery. Have compassion. Do the right thing. God will forgive you."

"You're asking the impossible, and I wouldn't do it anyway. I wouldn't forgive myself if I didn't give you every opportunity to believe."

"Let me die!"

"Chaim, I do not understand you. I really don't. You know the truth. Your suffering will be over in several weeks and—"

"I will *never* survive that long!"

"And you'll have something to live for."

Chaim was silent and still for a long time, as if peace had come over him. But it had not. "To tell you the truth, my young friend, I don't understand either. I confess I want to come to Christ. But a battle rages within me, and I simply cannot."

"You can!"

"I cannot!"

"Not being able to is not the problem, is it, Doctor?"

Chaim shook his head miserably. "I will not."

"And you deny my charge that your pride keeps you from God."

"I admit it now! It *is* pride! But it's there and it's real. A man cannot become what he is not."

"Oh, that's where you're wrong, Chaim! Paul, who had been an orthodox Jew, wrote, 'If anyone is in Christ, he is a new creation; old things have passed away; behold, all things have become new.'"

Chaim thrashed painfully for several minutes, but he said nothing. To Buck, that was progress. "Chaim?" he said softly.

"Leave me alone, Cameron!"

"I'll be praying for you."

"You'll be wasting time."

"Never. I love you, Chaim. We all do. God most of all."

"If God loved me, he would let me die."

"Not until you belong to him."

"That will never happen."

"Famous last words. Good-bye, friend. I'll look forward to seeing you again."

CHAPTER 19

RAYFORD LOVED HIS DAUGHTER with all that was in him. He always had. It wasn't just because she was the only family he had left. He had loved Raymie too and still missed him terribly. Losing two wives in fewer than three years was a blow he knew would be with him until Jesus came again.

But his relationship with Chloe had always been special. They'd had their moments, of course, when she was going through the process of breaking away from the family and becoming an independent young woman. Yet she was so much like him.

That had made it difficult for her to believe that God was behind the disappearances in the first place. Flattered that she took after him and yet afraid her practicality might forever keep her from Christ, Rayford had agonized over her. The greatest day of his life—excluding when he himself became a believer—was when Chloe made her decision.

He was thrilled when she and Buck married, despite the ten-year age difference. He didn't know what he thought when he heard they were expecting and that he would be a grandfather with fewer than five years left on earth.

But seeing Chloe in the full bloom of her pregnancy, he was transported. He remembered Irene, despite difficult pregnancies, looking radiant the further she progressed and, yes, the bigger she got. He had read all the books, knew the pitfalls. Rayford understood that Irene would not believe him when he said she was most beautiful when she was very pregnant.

She had said the same things Chloe was saying now—that she felt like a cow, a barn, a barge. She hated the swollen joints, the sore back, the shortness of breath, the lack of mobility. "In a way I'm glad Buck is stuck in Israel," she said. "I mean, I want him back and I want him back now, but he's going to think I've doubled in size."

Rayford took the occasion to sit with Chloe. "Sweetheart," he said, "indulge me. It may be politically incorrect to say that you are doing what you were meant to do. I know you're more than a baby-making machine and that you have incredible things to offer this world. You made an impact even before the Rapture, but since, you've been a soldier. You're going to make the world commodity co-op a lifesaver for millions of saints. But you need to do me a favor and stop bemoaning what this pregnancy is doing to your body."

"I know, Daddy," she said. "But it's just that I'm so—"

"Beautiful," he said. "Absolutely beautiful."

He said it with such feeling that it seemed to shut her up. She looked different, of course. Nothing was the same. With only a few weeks until her due date, she was full faced and ponderous. But he could still detect his little girl there, his Chloe when she had been a toddler, full of life and curiosity.

"I'm frustrated for Buck that he can't see you like this. Now don't look at me like that. I mean it. He will find you so lovely, and believe it or not, he will find you attractive too. You're not the first mom-to-be who equates pregnancy with being overweight. Husbands don't think that way. He'll see you the way I saw your mother when she was carrying you. He'll be overcome with the knowledge that you're carrying his and your child."

Chloe seemed to appreciate the pep talk. "I'm really stressed about him coming home," she said. "I know he's leaving Israel at six their time, but who knows how long he'll be in Greece?"

"Not long. He wants to get home."

"And it being a charter, they'll keep moving I think. I wish I could meet him at the airport."

"Doc says you shouldn't—"

"Ride in the car, especially on these roads, I know. I don't really want to endure that. But Buck and I have been apart so long. And as much as we worry about bringing a baby into the world at this time in history, we've both grown so attached to this child already that we can't wait to meet him . . . or her."

"I can't wait to be a grandfather," Rayford said. "I've been praying for this child since I knew it existed. I just worry that life is going to be so hard for all of us that I won't get the opportunity to be the kind of grandpa I want to be."

"You'll be great. I'm glad you're not still flying for Carpathia. I wouldn't want to worry about you all the time."

Rayford stood and looked out the window. The morning sun was harsh. "I'm getting back into the war," he said.

"What does that mean?"

"Well, I can blame it on you. You've taken Ken's idea so far that it's going to give me a full-time job. I'm going to be flying almost as much as when I was with Pan-Con."

"For the co-op?"

He nodded. "I've told you about T."

"Uh-huh."

"We're going to run the airlift operation out of Palwaukee. I'll be flying all over the world. If those fishermen in the Bering Strait are as successful as you seem to think they'll be, I'll have enough business up there to last till the Glorious Appearing."

Floyd Charles knocked on the doorjamb. "Time for a little checkup. You want Dad to wait outside?"

"What're we doing?" Chloe said.

"Just checking heartbeats, yours and Junior's."

"He can stay. Can he listen?"

"Sure."

Floyd took Chloe's pulse first, then listened to her heart with his stethoscope. He spread lubricating jelly on her protruding belly and used a battery-powered monitor to amplify the liquid sounds of the fetal heartbeat. Rayford fought tears, and Chloe beamed. "Sounds like a big boy to me," Doc Charles said.

As he finished up, Chloe asked, "Everything still fine?"

"No major problems," he said.

Rayford glanced at Floyd. He was not as light as usual. He had not even smiled when he joked about her having a boy. She didn't want to know the sex of the baby, and he had never tested to find out.

"How about other than major problems, Floyd?" she said, her voice flat. "You usually say everything's great."

She had spoken exactly what was on Rayford's mind, and his heart sank when Floyd pulled up a chair.

"You noticed that, did you?" he said.

"Oh, no," she said.

Floyd put a hand on her shoulder. "Chloe, listen to me."

"Oh, no!"

"Chloe, what did I say? I said no major problems, and I meant it. Do you think I would say that if it wasn't true?"

"So what's the minor problem?"

"Some reduction in the baby's pulse."

"You're kidding," Rayford said. "If I'd had to guess, I would have said it sounded too fast."

"All fetal pulses are faster than ours," Floyd said. "And the reduction is so slight that I hardly gave it a second thought last week."

"This has been going on for a week?" Chloe said.

Floyd nodded. "We're talking about a fraction of a percentage decrease in six days. It doesn't have to mean anything."

"But if it means anything," Chloe said, "what would it mean?"

"We don't want to see an actual slowdown of the fetal pulse. Like 5 percent, especially 10 percent or more."

"Because . . . ?"

"Because that could mean some threat to viability."

"English, Doctor," Chloe said.

"As the baby gets into position for birth, the umbilical cord could tighten around the chest or the neck."

"Do you think that's happening?"

"No. I'm just watching heart rate, Chloe. That's all."

"Is it a possibility?"

"Anything is a possibility. That's why I'm not listing everything that can go wrong."

"If this is so minor, why are you telling me?"

"For one thing, you asked. I just want to prepare you for a form of treatment should the symptoms persist."

"But you said the reduction in rate right now is not worth worrying about."

"OK, if the symptoms get worse."

"What would you do?"

"At least get you on oxygen for the better part of each day."

"I need to stand up a minute," Chloe said.

She started to move, and Rayford reached to help. Floyd didn't. "Actually," he said, "I'd prefer that you take it very easy until I can get out and get you some oxygen tomorrow."

"I can't even stand up?"

"For necessities. If it's just to shift position, try not to."

"All right," she said, "my dad and I are bottom-line people. Give me the worst-case scenario."

"I've dealt with enough pregnant women, especially at this stage of gestation, to know it's not best to dwell on all the negative possibilities."

"I'm not pregnant women, Doc. I'm Chloe, and you know me, and you know I'm going to bug you to death until you tell me the worst case."

"All right," he said. "I see the oxygen solving the problem. If it doesn't, I'll have you on monitors around the clock to warn of a significant change in fetal pulse. Worst case, we might want to induce labor. It might mean a cesarean section because of the likelihood of an umbilical cord problem."

Chloe fell silent and looked at Rayford. He said, "You don't like to induce, right?"

"Of course not. I used to say nature knows best. That baby comes when he is ready. Now I know that God knows best. But he has also given us brains and miracle medicines and technologies that allow us to do what we need to do when things don't go the way we wish."

Chloe looked uncomfortable. "I need to know one thing, Floyd. Did I contribute to this? Was there something I shouldn't have done, or something I should have done differently?"

Floyd shook his head. "I wasn't wild about your going to Israel. And if I never hear again about you running from helicopter to jet, it'll be too soon. But overexertion at that stage of pregnancy would have shown up in different problems."

"Such as?"

"Such as nothing that turned up, so I'm not going to talk about it. How's that? You've already been through all the predictable stuff—convinced you're going to have a monster, convinced the baby has already died, certain your baby doesn't have all its parts. You don't need to worry about stuff you might have caused but didn't. Now when do you expect Papa?"

"Sometime tonight," she said. "That's all I know."

Abdullah Smith seemed pleased that Buck showed up when he said he would. "I heard you were a man of your word," Buck said, "and wanted to show that I am too."

Abdullah, as usual, did not respond. He grabbed one of Buck's bags and led him briskly toward his plane. Buck tried to guess which one it would be. He passed the prop jobs, knowing they would never get him across the Atlantic. But Abdullah also passed a Learjet and a brand-new Hajiman, a smaller version of the *Concorde* and just as fast.

Buck stopped and stared when Abdullah pulled back the

Plexiglas cockpit shield of what he recognized as an Egyptian fighter jet. It would fly nearly two thousand miles an hour at very high altitudes but had to have a shorter than usual fuel range.

"This is your plane?" Buck said.

"Please to board," Abdullah said. "Fuel tank enlarged. Small cargo hold added. Stop in Greece, stop in London, stop in Greenland, stop in Wheeling."

Buck was impressed that he knew where he was going. It was clear his hope of stretching out, getting some reading done, even dozing, was not in the cards.

"Passenger must board first," Abdullah said.

Buck climbed in and tried to show that he knew his way around this type of craft, after having done a series of articles on ride-alongs with American fighter pilots. That was before the reign of Nicolae Carpathia and the wholesale marketing of such surplus craft to private citizens.

Buck was about to strap on his helmet and oxygen mask when Abdullah sighed and said, "Belt."

Buck was sitting on it. So much for showing off. He had to stand, as much as one could in that confined space, while Abdullah reached beneath him to retrieve the belt. Once strapped in, he tried to put the helmet on. Again the pilot had to assist—untangling his straps, twisting the helmet just so, and smacking it on top until it settled into correct, and extremely tight, position. It pressed against Buck's temples and cheekbones. He started to put the mouthpiece in until Abdullah reminded him, "Not until high altitude."

"Right. I knew that."

Abdullah fit just ahead of him, giving Buck the feeling they were on a luge, Abdullah's head just inches from Buck's nose.

Taking a jet fighter from a staging area, out onto the tarmac, into line, and then out onto the runway would have taken up to half an hour in the States. Buck learned that in Amman, the airport was like the street market. No lines or queues. It was first come, first served, and you were on your own. Abdullah sang something into the radio about jet, charter, passenger, cargo, and Greece, all while moving the fighter directly onto the runway. He didn't wait for instructions from ground control.

The Amman airport had only recently reopened after rebuilding, and while air traffic was down because of the plague of locusts, several flights were lined up. Two wide-bodies sat at the front of the line, followed by a standard jet, a Learjet, and another big plane. Abdullah turned to get Buck's attention and pointed to the fuel gauge, which showed full.

Buck gave a thumbs-up sign, which he intended to imply that he felt good about having lots of fuel. Abdullah, apparently, took it to mean that Buck wanted to get into the air—and now. He taxied quickly around other planes, reached the line of craft cleared and in line for takeoff, and passed them one by one. Buck was speechless. He imagined if the other pilots had horns, they'd have been honking, like drivers in traffic do to those who ride the shoulder.

As Abdullah passed the second wide-body, the first began

to roll. Abdullah slipped in behind it, and suddenly he and Buck were next in line. Buck craned his neck to see if emergency vehicles were coming or whether the other planes would just pull ahead and get back in their original order. No scolding came from the tower. As soon as the big jet was well on its way down the runway, Abdullah pulled out.

"Edward Zulu Zulu Two Niner taking off, tower," he said into the radio.

Buck fully expected someone to come back with, "Just where do you think you're going, young man?" But no one did.

"Ten-four, Abdullah," was all he heard.

There was no warming up and little building speed. Abdullah drove the fighter to the end of the runway, lined her up, and punched it. Buck's head was driven back, and his stomach flattened. He could not have leaned forward if he'd wanted to. Clearly breaking every rule of international aviation, Abdullah reached takeoff speed in a few hundred yards and was airborne. He rocketed above and beyond the jet in front of him, and Buck felt as if they were flying straight up.

He was pressed back in his seat, staring at clouds. It seemed only minutes later Abdullah reached the apex of his climb, and just like that, he seemed to throttle back and start his descent. It was like a roller-coaster ride, blasting to the peak and then rolling down the other side. Abdullah mashed a button that allowed him to speak directly into Buck's headset. "Amman to Athens just up and down," he said.

"But we're not going to Athens, remember?"

Abdullah smacked his helmet. "Ptolemaïs, right?"

"Right!"

The plane shot straight up again. Abdullah dug through a set of rolled-up maps and said, "No problem."

And he was right. Minutes later he came screaming onto the runway of the small airport. "How long with friends?" he said, taxiing to the fuel pumps.

Rayford reassured Chloe, and they agreed they'd rather Floyd tell the truth than sugarcoat it and run into problems later. But after he brought her water, Rayford moved upstairs to talk to Tsion. The rabbi welcomed him warmly. "Almost finished with my lesson for today," he said. "I'll transmit it in an hour or so. Anyway, I always have time for you."

Rayford told him of the potential complication with the baby. "I will pray," Tsion said. "And I would ask you to pray for me as well."

"Sure, Tsion. Anything specific?"

"Well, yes. Frankly, I feel lonely and overwhelmed, and I hate that feeling."

"It's sure understandable."

"I know. And I have a deep sense of joy, such as we get when we are in fellowship with the Lord. I have told him this, of course, but I would appreciate knowing someone else is praying for me too."

"I'm sure we all do, Tsion."

"I am most blessed to have such a loving family to replace my loss. We have all suffered. Sometimes it just overtakes me.

I knew this locust plague was coming, but I never thought through the ramifications. In many ways I wish we had been more prepared. Our enemy has been incapacitated for months. Yet while we count on them for so many things, like transportation, communications, and the like, this has crippled us too.

"I don't know," he said, rising and stretching. "I don't expect to find happiness anymore. I am looking forward to the birth of this little one as if it were my own. That will bring a ray of sunshine."

"And we want you to be another parent to it, Tsion."

"The contrast alone will be sobering though, won't it?

"The contrast?"

"This fresh, young innocent will not know why Hattie is crying. Won't know of our losses. Won't understand that we live in terror, enemies of the state. And there will be no need to teach the little one of all the despair of the past, as we would if we were raising it to adulthood. By the time this baby is five years old, it will already be living in the millennial kingdom with Jesus Christ in control. Imagine."

Tsion had a way of bringing perspective to everything. Yet Rayford was sobered by the rabbi's angst. Millions around the world expected Dr. Ben-Judah to be their spiritual leader. They had to assume he was at peace with his own mature walk with God. Yet he was a new believer too. While a great scholar and theologian, he was but a man. Like most others, he had suffered grievously. He still had his days of despair.

Rayford began feeling lonely in advance. Floyd would

have plenty of doctoring to do in the safe house with a new baby and Hattie still ailing. Buck had told Rayford he looked forward to some modicum of normalcy and permanence, so he could make his Internet magazine what it needed to be to compete with Carpathia's Global Community rags. Chloe would be busy with the baby and the details of the commodity co-op. And Hattie, when she finally recuperated, would itch to get out of there.

That left Rayford to be the one on the go. He looked forward to being back in the cockpit. He had resigned himself to the fact that his life would consist of hard work, being careful to remain free and just trying to stay alive. But the Glorious Appearing seemed further away all the time. How he longed to be with Jesus! To be reunited with his family!

His life as an accomplished commercial pilot seemed eons ago now. It was hard to comprehend that it had been fewer than three years since he was just a suburban husband and father, and none too good a one, with nothing more to worry about than where and when he was flying next.

Rayford couldn't complain of having had nothing important to occupy his time. But the cost of getting to this point! He could empathize with Tsion. If the Tribulation was hard on a regular Joe like Rayford, he couldn't imagine what it must be like for one called to rally the 144,000 witnesses and teach maybe a billion other new souls.

Early in the afternoon Rayford took a call from T Delanty. "I want to start digging tomorrow," he said. "You still willing to help?"

"Wouldn't miss it. If my son-in-law gets in at a decent hour, I'll be ready when you are."

"How about seven in the morning?"

"What's the rush?"

"I hear Ernie's getting better. Bo probably would be too, but he tried to kill himself three ways. He's a mess."

"Buy him out."

"I will, and that will be easy because the way we're set up, all I have to do is make him an offer he can't match. He was left some money, but his share in the airport is so small, I should be able to make him go away. I worry about Ernie."

"How so?"

"He was close to Ken, Ray. At least as close as a person could hope to get. I know Ken considered him a believer; he had me fooled too."

"I'm the third stooge on that list," Rayford said.

"It's possible Ken confided in Ernie."

"Nah. He only just told *me* on the flight to Israel."

"You say that like you guys have been buddies for years. He hardly knew you, Rayford, and yet he told you he buried his gold. I had heard the rumor myself, and I don't feel like I knew Ken well at all. Ernie worked with him, ingratiated himself. I don't believe for a second that Ken promised him a thing. That wouldn't make sense. But still I'll bet Ernie knows more than he'll let on."

"You think he'll get better and show up with a shovel?"

"I wouldn't put it past him."

"First, Mr. Williams, call me Laslos. It comes from my first name, Lukas, and my last name, Miklos. OK?"

Buck agreed as they embraced in the small air terminal. "And you must call me Buck."

"I thought your name was Cameron."

"My friends call me Buck."

"Then Buck it is. I want to take you to meet with the believers."

"Oh, Laslos, I'm sorry. I cannot. I'd love to, and maybe I will get back here and do that. But do you understand that I have been away from my wife for many months—"

Laslos looked stricken. "Yes, but—"

"And that she is in her last couple of weeks of pregnancy?"

"You're going to be a father! Splendid! And everything is fine, except that this is the worst time . . . well, you know that."

Buck nodded. "My father-in-law wanted me to discuss with you your role in the international commodity co-op."

"Yes!" Laslos said, sitting and pointing to a chair for Buck. "I have been reading what Dr. Ben-Judah says about it. It is a brilliant idea. What would we do without it? We would all die, and that is what the evil one wants, right? Am I not a good student?"

"Do you see a role for yourself or your company?"

Laslos cocked his head. "I'll do what I can. My company mines lignite. It is used in power plants. If there is any call for it in the community of believers, I would be happy to be involved."

Buck leaned forward. "Laslos, do you understand what it will mean when citizens of the Global Community are required to wear the sign of the beast on their hand or on their forehead?"

"I think so. Without it they cannot buy or sell. But I do not consider myself a citizen of the Global Community, and I would die before I would wear the sign of Antichrist."

"That's great, friend," Buck said. "But do you see how it will affect you? You will not be able to sell. Your whole business and livelihood are built on a product you sell."

"But they need my product!"

"So they will put you in jail and take over your mines."

"I will fight them to the death."

"You probably will. What I'm suggesting is that you look for another commodity to trade, something more internationally marketable, something your brothers and sisters in Christ need and will be unable to get when the mark of the beast is ushered in."

Laslos appeared deep in thought. He nodded. "And I have another idea," he said. "I will build my lignite business and sell it before they quit buying from me."

"Great idea!"

"It happens all the time, Buck. You make yourself so indispensable to your biggest client that it only makes sense that they buy you out."

"And who is your biggest client?"

Laslos sat back and smiled sadly, but Buck detected a gleam in his eye. "The Global Community," he said.

CHAPTER 20

RAYFORD RAN INTO Floyd Charles angrily slamming stuff around. "Which vehicle can I use?" Floyd asked.

"Makes no difference, Doc," Rayford said. "Rover's running fine. I'm taking Ken's Suburban to T tomorrow. See if his little church group can use it. It's rightfully his anyway."

"I'll take Buck's."

"Where you going?"

"I've got to get some oxygen, Ray. I don't want to be caught off guard without O_2 when I need it. And I don't want Chloe as stressed as I am."

"That bad? Should I be worried?"

"Nah! It's not Chloe as much as Hattie now. She thinks

she's better, so she wants to get up and get out. Well, she can't without help, and I'm not going to help her. She *has* made a turn for the better, but she's underweight, and her vitals are average. But, like you say, she doesn't report to us."

"You want me to talk to her? Maybe I can shame her into doing what you say, after all we've done for her."

"If you think it'll do any good."

"Where you getting O_2, Kenosha?"

"I don't dare show my face there again. I called Leah at Arthur Young. She's got a couple of tanks for me."

"You know who you can check in on over there? Hattie's young Ernie."

"No kidding?"

"T told me Ernie and his friend Bo were being treated there."

Buck was ill by the time Abdullah landed at Heathrow. Cramped, nauseated, exhausted, tense—he was a mess. All he wanted was to get home to Chloe.

Heathrow was a shell of what it had been before World War 3 and the great earthquake. But Carpathia had poured money into it and made it high-tech and efficient, if not as big as it had been. With the waning population, nothing needed to be as big as before.

Heathrow tower flatly rejected Abdullah's announced sequences. He seemed frustrated but didn't rebel. Buck wondered what he did before becoming a believer. Maybe he'd been a terrorist.

Abdullah seemed cognizant of Buck's wish to keep moving. He returned from refueling with two cellophane-wrapped cheese sandwiches that looked as if they'd been sitting for days. He offered one to Buck, who refused only because he was queasy. Abdullah must have assumed Buck was in too great a hurry to eat, because as soon as the deliberate ground control officer cleared him for takeoff, they were streaking toward Greenland.

Buck felt as if he were running a sprint that would never end. He assumed that at some point he could try to relax, but the jet seemed always on the verge of exploding or crashing. When his phone chirped in his pocket, Buck went through all sorts of vain gyrations to get in a position where he could reach it.

Abdullah noticed and asked if anything was wrong. "Need an emergency landing?" he asked.

"No!" Buck hollered, sensing the hope in Abdullah's question. Apparently a normal race from Jordan to America wasn't enough of a thrill for Abdullah. But where does one execute an emergency landing between London and Greenland? Surely he would have had to turn back to London, but Abdullah seemed more likely to find an aircraft carrier.

When they finally reached Greenland for the final refueling, Buck extricated himself from his seat and learned that his caller had been Dr. Charles. He called him back.

"I can't really talk to you right now, Buck, sorry. I'm picking up supplies at a hospital."

"Well, give me a hint, Doc. Everything OK there?"

"Let's just say I hope you're on schedule."

"That doesn't sound good. Chloe OK?"

"We all need you here, Buck."

"Spill it, Doc. Is she OK?"

"Buck, let me get free for a minute here so we can talk."

"Please!"

Buck heard Floyd asking someone named Leah if she would excuse him. "All right, Buck. Are you on schedule?"

"I'm surprised I'm not ahead of schedule, but yes, we're looking at a 10:00 p.m. arrival."

"That late?"

"You're scaring me, Doc."

"The truth is, Buck, I've been misleading Chloe and Rayford today. The fetal heartbeat has been dropping for a few days, and it's at the alarming stage."

"Meaning?"

"I'm putting Chloe on oxygen as soon as I get back there. I wanted to do it hours ago, but I ran into a snag at the hospital. I dropped in on somebody Rayford knows who was recuperating here. He sounded real interested in hearing about the judgments and what they meant, and I wound up spending way too much time with him. Hattie's been talking to his younger friend, who's apparently already been released."

Buck stood in the cold wind and hollered into the phone. "Doc, I haven't a clue what you're talking about. I'm sorry to be rude, but get to the point. Why did you think it necessary to mislead Chloe and Ray when they're right there and can deal with the problem, but you drop it on me in the middle of nowhere when I can do nothing?"

"If you had seen how they reacted when I just hinted at the problem, you'd know I was right. I need Chloe to stay upbeat, and if she knew how serious this is, she would not be in a position to do her part."

Abdullah signaled Buck to reboard. "Will I still be able to talk on the phone?"

"Yes, yes!"

But in the air the noise was awful. Buck and Floyd had to repeat almost every sentence, but Buck finally got the whole scoop. "Is there any chance you'll have to induce before I get there?"

"I'm through making promises."

"Do what's best for Chloe and the baby!"

"That's what I wanted to hear."

He needs permission for that? Buck wondered.

"And tell Rayford the truth, Doc! I think Chloe can take it too, but if you think it would put her into a tailspin, use your own judgment. She's pretty tough, you know."

"She's also very pregnant, Buck. That floods the body with a hormone wash and turns a woman into a mother hen."

"Just don't say or do something you have to apologize for later. She's going to want to know why she wasn't fully informed."

"Rayford will be there to get you, Buck. I've got another call. Godspeed!"

Rayford was relieved when Doc Charles finally answered. "Where are you, man? You've been gone for hours!"

Floyd told him of meeting Bo and getting sidetracked telling him about God. "The other guy was discharged this morning. Anyway, what's up?"

"Chloe is not feeling well, and of course she's worried. Is there anything we should do for her?"

"What's her complaint?"

"Shortness of breath. Extreme fatigue."

"I'll get there as soon as I can. Put her in a position where her lungs can expand the most. Can you handle the fetal monitor?"

"We'll get it done between the two of us if it's important."

"Call me with the results in ten minutes."

Buck liked Doc, and it felt strange to be angry with him. But a trained medical professional should be more buttoned-down, less hung up on periphery. Here he was, his own life in Abdullah's hands, rocketing through the air to get home to his wife, and he gets this news. What was he supposed to do but pray? Buck believed in prayer and exercised it to the fullest. But anxiety just about did him in, and he could easily have been spared it. There'd be plenty of time to worry once he got there.

Rayford felt all thumbs getting the fetal monitor working, and at first he feared the heartbeat had disappeared. "God, please, no!" he prayed silently. "Not this on top of everything else." For all the talk about the inadvisability of bringing a baby into the world during the Tribulation, everyone in the house had a huge stake in this birth.

Suddenly they heard the speeding heart. "Do you just count and multiply?" Rayford asked.

"I don't know," Chloe said, panting. "Can you count that fast? It's still fast, but is it slower than before?"

"It wouldn't change enough in a few hours that we'd be able to tell without precise measurement."

"Then get it to work!"

An LCD readout came to light. When Rayford called the figure in to Floyd, he told Ray to worry more about Chloe than the baby. "I want her to breathe deeply and get all the oxygen she can until I get there. But Ray, I've got a problem. I'm being followed."

"You're sure?"

"No question. I've taken several detours, and I can't shake him."

"What kind of car?"

"A motorcycle. One of those little jobs they race off road. No way I'm going to outrun him."

"Lead him around awhile. See if he gets bored. Some guys just get a kick out of worrying people."

"He's smooth, Ray. He's far enough back to not be obvious, but he's stayed with me for miles. I don't want to give away our location to anybody, but I also need to get this oxygen to Chloe."

"I'll take care of her. Keep me posted."

"Uh, I'm a little low on fuel, and those cycles can go forever."

"How close are you to Palwaukee?"

"Close."

"I'll call T. Whoever's following you isn't going to follow you into an enclosed area. And T will gas you up too."

"Great."

Rayford called T and filled him in.

"Oh, no," T said.

"What?"

"Ernie's a bike racer. He probably followed your man from the hospital, trying to find out where Hattie lives. They've been talking more."

"How do you know?"

"A phone girl here said Hattie called for Ernie, and she told her he was at Young Memorial. But if Hattie wanted to see him, wouldn't she just have told Ernie where she was?"

"She doesn't know where she is, T. She knows it's Mount Prospect, but there's no way she could tell him how to get here."

"If your man leads Ernie here, I'll give him what for. We'll keep him from finding you, you can be sure of that. What's he driving, and what does he look like?"

"The Rover and you."

"Come back?"

"He's driving Buck's Rover, and he looks a lot like you."

Rayford arranged pillows so Chloe could lie back and raise her arms over her head without hurting herself or the baby. That opened her lungs more, and she said she felt a little better. Rayford was startled when he turned and saw Hattie at the top of the basement stairs.

She looked awful, like a ghost or worse, a zombie. Thin, eyes dark, skin pale. She limped to Chloe.

"Hattie!" Chloe said. "It's been ages."

"I wanted to see how my godchild was doing."

"Not here yet, Hattie. We'll let you know."

"And I wanted to tell you I'm not jealous."

Rayford squinted, watching Chloe's reaction.

"You're not, huh?" she said. "I never thought you would be."

"Who would blame me if I was? I lost my baby, but you get to have yours. You're lucky, I'm not. The story of my life."

Rayford wanted to talk to her alone. No way he wanted Chloe to know what was going on. "We're sorry for your loss, Hattie," he said. "And we're grateful you still want to be godmother to Chloe's child."

"We were going to be godmothers to each other's," she said.

"It has to be painful," Chloe said.

"It's going to be for the one who did it," Hattie said.

"If you'll excuse us," Rayford said, "we're trying to do a little doctoring by phone here." He dialed Floyd.

Hattie drifted away without a word.

Floyd told Rayford he was within a mile of Palwaukee. "But this guy's still hanging with me."

Rayford didn't want to leave Chloe, but he didn't want to alarm her either. "If you're comfortable for a while, honey, I want to talk with Hattie."

Buck found himself fighting drowsiness. That should have been no surprise. He had been up since dawn in the Middle East. Despite the noise and thin air, he was desperate to talk with someone in Mount Prospect. He feared upsetting Chloe, and Rayford might be tending to her. He understood Hattie had been incoherent for months. That left Tsion.

What time was it in the States? Late afternoon? The rabbi should be putting the finishing touches on his daily missive. Buck called him. They'd have to yell and repeat themselves, but any contact was better than none.

"Cameron, my friend! How good to hear from you! Where are you?"

"First, Tsion, assure me I am not keeping you from your work. The world waits with bated breath for everything you—"

"I posted it not twenty minutes ago, Cameron. This is a

perfect time to talk. We're all excited about the baby and your return. Now where are you?"

"I wish I knew. We're chasing the sunset, but at high altitude in an old jet fighter, I can't even look down. I'd be looking at the Atlantic, that's all I know."

"We will see you in a few hours. There are few small pleasures left in this life, Buck, and rejoining friends and brothers and spouses is one of those. We have been praying for you every day, and you know Chloe is most excited. You'll be home in plenty of time for the birth, which will likely take place at the hospital in Palatine."

Buck hesitated. "Tsion, you will be honest with me, won't you?"

"Always."

"Are you trying to keep me upbeat because you don't know about complications with Chloe and the baby, or because you do?"

"Your father-in-law briefed me. Dr. Charles seems to have it under control. Rayford reached you with the news?"

"Actually, Floyd did, and it's worse than Rayford and Chloe know."

"Should he not tell them?"

"He has his reasons. I just wondered if Floyd had talked with you."

"No. I heard someone leave hours ago. I assumed it was he."

"He's worried I won't be back in time if he has to induce."

"Induce? Why did he not take her to the hospital then?"

"Frankly, Tsion, I've been killing myself with questions since he called. I don't know what Floyd expected of me."

There was a pause. "Cameron, there is nothing you can do until you get here, except to pray. You have to leave this with the Lord."

"I've never been good at that, sir. I know we're not supposed to worry, but—"

"Oh, Cameron, I think even the Lord himself allows some latitude on that during the Tribulation. The admonition to not worry was written to people who lived before all the judgments. If we did not worry about what was coming next from heaven, we would not be human. Don't feel guilty about worrying. Just rely on the Lord for the things you cannot control. This is one of them."

Buck loved talking with Tsion. They had been through so much together. It hit him that he was whining about his wife's complicated pregnancy to a man whose wife and children had been murdered. Yet somehow Tsion had the capacity for wisdom and clear thinking and had a calming effect on people. Buck wanted to somehow keep him on the phone.

"Do you mind talking a little while longer, Tsion?"

"Not at all. I was beginning to feel isolated anyway."

"How's Hattie?"

"Quieter. The worst is over for her, though she is going to require a long recovery."

"No movement spiritually, Chloe tells me."

"A tough case, Cameron. I fear for her. I hoped she was merely getting things off her chest and that once she spewed her venom she would turn to God. But she has convinced me she is sincere. She believes in God, knows that he loves her, and knows what he has done for her. But she has decided that she knows better than he, and that she is one person who chooses not to accept his gift for the very reason the rest of us jumped at it."

"She knows she's unworthy."

"It's difficult to argue with. She is an adult, an independent moral agent. The choice is hers, not ours. But it is painful to see someone you care for make a decision that will cost her her soul."

"I don't want to keep you, Tsion, but what was your message today? It's unlikely I'll get to read it for days, and I need all the encouragement I can get."

"Well, Cameron, as we come to the end of the suffering caused by the locusts, it's time to look ahead to at least the next two 'woes.'"

"So Trumpet Judgment six is next. What do you expect there?"

Tsion sighed. "The bottom line, Cameron, is an army of two hundred million horsemen who will slay a third of the world's population."

Buck was speechless. He had read the prophecy, but he had never boiled it down to its essence. "What possible word of encouragement could you have left people with after that bit of news?"

"Only that whatever we have suffered, whatever ugliness we have faced, all will pale in comparison to this worst judgment yet."

"And the ones after this get even worse?"

"Hard to imagine, isn't it?"

"Makes my worry over our baby seem insignificant. I mean, not to me, but who else can get worked up about it when a third of mankind will soon be wiped out?"

"Only one-fourth of the people left behind at the Rapture will survive until the Glorious Appearing, Cameron. I am not afraid of death, but I pray every day that God will allow me the privilege of seeing him return to the earth to set up his kingdom. If he takes me before that, I will be reunited with my family and other loved ones, but oh, the joy of being here when Jesus arrives!"

Rayford found Hattie outside. "What're you doing?" he asked.

"Getting some air. It's nice to be able to move around a little."

"Doc thinks it's too early."

"Doc's in love with me, Rayford. He wants to keep me here, incapacitated if necessary."

Rayford pretended to study the horizon. "What gives you that idea?"

"He didn't tell me in so many words," she said. "But a woman knows. I'll bet you've noticed."

Rayford was happy to say he had not. He had been surprised when Floyd told him of his feelings, but he was also surprised to know that Hattie had sensed it.

"Has he told you, Rayford?"

"Why do you ask?"

"He has! I knew it! Well, I'm not interested."

"He had a crush. I'm sure you've pushed him away by now."

Hattie looked disappointed. "So he's got the picture that there's no hope?"

Rayford shrugged. "It's not like we talk about it."

"Does he know you had a crush on me once?"

"Hattie, you sound like a schoolgirl."

"Don't deny it."

"Deny what? That I had a wholly inappropriate attraction to a younger woman? We both know nothing ever came of it and—"

"Only because a bunch of people disappeared and you started feeling guilty."

Rayford turned to go back into the house.

"I still make you nervous, don't I?"

He turned. "I'll tell you what makes me nervous. It's your obsession with this kid at the airport."

"Ernie? I want to meet him, that's all."

"Did you tell him where we are, how to get here?"

"I don't even know."

"Did you tell him Floyd was coming to the hospital?"

Hattie looked away. "Why?"

"Did you?"

"I might have."

"That was pretty stupid, Hattie. So what's the plan? His buddy, Bo, distracts Floyd long enough for Ernie to go get his bike and follow Floyd back to you?"

Hattie looked stricken. "How do you know all this?"

"You're working with a teenager, Hattie. And you're acting like one too. If you want to see this kid so bad, why don't you ask one of us to take you there?"

"Because Floyd is jealous of him and doesn't want me to even talk to him on the phone. Then he convinces you I'm too sick to go anywhere, so you won't take me."

"So Ernie's trying to come here to what, get acquainted?"

"Yeah."

"Bull. Do you know he faked being a believer to get next to Ken and might have infiltrated us if we hadn't caught on?"

Hattie appeared to be hiding a smile, which infuriated Rayford. "You knew about that too?" he demanded.

"When I told him I wasn't really part of the Tribulation Force, he told me his plan. It's what I kinda like about him."

"That he would endanger our lives? That he's an opportunist? A gold digger?"

She shrugged. "The other men in my life are getting boring."

Rayford shook his head. "I hope you're happy with him."

"Is he coming here?"

"Floyd's trying to shake him, but he may have to lead him here. We can't withhold oxygen from Chloe just because

Floyd has a kid following him. I hope you're happy. There's no way we can trust that kid once he knows where we are. We'll have to move again, and where will we go? And could we, with a woman about to give birth or with a brand-new baby? You go on about not being worthy of God's forgiveness, and then you try to prove it."

Rayford went in and let the door shut behind him. He hesitated, wanting to say more but not knowing what. She opened the door. "Come back, Rayford. Chloe's in trouble?"

"Could be. Needs that oxygen."

"Floyd obviously has his phone with him."

"Yep."

"Call him. Let me talk to him."

Rayford dialed.

"Hey, Rafe," Floyd said. "He didn't follow me into the airport, but after meeting T, I know why. We're thinking of switching cars and seeing if the kid will follow him. That's one advantage to our looking alike."

"Good idea, but Hattie wants to talk to you."

"Hi, Doc. Listen, Ernie will talk to me. Just hold the phone out the window of the car and stop. . . . Yeah, I think he will. It's worth a try."

CHAPTER 21

"I HAVE BEEN going too fast!"

Buck was startled awake. Had Abdullah said something? "I'm sorry?" he shouted.

"I have been going too fast!"

Had he been pulled over by the air police, or what? "We're ahead of schedule then?"

"Yes, but I burned more fuel than I planned, and we need to refuel in New York."

Buck just wanted to get home. "Where are you going to put down? New York was last on Carpathia's refurbishing list. Still blaming the U.S. for the rebellion, I guess."

"I know a place. You will be in Wheeling in two hours."

Buck checked his watch. It was seven in the Midwest. If they were on the ground by nine, he could be to the safe house before ten. There would be no more sleeping.

Rayford sat with Chloe, who looked pale, her lips bluish. This was getting ridiculous. He had the feeling the baby would be born in that house tonight, and he was going to do everything he could to be sure it had every chance.

"All right, sweetie?"

"Just exhausted, Dad." She seemed to keep shifting so she could breathe better. He knew she was unaware of how serious that was. When his phone rang, he flipped it open so quickly he dropped it.

"Sorry," he said, picking it up. "Steele here."

"Ray, it's Doc. We switched the oxygen to T's red Jeep, and I'm on my way. How's our girl?"

"Yes."

"You're right there with her?"

"Correct."

"On a scale of one to ten, one being the worst, how do you rate her?"

"Five."

"I'd ask for another fetal pulse, but there's nothing I can do until I get there anyway."

Rayford stood and turned his back to Chloe, moseying to look out the window. Hattie was outside, talking animatedly on her phone. "What's happening with T?" he asked.

"I think Biker took the bait, but he's going to recognize his old boss right away. We just hope he'll stop and talk to Hattie anyway."

"I'm only guessing, Doc, but I think he's doing that now. Please hurry."

"What's going on, Daddy?" Chloe asked.

"Doc got hung up at the hospital and had to run an errand on the way back. He's coming with the oxygen."

"Good. And he thought it could wait until tomorrow."

"He was only hoping."

"My baby's going to be all right, isn't it?"

"If you keep breathing deeply until the O_2 gets here," Rayford said, eager to talk to Hattie. "I'm going to get some air."

"Get me some," she said, smiling weakly.

"Just do it, Ernie," Hattie was saying, her back to Rayford as he stepped out. "Prove you're a man, and I mean it." She heard the door and slapped her phone shut.

"Cooled his jets," she said.

"Yeah? How?"

"Just told him the situation and that it was stupid of me to ask him to try to get here. I told him maybe you'd take me to Palwaukee one of these days if I take care of myself."

"Maybe. What's he going to do now?"

"Go home, I guess."

"He lives at the airport."

"That's what I mean."

"He got bit the same day you did. How's he feeling?"

"Pretty weak, I guess, but he said it was fun to get out riding again."

Rayford's phone rang. "Excuse me, Hattie," he said, but she didn't move. "Am I going inside?" he added. "Or are you?"

"Well, excuse me!" she said and left.

"Steele."

"It's T. Ol' Ernie turned three colors when he caught up and found out I was driving. He started to scoot away, but I said, 'Your girlfriend's on the phone.' He took it and the first thing he said was, 'No, it isn't.' I'm sure I didn't sound like Doc Charles, and she probably asked him if that's who I was. Then she really must have been reading him the riot act because all he did was apologize and say yes a dozen times."

"She claims she told him to back off and that she'd see him again some other time."

"Doc's long gone, so Ernie's out of options anyway. He headed back to Palwaukee. At least he said he did."

"You busy tonight, T?"

"I let everybody else go home, and I was going to handle Buck's arrival. We took a message out of New York that they've refueled and should be here by nine. You know they're in a Z-two-nine?"

"The Egyptian fighter? You're kidding."

"That's what it says. He could make it from New York in an hour if he had to. Anyway, what do you need?"

"Keep an eye on Ernie. I don't trust him or Hattie."

"What can he do? He doesn't know where you are."

"He might follow me when I pick up Buck. Who knows?"

"If he's around when Buck gets in, I won't let him out of my sight. Fair enough?"

Buck was claustrophobic by the time Abdullah streaked over Ohio airspace, but his discomfort was covered by excitement. Seeing Chloe was his end-all goal. Whatever was wrong with the pregnancy was out of his hands. All he could do was pray and get there. They could get through anything together. The next few years weren't going to be easy regardless.

He reached forward and gripped Abdullah's shoulders. "Thanks for the ride, friend!"

"Thanks for the job, sir! Tell Mr. McCullum what a nice ride you had."

Buck laughed but didn't let Abdullah hear him. He would never again use a fighter as a passenger plane, but he was grateful for the lift home. "Everything all right? On course, on schedule, got all our fluids?"

"OK, Mr. Williams. I will need a place to sleep."

"I believe there are accommodations at the airport. I'd invite you to our place, but we're in hiding and crowded as it is."

"I need very little," Abdullah said. "Just a place to sleep and a place to plug in."

"Your computer?"

"Ben-Judah."

Buck nodded. What more needed to be said?

Rayford was never happier to see a vehicle chug past the north side of the house. He ran out to help Floyd lug the oxygen tanks. "I've got these, Doc. Go check on her."

"Leave the other one in the car for now. She needs O_2 more than she needs anything else."

Rayford was only half a minute behind Doc, but by the time he hefted the tank close enough, Floyd had the fetal monitor on Chloe and looked grave. Tsion stood watching from the bottom of the stairs. Hattie was in the opposite corner looking warily from the top of the basement stairs.

Chloe looked worse than she had just minutes before. Doc swore. "Forgive me," he said. "I'm working on that."

"What's wrong?" Chloe said, gasping.

"OK," Floyd said, "listen up, starting with the patient. We're all going to have to work together here. I need as clean an environment as I can get. Hattie, if you could start a big pot of—"

But Hattie looked as if she wasn't listening. Her eyes were glazed, and she appeared shocked. She turned shakily and began making her way down the stairs to her basement room.

"I'll do whatever you need done," Tsion said, rolling up his sleeves and hurrying over.

"Am I having this baby tonight?" Chloe said desperately. "Before Buck gets here?"

"Not if I can help it," Doc said. "But your job is to be quiet. Don't talk unless you have to."

"All right," she said quickly, "but I have to know everything right now, and I mean it."

Doc looked to Rayford, who raised his eyebrows and nodded. "Just tell her."

"All right, Ray. Get the O_2 on her. Chloe, there has been a significant decrease in the fetal pulse. I don't have the equipment to check on the position of the cord, and I don't want to do a C-section here anyway. A ride to Young Memorial would not be medically positive."

Chloe pulled the oxygen mask from her mouth, though it had already made her face look pinker. "Medically positive?" she said. "You're not gonna keep me quiet with foggy language. You mean the ride might kill me?"

"That's a moot question. You're not going. Now be quiet. Tsion, just give me what I ask for when I ask. Keep your hands clean. Ray, you stay washed up too. Bring me those two chairs and pull those two lights over. Put that one atop the table. Give me that bottle of Betadine."

Once the room was set up and lit as brightly as possible, it took all three men to carefully lift Chloe into position on the makeshift delivery table. "So much for dignity," she said from behind the mask.

"Shut up," Floyd said, but he playfully pinched her toe.

"I must ask a question," Tsion said from the stove. "How will you decide whether an emergency cesarean is necessary?"

"Only if the baby's heart slows too much or stops. Then we'll have to do what we have to do. Chloe will be pretty much out of it by then, so she'll have to make that call now. You'll be anesthetized, Chloe, but not to the degree I'd like for a cesarean. Now—"

"Not even a question," she said, despite the mask. "Go for the baby and worry about me later."

"But if—"

"Don't even argue with me about this, Doc."

"All right, but all this stuff is just precautionary. I'd like to not have to induce. We may not have that luxury, but I'll hold off as long as I can, hoping the baby will stabilize."

"Just try to wait for Buck," Chloe said.

"Not another word," Doc said.

"Sorry, Floyd," she mumbled.

Rayford looked at his watch. "What happens when I have to leave to get Buck?"

"Frankly, I could use you. Buck's car is still at the airport. He can drive himself."

"That leaves T without a car."

"He can ride along and pick up his car here."

"T doesn't want to know the way. Makes it easier on him if he ever gets questioned."

"But you trust him," Doc said.

"Implicitly."

"It's a risk he has to take."

Abdullah crossed into Illinois a few minutes before nine, and Buck called Rayford. "So I'm to bring T with me?"

"And make sure you're not followed. It's a long story."

"We always watch for tails. Someone specific?"

"T will tell you. It's a guy who lives right there at the airport."

"Abdullah is staying there. I'll assign him guard duty."

"Abdullah! You're flying with Abdullah Smith?"

"I didn't know you knew him."

"Put him on!"

Buck tapped Abdullah on the shoulder. "My father-in-law wants to talk to you. Rayford Steele."

Abdullah turned almost all the way around in his seat. "Rayford? Are you serious?"

Rayford quickly filled Abdullah in on the situation. "I'll make sure he goes nowhere," the pilot said. "You know I can manage."

"How well I know. What's your ETA?"

"Fourteen minutes, but I'm shooting for eleven."

Rayford clapped his phone shut and said he was going to check on Hattie. He got three steps down and bent to see her in a fetal position on an old couch. He shook his head and went back upstairs.

"How're we doing, Doc?"

"We're going to induce, but I can start her slow and give Buck plenty of time. Everybody OK with that? Fetal pulse is not critical yet, but it will be in an hour. I'd start the drip if it was my call."

Chloe pointed at Floyd.

"That means it's your call, Doc," Rayford said.

"Small airport," Abdullah said as they descended.

"Not too small for you, though, right?"

"I could land on an envelope and not cancel the stamp."

Buck knew it was nervous tension, but he didn't stop laughing until he climbed out. He stretched so far he dizzied himself and thought he would break in two. He told Abdullah, "The guy on the radio was T, the one we're supposed to meet. He'll point you to where you're staying and hopefully introduce you to Ernie. You know what to do."

Abdullah smiled.

Fewer than ten minutes later, Abdullah was unpacking next to Ernie's room. Buck and T traded phone numbers with Abdullah and left, Buck driving his own car.

"You guys have had some excitement," Buck said.

"Not as much as you're about to have."

"I can't wait. I should call Chloe."

"I wouldn't do that just yet. I understand the doctor has her on oxygen and is going to induce labor, but they're trying to stall for you."

Buck sped up. They were already bouncing so that each had to brace himself with a hand on the ceiling. "What was that?" Buck said, studying the rearview mirror and then swerving to miss the giant concrete pile he had forgotten about on Willow Road.

"I don't see anything," T said, looking back.

Buck shrugged. "Thought I saw a bike."

T looked again. "If there's a bike back there, its light is off. Probably your imagination."

Buck looked again. His mind was playing tricks on him, and why not? He'd have let T drive if T knew where they were going.

"You want me to call Abdullah?" T said. "Make sure he's still got an eye on Ernie?"

"Maybe you'd better."

T dialed. "How are things going, my friend? . . . All right? . . . Yes, he's a fascinating boy. You won't let him hoodwink you now, will you? . . . Just an expression. It means put one over on you, ah, pull a fast one, um, cheat you, swindle you. . . . Attaboy, Abdullah. You should be able to get to sleep now. You've stalled him long enough."

Buck and T pulled into the yard behind the safe house just before ten, and Buck was out of the car before the engine died. Chloe, who had just experienced her first contraction, beamed when she saw him. Doc Charles greeted him with a point to the sink. "First things first, stranger."

Buck washed up and moved to Chloe's side, where he took her hand. "Thank you, God," he said aloud. "I would not want to have missed this."

"I would like to pray too," Tsion said.

"I was hoping you'd say that," Buck said.

"Doctor, you have a waiver on closing your eyes. Almighty God, we are grateful for your goodness and your protection. Thank you for bringing Buck to us, and just in time. We know we have no claim on your sovereign will, but we plead for a safe delivery, a perfect baby, and a healthy mother. We need this tiny ray of sunshine in a dark world. Grant us this, our Lord, but above all, we seek your will."

Rayford's head jerked up with a start at the sound of an engine coming to life in the yard. He scanned the room, looked at T, and said, "Hattie."

Buck shouted, "Catch her! She can't expose us like this!"

Chloe tried to sit up. "Relax, Chloe!" Floyd said. "I'll be fine with Buck and Tsion if you other two have to go after her. But just do it and stay out of here."

Rayford dashed past T and skipped down the steps and out the door. He heard a motorcycle engine, and the Rover was missing. He and T jumped into T's Jeep, but the keys were gone. Rayford ran back in the house. "Floyd! The keys!"

"Agh!" Floyd said. "Tsion, my right pants pocket, and then you'll have to wash again."

Tsion tossed Rayford the keys, and Rayford and T were soon careening back toward Palwaukee. "So Ernie followed you after all?"

"Impossible," T said. "We talked to Abdullah on our

way, and he said Ernie was still there. Buck did think he saw something a couple of times though."

"Maybe Ernie had the drop on Abdullah and made him say that."

"He was pretty convincing. Small talk, details, and all."

"Frankly that doesn't sound like Abdullah. Call him."

Abdullah answered on the second ring. "Did I wake you? . . . Listen, just answer yes or no. Is Ernie still there? . . . He is? What's he doing? . . . Digging? Put him on for me, will you?"

Rayford shook his head. "I'm telling you, he's not—"

"Ernie? Hey, how's it goin', man? Whatcha doin'? . . . Cleaning Ken's area? Nice of you. Abdullah said you were digging. . . . Just sweeping, huh? . . . Yeah, I can see how he could mistake that for digging. Well, tell him we'll see him in a few hours."

Buck could not imagine what Hattie was up to. He had long since quit trying to figure her out. Where would she go in the middle of the night besides crazy? Maybe that was it. She'd got cabin fever and just had to escape. It'd be just like her to get lost and wind up leading someone to the safe house.

Chloe gripped his hand and grunted. Buck looked to Doc, who had attached a fetal monitor to the baby's skull through the uterus. He said it was as accurate as it could be and that he was encouraged. "We're going to have a baby tonight," he said. "And it's going to be all right."

Buck sighed heavily, too excited to notice his fatigue. He also held out a sliver of realism, knowing that for the sake of the patient it was just like Floyd to sound more optimistic than he felt. Buck was glad he was there, no matter what happened. He would not have wanted Chloe to go through this alone, regardless of the outcome.

"So Ernie really *is* a gold digger," Rayford said.

T nodded. "And I'll bet you dollars to donuts we'll find Bo has been released from Young Memorial too. Shall I find out?"

"Sure."

"Humph," T said a few minutes later, his hand over the phone. "They say he's still registered."

"Ask to talk with him. No wait, ask for Leah and let me talk to her." T did and handed him the phone. "Leah, it's Rayford Steele, friend of Dr. Charles."

"What now?" she said, but not unpleasantly.

"We just need to know if a patient who has not checked out or been released might be gone anyway. Name's Bo something. Just a minute, I'll get the—"

"Beauregard Hanson," she said. "We don't get a lot of Bos, you know. Yeah, he's still here."

"You're sure?"

"You want me to check?"

"Would you?"

"I've done more than that for you guys."

"That's why we love you."

"Hang on."

Doc Charles seemed elated, and that made Buck feel better. "We're doing the right thing," Doc said. "This could not have waited, but the pulse is steady and has been for a while. We're going to be OK. You doing all right, Mom?"

Chloe nodded the perspiring nod of the extremely pregnant.

"He's gone?"

"Cleared out," Leah said. "I didn't like him anyway, him or that kid who was in the same room. He disappeared earlier today without a word, so I should have known."

"We owe you one, Leah," Rayford said.

"One?"

"Touché. Someday we'll make this all up to you."

"Yeah," she said. "I'm guessing in five years or so."

"I wish Daddy could be here," Chloe said.

"Maybe he'll be back in time," Buck said. "What's your guess on timing, Doc?"

"I don't want to rush her. Sometimes even a moderate

drip will cause fast action. All depends on mother and child. But we're still doing well, and that's what counts."

"Amen," Tsion said. And Buck thought the rabbi looked as excited as Buck felt.

"Do you believe this?" Rayford said, shaking his head. "Like the idiots they are, they don't even know they've been followed."

The Rover sat idling in front of the Quonset hut that had housed Ken and now Ernie and the temporary guest, Abdullah. T parked the jeep back about fifty feet and turned off his engine and lights. They sat watching. "Abdullah can take care of himself," Rayford said, "but he *is* outnumbered."

T got out. "Let's see what they're up to."

When they got to the Quonset hut, they heard conversation. "Let the Rover idle," Rayford whispered, "so they don't know we're here."

They crouched near the curtained window and listened.

"Let me get this straight," Abdullah was saying. "You'll give me a brick of gold bullion for flying you to New Babylon."

"That's right," Hattie said.

"And this gold belongs to you?"

"It belongs to my fiancé."

"This young man is your fiancé?"

"Yes, I am!" Ernie said. "Soon's I give you this gold. Now take it."

"Do you realize," Abdullah said, "that this gold is worth ten times the cash I would charge for the same flight?"

"But we want to go now," Hattie said. "And I know that's worth something."

"If you want to go now, you picked the wrong pilot. I cannot fly for twenty-four hours."

"Carpathia rescinded international air laws," Hattie said. "I know. I used to work for him."

"You did more than that for him, ma'am. Were you not engaged to him, too? How many fiancés do you have?"

"One fewer if we don't get going," she said.

Rayford signaled T to follow him about a hundred feet away. He phoned Abdullah.

"Hello, yes?"

"Abdullah, it's Rayford Steele, but don't say anything. Just repeat after me, all right?"

"All right."

"Global Community Militia? . . . A stolen Range Rover? . . . Gold? . . . Prison? . . . Yes, you come and question me, but all the gold is here and the automobile too. . . . Yes, I will be here when you get here. . . . No, I do not want to go to prison."

Abdullah broke in. "It's working, Rayford."

"Rayford?" he heard Hattie scream. "Ernie, wait!"

But Ernie and Bo were already riding double on the motorbike, leaving a plume of dust as they hightailed it from the airport.

Rayford and T found Abdullah looking fatigued but

proud of himself, sitting across from Hattie, who sat on the floor with her back pressed against an army cot. "Let's go, Hattie," Rayford said. "Maybe we can get you back in time to see the new baby."

Four hours later, in the darkest hour of the morning, Chloe Steele Williams gave birth to a healthy son. In tears she suckled him and announced his name.

Kenneth Bruce.

Even Hattie wept.

EPILOGUE

One woe is past. Behold, still two more woes are coming after these things.

Then the sixth angel sounded: And I heard a voice from the four horns of the golden altar which is before God, saying to the sixth angel who had the trumpet, "Release the four angels who are bound at the great river Euphrates."

So the four angels, who had been prepared for the hour and day and month and year, were released. . . .

REVELATION 9:12-15

ABOUT THE AUTHORS

JERRY B. JENKINS, former vice president for publishing at Moody Bible Institute of Chicago and currently chairman of the board of trustees, is the author of more than 175 books, including the best-selling Left Behind series. Twenty of his books have reached the *New York Times* Best Sellers List (seven in the number-one spot) and have also appeared on the *USA Today*, *Publishers Weekly*, and *Wall Street Journal* best-seller lists. *Desecration*, book nine in the Left Behind series, was the best-selling book in the world in 2001. His books have sold nearly 70 million copies.

Also the former editor of *Moody* magazine, his writing has appeared in *Time*, *Reader's Digest*, *Parade*, *Guideposts*, *Christianity Today*, and dozens of other periodicals. He was featured on the cover of *Newsweek* magazine in 2004.

His nonfiction books include as-told-to biographies with Hank Aaron, Bill Gaither, Orel Hershiser, Luis Palau, Joe Gibbs, Walter Payton, and Nolan Ryan among many others. The Hershiser and Ryan books reached the *New York Times* Best Sellers List.

Jenkins assisted Dr. Billy Graham with his autobiography, *Just As I Am*, also a *New York Times* best seller. Jerry spent 13 months working with Dr. Graham, which he considers the privilege of a lifetime.

Jerry owns Jenkins Entertainment, a filmmaking company in Los Angeles, which produced the critically acclaimed movie *Midnight Clear*, based on his book of the same name. See www.Jenkins-Entertainment.com.

Jerry Jenkins also owns the Christian Writers Guild, which aims to train tomorrow's professional Christian writers. Under Jerry's leadership, the guild has expanded to include college-credit courses, a critique service, literary registration services, and writing contests, as well as an annual conference. See www.ChristianWritersGuild.com.

As a marriage-and-family author, Jerry has been a frequent guest on Dr. James Dobson's *Focus on the Family* radio program and is a sought-after speaker and humorist. See www.AmbassadorSpeakers.com.

Jerry has been awarded four honorary doctorates.

He and his wife, Dianna, have three grown sons and six grandchildren.

Check out Jerry's blog at http://jerryjenkins.blogspot.com.

DR. TIM LAHAYE (www.timlahaye.com), who conceived and created the idea of fictionalizing an account of the Rapture and the Tribulation, is a noted author, minister, and nationally recognized speaker on Bible prophecy. He is the founder of both Tim LaHaye Ministries and The PreTrib Research Center.

Dr. LaHaye speaks at many of the major Bible prophecy conferences in the U.S. and Canada, where his prophecy books are very popular.

Dr. LaHaye earned a doctor of ministry degree from Western Theological Seminary and received an honorary doctor of literature degree from Liberty University. For 25 years he pastored one of the nation's outstanding churches in San Diego, which grew to three locations. During that time he founded two accredited Christian high schools, a Christian school system of ten schools, and San Diego Christian College (formerly known as Christian Heritage College).

There are over 59 million copies of Dr. LaHaye's 50 nonfiction books, some of which have been published in over 37 languages. He has written books on a wide variety of subjects, such as family life, temperaments, and Bible prophecy. His fiction works include the Left Behind series and the Jesus Chronicles, written with Jerry B. Jenkins. LaHaye's other fiction series of prophetic novels consist of the Babylon Rising series and The End series. Dr. LaHaye is the father of four grown children, grandfather of nine, and great-grandfather of eleven.

THE TRUTH BEHIND THE FICTION

THE PROPHECY BEHIND THE SCENES

The Locusts of Apollyon Attack (Revelation 9:1-11)

This book in the Left Behind series gets its name from the fifth of the seven Trumpet Judgments—the attack of the locusts of Apollyon. Tim LaHaye and Jerry B. Jenkins describe the background for this event in chapter 13 of their nonfiction book *Are We Living in the End Times?*

The fifth Trumpet Judgment is also the first of three woes pronounced by the angel of Revelation 8:13—a frightening

TEST YOUR PROPHECY IQ

+ Is it possible that the 200 million horsemen of the sixth trumpet could be an army from China, as many have suggested?

See answer at the end of this section.

sign of the ferocity of the coming judgments. When this trumpet is sounded in Revelation 9, an angel unlocks the "bottomless pit," and out of the pit belches smoke and "locusts" with the scorpion-like power to sting and torment unbelievers for five months. Their sting is never fatal—in fact, John says, "In those days men will seek death and will not find it; they will desire to die, and death will flee from them"—but the pain they cause will be unbearable. Victims of scorpion bites say the animal's venom seems to set one's veins and nervous system on fire, but the pain is gone after a few days; not so with these locusts. They are given power to torment "those men who do not have the seal of God on their foreheads" for five long months. Yet unlike normal locusts, these beasts attack only unregenerate human beings, never foliage.

The appearance of these locusts is both frightening and repulsive (verses 7-10), and they do not act in an unorganized way; in fact, John says, "They had as king over them the angel of the bottomless pit, whose name in Hebrew is Abaddon, but in Greek he has the name Apollyon" (verse 11). Both names mean *Destroyer*.

This seems to be one of the plagues that God sends on the followers of Antichrist to hinder them from proselytizing among the uncommitted of the world. It may also give Tribulation saints some time to prepare themselves for the horrors of the soon-to-come Great Tribulation. In *Apollyon* the attack of the locusts accomplishes just this purpose. A character named Mac writes to a fellow Tribulation saint:

A few of us believers have been able to pretend we are simply recuperating more quickly, so we don't lie around the infirmary twenty-four hours a day listening to the agony. Carpathia has sent me on some missions of mercy, delivering aid to some of the worst-off rulers. What he doesn't know is that David has picked up clandestine shipments of literature, copies of Tsion's studies in different languages, and has jammed the cargo hold of the Condor 216 with them. Believers wherever I go unload and distribute them.

The Two Witnesses

Prominent in *Apollyon* and woven through the Left Behind volumes covering the first half of the Tribulation are two characters known as the Two Witnesses. Chapter 23 of *Are We Living in the End Times?* describes them as two of the most colorful characters in all of Bible prophecy. These two supernatural prophets burst on the scene during the first 1,260 days of the Tribulation. Some try to identify these witnesses as Enoch (because he never died, Genesis 5:24), Elijah (who also never died, 2 Kings 2:11-12), or Moses. Left Behind author Tim LaHaye is inclined to think they are Moses and Elijah, but whatever their identities, God calls them "My two witnesses." They dress in sackcloth, they prophesy, they dispense astonishing miracles, and they witness to the grace of God in a hostile Jerusalem culture.

Of course, this does not make them popular with the authorities or with the unredeemed multitudes. And it sets up a final confrontation that leaves the world breathless.

The Assassination of the Two Witnesses

For reasons known only to God, the Lord allows the Antichrist to overcome and kill the two witnesses once they "finish their testimony." Before that time they are untouchable; anyone who threatens them must be killed by flaming fire out of their mouths. But after they have accomplished the mission God entrusts to them, the Antichrist "makes war" on them and kills them.

And then the unsaved people of the world who so hate the witnesses commit an incredibly evil deed. They refuse them a decent burial, leaving their dead bodies to decay in the streets of Jerusalem. They even make a Christmas-like celebration out of their murders by sending and receiving gifts "in honor" of the occasion.

Then an even more incredible thing happens. John prophesies that "those from the peoples, tribes, tongues, and nations will see their dead bodies three and a half days" (Revelation 11:9). How could the whole world see their dead bodies? Only a few years ago it was impossible to fulfill that prophecy—but today, with round-the-clock cable news, it could happen at any moment.

That's Not All, Folks!

Why God allows the Antichrist to kill the two witnesses, we are not told. But we do know the story doesn't end with their deaths! While the world is watching, God will do a mighty miracle.

> Now after the three and a half days the breath of life from God entered them, and they stood on their feet, and great fear fell on those who saw them. And they heard a loud voice from heaven saying to them, "Come up here." And they ascended to heaven in a cloud, and their enemies saw them. In the same hour there was a great earthquake, and a tenth of the city fell. In the earthquake seven thousand men were killed, and the rest were afraid and gave glory to the God of heaven.
>
> REVELATION 11:11-13

The most supernatural event of those times will be televised instantly around the world Among other things, this will be a loving gesture by God Almighty, not only to resurrect and take to heaven his two prophets, but also to make known his existence and power around the world. We have no doubt that millions of souls to whom the 144,000 Jewish witnesses will be speaking and whom the Holy Spirit will be convicting will see this demonstration of the divine and respond to the Savior.

IN THE MEANTIME . . .
since the Left Behind series was first published.

How do we know when events are really setting the stage for the end times? As the publication of the main Left Behind series proceeded from 1995 to 2003, and especially since 9/11, it increasingly seemed as though the major headlines had a prophetic ring to them. However, any speculating must be done with caution. We really do have some powerful evidence for supposing that our generation has more reason than any before us to believe Jesus could come in our lifetime! Still, although there are several signs of the end in existence today, it is unwise to set limits on the season. But it is worth pointing out that some of these signs did not exist even a half generation ago.

An example of looking back with a long view is a May 15, 2005, article in the Left Behind Prophecy Newsletter (2003–2009) by Mark Hitchcock on the occasion of the sixtieth anniversary of the end of World War II in Europe.

> Without a doubt, the end of the European theater in WWII stands as one of the enduring moments of the twentieth century.
>
> But many people may have never stopped to consider the significance of WWII as a stage-setting event for the end times. The last half of the 20th century brought some incredible changes that produced effects that are still with us today.

None of the events in the last fifty years are direct fulfillments of Bible prophecy but they bear amazing correspondence to the picture the Bible paints of the end times. They show how world events seem to be shaping up for the final Middle East conflict presented in the Bible. I believe that WWII may the single greatest stage-setting event for the end times.

World War II helped set the stage for the end times in at least two key ways. First, along with World War I, it provided the necessary impetus for the reuniting of Europe, which was the core of the historical Roman Empire. Ever since the break-up of the Roman Empire in AD 476, the nations of Europe fought one another again and again. For centuries, Europe was a battlefield with only brief respites in the ongoing conflict.

But in the aftermath of WWII, a dramatic change occurred. The severity and brutality of the conflict left Europe with no alternative other than to make some attempt to end the constant warfare. Instead of building up for the next great armed conflict as they had done for almost 1,600 years, six of the nations of Europe decided to come together in a coalition of nations that was originally called the Common Market.

The second way that WWII helped set the stage for the end times is the creation of the nation of Israel in 1948. The collective angst and guilt of the world for allowing the Holocaust was a powerful incentive for the establishment of a national homeland for the Jewish people. And the regathering of the Jews to their land in unbelief is the key event that must occur for the events of the end times to unfold.

Thank God for his sovereign hand in bringing the horror of the Third Reich to its knees. But also thank God for using such a tragedy, in His providence, to set the stage for the end times.

A lot has happened in the world since the momentous events of World War II. Try to list a few and see how many could have prophetic implications.

TEST YOUR PROPEHCY IQ—ANSWER

No, as we'll see both in the story of *Assassins* and our ending notes in that volume, Tim LaHaye and Jerry B. Jenkins remind us that the 200 million horsemen are not humans but demons, and their steeds are not horses but creatures "so awesome to look on . . .that they actually frighten people to death."